FACES OF COURAGE

SUSAN K. BEATTY

Jessie,
Take courage —
Susan K Beatty

ISBN: 978-1-951839-21-5

Celebrate Lit Publishing

304 S. Jones Blvd #754

Las Vegas, NV, 89107

http://www.celebratelitpublishing.com/

With love to my daughter Melanie Bernhart, whose example of courage during her breast cancer journey has inspired my passion for writing stories of courage at the intersection of faith and grit.

Chapter One

The back of Olivia's neck prickled. Too close, Frank. Too close.

If only she could tell her husband to move that former linebacker body away from her. For the briefest of moments, she watched from her front door as their Bible study guests wandered down the driveway illuminated by inlaid lights. She eased the door closed.

"I'm sick and tired of those church hypocrites." His voice boomed, echoing in the marbled-floor atrium.

Her ears rang, but she didn't dare put her hands to the sides of her head. Didn't he realize he might wake up the kids and frighten them? It was a good thing she'd sequestered the dog in Dylan's room. She tucked her chin to her chest and, without turning around, tried to edge past him in a well-practiced escape.

He seized her arm and whirled her around to face him. "Did you hear me?"

Olivia shrank into herself. "They're our friends." Her voice wobbled.

Frank gripped her arm harder, his turbulent gray eyes flashing above his scruffy-looking facial hair. "Friends! They're just holier than thou hypocrites. Always telling me how to act when they're just as bad."

What was he talking about? He'd been a deacon and always around the church. Well, until lately. Her mind skipped to the empty pew beside her these past few Sundays. And his disappearances after the beginning of Bible study, showing up at the last minute as everyone was leaving. Tonight, he hadn't bothered to appear until she stood at the front door. And he'd never called their friends hypocrites before.

He clenched and unclenched his fist by his side.

"I'm sorry." She tried to make herself smaller. Questioning him was pointless, riling him more, making everything her fault. It was always her fault. What could she say anyway? Or do?

"Sorry?" He gripped her arm even tighter, his fingers no doubt leaving their mark. "You're sorry all right. Sorry excuse for a wife. I won't put up with those do-gooders anymore."

Olivia made no noise, but she couldn't control the twitch in her cheek.

Frank blinked, and his eyes seemed to clear. He dropped his hand, spun, and stomped out of the entryway.

Still feeling his fingers lingering on her arm, she willed her legs to carry her toward the living room. She perched on the sectional, trying to make sense of what he'd said. And not said. But no doubt before she was allowed to sleep tonight, he would say more with shouting and streams of epithets. More often than not lately. At least he hadn't ever hit her.

Without really seeing, she stared at the atrium lights beyond the glass wall that flanked the opposite end of the room. An ache slammed into her head, bringing her to the reality of her surroundings, judging the mid-century modern furniture underneath her as not fit for relaxing. If only she could lie down on her plush couch in the family room.

What felt worse, the pounding in her head or seeing the usually pristine room littered with the debris of sixteen guests?

At least the busyness would distract her from Frank. She forced herself up, got a trash bag from the kitchen, and stuffed it with used paper cups and napkins. *Lord, I know marriage is forever. Help me learn to stay out of his way.* She picked up another handful of trash, but a small notebook-sized sheet of paper lying on the travertine coffee table caught her eye. She recognized the verse from the night's Bible study. "Be strong and courageous."

Maybe for everybody else, but not for me.

"Aren't you done yet?" Frank stood in the doorway in his T-shirt and flannel sleep pants, fists firmly planted on his hips, and a scowl, just as firmly planted, on his forehead.

Go to sleep. I can't deal with you now. "Almost." Olivia scurried to finish clearing the room. *Don't look at him. Maybe he'll go to bed.*

"Can't you do that in the morning?"

Her throat tightened, and her weariness increased, as if someone had dropped a twenty-pound weight on her already fragile shoulders. "There. All done. Just have to set the trash in the kitchen." She offered him a small smile before scurrying away.

Frank harrumphed and followed her. His reflection in the kitchen's plate glass window showed him waving his arm around the disorderly room. "You're gonna leave this for tomorrow, right?"

"Of course, Frank. Let's get to bed."

He left her to follow him.

Was she being an unsubmissive wife? Hah! She couldn't be anything but. She had no power, no guts. Never had. She checked the door locks and, after surveying each room, turned off the lights. She stood in the atrium between the living room and the family room. She used to take comfort in the large, comfortable chairs, the well-stocked bookcases, and the stone fireplace in the family room.

Now, she willed the lingering aroma of coffee, the smoky scent of cooling ashes in the living room fireplace, and the soft tick-tock of the family room clock to wrap around her, to envelope her in peace.

"Olivia!"

So much for peace.

Why were their church friends suddenly hypocrites to Frank? She shook her head.

"Checking on Zoe and Dylan. Be right there."

Olivia padded into Dylan's room. King raised his head from where he sprawled his ungainly body across the throw rug next to Dylan's bed. Satisfied she wasn't an intruder, he closed his eyes. Her five-year-old lay spread-eagle across his race car bed, the matching bedding bunched underneath him. She stepped around King and moved Dylan enough to get the blanket over him. She kissed his cheek.

In the next room, Zoe's favorite Amish country hearts quilt lay without wrinkle across the bed, the top edges folded by her cheek, the sides draping in precise folds. Only the small telltale mound that was the sleeping seven-year-old disturbed the flat neatness of the bed.

Olivia stroked Zoe's bangs away from her face and kissed her forehead. Her shoulders slumped. *Continue to get along. For the kids. And we'll be fine.*

In the master bedroom Frank sat up against the bed pillows, his arms folded across his chest. "Tell Pastor David to impose on someone else for Bible study. I don't want those people here anymore."

"But, Frank—"

"You heard what I said."

The force in Frank's voice pushed Olivia back, her father's voice reverberating in her head—the same hot anger, an anger that scorched her soul and often ended in a beating. Olivia slipped off her dress and hung it in the closet with a shaky arm. "Okay." Olivia whispered, looking back at her husband through lowered lashes.

With a glare that sent heat rising up her chest, Frank

snapped off his bedside light and jammed himself under the covers, turning his back to her.

Olivia's chest and neck burned as she silently shut herself in the bathroom. *Just get along. As long as we're safe and healthy, that's all that matters.*

But where would she get the courage to keep them safe if he became violent?

———

Olivia plunged her hands into the dishwater, taking comfort in its warmth, hoping to dispel the lack of sunshine outside the kitchen window and the sleepless night Frank's diatribe caused.

How could he demand she cancel Bible study? And ignore her this morning? She should stand up to him and refuse. It was her house too. And her friends. But no, she wouldn't—couldn't—do that. Besides, wasn't she supposed to respect her husband, be a good wife?

Olivia finished rinsing the silverware, stuck it in the dishwasher, and slammed the door. She was lucky to have a husband and children. She needed to deal with the hand she was dealt. She stuffed down thoughts of rights and respect and stepped out of the sliding glass door onto the patio, wrapping her sweater around her chest against the wind.

Inhaling the crisp early morning air, she sought a whiff of something in the cold scent-barren day to prove she wasn't alone. At least cold was relative here in Southern California, not below zero like in Buffalo where she spent her childhood. Was it only February? Spring was still around a corner. Or two.

The yipping of the terrier next door and the soft chirping of a cedar waxwing broke the quiet. Isn't that what Frank told her the bird was called? It was hard to remember those complicated names of trees and animals, despite his attempts to teach her. She shuddered. Why did those lessons always end badly?

She basked in the stillness, soon to be broken by the children clamoring for breakfast. Who needed sunshine? Frank was at work. A fun field trip lay ahead with her kids and friends. That was better than sunshine. She hummed to the words "out of the darkness, into your glorious day," from her favorite praise song, and smiled. Better get a shower before Zoe and Dylan super-charged the day.

She returned to the kitchen and walked into a sword fight between two miniature combatants—one wielding a flyswatter against the other's empty paper towel tube. A third body, bouncing on four then two paws, wriggled in the middle.

So much for that shower.

Zoe parried and thrust.

Dylan waved the flyswatter in all directions in a wild attempt to connect with Zoe's tube. "See, Mommy. Just like the three muss cat ears we saw on the video." He giggled.

Zoe stopped the action to cross her arms. "You mean *The Three Musketeers*, goofy." She giggled and collapsed on the floor, joining the human pile consisting of Dylan and their mom. Humans plus doggy in the middle.

If only King realized he was no longer a puppy. Are all four-year-old black Labradors normally like this?

Still on the floor, Dylan brought his face inches from Olivia's, his eyes serious. "Can we have pancakes? Please."

Olivia kissed and softly pinched his chubby cheeks. "Pancakes it is." Olivia scrambled to stand. "Then we better get started. Zoe, can you please grab the pancake mix out of the pantry? Dylan, please put away the muss cat ears' swords."

Tummies full and the powdery and maple syrup messes cleaned up, Zoe and Dylan picked up their swordplay weapons.

Olivia stepped between them. "My good Musketeers, no time for battles. Time to get ready for a field trip to—"

"Where? Where are we going?" Dylan tossed his flyswatter at his feet.

"I know! I know! The Discovery Center, right?" Zoe retrieved Dylan's flyswatter and laid it and her paper towel tube on the table. "Right?"

"Yep! And Auntie Carmen and the boys will be here soon, so we better get ready. Dylan, did you feed and water King?"

After a mad scramble to finish the chores and dress, Olivia held Dylan's coat as he slipped his arm into one sleeve.

"Mooom! Where's my new jacket? Can't find it anywhere." The fashion diva's voice echoed down the hallway.

"I have it right here." She helped Dylan with his other sleeve.

"Will they pick us up in their new SUV?"

"What new SUV?" Carmen had said nothing about a new car last night.

"A Cadillac Escalade. I bet it's really cool." Dylan's eyes lit up with any discussion of vehicles.

"They're here!" He scooted out the front door in a flash.

"Wait! Dylan—" Olivia sighed, plucked up his backpack along with her own as Zoe grabbed her jacket and dashed out ahead of her.

Carmen's cherubic face popped out of the open driver's side of a sleek Escalade, the wind swirling her mane of black curly hair about her head. "Hey, guys! Looking forward to a super fun trip?" Her grin pushed her cheeks into puffy pillows.

The kids clamored into the SUV, greeting their pals Gabe and Arturo with squeals and high fives.

Olivia hoisted herself onto the running board, barely landing on the seat before sliding across the leather. The unmistakable new car smell greeted her, and a little monster nipped deep inside her belly.

"Nice car. You didn't tell me."

"No? Jorge picked it up yesterday. Didn't want me driving

an old car when he's out of town." Carmen prattled on as she made their way to the freeway, merging them into stop-and-go traffic. "He's taking me to the Summit House for dinner tonight. Anniversary date night. Then he's taking the boys on an outing Sunday. All day. After church. Said I needed a real day of rest."

With barely taking the time to breathe, she continued to chatter. "And don't forget our family anniversary party tomorrow. Got a bounce house for the kids, a taco man for the adults, and a Mariachi band. Can't have a Mexican party without the Mariachis. And since it is our tenth anniversary, we want to honor our parents' heritage with a real fiesta, so I'm gonna wear a traditional costume. But you don't have to. Jorge won't go that far..."

No, Olivia wasn't jealous of the new SUV, not really. She had her own SUV purchased last year. But what she didn't have was a husband like Jorge, thoughtful of her safety, her needs. She'd seen Jorge's look of tenderness toward Carmen while they were amid a group. Frank bought her a new vehicle because he couldn't have a five-year-old one be seen in their driveway next to his Stingray, his reward for having survived a car accident that kept him in the hospital for a week with head injuries.

These days Frank rarely looked at her with anything but scorn. Or lust.

"Bible study next week—"

The words snapped Olivia to attention. "Sorry. What did you say?"

"Oh, that we may be late to Bible study next week. Picking Jorge up from the airport at six. Coming back from Atlanta. He was promised a promotion and big raise..."

Bible study? What to tell Carmen? Should she talk to Pastor David first? But a neighbor, well, best friend, would wonder why she hadn't told her. Carmen hadn't told her about their new Cadillac. She'd wait.

Olivia stared out of the side window, but only the vague outlines of buildings along the 55 Freeway passed by.

Without turning her head toward Carmen, she blurted out, "Bible study may not be at our house next week. Frank wants to take a break for a couple weeks."

"Oh?" Carmen reached across the console and squeezed Olivia's hand. "Everything okay, *chica*?"

Yeah. No. My husband's being a jerk. She bit back the words and produced a smile. "Oh, sure. Frank just needs a break."

She didn't look forward to calling Pastor David. She could stall.

Chapter Two

The four children bickered as Zoe and Dylan tumbled out of the black Escalade into the late afternoon gloom.

Olivia missed the running board, her feet plopping onto the pavement. "See you tomorrow." With a final wave, she shuffled the kids and their grumbling toward the house.

Thank goodness Frank's Stingray wasn't parked in front. She had a reprieve before dealing with whatever mood he brought home. Before she could get the front door unlocked, the thrum of the Corvette's engine invaded the driveway behind them. Her shoulders tightened.

Scuffling and a hey-I've-been-cooped-up-too-long Labrador filled the atrium entryway as Dylan abandoned his jacket and backpack.

Dylan rushed to Frank. "Daddy, guess what I did today? It was just like being in a rocket ship and a helicopter. It was so cool."

"That's great, sport." Could Frank have said it with any less enthusiasm? His foot, clad in expensive Italian leather, booted Dylan's backpack out of his way, brushing King's coat. "Outta the way, mutt. Didn't know you guys were going out."

"You're home early." She turned to pick up their backpacks and organized them on the slatted walnut bench.

Zoe sighed. "Hi, Daddy. Mommy, is it okay if I go watch Nickelodeon now?" At Olivia's nod, she wandered away to the family room, trailed by her brother and his four-pawed shadow.

In their bedroom, Frank slipped off his shoes, wiped them, and lined them up on his shoe rack. "So why didn't you mention you were going on a field trip today?"

Did Frank's cool tone mean he was reserving his anger, or was he merely being the calm, inquiring husband?

"Sorry. Thought I did." Olivia steeled herself for a tirade as she shed her coat and hung it in the closet.

"You didn't."

She held her breath for a moment. That's it? No, surely, he'll launch into a fit any minute. Olivia scuttled out of the room. Better start dinner. The smell of a sizzling steak should calm the temper she was sure he was gearing up for.

Later, after an eruption-free dinner and bedtime ritual, she eased onto the oversized family room couch and relaxed her body. Her new romance novel beckoned.

The cushions next to her sank under Frank's weight as he sat, his hip touching hers. Her back tensed. He never sat here.

Frank stroked her arm. "You should have told me you were going out today." The stroking stopped, and he squeezed. "I don't like those kinds of surprises."

"Ouch! Stop!" Olivia pulled away, her book dropping to the floor.

When he released his grasp, her breathing stopped for a split second, but he grabbed her chin and angled her face to his. "I told you. I don't like those kinds of surprises." He pinched with increasing pressure.

"Please. Hurts." The words jammed up against her teeth so that she mumbled. She struggled to twist aside, but he only pinched harder. Maybe it would hurt less if she pressed her lips shut.

Letting go of her chin, he gripped both of her arms and shook her. "How many times do I have to tell you I don't appreciate it when you don't tell me where you're going?" A muscle in his jaw twitched.

Her teeth clattered, but she whispered, "I-I'm sorry. I won't let it happen again."

"See that it doesn't." He released her and moved to his recliner, flipping on the remote. A basketball game bloomed on the screen.

To hide her heaving chest, she turned her back on him. Mustn't show fear. Her chin pulsing with pain, she kept her back to him and rose. "I'm going to bed now."

"No. Sit here with me."

Olivia sank back down. She dropped the book on the coffee table, and clenched her fists, hiding them under her thighs. He couldn't order her around. Why did he treat her as if she were a child? No, a slave. Because he could. He was her husband, and it was her job to be a good wife.

And, besides, she had no guts to stand up to him.

She perched ramrod straight.

"You can read your cheap novel. I just want your company." His voice was low and hard.

Olivia cleared her throat as she picked up the book. Although she held the tears back, the print blurred on the page.

The basketball game disappeared from the big screen and all went quiet, pulling Olivia out of her cocoon. How long had she remained there?

Frank stood, stretched, and headed out the door, throwing his next challenge over his shoulder. "You did call Pastor David and tell him no more Bible study here, right?"

———

Olivia tip-toed into the bedroom, hoping Frank slept, but he sat up and snapped on the light. Wincing, she steeled herself to be pinched, or at least upbraided, again.

"Sorry I was so nasty. I dunno what came over me."

She tried to keep the surprise from her face. Frank used to apologize often, but not so much lately.

"But, look. I really need to know where you are. In case of emergency. To keep you and the kids safe."

Safe? When he yelled and pinched her right here in their own home? Really? Now who was the hypocrite?

"You understand, right?"

What could he do from work? Or from out of town? She may be spineless, but she took care of herself and her children. Locked doors, cell phone, AAA. Carmen lived down the street while Frank worked an hour away. Speak up. If they talked about this infraction, it kept the discussion away from her calling, or not calling, the pastor about Bible study. Her heart pounded in her ears.

"I have a cell phone."

His face hardened for a split-second and softened again. "Of course, babe, but what if you run out of battery or there's no reception?"

Frank made no sense. Even if she told him where they were every minute, how would he know they needed help if she had a dead cell phone? She opened her mouth to challenge him but snapped her jaws. His controlling nature made it impossible for her to challenge him, let alone win a debate. Ever. Even if her point was more logical. And it probably wouldn't keep the conversation away from the dreaded Bible study topic, anyway.

"You get it, right?" He looked at her, his eyes soft with desire.

She recognized the look. Was he sorry? Was his talk of keeping her safe a way to woo her into bed? As her husband, he didn't have to woo her because he ruled the bedroom. But at least they wouldn't be talking about Bible study.

"Sure. I get it."

Frank patted the bed again.

Chapter Three

The next afternoon Olivia followed Frank as he pushed open the side gate and strode into Carmen and Jorge's yard.

Olivia caught the wrought iron spindles as they slapped toward her. He wouldn't think of holding a door, much less stepping aside so his family could enter first. Olivia huffed, but kept her mouth shut.

He wouldn't have heard her, anyway. Only the children's squeals in the bounce house echoed over the lively sound of the Mariachis, punctuated by the *grito Mexicano*, the traditional Mariachi yell.

Zoe and Dylan rushed to the air-filled fun house beyond which the palm trees reached high into the sky, swaying with the music.

Still near the gate, Olivia stood alone, the noise and chaos and Frank's rudeness receding as she admired the sun glittering off the palm fronds. God's creation. How wonderful to see the sun after a gray week.

She tried to shed the gloom inside her and enjoy the sense of celebration evident in the large, rustic yard. In contrast to the yard, Jorge and Carmen's home was a showpiece, an award-wining Craftsman home. Jorge had explained to them

16

when they first met that the house was a rare find because it was much larger than the traditional Craftsman bungalow. Someday, they said, they would transform the backyard to match the house. Olivia had to take Jorge's word about the home's origins, but she admired the covered front porch and dormer windows on the outside, and the nooks throughout the house. It may be award-winning, but they had made it an unpretentious, homey kind of place.

Her own award-winning home, with its banks of glass walls, many atriums, and single story, was a stark contrast to the Delgados' house.

"Livie! Over here!" Carmen waved from beside the taco cart. The smoky smell of steak and peppers searing on the grill tantalized her closer. True to her word, Carmen was clad in a Mexican peasant skirt and off-the shoulder blouse, with large hoops dangling from her ears. All Carmen's flowing costume needed was a Spanish-style hacienda. Olivia ran her hands over her own pressed jeans and fitted Oxford shirt. Nope. She could never pull off Carmen's Spanish *doña* look.

"I'm so glad you're here. Could you help me get everything on the buffet table? I've got pots and platters in the kitchen. I promised myself I wouldn't overfeed everybody, but ..." Still chattering, Carmen grabbed Olivia's hand and pulled her into the kitchen.

The butcher block counters were now covered with pots of beans or rice and platters of *tamales* and *chili rellenos*. Various salsas pooled in stone dishes.

Members of Carmen's family greeted her with hugs and spirited shouts. What would it have been like to have a large and loving family? Her heart fluttered. She'd never know.

A hefty pot of beans was thrust into her hands. Shaking the thoughts away, Olivia headed to the patio.

She skidded to a stop.

Pastor David's bulk towered over Jorge's more compact form as they talked near the pool. What had she been thinking? Of course, Pastor David would be here today. Half of the church was here. Frank might choose not to talk to Pastor David. After all, wasn't Pastor David the "hypocrite"? And why would he broach Bible study here? The pastor had many other people to chat with to keep him busy. It wasn't as if Frank and Pastor were buddies. Ha, far from it. And not Pastor David's fault.

Where was Frank? As she made room on the table for the large pot, she spotted him across the flagstone patio. How long would they stay on opposite sides? After several tries, she found enough saliva to swallow. Her eyes darted from Frank to Pastor David to the buffet table and followed the pattern again even as she set down the pot and backed toward the kitchen for another load of food.

"*¡Cuidado! hija!*" Watch out, daughter. Ramona, Carmen's mother, blocked the doorway, a pot of steaming *pozole* in her gnarled hands. "I almost dumped this on you. This not day for accidents." Olivia was grateful that Ramona's gentle smile eased the reprimand.

"I am so sorry. Here, let me take it for you." Olivia tried to take the pot, but Ramona turned aside.

"No. No. Will spill if I give to you. Is okay."

Olivia stepped back to allow Ramona by. She turned again toward the crowd. Where did Frank go? Her gaze flitted around the backyard, but not finding him, returned to examine each group. He shouldn't have been hard to find. He was a head taller than most of the others, except Pastor David. Where was the pastor? She spotted him still by the pool. She let out a breath. At least Frank wasn't talking to him.

"Hi, Olivia. Great to see you." Friends wandered by greeting her. Was her smile at each person warm enough? Were they judging her? Her eyes went back to the crowd.

A heavy hand clamped her shoulder. Olivia whirled around.

"Frank! You scared me."

"Why should you be scared of your husband?" His jaw was tight, but he ran his hand up and down her arm.

Olivia stammered but managed, "I didn't know you were behind me."

He continued to caress her arm even as his gaze flitted to somewhere over her shoulder. Pastor David?

"Excuse me, Livie. Can you take this to the buffet table?" Carmen handed her another tray piled high with steaming roasted corn on the cob, the earthy scent wafting in the breeze.

Olivia wanted to stay and continue diverting Frank's attention away from the pastor, but she couldn't ignore Carmen's request for help. Olivia moved away. Was she putting off the inevitable? She had to hold off discussing Bible study until they were home at least. She found a place on the buffet table for the corn, and another guest chatted with her.

The Mariachi music ceased, but the chatter and laughter grew louder. A trumpet blasted, long and sharp, and Jorge was at the microphone.

"*Amigos.* Friends." Another blast, and the hubbub subsided to a murmur.

Jorge gave a short welcome speech, prayed, and invited his guests to feast at the buffet table. The Mariachi band, clad in black and silver-studded charro suits, launched into another number, the trumpet, violin, and guitar pumping the air with a cheerful tune.

Olivia allowed the music to distract her.

"Hey, *chica.*" Carmen sidled up to her. "Frank's in the house watching a soccer game."

"Soccer?" Olivia figured she looked as surprised as she felt. "Frank can't stand soccer." Her hand flew to cover her mouth. "Oh, sorry." She mumbled behind her hand.

Carmen giggled. "That's no surprise. He hasn't exactly been shy about his opinion of soccer. But I hear it's a good game."

Olivia relaxed her shoulders. Frank was safely out of the way. For now.

"Have you had anything to eat? You need to have some of my *mamá's Menudo*."

Olivia wrinkled her nose. "Over my dead body."

Carmen laughed at their private joke. "Okay, then, *chica*. I think *mamá* saved you some *pozole*." Carmen put her arm around Olivia's waist and led her toward the kitchen.

Later was early enough to worry about Frank.

A silver-haired man stood in the middle of the kitchen speaking to Ramona in Spanish. Shouldn't she know him? His military posture looked familiar.

Carmen led Olivia toward the two. "Lance. I'm so happy you decided to come. Olivia, do you remember Lance Gordon? He's been out of the country for a while on a medical missions trip, but he's back now working at City of Hope. Lance, this is my good friend Olivia."

Olivia held out her hand. "Dr. Gordon? Nice to meet you." His square jaw and light gray-blue eyes reminded her of Frank's darker ones. She shuddered.

"Yes. Doctor. But just Lance, please. Isn't your husband Frank Stanford, former linebacker for the Philadelphia Soul?"

Her eyebrows shot up. How did he come by that little-known fact? "Yes. That's my husband."

"What's he doing now? Coaching, I bet."

"Oh, no. He's a VP in charge of production at Hollyfield Engineering."

Carmen put a hand on Lance's arm to interrupt the conversation. "Excuse us, Lance. Gotta get this girl some food." With a wave to Lance, she led Olivia toward the *pozole*.

"Wow, Livie. I didn't know Frank played pro football." Carmen locked arms with her.

"Not pro...exactly. It was an Arena Football team."

"A what?"

"Never mind. Some other time. I'm starved." Olivia

rushed her friend toward the food and away from the football conversation.

How did Dr. Lance Gordon know about Frank and the Soul? And why did he disturb her?

———

The nighttime temperature fell, and the buffet tables looked like a swarm of locusts had dropped in for the fiesta. Empty pots and platters looked abandoned, the tables dotted with globs of beans and puddles of salsa.

Many of the guests and the Mariachi band had gone home. Carmen's family worked on cleaning up the kitchen.

Olivia checked on Zoe and Dylan, so worn out they slept on Gabe's bedroom floor, snug under Amish quilts. Olivia stroked the colorful checkerboard garden quilt covering Dylan. It was her favorite of the many Amish quilts she had on her wish list. How did Carmen always snatch up their favorite patterns before she did? Olivia chuckled. Amish quilts in Carmen's house looked much more at home than in her own mid-century modern one.

Satisfied, Olivia wandered through the house looking for Frank. Maybe he went home by himself..

Moira, also affectionately known as Quirky Moira, a church deaconess, greeted Olivia as they met by the front door.

"Oh, Olivia. I wanted to thank you for how much work ye put into the homeless mission. We raised more this year than ever, we did." Moira's wrinkles left no doubt about the eighty hard years she'd lived, but her smile was like a summer day.

Olivia grasped Moira's cool, veined hands and caressed them. "I only handle the applications and other paperwork. And, of course, you're welcome. Always happy to help."

Moira beamed even brighter, if that was possible. "Oh, thank you. You're a saint, you are. Time ta get me home. Ta."

Olivia hugged her as she said goodbye. Moira was one of the few church acquaintances she felt comfortable hugging. Such a sweet soul, if a bit eccentric. Must be the Irish fairies in her.

Now where was Frank?

Pastor David's low tones drifted to her from the family parlor down the hall. Another, louder voice mingled with Pastor David's.

Frank.

Olivia stopped just short of the doorjamb, out of sight. Theology. They argued theology. Well, Frank was arguing. Pastor David was countering, pointing out Frank's errors in thinking as gently as possible.

"Your mind's so closed. You won't even consider I might be right." Frank's voice bounced off the walls.

"Frank, I listened to what you had to say, but it doesn't line up with Scripture. Romans says—"

Thunk! Frank pounded on something. "I'm done here! And with Bible study. I assume Olivia told you I don't want it at my house anymore."

Olivia's legs became as wet noodles, and she grabbed at the hall table for support.

"I'm sorry to hear that. What can I do—"

"Drop our church membership too. We won't be coming back."

What? This was new to her. He was going too far.

"Are these Olivia's wishes too?"

Strength charged through the bones and muscles of her legs, and she whipped around the corner. "No! These are not my wishes." Sweat beaded her upper lip as she confronted her husband. Oh, no. Where did that come from? Don't step back. Don't step back.

He stood on one side of a low, wooden mission-style table, the pastor sitting on the other side. Frank stared at her, rage boiling in his eyes. "Olivia. You will keep quiet."

Pastor David raised his hand, palm outward. "Now, Frank. Olivia has a right to an opinion, and her wishes should be taken into consideration."

God bless Pastor David.

Frank swung his face to Pastor David while simultaneously pivoting on his left foot, positioning himself perpendicular to the pastor, with his right arm cocked back and low, his fist clenched. "This isn't any of your business. Stay out of it."

The pastor remained seated, his features soft, and his hands loosely folded in his lap. "That will accomplish nothing. Please. Both of you sit down and let's talk it through."

Frank reared as if someone had slapped him, and then plunged his arm to his side.

Hope welled in Olivia's chest. Hope that the pastor had reached Frank's heart. If he listened to the Lord through the pastor, perhaps life could be better. Frank could be different. Olivia pled with the Lord.

"No." Although Frank muttered it, his face was flushed, his neck corded. He rushed to Olivia, grabbed her hand, and pulled her toward the door.

Had someone doused her with a bucket of ice water, melting her hope? She locked her gaze on the pastor's. Did he see her pleading for forgiveness?

Pastor David stood. "Frank. Wait."

Frank stopped at the door, turning toward the pastor. "This conversation is over." With that, he dragged Olivia out of the room, his hand in a vice grip around her wrist.

"Where are the kids?" He asked through gritted teeth.

"Gabe's room. Upstairs."

Olivia stumbled as he rushed them up the staircase. She tried to swallow, the fear rising in her throat, but the fear glued itself to her tonsils.

At Gabe's door, he released her wrist. "Get Zoe."

Olivia bent and whispered to Zoe as Frank threw back the

quilt and scooped up the sleeping boy, throwing him over his shoulder as if he were an infant needing a good burp.

"Let's go!"

Zoe mumbled, and Olivia clasped her hand, helping her to her feet. Frank again grabbed Olivia's wrist, pulling the four of them out the door and down the stairs.

As Frank swept them through the kitchen without a word, Olivia glanced at the remaining crowd, and then turned away but not before heads had turned and their curiosity turned to surprise.

How could she face these people again? They will think this was all her fault. Discard their friendship. Shame weighed her down like a wet, woolen blanket.

Dr. Gordon stood near the gate, his mouth a thin line as Frank dragged his family home.

What was in store for her when they got home? He would not touch the children. Even if she had to prevent it with her dead body. She was thinking about her dead body a lot tonight. She shivered.

———

The moon now hid in the clouds, the walk home lit only by the one streetlight between the Delgado and Stanford houses. How could a walk five houses away take so long? Yet be so quick?

Frank muscled them in through the front door and to the children's bedrooms. He slammed the door behind them, his face a thundercloud. He didn't give Olivia time to tuck the children in, grabbing her elbow and pulling her down the hall.

In their bedroom, Olivia backed up, the doorknob hitting the small of her back. Her leg muscles tightened, but there was no place to run. She wrapped her arms around her belly as Frank brought his face to within an inch of hers.

His breath fogged her face with the stench of old garlic

and onions. She pushed back the bile adding to the roiling in her gut.

Oh, God.

"You dare argue with me in front of that hypocrite! You worthless piece of trash."

He grabbed her arms and shook her, her head banging against the door. She bit her tongue and tasted blood.

"Don't you ever do that again. And you lied to me. You said you told him we didn't want those phonies here anymore."

"F-Fr-Frank." She stuttered out his name, each syllable punctuated with a bang of her head. "Pl-Please stop. I didn't lie. I didn't tell you that."

But he didn't stop.

His eyes lit with a "Gotcha!" smirk. "So, you didn't tell him. Like I told you to, right?"

"N-No."

Frank stopped shaking her. Olivia slumped in relief, until he took a hand from her arm.

Thwack!

His slap blossomed on her cheek and knocked her head to the side. The sting drove the tears from her eyes to gush down her face. Her knees buckling, she hung in the grip that still clutched her arm.

Had that really happened? A scream echoed in her skull.

"You ever disobey me again, and I'll knock you to forever."

He released her, throwing her against the door. The knob jabbed her again. She turned to the door, clutching the knob that had gone from tormentor to lifeline.

Leaning her forehead against the door's satiny smoothness, she machine-gunned herself with questions. How had she allowed a man to hit her when she had promised herself immunity against such violence? It was not ever supposed to happen to her. Even though Frank bullied her verbally, she told herself Frank was not violent. But somewhere deep inside she had known the idea was a lie.

As the roaring in her ears subsided, muffled sobs penetrated her hearing. Zoe.

She tried to open the door, but Frank must have heard Zoe too because he thrust Olivia aside.

He spat out, "I'll take care of Zoe. You. You stay here." He knocked her aside and charged out, slamming the door behind him.

Would he hurt Zoe? If he did, she was through. She wouldn't—couldn't—stay with a man who hurt her children.

I will not become my mother!

Olivia relived her father's blows against her little body as her mother hid her face. She heard her own moans and her mother's pitiful whimpers.

Now the absolute stillness surrounding her thrust her into reality. What was going on? Why didn't she hear Zoe or Frank? She fought the urge to throw herself on the bed and curl into a fetal position.

No. She would not be her mother.

She swallowed the blood pooled in her mouth and slipped toward the barrier that separated her from Zoe. No sound. Nothing. She couldn't just stand there. Cracking open the door, she put an eye against the merest of open space. Her view of the hallway went as far as Zoe's room. All was quiet.

Was Zoe in her room? Was Frank in there?

He better not touch Zoe. Or Dylan. She might endure him saying nasty things to her, maybe a slap or two, but she would not allow him to hurt her children. Why had her mother not intervened to protect her? Her mother was afraid. She got that. But her father beat her mom, anyway. And her mother paid for it with her life. Not once having protected her daughter.

No, sir. She would not be like her mother.

Trembling, she crept toward Zoe's door. Deep murmuring and a soft giggle came from inside. She let out a breath.

The murmuring grew closer, and the floor creaked.

Olivia shot back to her bedroom, clicking the door closed. Was that Zoe's door shutting? She retreated to the furthest corner of the room where she maneuvered herself between her vanity and the slipper chair. As if the little chair could protect her from him.

Every muscle taut, she waited. A minute or two ticked by. She didn't know how long. Where was he? If she'd only obeyed Frank in the first place, he wouldn't have struck her, and she wouldn't be worrying about Zoe. It was her own fault, wasn't it? She must learn it was better to just obey him.

Such a coward. Did she think she'd really act any different from her mother? Challenging Frank required courage if he threatened the kids. Courage was not in her genes.

She lost track of the minutes. Had it been two or ten? Where was Frank? What was he doing? Throwing her shoulders back, she marched out of the room, but once over the threshold, she stopped. Was she nuts?

Frank was not in sight, so she tiptoed to Zoe's room. Zoe was curled up asleep, her face peaceful.

Where was he? She didn't want to know. But she had to.

She continued to Dylan's room. He, too, slept peacefully as sometimes only children could. King softly snored at the foot of his bed.

The house sat silent, not revealing its secrets. Where did danger lurk? Olivia held her breath as she peeked in every room, ending in the vacant kitchen.

The garage.

Only Frank's accident-scarred Honda occupied the garage.

Olivia sagged against the doorjamb. The driveway. She flew to the front windows. Only her white SUV hunkered there. No red Stingray.

Frank didn't frequent bars or lounges. At least that she knew of. The living room clock bonged once, then clanged out twelve more times. So where had he gone at midnight?

Ahh, sweet relief. She'd better not get too comfortable. No telling when he'd be back. Would he try to slap her again?

The night crashed in on her, landing in the pit of her stomach. If only it had stayed there. She ran to the bathroom and spewed pozole and who knew what else into the toilet. When it stopped, she brushed her teeth and succumbed to the beckoning of her bed. Temporary or not, she would take advantage of his absence and curl up like the kids.

Maybe even sleep. If she dared.

Chapter Four

Olivia swam up through the murky waters of deep sleep. As she broke the top, barely awake, she felt a hand on her shoulder.

"Livie."

Wha?

She cracked open one eyelid. Daylight seeped around the roman shades. Morning? Already?

"Babe!" The hand shook her again.

"Frank? What's goin' on? What time is it?"

"10."

Olivia shot to a sitting position. "The kids! Where are the kids?"

"S'okay. Gave them breakfast. They're playing in the yard."

Frank fed them breakfast? Without waking her.

"Where were you?"

Irritation flashed across Frank's face, but then was gone. "Babe, I'm sorry. I didn't mean it." He slid his hand up and down her arm. "Can we forget it? Won't happen again. I promise."

Didn't mean it? What didn't he mean? The horrible things he said? Slapping her was—what? An accident? She wanted to laugh in his face. But as quick as that, his apology would be forgotten, his hand accidentally on her face again.

Frank curled his fingers around her arm. She stiffened.

"But you know. You made me do it. If you'd just done what I told you."

Her fault? Maybe it was. But slapping her?

"Come on, babe. I'll make you waffles." He tugged gently on her arm.

Just give in already. Don't rock the boat. Everything will be fine if she just accepted his apology and moved on.

But her heart—or was it her gut?—rebelled at the thought. God surely didn't approve of her being hit for whatever reason. Right? What provoked her father to beat her mother?

She had to stand up to Frank. Tell him slapping wasn't right. It was not her fault. Could she find the teeniest bit of courage?

Olivia sucked in a breath and pulled her arm away.

"No, Frank."

His features hardened, and he grabbed her arm again. Not gently.

Oh, Lord. What have I done?

"I just said I was sorry. Stop it and let's get those waffles." He pulled her off the bed and dragged her toward the door.

A battle raged inside her head. Did she dare resist and risk certain wrath? Did she have the backbone? Or should she just give in? She wanted it to be over, for there to be peace. But he continued to tow her down the hall, so she ignored the screaming inside her head.

"Okay, okay."

Soon a platter loaded with waffles, bacon, and eggs sat before her. How was she supposed to eat all of this? She nibbled at the pile, worried she'd never make it look like she'd eaten enough to matter. She cut, pushed it around, and nibbled a little more.

Thwack! Frank's hand slammed the counter next to her. She jumped, her knife and fork clattering to the tile.

"I went to all the trouble of making that for you. The least you can do is eat it."

"I'm working on it. You know I'm a slow eater." Olivia kept her voice calm.

She tried to take a larger bite while glancing at the clock. Yep, too late for church today. Better not bring up that subject. Would her life get back to normal? What was normal? The large bite had glued itself to the back of her throat. She washed it down with a gulp of orange juice and nipped at the next bit of waffle on her fork.

Frank turned to the wall of glass that separated them from the yard where the children played. "Well, eat faster. I want to take the kids to Disneyland."

Talk about whiplash. Frank wanted to spend a lot of money on a family outing? That was almost as rare as a blizzard in July.

"Disneyland?"

"Call your friend Vanessa and have her husband what's-hisname sign us in."

Ahh. "I don't know if I can just call Vanessa and ask that. Jim might not even be working today." She hadn't spoken to Vanessa in a couple weeks, not even about mutual businesses matters.

He kept his face toward the door.

Great. She was talking to his back, and her words bounced off.

"Yes, you can. And you will." Frank turned to her, a smirk playing at the corners of his mouth. "Clean up the kitchen. I'll tell the kids."

"Bu—"

He slammed the sliding glass door shut before she could get the word out. He strode toward the children, who immediately began hopping and twirling, their four-pawed sidekick in the middle of the excitement.

Olivia shoved her plate aside, the sticky piles careening over the edge onto the counter. She stalked toward her haven, sometimes called her office. Too bad Frank couldn't hear the protest as the door slammed.

"Livie! My dear friend. How the dickens are you?" Vanessa's welcoming, although somewhat loud, voice greeted her.

Olivia sighed into the phone.

"Uh oh. What's the matter?"

"I'm so sorry to ask you this. I know it's an imposition, and you won't believe this, but Frank wants to take the kids to Disneyland today—"

"And he wants Jim to sign you all in? It won't be a problem. He's at work. Don't *you* worry about it."

"But, Van. It's so last minute. I'm sorry."

"Look, *you* have nothing to be sorry about. Frank, on the other hand. He shouldn't have put you in the middle. Made you call me, didn't he? He could have called Jim directly."

All Olivia could manage was another sigh.

"Frank can be such a jerk. I don't know why you stay with him. But listen, this won't be a problem for Jim. I'll call him right away. Love you, girl."

Olivia laid her head back against the chair's headrest. Vanessa tried to support her, but how could she as an unbeliever understand why Olivia couldn't leave Frank? Not having any children, Vanessa didn't get that part of her life either.

How could she thank the Lord enough for giving her the Hunters to be her forever family when she was twelve, and then giving her Vanessa, her next-door neighbor and first friend? The memory of Adam and DeeDee Hunter brought an ache to her throat. Twelve years didn't dim her loss.

Vanessa was the only one left from that singular, really happy time of her life.

Please, please draw Vanessa to you.

Little feet stampeded down the hall toward her door. She hauled herself out of the chair. Better clean up the kitchen and get ready to go.

Chapter Five

Mondays were always hard, but the day after Disneyland, Olivia wasn't surprised the kids still slept soundly at eight in the morning.

Her early risers didn't often allow her to work in the morning, so today Olivia took advantage. Regardless of the battle over what to do about Frank, she had children and a business to take care of. She sat at her desk and flipped through her files.

Three clients with events two years out. Those could wait. Two that needed follow through with the contracted hotels. Better do those today. One new client looking for a large resort hotel with pizzazz meant a fat check. That one first? No. Tempting, but she couldn't let her faithful clients down.

Olivia made three calls, handwriting notes on her conversations as she talked. She filed each note in its proper file and stacked the folders, aligning the edges. She patted the stack of folders and leaned back in her chair. She really should start entering her notes in the computer. But writing them in longhand helped her remember.

Not bad for an hour's worth of work. Her desk phone trilled, and she sat straight in her chair.

"Livie! Girl. How'd yesterday go?" Olivia pulled the phone away from her ear. Vanessa's welcome but enthusiastic greetings demanded distance.

"Everything was good. Jim was a lifesaver."

"And Frank? Did he behave himself?"

Sometimes Olivia wished she hadn't shared so much with Vanessa. She was always quick to check up on Frank's behavior, even though she didn't appreciate it when Olivia asked questions about her private life. And Vanessa didn't know the half of it. She certainly didn't know about the slap.

"Actually, he did well."

"Humph! Thank God for small favors."

What possessed her to share so much with Vanessa and not with Carmen? Must be that Vanessa's own marriage was a little rocky. Carmen's seemed idyllic. Despite being a believer, she probably wouldn't understand. It was hard to know who to trust.

Frank may have done well at Disneyland, but he hadn't forgotten to remind her this morning that Bible study was over. And attending church was out of the question. She should have protested again, but it seemed like a waste of time. To say nothing of dangerous. She had to develop a plan.

Vanessa broke into her careening thoughts. "Been thinking about that San Francisco hotel tour we have booked week after next. Thought we could add a couple a days and combine pleasure with business. Whattya say?"

Olivia was tempted to agree without much thought. Then again, what would Frank say, especially after the recent tirades? Did she dare tell him she wanted to be gone three days instead of one? Carmen wouldn't mind watching the kids an extra two days. Carmen and Jorge's two boys loved having Zoe and Dylan over, and Carmen often mentioned the four kids were easier to handle than when it was just her own.

She worried a cracked spot on her lip, increasing the soreness, while debating with herself over whether she should broach the idea with Frank. But wait. Vanessa wanted to fly out Saturday. Carmen would only have to watch the kids on Monday. It would be good for Frank to have responsibility for the kids over the weekend, and the kids would get to spend more time with their father. They loved being with him at Disneyland yesterday. Well, what kid doesn't love being at Disneyland? But Frank had been cheerful for a change.

Three days of freedom and fun, away from Frank, even if one day was business, sounded heavenly. Time with her oldest friend—what a bonus.

He would never go for this. Frank had already been complaining about the time she devoted to activities other than what he wanted.

On the other hand, he liked that she worked and brought in money, even though his salary was more than adequate. Truth be told, he'd have the kids in traditional school and her work full time. *Frank, why can't you more than half-heartedly support our homeschooling?*

Maybe if she didn't mention that the tour was only one day and the other two were just for fun? *Liar!* Conviction weighed on her chest. No, she couldn't lie to him, a temptation that stole over her way too often, but the Lord had been faithful at convicting her in time, protecting her.

Her mind snapped to her other problem. What kind of plan could she come up with to get her husband back to church, back to Bible study? She groaned. That sounded too much like scheming, manipulation. That's not who she was. A schemer. A liar. Right?

And your rebellious thoughts against submitting to your husband? Hmmmm? Still, you don't really need to submit to your husband. And hasn't he been mean to you lately? Remember that slap? You should get away. Whatever it takes.

The thoughts battled within her. Slouching, she reminded herself where these thoughts came from, the enemy.

Vanessa waited on the line.

"Sounds great, but I'll have to let you know."

"Well, you just tell that no-good husband of yours you're going. I'll make the arrangements. Later!"

And Vanessa was gone before Olivia could protest.

Olivia put away her files. 9:30 a.m. Already. She'd have to get the kids up soon. Maybe a minute or two on Instagram first.

———

The Rockfire Grill was nearly empty two days later when Olivia hurried in out of the March wind, stepping over the welcome mat strewn with vegetable designs. She cheered at the drawings on the colorfully adorned chalk boards and the bright green walls.

Was that Vanessa in the corner? It looked like her except for the white platinum hair shorn close to her head with spiky wisps on top.

"Van? That's quite a do-over!"

Vanessa produced a throaty laugh. "Jim wanted me to keep it dark and long, so of course I had to go short and blonde." She laughed again.

"Of course, you did. How did he take it?" Olivia took a seat across from her.

"He hasn't seen it yet. Tonight. But I'm ready for him."

Olivia thought she detected a glint in Vanessa's eyes.

"Discovered how much money he's been spending without mentioning it. He won't complain about a little ol' new hair-do." Vanessa lifted her chin.

"I'm sure you two can work it out." At least she hoped so.

"Already ordered for us. Ready in a minute."

On cue, a server brought them their food. A can't-get-your-mouth-around-it burger with truffle fries for Vanessa and a turkey salad for Olivia.

"Ah, thanks. You always know what I want."

"Yeah. Rabbit food."

They shared a grin and then tackled the dishes in front of them.

Only the crunch of carrots and cucumbers in Olivia's salad punctuated the companionable quiet for the first few minutes.

It didn't take long for the cheerfulness of the decor to wane in Olivia's heart. What was going on with Frank? He hadn't harassed her the last couple of days or mentioned Bible study or church. She certainly wasn't going to bring it up. She hadn't brought up Vanessa's invitation either.

"Okay, my dear friend. What's up? You're seldom available for lunch."

Olivia took her time chewing, then spoke from behind her paper napkin. "Our trip."

Vanessa arched an eyebrow at her. "Frank did say you could go, right?"

"Uh, well…"

"You didn't tell him?"

Olivia put down her napkin and sat back, letting out a breath that puffed her cheeks. Would she be a disloyal wife if she divulged Frank's recent rages and demands? She and Vanessa had shared many secrets over the years, but Olivia hated to speak against her husband, even though Vanessa often railed against her own. Wasn't loyalty a part of respecting your husband? How would she feel if Frank talked about her to his sports night buddies? How did she know he didn't? The uncertainties about Frank had her at sea.

The story seeped out softly and slowly at first but built to a crescendo as she finished with how kind he'd been the last couple days. The rage, the demand, the slap. Then his audacity with the apology and sweetness. Shame pricked her heart. She was complaining about him being nice.

"Something's troubling Frank. That's not normal behavior."

Ah, yes. That's why she was complaining. The before he was nice part.

Olivia poked at her salad. The tinkling of the shop door diverted her attention to the four black-clad teenagers who surged through the doorway, jostling and laughing. The shortest boy of the group became the tallest with a foot of spiked hair.

"Doesn't that hurt?" Olivia nodded her head toward the group.

"What?"

"You know." She whispered. "Getting all those tattoos and piercings. I would never be brave enough to even try."

"I wouldn't call it brave. I'd call it stupid," Vanessa whispered back a little too loudly.

"Said the woman with spiked platinum hair."

Vanessa chuckled.

Still. It had to hurt. Where does one get the courage to step out even if it's going to hurt? How could Vanessa be so brave to do the exact opposite of what she knew her husband wanted? Even if it was only hair. Was that brave or foolish? Does it hurt less to act when it is in the must-do-the-right-thing category? What's the right thing to do?

"You really need to have a heart-to-heart with Frank."

What? Had she asked that question aloud? Was Vanessa right?

"I don't know, Van. Why rock the boat? He's apologized, and things are good right now." Olivia balled her napkin and tossed it onto her plate. She ran her hand over the pebbly surface of the bistro table, the cold of the tile seeping into her hand. She stopped, not looking up from her splayed fingers on the table. Confronting Frank now would only make things worse. Besides, it was probably her own fault.

"Hey, let's plan our trip." Vanessa's voice bubbled with excitement. "Tell Frank tonight! Don't ask. Tell."

Olivia glanced up to see the set line of Vanessa's mouth.

"I guess I'll talk to him tonight." She held back a sigh. "What are the must-see sights in San Francisco? It's been years since I've been there."

Alcatraz, of course. She'd feel right at home.

Chapter Six

As usual, whenever she made up her mind to talk to Frank, something happened to derail the conversation. He had worked until late last night, and today was his every-other-Thursday sports night out with the guys. And he would really be looking forward to it after his long work hours.

As if on cue, Olivia's phone began to play the *Cops* theme "Bad Boys," and Frank's face appeared on the screen. Good thing *Cops* was one of Frank's favorite TV shows or she'd have a hard time explaining why it was her theme song for him.

"Hey. Take my brown suit to the cleaners, will ya? I'm heading straight to Dave and Buster's to watch the game with the guys. It's gonna be a great game. Don't wait up for me."

The excitement in Frank's voice pricked her heart. He seldom seemed that eager to plan a night out with her. He never suggested they go out, much less plan the evening like Jorge did for Carmen. Did Jim do that for Vanessa?

"But, Frank, I wanted to talk to you about something."

"Don't nag. You know how much I need this. Talk to you in the morning."

The silent phone remained at her ear as if she could will him back on the line. Olivia finally dropped the hand holding the phone to her side. What about what *she* needed? She needed time away too. She was definitely staying those extra days in San Francisco.

Before she could change her mind, she punched in Vanessa's number and told her to make the reservations.

"Kids, grab your jackets. We gotta take Daddy's suit to the cleaners."

The chores and dinner done and the kids in bed, Olivia straightened up her already tidy desk, jerking files from one stack to another, muttering all the while.

He's just not going to have a say about this trip. She could back down about Bible study and church attendance, at least until she could convince him otherwise, but she had to stand up somewhere. Sometimes. Pick your battles, her adoptive mother always told her. But why pick them when you know you won't—can't—fight? Shrugging off that thought, she decided it was time. Okay, she'd pick this one.

Olivia clutched a stack of papers to her chest and stilled herself for a moment, and then slammed the stack to the desk. *Stop, Olivia!* She had to shut down her mind for a while.

Now where was that romance novel she had started last week?

Curling up in the corner of the big grey couch Dylan had nicknamed the elephant, she blew out a breath as she put on her headphones and selected her praise playlist. Okay, let's do this. The type on the page stared back accusing her of neglect. Shaking her head to dislodge the cottony feeling, she tried to read. How many sentences had she read without really reading them? Three? A dozen?

Her cell phone began playing "She's a Lady," her mother-in-law's ringtone.

"Katherine! What a nice surprise."

"Hello, sweetheart. I hope I am not calling too late."

Olivia smiled at the sound of her mother-in-law's deep, but raspy voice. "No, of course not. I'm so happy you called."

"I tried calling that son of mine yesterday and today, but he didn't answer. Is everything okay?"

It wasn't like Frank to ignore his mother's calls. "Everything's fine. He's at his guys' sports night right now. Did you leave him a voicemail?"

"I don't like leaving messages."

Olivia chuckled. "Katherine. If you want him to call you back, you have to leave a message, or texting him is even better."

"Oh, pooh."

They giggled like teen girls.

"What are you doing up at…" Olivia glanced at the clock as she combed her fingers through her hair, calculating Katherine's east coast time. "12:30 in the morning?"

"I just wanted to talk to my son."

"Are you okay? Everything okay at church?"

It was only a brief moment of silence, but the moment was there. "I resigned as the women's ministry administrator and the food bank program manager."

"What? Why?"

"Should say *retired*. Get to a certain age, and, well, they needed a younger woman in charge."

"But you're only sixty!" Whose decision was it for her to retire?

Katherine snorted in a most unladylike way. "You wait until you're sixty."

"What are you doing with all of your free time?"

"This and that."

Her heart ached at the thought that despite her protests, her mother-in-law may have been forced out of her job. A job she had loved for ten years at least. The loss of income was not a likely problem, but loneliness whispered in the shadow of Katherine's words.

Olivia bolted to her feet. "Can you come for a visit?"

Katherine was often reluctant to leave her church duties to venture the three thousand miles. But now?

"I was hoping you would ask. As long as I won't be too much trouble."

Olivia felt lighter already. "Can you stay for Zoe's birthday? On the 25th? How soon can you come?"

"Is next week too soon?"

Plans laid, Olivia pushed the screen icon to end their call. Zoe and Dylan will be so excited. Heck! She was excited. Katherine was such a treasure, accepting her not just as a daughter-in-law, but as the daughter Katherine never had.

Frank should be happy with his mother here. Frank. Would he be happy? Would he stop acting like a jerk? Or would he act up in front of his mother? Katherine's last visit was before he started acting so irrationally.

She sank back to the couch, and her head fell back against the gray velvet-like fabric. As she worried about Frank, the joy of having Katherine with them dimmed. He would never disrespect his mother and act up. Would he? But a couple of weeks ago she would never have expected him to call their church friends hypocrites, or argue with their pastor, or haul her out of a party in front of their friends. Or slap her.

Truthfully, she couldn't count on how Frank would act in front of his mother now. She'd just have to pray and leave it in the Lord's hands. *And how's that been working out for you, Olivia?* She clamped off those thoughts and began making a mental list of everything she had to get done before Katherine arrived next week.

Somewhere between grocery shopping and changing the guest room sheets in her thinking, Olivia remembered her work-turned-needed-getaway trip with Vanessa. She grabbed her cell phone and thumbed her way to her calendar. The site visit was Monday, March 20, but Vanessa wanted to leave Saturday morning for their getaway. Not only was that during

Katherine's visit, but how had she missed the fact it was just a few days before Zoe's birthday party? What an idiot she was.

The pattering of rain on the windows brought the living room temperature down and a chill swept through her. Turning the gas on in the fireplace was tempting, but it was almost eleven and time for bed. Should she stay up and tell Frank his mother was coming? He had told her to not wait up for him. She mentally chastised herself. Why was this even a thing? Shouldn't she automatically know the right thing to do? She shouldn't even have to think about it.

Fatigue befuddled her brain, and she couldn't think any longer. She hoisted herself up and dragged her feet toward the bedroom. She'd get ready for bed and see if she could stay awake until Frank got home.

Clad in her warmest flannel pajamas, she snuggled under the comforter trying to warm up the chilled sheets. Her eyes drooped, and she snapped them open again. Maybe she should get up and write him a note. She nestled further into the bed.

———

Although it was morning, no early light peeped in around the shades. The warmth from Frank's muscled body radiated to her side of the bed. No matter how many times she closed her eyes, they popped open again as if they were eager to see the day, and each time her mind whirled faster.

She slipped from the room and settled into her office. Might as well get to work.

As Olivia looked over the wall calendar posted above her desk, she winced. Zoe's birthday. She hadn't forgotten about it. Exactly. After all, the basic plans were laid a month ago. Recent days had buried the date in her subconscious.

And asking Katherine to come during her trip? What was she thinking? Canceling either was out of the question. The business portion was only overnight, anyway. Was it rude for her to go away for a few days during Katherine's visit? Or would she enjoy having the children to spoil during her absence?

Humph. Frank would never allow it.

Wait. It's not up to Frank on this one. She had to admit Katherine's stay changed that.

What about Vanessa? She pictured Vanessa annoyed. She wouldn't let a visit from her mother-in-law change her plans. No, siree. But then, she didn't much care for her mother-in-law. Or, so it seemed, her husband.

She shuddered at the thought of hurting Katherine's feelings.

How had she allowed her life to get so complicated?

Church. Frank wouldn't dare put up a fuss over attending services with his mom here. As the image of Katherine taking a hairbrush to his backside formed in her mind's eye, a chortle escaped.

Remember? It's time to take a stand. She leaned toward the calendar and with a bold marker wrote "Getaway" in the Saturday, March 18 square. The hotel appointment winked at her from the March 20 box. She immediately regretted adding the getaway to her calendar. What if Frank saw it before she spoke to him? Thank goodness he seldom came into her office.

Heavy footsteps sounded in the hall. He was up so soon? She whirled around, and he filled the open doorway, jamb to jamb. He had elected to go scruffy, or as he called it "his permanent five o'clock shadow." Getting used to it might take a while.

Scrubbing a hand over the scruff, he yawned. "You're up early. My breakfast ready?" He shifted away without waiting for an answer.

She moved sideways, making sure her body blocked the ink that screamed from its March 18 box.

"Wait." Would she have to grab his shirt tail to force him to stop and listen? So many of their conversations occurred on his way out of the room.

He turned back and scowled. "Well?"

She wanted to rant, but she took a moment to adjust the words and soften her tone.

His look blackened. "What? I'm going to be late."

"You missed some calls from your mom. I talked to her last night."

Olivia relayed the conversation, and Frank's face softened into a grin that only the kids and Disneyland had produced.

"Awesome!" And he was out the door.

At least something got him to smile. His mother's visit might show him how unacceptable his belligerence was. If he behaved, everyone benefitted from her visit. Did she dare suggest Katherine watch the children to make her getaway possible?

She stared at the March poster, her hand hovering over her phone. Who had desk phones anymore? Hers was red, a gift from Frank when she first started her business. He told her it was her hotline to success.

It was only six. Better not try Vanessa right now. Anyway, the only thing she could say was she wrote it on her calendar. That wasn't telling him.

"Olivia? Where's my breakfast?"

She scuttled to the kitchen.

———

Frank finally out the door, she clicked Van's photo on her favorites screen, but the call went straight to voicemail. Hmm. Well, the clock showed only seven. She thumbed the off button. Why didn't she leave a message?

Zoe and Dylan stirred, signaling time to get their morning started. She'd try Vanessa again later.

As expected, they squealed with excitement when Olivia told them their grandmother planned to visit. Maybe she should have announced it at after schoolwork. Getting them to settle down to study now was like cleaning Jell-O off the floor. Tedious and almost impossible.

Last night's rainfall hadn't let up, contributing to Zoe and Dylan's constant chatter and their bodies' need to stay in motion all morning. King was similarly infected, barking and prancing between the kids.

Somewhere in her deep past, she thought she had wanted six children. Today she felt as if she had gotten her wish. The entire house seemed to bounce. *Love those two, but oh so glad it is only two.*

Only the normal rainy-day ups and downs colored the day. When Frank joined them at dinner, it was also with only the normal ups and downs. He idled in neutral throughout the evening.

Rain pattered on the roof, a fire blazed in the stone fireplace, and the buttery aroma of fresh popcorn and the sweet smell of hot chocolate pervaded the family room. Frank and Dylan sat riveted by a basketball game, while Olivia allowed Zoe to trounce her in checkers. Yep, that was her story, and she was sticking to it.

She longed for this scene to be their reality. But she couldn't shake the vision that they performed on a stage, all of them actors. She waited for the curtain to fall while they exited into their real life.

Chapter Seven

Olivia's Honda CRV screeched to a halt in her driveway. She'd told Frank she'd be gone only two hours, yet the clock on the dash told her it had been three. Dread twisted in her gut.

He had agreed to watch the kids while she shopped for his mother's visit while emphasizing his patience had a limited window.

Now she grabbed her shopping bags and dashed out of the car. She scooted around the back of the house, hoping Frank was anywhere but the kitchen. Maybe if she came in quietly, he wouldn't notice how long she'd been gone. *Yeah, right.* Why hadn't she paid more attention to the time? Now Frank would have something to complain about, maybe explode again. She couldn't help that the traffic was backed up near the mall or that the first three stores didn't have what she needed.

Olivia slid open the glass door from the patio and stepped into the kitchen. The acrid scent of burned grease assaulted her nose, the offending grease-filled frying pan still sitting on the stove. Pancake batter caked the side of the bowl and puddled to a dried mass at the bottom. The box of pancake mix lay on its side with its former contents blanketing nearly every inch of the counter.

She dropped the bags onto a nearby chair and stared, arms akimbo.

"Mommy! Look, we made breakfast. All by ourselves." Zoe's face shone with pride from where she sat in front of half-eaten, very black pancakes.

"So I see. Where's your daddy and Dylan?" Frank could not have seen this mess yet. He didn't like it when she spent too much time cleaning up when he had other plans, but neither did he tolerate the kids making such messes.

"Right here!" Dylan sat under the table running Hot Wheels through the pancake mix that had found its way to the floor. "Look! I'm making roads. *Zoom! Zoom!*" Behind Dylan, King sprawled, sporting telltale white paws.

"Daddy's in the shower." Zoe forked another bite of pancake into her mouth. "We're gonna surprise him with pancakes," she said around the mouthful.

A groan slipped out unbidden. What was Frank going to say to this?

Wait! What was she thinking? Was she only concerned about the mess? The kids had been using the stove unsupervised. With grease yet. They could have been seriously hurt, burned the house down.

Why wasn't Frank keeping a better eye on them? He could scream all he wanted about the mess, but the danger he had allowed the kids to get into was unacceptable. She hated to chastise the kids when they thought they were doing something nice, but this couldn't happen again.

"You two know you aren't to use the stove without help. What were you thinking?" Her voice became shrill. Need to be calm here. She softened her voice. "You could have been seriously hurt. Don't ever do this again without adult help."

Dylan crawled out from under the table and laid his

powdery hand on her arm. "But we weren't hurt, Mommy. See?" He twirled around for inspection.

Olivia put her arm around his shoulder. "This time. But next time you could be. No stove without an adult."

"What the…?" Frank stopped on the threshold, his eyes bulging and his face reddening.

"Daddy, we made you pancakes and—"

Frank rent the air with a roar that sounded like thunder reverberating in the room. "You two clean up this mess now!"

The children stood momentarily transfixed. Olivia started toward the counter to clean up, when another bellow assailed her. "Don't help. They made the mess. Let them clean it up by themselves. Now!"

Zoe and Dylan moved slowly toward the counter, heads down.

"Now!"

King bolted from the room while the children scurried, grabbing rags and a broom. Zoe dropped the rags on the counter and wrapped her fingers around the handle of the frying pan.

"Stop! No, Zoe. That could still be hot. Frank, she could get hurt. Let me take care of that at least." Olivia held her breath.

Frank nodded.

When Zoe unwrapped her fingers from the pan, Olivia exhaled in relief, picked up the pan and set in the sink, preparing to dispose of the grease.

"This is all your fault, you know." Frank's voice was hard and low, and when she turned to him, his gray eyes looked as unrelenting as steel. "Where've you been? It's been hours."

Her insides knotted up and seemingly moved into her throat with such real pain that her hand flew to the base of her throat.

"Answer me, woman!"

Woman? Oh, Lord, he sounds so much like Dad. She started to reach toward him, but he jerked his arm up. She shrank back. Olivia's mind was a maelstrom. Was he going to slap her again? Or worse, hit her like her father had? What was the matter with Frank? What could she say that would cut through his anger?

Frank halted, his arm in mid-air. He stared at it as if it had materialized on its own, then his face morphed into an expression of shock. He dropped his arm, strode to the sliding glass door, and stood looking out with his arms crossed against his chest.

Olivia grabbed the counter and sank onto the nearest barstool. Zoe and Dylan worked with their heads still down. Hopefully, they hadn't seen what had happened.

What did happen, Lord? Would Frank have hit her? She didn't want to believe that he would do more than slap her and was reassured by the jolt in his expression. Surely, that meant something in his favor?

She remembered seeing a similar expression on her father only once. The day he beat her mother so severely, she was taken to the hospital. The last day of life as Olivia had known it.

Now Frank uncrossed his arms and clenched his fists by his side. After a moment, he splayed his fingers and turned toward the kids.

"Kids. Stop. Your mother will finish up. Sorry I lost my temper."

Zoe and Dylan beamed and shot out of the room without a backward look.

Olivia held her breath for a moment. His apologies often turned into the blame game.

"You wanted to clean it up. Do it." He started toward the door but stopped and turned. She was sure she saw pain in his eyes. "I need some file folders for work."

She plunged her hands into the soapy water. "In the left-hand door of the black supply cabinet in my office."

No sooner had the words left her lips then she sucked in so much air her lungs hurt. The calendar. Maybe he won't look at it. Her body tensed as she gripped the sink's edge. In her office, the cabinet door slammed. Somewhere in the house, the kids giggled.

Her shoulders began to ache from the tension, so she concentrated on relaxing them. Maybe he hadn't looked at the calendar. Why would he?

Heavy steps echoed down the hallway. Without turning around she knew he was in the room. Her shoulder blades prickled.

"What. Getaway." His voice was low and deliberate.

"I have that Visitor's Bureau Familiarization Tour in San Francisco." She turned her body toward him, but focused everywhere but Frank's face, and rushed through the words. "Vanessa and I want to spend a little time there before the meeting."

"And what about the kids?"

"Your mom will be here next Saturday."

"So?"

"And I'd leave on the weekend."

"You expect me and my mom to babysit the kids while you go off gallivanting. Doing who knows what?" His jaw twitched.

Babysit? That's not babysitting. That's spending time with his kids. She choked back the thoughts. Out loud was not an option.

"Your mom is so looking forward to spending time with you—and the kids. I thought you would want to spend time with her and *your* kids." Had she really dared sarcasm?

"You going to be bar hopping or something?"

Olivia choked on her saliva and sputtered. "What? You know me better than that!"

The twitch in his jaw disappeared and his shoulders slumped—a fraction, but she caught it.

"Yeah. Yeah. Miss goody-two shoes. Okay. Okay. But have Vanessa's husband get us into Disneyland one of those days."

Olivia was glad she was still holding on to the counter because she almost sagged to the floor. What? He agreed? Maybe this was a trick. She waited for an even bigger "but" coming. Something more dreadful than asking Jim for tickets.

Frank's cell phone chirped. Pulling the phone from his shirt pocket, he turned and strode out of the kitchen.

She gritted her teeth. Should she be relieved or irritated at the phone call? Had it just delayed the inevitable big demand?

————

What was the phrase her adoptive mother always used to use? Oh, yeah. "Waiting for the other shoe to drop." She hadn't understood it before, but now the feeling sat on her chest. The next six days were like walking on broken glass with not just one shoe on, but no shoes. Which was worse? Waiting for Frank to make more demands? Or actually getting the ultimatum? Get it over with already.

But no demands had come. Olivia tried to focus on getting ready for company, keeping up with the kids' schoolwork, and taking care of her clients.

But it wasn't easy.

Frank's mother would arrive tomorrow, and as she put clean sheets on Katherine's bed, her mind would not be quiet.

Katherine wouldn't mind spending time with the kids while she was out of town. Right? She and Katherine had a whole week before Olivia had to leave for San Francisco. Then there was another week before Zoe's party. And who knew how long Katherine would stay beyond the party? Katherine said she purchased a round-trip ticket with the return date open.

Frank had been so well behaved this week. Katherine's

visit was already working wonders. Would it continue? He had apologized to the kids. Without blaming her. Miraculous.

After making the bed, she dusted every spot imaginable, and some she was sure she never considered dusting before.

Maybe this was the perfect time to get back to church on Sunday. He wouldn't want to disappoint his mother by refusing to go or preventing them from going. Church attendance had been ingrained in him from babyhood. Pastor's kids didn't really have a choice. And in spite of the tragedy of his father's sudden death, his mother was not just a faithful attendee, but an integral part of his father's church since. She would not take kindly to her only child slacking in that respect.

Olivia stopped in the middle of the room. It was very quiet. Had she heard from the kids in the last few minutes? She had been so focused on her own thoughts, she wasn't sure. The sound of Zoe instructing Dylan on the finer points of coloring between the lines reassured her all was well. She dusted the knickknacks on the dresser. Again.

And maybe they could resume hosting Bible study. Okay, perhaps that was too much to ask right away. So maybe not in their own home. Would Frank consent to go to someone else's house? Yeah, but they'd still be hypocrites in his opinion. Wouldn't they?

She had to admit that sometimes she also thought they were hypocrites. The gossip. The holier-than-thou attitude when someone's sin became public. Wasn't everyone a hypocrite? *All have sinned and come short of the glory of God.* People somehow think if no one sees their sin, it's okay. Or if it was only a little sin, that too was okay. Not a big sin like adultery or theft.

Yes, she was guilty of being a hypocrite. Judging someone else's sin as greater than her own. But then, being so worthless and cowardly, who did she know whose sin was greater than hers?

And Frank. Did he consider his own sins? Did he try to

take that tree out of his own eye before looking for the sawdust in someone else's? Or did he even think his actions wrong? He must. At least sometimes or he wouldn't ever apologize. Although that was rare. What about after the kitchen fiasco? Had she really seen pain in his eyes? Yes, she was sure she did. She hoped it meant repentance.

Had she dusted the lampshades? How about the rocking chair?

She needed to figure out the best way to broach the subject of Sunday church. If she talked to him alone, he'd feel freer to say no. Asking him in front of Katherine would be better. Maybe she shouldn't ask. She'd just talk like it was already decided.

People. She needed more people.

Olivia whipped her phone out of her back pocket and tapped Carmen's name on her favorites list.

"Carmen! How about coming over for dinner tomorrow night? Katherine will be here in the morning, and I know she'd love to see you. Kind of a welcome party?"

"As a matter of fact, our plans for tomorrow night just cancelled. So, yeah, we can come over. What do you want me to bring? Jorge already planned to make some carnitas." Carmen babbled for a few more sentences before Olivia could break in.

"Great! Gotta run. See you at six." She jabbed the end call button before Carmen could start another line of conversation. She loved Carmen like a sister, but man, could that girl talk.

When she moved to dust the rocking chair, her leg was pinned to the floor. How had she not noticed the child-sized barnacle attached to her?

"Mommy! Zoe says I can't color outside the lines. Tell her she's not the coloring police." There was no hint of amusement in Dylan's face.

Olivia stifled a laugh. "You're right. She's not the coloring police."

"Then tell her!" A child-sized stomp punctuated his words.

"None of that. We don't stamp our feet and demand our own way. Remember?"

Dylan scowled then allowed his face and his shoulders to sag. "I 'member. Sorry, Mommy. But tell her. Please?"

"Do you remember who's coming in the morning?" She knelt in front of him, taking his picture and his hands in hers. "Grandma's going to be here, and we don't want to be fighting while she's here. You want her to have a good time, don't you?"

"Can I give her my pitcher? Grandmas don't care 'bout coloring outside the lines. They just love us. Right?" Expectant hope shined in his eyes.

"Yes, they just love us."

The hope moved from his eyes to his mouth in a full-size grin.

"Let's go talk to Zoe and then start dinner. Daddy will be home before too long."

Was she scheming too much? She banished that thought. Too late, the plans were already drawn. Heartburn inched its way up her throat.

Chapter Eight

Standing at the airport baggage claim the next morning, Olivia's mind churned, looking for but not finding an answer. Why hadn't Frank wanted to pick up his mother himself? She didn't mind picking her up. In fact, she was rather glad to have the twenty-minute drive to John Wayne Airport alone. It gave her time to think without Frank hovering. Too bad Katherine hadn't flown to LAX. She would have had an hour and a half to wonder why Frank asked her to pick up Katherine.

So much for twenty minutes to think about more important matters. No carousels moved. Rumpled travelers trudged back and forth with irritation and the red-eye travel weariness etched on their faces. The crowds grew bigger as loved ones and business associates arrived to wait with them.

Olivia moved away from the baggage claim area to find an arrivals screen. Finally, it listed Katherine's flight as landed. The bad weather delay could have been much worse than an hour.

Her phone vibrated in her pocket. Frank.

"Are you on your way home yet?" He didn't bother to disguise his irritation.

As she explained Katherine's plane had just landed, the thumping and whirring announced the arrival of the passengers' luggage.

"Too much noise. Be home soon." She cut off Frank's call. She might pay for that later.

The baggage claim screens still didn't list Katherine's flight. None of those bags would be hers.

Her phone vibrated again, and irritation at Frank began a hitch in her breathing until she realized it was Katherine.

"Hi, sweetie! It's me. I just called Frank and he said you were picking me up. I'm walking down the jetway."

Her suitcases couldn't be too far behind. Yep, within minutes, her flight finally showed up on the screen for carousel two. Passengers swarmed up to the thumping and bumping silver behemoth like ants on honey. Good luck at catching sight of your bags with the swarms blocking your path.

Olivia tore her eyes away from the melee and watched for Katherine. Chances are her bags weren't in that batch.

Katherine's five feet, zero inches would be camouflaged in the decidedly taller crowd, so Olivia kept her eyes at the other travelers' chest levels. At last Katherine's head of mostly jet-colored hair, with a few strategically placed silver strands, stood out against a bright red jacket on the man walking near her.

Arms lighter than they had been in months, Olivia hugged Katherine, barely containing the joy bubbling up from her chest.

"I am so sorry, sweetie, that my flight was delayed. You must be exhausted waiting for me." Despite her cross-country overnight trip, Katherine's gray eyes showed concern for Olivia rather than herself.

Frank may have inherited the color of his mother's eyes, but Frank's hadn't shown the same concern for her in some time.

The baggage monster finally coughed up Katherine's bags, and they were on their way.

Not even on a Saturday morning could one get a break from a clogged north bound 55 Freeway. Was there a day or time that she could remember that it wasn't jammed up?

"Sorry for the traffic. I'll get you home as soon as possible so you can get some sleep. Red-eyes always wear me out."

Katherine laid her head back against the headrest. Olivia couldn't see behind Katherine's dark sunglasses, but she'd take bets her eyes were closed.

"Do not give it a thought, dear. I may be old, but I can still handle a flight."

Again, Olivia glanced sideways at Katherine and back to the cars in front of her. The grin on Katherine's face produced an identical grin on her own.

"Old! You're not old."

"You might think differently when you are my age."

At thirty-one, Olivia did view, privately of course, sixty as old, an almost-to-the-end-of-life age. Her mother-in-law's birth certificate may reveal one age, but Olivia found it impossible to think of Katherine as old. Well, except maybe her refusal to text. Olivia grinned again.

———

"Gramma's here! Gramma's here!" The children squealed as they ran down the driveway to meet them.

"Hey, munchkins." Katherine threw her arms wide as her grandchildren hurled themselves at her, chattering away.

"Whoa! I'm glad to see you, too, but let's slow down so I can understand you." Katherine's throaty voice always seemed to be anointed with kindness.

"Kids, let Grandma settle in her room before you wear her down." Olivia's heart warmed at the kids' enthusiasm.

"Hey, Mom." Frank wrapped his arms around Katherine

in a full-bear hug and pecked her porcelain cheek. "Glad you're here. Let's get these to your room." He grabbed her bags and moved down the hall.

The settling in complete, Zoe and Dylan led their grand-mother into the family room and to the big couch with its high, humped back.

Katherine stroked the couch's gray arm. "What is it you call this couch? I know it's something funny."

"Gramma! It's the elephant. Doesn't it look like one?" Dylan was proud to have named it when he was two.

They giggled, collapsing onto the elephant. King panted for attention. Olivia's heart was happy watching and listening to Frank, her children, and their grandmother share stories and laughter.

Thank you, Lord, for this gift, this wonderful woman. Even Frank seemed happy and at ease for a change. She looked forward to the next few weeks soaking up Katherine's joy.

Why can't I have the same joy, Lord?

Obviously, Katherine's life had been far different than her own. Except for the death of Frank's father, it was nearly perfect from what she could see. Katherine didn't have the past to deal with as Olivia did. Yes, Isaac, Frank's father, died suddenly of a heart attack. Olivia knew the sorrow of suddenly losing a parent. Not one parent, but both. At the same time. Twice.

At least Katherine and Frank had the memories of Isaac, the beloved pastor of their large congregation, as well as the memories of all the good works he did on behalf of the community. She wished she'd known Isaac. Frank never wanted to talk about his father. Twelve years and still too painful. Twenty-one years since her birth parents died, and twelve since her adopted parents. Yes, still way too painful.

Isaac and the Hunters died the same year? She hadn't put that together before.

Now that Olivia thought about it, Katherine seldom

wanted to talk about Isaac either. They must have loved him very much to still be grieving so intensely that they couldn't talk about him.

Did she grieve over her own birth father? She wanted to, but her grief seemed to be more about the father he wasn't than for the father he was.

Yet grief shackled Olivia like she was bound in a too-small burlap sack. Tight, shapeless, and scratchy. With hidden pockets in which she stored her griefs. One for her father's "You're worthless." "Get out of my way." "You're bothering me." One for her mother, whose life seemed so wasted. Another for the three years in foster care homes, some good, some bad. Another for the loss too soon of her beloved adoptive parents.

Tucked way down was a treasure box filled with the love the Hunters showed Olivia by miraculously adopting her when she was twelve and not so lovable. Filled with thanksgiving for helping her see Jesus and getting to know Him.

She wanted to remove that treasure box, put it on display in a trophy case, a place without grief. Even after so many years, Olivia's soul-scars kept the treasure box buried so deep she couldn't reach it. And even if she could, tentacles of the sisal fibers wound themselves around the box, imprisoning it in place.

How long, Lord? How long?

———

That evening, warm and spicy aromas filled the house, along with bright conversation and the children's laughter. Jorge was the lead circus clown entertaining with antics that ended in raucous hoots from all of the little clowns. Even Frank joined in. King, infected by the excess energy, earned a time out in the backyard.

"Hey, gang. Let's play the new game we brought!" Carmen's love of games always enchanted Zoe and Dylan.

"Oh, yes! Let's." A brief nap had revitalized Katherine who was now happily in the center ring.

Thank you, Katherine, Jorge, and Carmen for always adding fun.

After an hour of Bamboozle and Pie Face, Katherine suggested a change of pace with a video in the family room for her and the four children.

Devoid of the circus, the decibel levels fell within reason. The four adults who remained sprawled in companionable silence sipping the cinnamon-spiced Mexican hot chocolate Carmen had brought.

Jorge leaned forward on the mid-century sectional and rested his forearms on his thighs, cradling his steamy mug between his knees. "Frank, Lance Gordon mentioned to me that you were a linebacker for the Philadelphia Soul Arena Football team. A star until the major concussion. I didn't know."

"Gordon? Who's that?"

"Dr. Lance Gordon. You remember. He spoke at church a couple of weeks ago about his mission trip. He's a radiation oncology doctor."

No, Frank wouldn't remember. He had refused to go to church that week. Dr. Lance Gordon? Oh, must be the doctor she met at the Delgados' party.

"Huh. Yeah. I played for the Soul." Frank leaned further back into the far corner of the sectional, propping his right ankle on the opposite knee, and stretching his arm along the back. "I was their best mike linebacker. Could call out the plays so the linemen always knew exactly what to do. Made the most tackles, too. They shoulda renewed my contract. One little concussion. They wouldn't have lost the next season."

Olivia blinked. She was sure that instead of seeing Frank

sitting, she'd see him strutting around the room and unfurling his plumage.

"Lance said he read you had several concussions." Carmen cut a glance to Olivia. "You must have suffered side effects. Headaches and such?"

"Oh, well, yeah. A few headaches. But nothing I can't—couldn't—handle."

Headaches? Yes, there had been a few lately. But he'd had headaches ever since college football. Nothing new. How many drugs did he take for them? Could the drugs be altering his moods?

A yawn made its way around the room, and all seemed to arrive at the same conclusion—it must be time to call it a night. They stood and Jorge whistled *Reveille*. A signal for his children that was far better than yelling.

But did he realize *Taps* would be more accurate? How do you whistle taps? Olivia tried it, but no sound passed her lips. Just as well. It would have been pathetic.

Of course, Jorge knew the difference between *Reveille* and *Taps*. Hadn't he served a tour in Afghanistan? Olivia remembered a photograph in the Delgados' living room. Both Carmen and Jorge in Army uniforms. Taken at a stateside base.

Talk about courage. No one was talking about courage except the voices in her head, and they constantly nagged on the subject. How could Carmen have had enough courage to leave her close-knit family, travel across the country alone, and live through basic training? Earning commendations, even. Olivia couldn't fathom that kind of bravery. Any kind, really. God must have left that out of her own gene pool.

Did foster care count? She was always alone in foster homes. But she wasn't brave then. She hid inside her shell, emerging only when Adam and DeeDee adopted her.

What about leaving the only real home she'd known to go away to college? That had to count for something. Even though it was less than 200 miles from home. Then didn't she have to go at it alone when Adam and DeeDee died two months later? That took courage. Right? No. She had retreated into her shell again. Until Frank.

Frank had shown up three months later, and Olivia fell into his arms and under his spell, trusting for a change. He was her cowboy riding in on a white horse to save her.

Had she asked the Lord whether she should marry Frank? Whether it was His will? It seemed so unnecessary. After all, he was a PK, a pastor's kid. Handsome, charming. Except his horse turned out to be black. So did his hat. Misplaced trust. At least for the last couple of years.

Katherine and the children answered Jorge's *Reveille* call.

As the packing up began, the voices in Olivia's head resumed their nagging. Courage. She straightened her spine. The time was now. "Don't forget. Daylight savings. Turn your clocks forward. We don't want to be late for church tomorrow."

All adult eyes turned to her. Katherine's and Jorge's smiled. Carmen's questioned, and Frank's were stormy.

"Of course. We won't let a lost hour of sleep keep us from church. Right, son?" Katherine's eyes questioned Frank.

Olivia caught the look, and her heart hammered. What did Katherine know? It was as if she knew that Frank had stopped going to church, in fact had prevented all of them from going to church. But how could she?

Frank set down the game he had been re-packing, glared at Olivia, and put his arm across his mother's shoulders. "Of course, Mom. We wouldn't want you to miss church."

Although she tried, Olivia couldn't detect any rancor in his tone.

Katherine patted Frank's cheek.

The Delgados' departure seemed to suck all the air out of the house. Olivia could hardly breathe as she went through the motions of getting the kids to bed and saying good night to Katherine.

Maybe Frank would be asleep if she took her time tidying up. Yeah, right. Like that had ever worked before.

As Olivia moved toward the open bedroom door, Frank appeared in her line of vision, pacing the length of their bedroom, pounding his fist into his thigh followed by repeatedly flexing his fingers. He turned at her footsteps, still flexing his fingers. Olivia sucked in a breath.

"What did you tell my mom?" He spoke through clenched teeth, his jaw twitching.

"What do you mean?"

"You told her I've been a bad little boy. That I haven't been going to church."

"No. Honest."

"Clever little trick. Sucking me in like that."

"You want your mom to know how you've refused to go to church? That would kill her."

Rage blossomed on his face, and Olivia stepped back.

He wouldn't slap her with his mom in the room down the hall, would he? Her face tingled at the possibility she could be wrong. She stepped back again, but one more step and she'd be in the hall.

Frank scrubbed his five o'clock scruff and the rage was gone. He looked at Olivia, and she thought she saw the pain in his eyes again. But as before, it was gone before she could be sure.

"All right. Yes. I...I don't want to hurt my mother." His brawny shoulders slumped.

She longed to throw her arms around him. Confusion over whether he needed consolation or a kick in the pants held her back. Was he giving in because he truly didn't want to hurt his mother? Did he realize his recent choices already hurt his family? She longed to think this was the road back. It couldn't be that simple. Could it?

Frank grabbed his head and moaned slightly.

"Frank?" She took a tentative step toward him.

"My head is splitting. Where's that pain medication? I gotta get to bed."

Olivia heard him rummaging in the bathroom cabinet and the water running as she changed into pajamas. He emerged from the bathroom, slid into bed, and eased his head to the pillow.

"Frank? What's wrong?" He *had* been complaining of headaches more and more lately. Was he taking the heavy duty drugs the sports doctor had prescribed or meds the doctor gave him after his accident last year? How much? Were they the culprits?

"Just a headache. Now let me get some sleep." He turned off the light and scrunched his eyes closed.

Time to drop the subject and get some sleep herself. He would only lash out. She turned her light out and tried to relax, but the more she tried, the more her mind continued to churn. *What's up with these headaches? Did he have a brain tumor or something? Is that where the rages came from?*

She tossed about like a ship in a storm. That's what she was, a little boat in a big storm. And the raging waves of her plush comforter threatened to drown her as she thrashed about.

Need to put one of the Amish quilts on the bed instead of this deadly comforter. But Frank didn't like the Amish quilt. Instead, he preferred the downy softness of the expensive comforter.

Frank grunted and then babbled in his sleep. Olivia lay still trying to understand what he was saying. But it was all gibberish. She sighed and once again tried to relax. The clock glowed 1:00 a.m. No. Make that 2:00 a.m.

Chapter Nine

"I enjoyed meeting your church family yesterday. I don't remember any of them from my last visit. But that wasn't your regular pastor, was it?"

Sunday church had gone better than expected. Pastor David was gone on a pastor's conference, and none of their friends mentioned the Stanford family's two-week absence. Best of all, Frank hadn't made any snide comments. Must be due to his mother's presence. Whatever the reason, she'd take it.

They sat at the kitchen table, the white painted wood covered with lists for Zoe's party. Guests. Decorations on hand. Decorations to buy. Menus, several variations worth. Zoe and Dylan reluctantly filled in math worksheets at the breakfast bar. Dylan's was mostly coloring and drawing objects. The five-year-old boy's attention span was shorter than their guinea pig's legs.

"And you are working with the homeless on the homeless missions team? Is that right?"

"I only handle the paperwork, arranging for shelter or motel space, paying grocery bills. I'm not out actually working with the homeless."

"Oh?"

"You know me. I prefer behind the scenes."

"I never understood that, dear. You are so capable, and so good with people." Katherine started a new list for party favors.

What? Where'd she get that idea? Maybe with people she knew. Maybe.

"You do well in your business. That's dealing with people."

"That's different. It's mostly by phone. It's not personal. Business."

She'd learned quite young that it wasn't safe to share your story with just anybody. The twins, Christy and Shelley, 13-year-old divas more spoiled than last week's fish, taught her that in her first year of foster care. How foolish she was to think that she'd have sisters to play with, to share secrets with. Olivia made the mistake of telling the twins from heck (she banished the word she really wanted to use) who looked at her with horror as if she were the murderer. Then they giggled their way to taunting her with "little orphan girl." Yeah, that first year was one bad year. She was happy to shake the dust off her feet as she moved on to another foster home. Not that it was much better.

The trip. Better get back to the task at hand. Olivia hadn't brought up her trip yet, and this was the perfect segue.

Olivia stopped making notes about the menu and two-handedly fiddled with her pen. "Speaking of my business. I have this trip planned."

Katherine didn't hesitate in her own notetaking.

"A site tour scheduled in San Francisco. We've been invited by a new hotel to stay and check it out. For our clients."

"Who's 'we,' dear?"

"Vanessa and me. Remember my friend Vanessa?"

"Your childhood friend. And she helped get you the job

with the company, right?" Katherine continued writing notes without looking up.

"Mmmm." Olivia ran her hands over the smooth plastic, re-reading the maker's name, clicking the silver button on top. *Click. Click. Click.*

"When are you going?"

"Well, that's the thing. See. The hotel is putting us up Sunday night and the tour is Monday—" The rest stuck in her throat.

Katherine finally looked up. "Okay. And?"

How did Katherine know there was an "and"? *Maybe because you forgot to say when you were leaving? Maybe because you sound guilty?*

"And—before I asked you to come for a visit, Vanessa and I had planned a kind of getaway. Just for a day or two."

Not taking her gaze from Olivia's face, Katherine folded her hands over the notepad. Olivia examined Katherine's expression searching for any sign of judgment. She found nothing but gentleness.

Breathe. Swallow. "We had planned to leave Saturday morning. Come back Monday night." Swallow. Breathe.

"Sounds like fun." Katherine concentrated on shuffling the papers in front of her. And suddenly looked up again. "Oh, and you're worried Frank and I can't handle the kids alone. Don't give it another thought. Frank probably already has a plan."

Olivia resumed the fascinating examination of her pen. "Well—you see—Frank isn't really good at that." Unless it's going to Disneyland and imposing on Jim. Now what would Katherine think of Frank? Would she judge her for saying such a thing? *Now you've gone and done it.* She would ask Frank what kind of wife would say such a thing about her husband. Dare criticize him in front of his own mother.

"He did say something about Disneyland." Squirming in

her chair, Olivia finally looked up and focused on Zoe and Dylan.

Zoe concentrated on the paper in front of her, her tongue peeking out the corner of her mouth, and Dylan scribbled fast and furiously, accompanied by little motor noises.

Spring was still a week away according to the calendar, but according to the backyard, it was showing up early. Nasturtiums, geraniums, and poppies dotted the garden beyond the courtyard. Olivia wished she was out there. Free and light like the little brown birds who twittered and danced from bougainvillea bush to bougainvillea bush that surrounded the gazebo in the far corner of the yard.

Frank built the gazebo for her the first year they lived in the house. He added built-in benches and a little wrought iron bistro table and chairs. It was supposed to be their getaway. But it now sat as neglected as the wife. Lonely for visitors.

"I mean—it's not that he doesn't want to." She turned her face back to her mother-in-law, whose eyes held a question, but her face still soft. "He just doesn't remember." Really? Such a lie. He doesn't want to. And he doesn't remember. Because he doesn't want to. Lately.

Katherine smiled and patted Olivia's arm. "It'll be fine, sweetie. Frank and I can handle it."

"Are you sure you don't mind me leaving so soon after you get here? And so close to Zoe's party?"

Laughter bubbled from Katherine like a tinkling fountain. "Honey, I am just pleased to be helping. To be needed." Katherine's expression changed ever so slightly, and the fountain dried up. "Really. I have not been needed for a while. Thank you for inviting me to come."

A little breeze wafted in through the open door, caressing her cheek. She felt a little lighter. Now if only Frank would continue to cooperate. Olivia was still waiting for that second shoe, more like a brick wall. Forgetting he ever agreed to the whole trip. Upending everything.

"Hey, mommy!" Dylan slid off the stool and stood at his grandmother's side. "Can I give my picture to Grandma?"

"Of course."

"And can I tell her my new joke?" Dylan bounced on his toes.

Olivia scrunched her eyes, surely creating too many folds on her forehead. "Ummm. What joke?" What was going to come out of his mouth this time?

"Do you know why there aren't hardly any jokes 'bout popcorn? Because they're corny." Dylan and his grandmother laughed at his joke while his mom and sister groaned. Olivia would have to work on Dylan's grammar.

"I think we're about ready to go party shopping. Who wants to go?" Olivia anticipated Dylan's response, but not Zoe's.

"Nah. I wanna stay with Gabe and Artie."

"Me, too. Can I stay at Auntie Carmen's?"

"Zoe, you don't want to go shopping for your birthday party?"

"Well, Artie's gonna show me his new book 'bout space. And he's got a new space video." Zoe loved books, outer space, and the ocean. Two out of three would be a magnet.

Carmen had said Dylan could stay while they shopped, and adding Zoe was never a problem.

"Okay. If you're sure."

"I'm sure. Gramma knows what I want."

Grandma knows? Not her own mother? Now that she thought about it, Olivia realized she hadn't talked to Zoe about a theme. How had Katherine accomplished that in two days? Where had Olivia's brain been? Obviously self-centered.

"Mom, do we still have those creation videos with Mr. Ham? I think Artie would like to watch 'em too."

"They're in one of the storage bins in the garage. We can look for them later in the week and show Artie when they come over."

Zoe flashed a frown. "But—"

"No time to look today. I don't even know which bin they're in. You have plenty to keep you busy today."

The nearly eight-year-old exhaled. "Okay."

Katherine re-shuffled her notes and stuffed them in her handbag at her side. "I guess I better go put on my face then."

Dylan recoiled from his grandmother, his mouth a perfect "O." "But, Gramma. You have a face." He leaned toward her an inch. "Can you really take it off?" His face was as serious as the day he learned he couldn't ride a motorcycle until he turned sixteen.

Katherine's mouth worked, and then she coughed to cover the laugh trying to escape. "That's just an expression. My grandmother used to say it to me when I was a little girl. It means I have to put my makeup on. On my face."

Disgust spread across Dylan's features. "Oh. Is that all?" His grandmother didn't have that special power after all.

Zoe poked Dylan in the ribs. "You doofus. Everybody knows that." What wisdom is granted to siblings two and half years older.

Hours later, the SUV loaded with birthday party supplies, Katherine asked to see the beach. Reluctantly, Olivia agreed as long as Katherine called Frank.

The sun and breezes at the Huntington Beach Pier enticed them to loiter.

As the sun began to sink a little low, Katherine looked at her watch. "Well, I guess we better go home. We've been gone a bit longer than I told Frank."

Olivia sucked in a deep breath. Frank would not be happy. He may be irritated, but he wouldn't dare get really angry or explosive with his mother. Right? Olivia counted on that. She realized Katherine hadn't addressed her earlier request to know more about Frank's father, Isaac. Did she forget? Katherine wasn't forgetful or easily distracted. Was she avoiding the subject? Why should she do that?

Chapter Ten

"What's the matter with you?" Frank greeted her as they returned home from the beach, the sun completely gone, the night taking over. He stood inches from Olivia, his face flushed and spittle pooling in the corners of his mouth. "Don't you have any consideration? I've been working all day!"

She stepped back, her throat aching with guilt. It was her fault—again. She should have known going to the beach would take too much time. What *was* the matter with her? Her husband had worked all day, earning a living.

Pinning her arms around her middle, Olivia stammered, "I-I'm sor-sorry. I guess I wasn't thinking."

Her eyes darted around the room. Where were Zoe and Dylan? Although she needed to know where they were, she was glad they weren't here witnessing her humiliation.

"You got that right! You never think. Never think about me." He stepped toward her again, closing the gap she'd tried to create, bellowing curse words she had never heard from him before. "You are a sorry, stupid woman."

A diminutive wall of human flesh thrust itself into the few inches that separated Olivia and Frank. Katherine's back was rigid against Olivia's arms and chest. Olivia almost missed Katherine's words, so quietly spoken.

"Frank, calm down. Now. It wasn't Olivia's fault. I told you on the phone. I wanted to go to the beach, and I insisted."

The vein in Frank's neck pulsed faster, and he jabbed a finger toward his mother. "This is not your business. Stay out of it."

The scene seemed to morph into slow motion, and Frank and Katherine's voices were eerily deep and distorted. Olivia wanted to step back but found herself leaning forward into Katherine for support. Could one actually faint from fear? Olivia was sure she was about to.

Her eyes snapped wide when Katherine's next words softly but clearly came to her ears. "Leave this house now."

She could only imagine Frank's gaping mouth.

"Don't come home until you calm down. Then I will expect an apology to Olivia and myself." Katherine pointed toward the door. "Go. Now."

He would never let this pass. Never let his mother tell him what to do. Interfere. At least in his eyes. Olivia held her breath for the roar she was sure was coming.

Frank turned on his heel and stormed out of the room. *Whoosh.* The room's turbulent air was sucked out with him. The front door slammed.

Katherine turned and reached up to put her arms around Olivia's shoulders, pulling her into a tight hug. Olivia sank into her mother-in-law's embrace, her nose tingling with unshed tears. She would not cry. Beyond that thought, her mind was a jumble. Frank never backed down in the throes of a rage. How did Katherine manage to do that? Never had Olivia expected to see her husband relinquish the last word. Even to his mother.

Three little bodies joined the hug, including one with four feet. "What's the matter, Mommy? Why is Daddy shouting?" Zoe's cheeks were wet with tears.

"Doesn't he love us anymore?" Sobs punctuated Dylan's question.

King whined.

What has he done to my babies? Rage began to build up, not for herself but for the two little innocents entrusted to her. Blood poured back into Olivia's extremities, and she knelt, encircling her children in her arms. Katherine, too, knelt, holding all of them.

Between them, Olivia and Katherine managed to calm Zoe and Dylan, feed them some dinner, and tuck them in.

Frank had not returned from wherever he had slunk off to. She didn't much care at the moment that he hadn't returned.

———

The only words Olivia and Katherine shared while managing the children related to their care. But now they sank onto the elephant, enveloped in its comfort. Katherine turned to Olivia, her brows forming a deep V.

"We need to talk about this."

Olivia turned her head aside, but Katherine continued. "Has he treated you like this before?"

How to tell a mother her son has been a monster? Ok, maybe not a monster. He hadn't hit anyone. Just a slap. A shake. Unlike her own father. Now *he* had been a monster. But Frank had been acting like a tyrant the last couple years, and more so in recent months, not like himself at all. He had been loving and kind during their courtship and early marriage. Sure, sometimes he got a little unreasonably angry, but never had he raged as he had recently. And curse words?

"O-only recently. Really, this isn't like him."

"Tell me." Katherine whispered.

Would telling his mother be disloyal to her husband? Would she be on his side? Probably not, if Olivia judged by how Katherine told him off a few hours ago. Olivia twisted the tissue in her lap as she related the last few months—his sudden rages, his mood swings, his apologies, and his mind changes. She kept her ears alert, worried that Frank would steal in and hear her revealing her secrets, his secrets. Katherine remained calm, quietly listening, only asking a question or two.

At the end of her story, Olivia raked her fingers through her hair, spent, as she sagged into the couch. *So tired.* Sleep was all she could think about. But she knew she wouldn't be able to sleep tonight.

"My dear, I am so terribly sorry Frank is acting this way. I can't be sure why, but I think there are some things I need to explain."

Olivia sat up straight, sleep forgotten.

"I love my boy, but Frank is responsible for his own actions...You may think Frank's father was a saint. That's what you've been led to believe." It was Katherine's turn to avert her gaze from Olivia. But only for a moment. She turned her head toward Olivia again, her back as straight as a soldier at attention.

"That's my fault, dear. I've spent the last twelve years trying to protect Isaac Stanford's reputation. That he was the fine, upstanding pastor everyone thought he was. But it's all lies. I couldn't bear the thought people would judge me, as if it were my fault. What was the matter with me? Why wasn't I good enough to hold Isaac, keep him from evil?"

She became quiet. The only sound in the room was Katherine's rapid breathing, the *tick-tock* of the antique clock on the wall, and the hum of the tires from a car passing in the street.

Don't stop now! Olivia's mind screamed so loud, she looked around, thinking she'd said it aloud. But she hadn't. She waited, staying silent with great effort.

Evil? What had Isaac done? Surely it couldn't have been

that bad? Could it? Was Isaac like Olivia's father? Was it worse? Criminal?

Olivia reached for her hand and started to speak, but Katherine jumped up and put out a hand to quiet her.

Pacing the room, not looking at Olivia, Katherine continued. "A couple years after Frank left for college, Isaac had a massive heart attack and died—almost instantly. The funeral was huge. The eulogies went on and on. I thought it was Isaac's due. Until—"

Katherine stopped and sank back onto the couch. "About a month after his death, we discovered Isaac owned several pieces of property, some commercial spaces, some with homes. We have no idea where he found the money to buy the properties. The church even had their books audited to make sure he didn't embezzle. He hadn't, but no one has yet discovered the source of the money."

"That's good news, right? He left you with a source of income."

"As far as it went, yes. But the bad news was he had another family living in one of those homes, and a lot of the money went to her."

Olivia sucked in her breath, almost choking. Another family?

Isaac had another family, wife and children? No, that can't be. Why wouldn't Frank have told her that? Unless Frank's following in his father's footsteps. Is that why he's changed so much lately? No, he's not out of town that often and only for a day or two. What if he had another family right here in Orange County? It was not like a small town here. No one would ever know. Right?

"He was married to someone else? While he was married to you?"

"Apparently they were never legally married during the seven years they were together. And the children were hers by previous relationships."

A sadness pressed upon Olivia, leaving a gummy sensation to her eyelids. "Seven years." How could Isaac have hidden it all that time? "So, was it a common-law marriage?"

"No. New York generally doesn't recognize common-law marriage if a couple just lives together. The property was only in Isaac's name, and there were no joint bank accounts. It seems Isaac had hidden bank accounts, and he just wrote her checks that she deposited in her account."

What must Katherine have gone through? But Olivia could detect no emotion in Katherine's recitation. Was it because she'd already worked it out? Olivia had never noticed any bitterness in Katherine over the years. In fact, she always seemed so full of love and joy. *Not me. Not really.* Or had Katherine been faking it? *What have I been faking?*

"Frank has been unable to forgive his father."

"You got that right!" Frank's guttural cry as he stepped into the room rent the air.

Katherine jumped up. Olivia couldn't see Katherine's face, but the stiffening of Katherine's back was obvious. Olivia's mind scrambled for something to say, but she sat mute.

Oh, Lord. Oh, Lord. What now? How much did Frank hear? Maybe he'll be glad this is finally in the open. Or not. Olivia gripped the arm of the couch as if it would save her from whatever was coming next.

"Mother, this is none of Olivia's business." Frank ground out the words through jaws clenched so tight Olivia thought his face would break. "You had no right to talk to her about him."

No right? Shouldn't a wife know these things about her husband's family? Especially since it may have explained so many things. Was his father's betrayal the source of his rage? And why only recently? It didn't excuse his actions, but perhaps she could understand Frank a little better now. Maybe it was the beginning of something.

"Frank—"

"Shut up, Olivia." The ice in his voice should have stopped her.

"I won't shut up!" Olivia heard herself shout. She never shouted. *Where did that come from?* She jumped up and skirted around the far end of the couch, stepping behind it, her hands clutching the high humpback. From the safety behind the elephant, she whispered, "We need to talk about this. You and your mom need to talk this through, so you can forgive him."

Barrier or not, Olivia trembled at her audacity.

Was that fear she saw flit across Frank's face? No, couldn't be. His face hardened even more than she thought possible.

"Forgive him?" He scoffed. "Why should I?"

"God wants you to forgive him."

Frank sneered at Olivia. "God? Where was he while my father two-timed us with another family?"

Olivia glanced at Katherine who was mute and seemingly rooted to one spot on the Berber carpet.

"Frank, you…you're not blaming God, are you?"

"God and my self-righteous, pillar-of-the-church father!"

Visibly trembling, Katherine reached toward the side chair and eased down.

Olivia clutched the couch in front of her until her hands hurt. "But that's in the past now."

Like her own father was in the past. *You hypocrite. You preach forgiveness, but you haven't forgiven.* A whispered response welled up. *But that's different!* Still, a question nagged. *Why?*

Her chest felt as if the dental x-ray technician had thrown the protective lead apron over her.

Katherine held up her palm to Olivia. "He has a right to be angry. With me, too. I should have known. For the first several years after I found out, I couldn't help think I should have been able to hold my own husband."

Frank managed a strangled cry. "Why couldn't you?

Weren't you a good enough wife?" His look toward Olivia said, *See?*

"Son. A counselor helped me realize it had nothing to do with that. It was your father's sin. A sin that a loving God would forgive. A sin that we must forgive if we want to be forgiven."

"Hah! Did Dad ask God for forgiveness? I doubt it."

"We don't know what went on between your father and God as he took his last breath. We have to hope that he asked and was forgiven. Even if he didn't, one sin doesn't separate us from the love of the Father."

"Enough of this bull. I'm going to bed." Frank ran out of the room as if demons chased him.

Maybe they did.

———

After the previous day's emotional revelations, Olivia tried to keep the children to their routine, but a funk hung over her like ninety-five-percent humidity. Frank hadn't spoken to her before he left for work. Again.

Katherine had claimed a headache after the altercation with Frank, so there had been no more discussion. This morning Katherine had eaten a quick breakfast and returned to her room.

Yesterday's sunshine melted into drops that looked suspiciously like rain. Talk about humidity. At least the March rain was cool, not hot and sticky. With every drip falling from the trees outside, the kids inside became more restless.

Maybe taking them and Katherine someplace special would lift everyone's spirits. Would that send the children the wrong signal? Every time something ugly happened, they got a treat? Children should enjoy their childhood but spoil them with too much activity, and they may begin to expect it as their right. Sure, lots of household chores could be done together. When did housework ever quit? Where did she draw the line between having the kids work together as a family and overburdening them? Balance. She needed to get the kids busy. For them and herself.

"Hey, guys, we're going to play a fun game!"

Zoe and Dylan looked up from their tablets. They'd finally settled down to play, but they'd been staring at their screens for about an hour.

"Funner than this game?"

Zoe gave her mother an indignant look. "But I'm reading. Besides, when you say that you usually mean work."

"We're going on a treasure hunt."

Now interest sparked in their eyes.

Olivia led them to the garage and rolled up the large outside door for light. The rain just beyond was soft and steady. Frank's bronze Honda Accord, sporting reminders of Frank's accident, occupied one half of the space. He wouldn't drive the car but refused to get rid of it. Piles of boxes, sports equipment, and, well, junk was the only word to describe it, occupied most of the other half. Shelves rimmed the three walls, each shelving unit packed with boxes. Some neatly taped and labeled. Some overflowing. All of it dusty. The space matched her soul, dusty and overflowing with junk.

Olivia wrinkled her nose. Did she really want to tackle this stuff? It was for a good cause. Getting her kids busy.

"What's the treasure?"

"Is there a treasure map?"

Olivia managed a little quirk on one side of her mouth. "No treasure map."

Dylan continued to press. "But what is it? Is it gold? Will it be in a treasure chest?"

"This is what we're going to do." Olivia explained they would look through all the open boxes and if they didn't find the treasure, they'd throw away what was in the box.

Zoe got into the discussion. "How will we know if we find the treasure?"

Dylan fisted his hips. "Well, duh! Don't you know what treasure looks like?"

Zoe looked down, in more ways than one, at her little brother. "No. And neither do you."

"Sure, I do. We watched *Pirates of the Caribbean*. Doncha remember?"

Olivia suppressed a laugh and asked Zoe to grab the step stool and Dylan to grab an empty trash can.

For the next hour they pawed through dirty boxes finding very little of interest or worth, much less anything that resembled treasure. The trash can began filling up.

"Mommy, I'm getting tired. Aren't we ever going to find a treasure?" Dylan rubbed his eyes with dirty fists.

"Hey, Mommy! I think I see the Mr. Ham videos." She put one hand on the cardboard box in front of her that was beginning to sag under the weight above, then leaned far to the right to reach the clear plastic tote full of videos.

A scream and a crash and Zoe was on the ground where she lay with her arm underneath her, cardboard boxes and their contents scattered.

"Zoe!"

"Mommy, my arm hurts." Tears created a waterfall down her cheeks.

Olivia felt Zoe's arm, eliciting great whimpers.

"We need to take you to the hospital, sweetie. You may have a broken arm—at least a sprained wrist."

She helped Zoe stand and guided her through the rain out to the CRV, helping her get settled on the back seat.

"Dylan, in the car with Zoe, please. I'm running in to get Grandma and an umbrella. Be right back."

The trip to the Children's Hospital was like Mr. Toad's Wild Ride, between dodging the larger puddles and glancing frequently in the rearview mirror at Zoe who bit her lip and held her arm. As they neared the hospital, Olivia took the gamble of using her cell phone and driving to call Frank. As usual, he didn't answer.

"Frank. It's me. Zoe may have broken her arm. At the Children's Hospital now."

They pulled into the hospital parking structure, and the race to the ER was on. Thank the Lord Katherine was here to stay with Dylan in the waiting room.

Olivia and Zoe waited in a curtained area. The child tried to remain brave during the probing and x-rays. Braver than Olivia.

"Mrs. Stanford, Zoe's arm isn't broken, just a grade one sprain to her wrist. We'll wrap it." The doctor pulled supplies from drawers and cupboards. "Have her ice it. And rest it. It'll be sore for a while, and she should be careful for the next two or three weeks, but it's nothing serious. Nurse? Where are the...? Excuse me. I'll be right back."

Before the doctor could get to the opening, a nurse pushed back the curtain. Frank stormed by the woman in scrubs, nearly knocking the doctor over.

"What have you done? Allowing Zoe to get hurt?" Even if they had been separated from the rest of the ER by walls two-feet thick instead of thin curtains, Frank's shouts would have been heard. "You don't watch them carefully enough. How in the world did you let this happen, anyway?"

The blue-clad doctor, his halo polished, stepped toward them. "Mr. Stanford. There is no need to shout. Calm down. You are disturbing the patients."

Frank's face reddened further, not from embarrassment but rage, and his voice became even louder. "Don't tell me to calm down! How did this happen? I want some answers."

"Mr. Stanford. I said calm down or I will have security escort you out."

Zoe shrank back against Olivia. *Yes, escort him out. Please.*

A uniformed security guard appeared next to the curtain. "Everything okay here, Doc?"

Sputtering, Frank looked from the doctor to the security guard. Olivia thought he was weighing his options. He finally asked quietly, "What happened to my daughter?"

The doctor and security guard exchanged a look, and the security guard walked away, but Olivia heard the creak of his leather belt stop within seconds. He must have stopped only a few feet down the hall.

"Your wife could answer that better, but I can say Zoe sprained her wrist. We'll wrap it and have her rest. I don't foresee any problems."

The doctor looked at Zoe. "You will be just fine, Zoe. If your arm hurts too much, your mom can give you some children's Tylenol." He turned his attention to Olivia.

"Will you be all right?" His halo shining even brighter, his eyes seemed to be asking about more than Zoe. Wasn't he a mandatory reporter? Would he have to report this incident to someone?

Olivia brightened her smile. "Oh, yes, of course. My husband will help us get home, and we'll be fine. Thank you."

The doctor finished wrapping Zoe's wrist.

His face only slightly tinged with pink, Frank nodded at the doctor, draped his arm around Zoe, and escorted his family out.

Trailing behind Zoe and Frank, Olivia's arm was caught gently by the doctor. He leaned into her and said under his breath, "Everything at home okay?"

Olivia pasted on her best smile. "Of course, doctor. Thank you." She quickly put distance between her and the doctor.

They made it all the way to the waiting room before Frank spoke through clenched teeth. "How could you let this happen?"

"Daddy, it was my fault. I stood on my tippy toes on the step stool."

Katherine and Dylan came over to inspect the newly adorned wrist.

Frank knelt in front of his daughter, stroking her uninjured arm. "Zoe, do you want to ride home with me?"

"Um, can I ride home with Mommy?"

"Sure. Okay. I'll walk you to the car."

When they stepped outside, the leaking from the sky had stopped. Frank finally looked at her as they approached Olivia's vehicle and stared with his jaw clenched and his temple visibly throbbing. Long moments later, he turned away, heading toward his car in another row.

Olivia sagged against the car.

"Mommy, can we go home now? My arm hurts."

Chapter Eleven

Once Frank was sure Zoe had been settled as comfortably as possible, he went back to work, leaving Olivia mentally exhausted. Dylan dragged too, so she suggested he go to his room to rest with King or at least play with his racetrack. It had been a long morning for him, too, so she wasn't surprised when he readily agreed, taking his sidekick with him.

"I think I'll nap while Zoe and Dylan do." Katherine ambled to her room, Olivia nodding at her retreating back.

She looked in on Zoe again. Sleeping peacefully. As she came out of Zoe's room, Olivia turned toward her own room. So tempting to curl up and sleep away the strife. Maybe after she checked on the damage left in the garage by Zoe's tumble, she could at least rest. It wouldn't be so easy to take away Frank's problems. Or hers. Could it? *Could you, Jesus?*

The kitchen door to the garage still hung open, lights on. Olivia stood in the doorway. Two overturned cardboard boxes had spewed their files, envelopes, and papers that now scattered the floor in slippery piles.

Olivia groaned aloud. Where to start? She righted both boxes, then bent down at the nearest pile and began shuffling and stacking as if vying for a speed record. The lure of a nap reached her even out here.

Halfway through filling one box, she picked up another box that in its former life held a ream of paper. A brand she didn't recognize. A box she didn't recognize. Curiosity got the better of her and she took off the lid to peek.

The box was full of envelopes, crushed with age. Hannah Sampson Baines was printed on a sticker in the upper right-hand corner of the top envelope. Her birth mother. What did she have of her birth mother? A small note card lay on top of the envelope.

Olivia Hunter, her adopted name, was neatly lettered on the front of the card. Such beautiful calligraphy. Only DeeDee could have written it. How had she not seen this before? She opened the card.

Dearest daughter,

Since you now have this card in your hands, you probably found the box after your dad and I are gone. Otherwise we would be handing you the box in person. These are your mother's medical records given to your dad and me after your adoption. We didn't believe it was a good idea to give them to you until you were much older or upon our death. Hope-fully that's a long time after I write this card. Your dad and I thank God every day that He brought you into our lives.

With much love, Mom.

No date. Considering she had Adam and DeeDee in her life for six years before their deaths, no, it wasn't a very long time after she wrote the words. A lonely ache stole over her. She hadn't known real love until the Hunters took her in and adopted her, introducing her to their Savior and His love. A boating accident just two months after she left for college took them and their love away. Jesus' love seemed a little more distant since that day. Maybe God thought she didn't deserve their love. Did she deserve His?

The Hunters' will had provided a trust for her that paid for her college and gave her a little nest egg. Her college living expenses ate through a great deal of her funds. The little remaining was being used for someone's home loan or small business loan, but it was protected for her on paper whenever she wanted to cash it in.

Thank you, Mom and Dad Hunter, for the college education. But did they have to go out in the boat that day? Officials said they warned them of the pending storm. It's not like they were young and strong. Not even middle-aged anymore, already in their sixties.

Did she now hold a Pandora's box? Did she really want to see? Olivia took a deep breath and opened the envelope. Another deep breath. She slid the stack of papers from its hideaway.

A jumble of something resembling a foreign language swam on the page. Medical terminology. It might as well have been Russian. Flipping through the pages, she prayed for something to make sense.

Stage IV metastatic breast cancer. That flashed like a neon sign. Her birth mother had cancer? Olivia flipped through her mental calendar. The diagnosis was dated six months before her death. Sadness and hope fought for dominance in her heart. Maybe her father hadn't killed her mother after all. Maybe it was the cancer.

A death certificate. Hope lost the battle. Her mother lost her battle to the injuries sustained by her husband's beating. The ages-old grief she thought she had banished returned from exile taking her heart captive, and the weight of it forced her against the pile of boxes for support.

Now what would she do with the bitterness toward her father? Hannah would have died anyway. He just hurried it up. Maybe he wanted to save her from more pain.

No! He will not be a hero. Only God can make that choice. Lester Hunter had no right.

"Olivia?"

Katherine's voice pulled her back to the garage.

"Here, Katherine." Olivia stepped from behind a stack of boxes and turned toward her mother-in-law, clutching her mother's medical records.

"Zoe woke up in a little pain. I gave her more children's Tylenol, and she went back to sleep. I hope that was okay. I didn't know where you were."

Olivia swallowed the ping-pong-ball-sized lump in her throat. "Of course. Thank you."

"You okay? What do you have there?" Katherine padded over to Olivia on stockinged feet. "Sorry. If you don't mind me asking."

She handed Katherine the stack of papers. "I don't know where these came from." Olivia rubbed her hands against her pant legs, leaving the grime on her khaki-colored jeans. Too bad she couldn't wipe off the grime of her father's deeds. The residue of her mother's death sentence. "I've never seen these before."

"This is your birth mother? She died from breast cancer?" Katherine continued to skim the file.

Olivia had kept her origins close, only sharing with Frank before they married. Hiding from the rest of the judgmental world who she was. *No, this isn't me! Is it?* Katherine wouldn't judge her. Would she?

Another opportunity to stand up.

The CliffNotes version of her family history tiptoed from her soul to Katherine's, a slight lifting of her burden, sharing it with someone who cared.

"Oh, sweet girl. I did not know. I am so sorry your childhood was so traumatic." She hugged Olivia, crushing the papers between them. "And you don't know how you got these records?"

"From my adopted mother, but she's been dead for twelve years. I'm sure I've never seen this stuff before. So, I don't know how they came to be in our garage."

Katherine handed the papers back to Olivia, who returned it to the envelope. "Later. I'll think about this later."

She had been so stunned by the contents of the first envelope that she'd forgotten there was more in the box. Opening another envelope, she was stunned again. Her child face grimaced at her from a handful of photos. A small handful. Her mother and father fake smiled from two of the photos. Olivia turned the photos over. Only one of the small, unhappy family in front of an anonymous motel carried a date. January 1993.

"Six. Maybe it was my birthday. Probably not. Celebrating birthdays was a waste of time. According to my father."

Full weight of the burden returned to Olivia, settling over her heart. And apparently her lungs. She struggled to breathe properly. She hurriedly stuffed the photos back in their envelope and jammed all the incriminating evidence back into the ream box. As she forced the lid in place, she forced air into her lungs, and out again.

"We better go check on Zoe and Dylan." Olivia put her arm through Katherine's and steered them toward the house. She didn't want to look back at the box again. Yet as she switched off the light, her head, of its own free will, turned to steal a glance over her shoulder. The box's phosphorescence gleamed in the dark. Mocking her.

———

The scene had been ugly. No matter how many times she told herself to forget it, the scene replayed in her mind over and over. And over again.

After everyone had been settled in later that night, Frank had allowed the wrath that had been building full vent.

Even two days later she squeezed her eyes to shut out the memory. *No, I will not go there!* Frank's moratorium on talking to her was a mixed blessing. No harsh words, but…

Solitary confinement. Harsh words. Which was worse? And a box of mysterious origins glowed in the garage.

Zoe lay propped up on the elephant, a dozen pillows behind her and one under her arm, her attention commanded by the Mr. Ham creation video she had been so intent on reaching in the garage.

Olivia stroked Zoe's forehead. "How are you feeling, sweetheart?"

Zoe waved her arm about. "Mom, did you know dinosaurs in the Bible are called leviathans? And they walked on the earth with people?"

"You should probably keep that arm still a while longer."

"It's hardly sore at all."

Olivia wished she could recover from Frank's diatribe as quickly as Zoe seemed to be recovering from her fall. But was she recovered enough for Olivia to leave for San Francisco in two days? Katherine had assured her Zoe would be fine and that Grandma could handle everything.

"I can't wait to show this video to Artie. When's he coming over?"

"Mmm. We'll see."

Would she be a bad mom if she left her daughter in pain? Zoe said it didn't hurt. Much. Katherine said they would all be fine if Olivia went on her trip. Vanessa had encouraged her not to cancel. Vanessa who had no children. Frank? Ouch. The one person who hadn't weighed in.

Maybe she would start packing. See how Zoe was feeling tomorrow.

Olivia re-situated Zoe in the master bedroom and pulled a suitcase out of her closet. So as to not disturb Zoe's arm, Olivia wedged the suitcase onto the window seat to pack.

"Are you going somewhere, Mommy?"

Obviously, she had completely forgotten to clue the kids in before the accident. She should have started talking about it two weeks ago, as soon as she had made the decision to go, knowing Zoe and Dylan did so much better with her absence if they had time to get used to the idea. With only two more days to go, they would not react well. *Where has my mind been? And now with Zoe's injury?*

The maple tree outside her window tapped rhythmically on the glass in the gentle breeze. The brief rains had been replaced by the glorious California sunshine. She leaned toward the window and raised the lower portion, allowing the earthy scent to waft into the room.

"Going on a short business trip with Auntie Vanessa." Olivia patted the case and moved to her closet.

"But, Mommy!" Zoe drew out the word mommy in the universal way of kids. "What about my arm?" She waved it again for emphasis.

"I thought you said it hardly hurt." Like her heart hardly hurt? She sighed and perched on the edge of the bed beside Zoe.

"Whattya talkin' bout?" Dylan barreled into the room and bounced on the bed next to Zoe.

So much for keeping Zoe's arm from being jiggled.

Dylan eyed the suitcase. "Ya goin' away, Mommy?" He drew his lips into a pout.

Both sets of eyes, the female set of pure chocolate, the other flecked with amber, took on a sheen that threatened to spill out into tears.

Olivia's heart quivered, and she held a child's hand in each of hers. How could she leave these two? Then again, when would she have another chance to get away for three days to regroup? To escape a neon box. She needed female adult companionship, her sweet mother-in-law notwithstanding, and chatter. She needed that.

"Auntie Vanessa and I have to do business. I'll only be gone three days. Back before you know it."

Dylan narrowed his eyes and put his little hand on his hip, mimicking his father. "Why d'ya hafta *do* bizness?" Zoe nodded in agreement.

It was hard not to laugh at Dylan's stance. "Well, it's how I earn money to pay for your karate lessons and Zoe's dance lessons. You know some mommies go to work all day, away from home, and their kids go to school or babysitters all day. But I get to work from home so I can stay with you and teach you at home."

"Ya ain't stayin' home if ya leave." Dylan scowled and now had both hands on his hips.

"Aren't, not ain't, sweetie."

But she couldn't argue with Dylan's logic, and her chuckle slipped out. Her work-away-from-home speech usually diffused objections to her working or going away on business. Apparently not this time.

She listened for the brown birds that usually sat in the tree. Their twittering usually brought her joy, but all she could hear was the clanking of the trash truck approaching the front of the house.

Chapter Twelve

Watched pots never boil, and pressure cookers never release their pressure. Olivia stood over the Instant Pot, jiggling the pin again. There could be no delays in serving dinner so that Frank would have fewer items on his list of grievances tonight.

Finally! The hissing had stopped. She rotated the cover and pulled it free, releasing the spicy aroma of chili powder and the rich bouquet of chicken broth. Olivia breathed in deeply and sighed in satisfaction.

"That smells so good, sweetheart. Can't wait to taste it." Katherine moved around the table laying the placemats and napkins, the silverware clinking in her hand as she placed them on the napkins.

"I'm home! Daddy's home!"

Frank? He hadn't sounded that jovial in, well, she couldn't remember when. It seemed out of place considering the discussion about his father and Zoe's accident. Suspicion crawled into her chest. *Wow.* She was being upset because he was happy? What was the matter with her? She forced distrust to crawl out and went to greet her husband.

Olivia traipsed down the hall, followed by Katherine. The kids were already at his side. Dylan grabbed his father around the leg with both arms, and Zoe gave him a one-arm hug on the other side. Frank patted them and looked up at her, his face sporting a broad grin. Where had that smile, that happy face, been all these many months? This was the old Frank. The one she fell in love with.

She joined the hug fest. "You must have had a great day today. What's going on?" Sure. Spoil the mood by implying this happy face was so unusual.

"I had a greaaaaat day!" Frank pulled out the word great like the old Tony the Tiger cereal commercial they'd seen once in a retro TV show. "So great that I'm getting a raise and a bonus."

"Congratulations, son. I'm sure you deserve it." Katherine's grin almost matched Frank's.

"Whatza raise?" Dylan's face was one big question mark as he peered up at his father.

"Yes, congratulations, dear. Dylan, a raise means Daddy's going to bring home more money."

"Daddy, does that mean you can buy me that mini-bike now?" The question mark morphed into a hopeful exclamation point.

"Sorry, bud. You have to be a little older."

"Aw, nuts." Dylan wore his emotions on his face. Rare for a boy, but maybe not for a five-year-old.

Olivia helped Frank take off his jacket and hung it in the hall closet. "So, what was the occasion? Why the raise now?"

"Finished the Kilpatrick space project. Two years. Finally, in the can. Never so glad to see something completed. We finished ahead of schedule, too, so raises for the team." Frank loosened his tie and headed toward the bedroom. "Dinner ready? Let me wash up."

"Just have to dish it out. Tortilla chicken soup doesn't seem quite fancy enough for a celebration."

"It'll be great." Frank tossed the words over his shoulder as he walked away.

Olivia danced on light feet toward the kitchen. She had missed the warmth that Frank's smile could produce. Maybe it had been the pressure of the project causing his moods and undue anger. Dare she think their lives could get back to normal? Could it be that simple?

Don't look a bonus check in the mouth, Olivia.

She and Katherine made quick work of ladling the soup thick with chicken and dotted with tortilla strips and cilantro, into her special, wide soup bowls. A crisp green salad with colorful vegetables and fragrant warm tortillas snugged into a basket added to the table.

It needed something more. While Katherine called everyone to the table, Olivia ducked out the sliding door and snipped a geranium. She cut the stem short and slipped it into a small stoneware bud vase, setting it in the center of the table as the hungry troops surged through the door.

"A feast for the conquering hero." Frank caressed Olivia's shoulder. "Thank you, babe. Looks delicious."

Olivia melted at this touch, his soft voice. This. This was the man she married. Who was that other Frank? The one who kept showing up and tearing their lives apart?

The laughter and good-natured teasing bounced around the table, mingling with the soup slurping and vegetable crunching. Frank described the scene in his boss's office when he told Frank he and the entire team received raises. Dylan told a new joke. And Zoe even laughed at it. Katherine punctuated the conversation with a joke of her own. Olivia knew that if she could look in the mirror, she'd see a silly grin on her face. Thankfulness bloomed so large in her chest, she thought it would burst.

Finally, at Olivia's "Ice cream for dessert, anyone?" the table erupted with cheers.

A couple of hours later, bringing Zoe and Dylan down from their high and getting them to bed was not cheerful.

"Zoe, I know you're extra tired and your arm probably hurts, but no more whining."

"Dylan, put away the Hot Wheels. It's time to sleep." For the fifth time.

She curbed her frustration. *Don't ruin the perfect evening. The kids are just being kids.* It was her own fault for serving them ice cream *and* cookies.

The kids settled in, Katherine retired to her room, and Olivia joined Frank. He emerged from the bathroom clad just in pajama bottoms, his muscles flexing as he towel-dried his almost-black hair. When he pulled the towel away, his hair curled tightly about his head. And love curled around her heart.

"What's with the suitcase?" Frank asked gesturing towards her bag on the window seat.

"Thought I'd get a head start on getting ready for the weekend." She turned down the comforter and sheets.

"You can't go now." His voice was Teflon and steel.

"Zoe's doing so much better. Your mom is perfectly capable and happy to take care of her and Dylan. Besides, I don't leave until Saturday morning, and you'll be home Saturday and Sunday. I'll be back Monday evening. Oh, and Jim will sign you in to Disneyland on Sunday."

"No. Disneyland is inappropriate for Zoe's sprained wrist. And inappropriate for you to leave considering your daughter's been hurt." Frank slowly put on his pajama top, buttoning it in slow motion. Or so it seemed to Olivia.

"Besides, I have to leave Tuesday for four days in Vegas. New project. Price of finishing the old one."

"But I'd be back Monday."

"No."

His gaze never left hers.

———

What kind of mother resents not getting away from her injured child? Olivia stared at the calendar box that had proclaimed *GETAWAY* so recently, but now seemed faded, as faded as the opportunity. Frank had been right, of course. As a mother, it had been her duty to stay with her child. No, not a duty, a loving sacrifice.

Then why was she angry? After all, in spite of having laid down the law that she had to stay home, Frank had been a model husband this past week. But then he hadn't been home for the last three days. A rare business trip to Las Vegas had demanded he get away.

Getaway. Why was Frank able to have a getaway and not her? She was the one who had needed it. Still did.

Not fair, Lord.

Was it fair that I was beaten for your sins before I was hung on the cross?

Ouch. Guilt took anger's place in her pocket of failures. She was such a sorry excuse for a Christian. For a human being.

Tomorrow's calendar box finally got her attention. Zoe's birthday. She had no right hiding here in her office, letting Katherine do all the work. They had a party to get ready for, and she'd better hop to it.

Frank promised to be home tomorrow for Zoe's party.

Chapter Thirteen

Southern Californians played Russian roulette when scheduling outdoor parties in March. Zoe's birthday party lost. A downpour dictated they move the party inside, so with little time to spare, they scrambled Friday afternoon and Saturday morning to adjust the plans.

It didn't matter that the sun outside was MIA. The lights twinkled brightly within. And so did the chaos.

Princes and princesses filled the room, their adult pages standing at attention by their side, ready to fulfill their every command.

Music blared, children squealed and ran about, cake was mashed into the carpet, and punch had somehow become Rorschach blots on one of the chairs. Wrapping paper and ribbons decorated every other available spot in the room. King's shrill let-me-out bark echoed from behind the closed door of the laundry room.

Olivia willed herself not to hyperventilate over the mess. *Good hostesses don't worry about the mess—until after everyone goes home.* She continued to give herself *The Pep Talk*, one her OCD self had to recite at every party she threw. *Think about something else.*

Frank. Yes. That's a less stressful topic. Where was he? Four o'clock already and no word. Zoe had asked about her father earlier in the day, but she seemed to have forgotten about him. If he misses his daughter's birthday party completely…She didn't have a rejoinder to that idea.

At least Vanessa had finally shown up. Her deep-throated laugh transcended much of the din as she flirted with one of the single fathers. Where was her own husband today? Vanessa had shown up alone and in a sour mood. Flirting seemed to have put her back in good humor.

Zoe called to Olivia from the other side of the room.

"Look! Auntie Nessa gave me a pass to Disneyland. How soon can we go?" Zoe's feet barely touched the ground as she showed Olivia her new pass.

Olivia felt a twinge of irritation that Vanessa hadn't asked Olivia if it was okay to give her a pass. No one else in the family had one. Now they'd have to spend the money for three more or Zoe's would go to waste. Olivia tried to hide the sputter.

"Hey, Livie, dear friend. You okay? Hey, here's passes for the rest of you. Can't have Zoe going to Disneyland alone, can we?" Vanessa winked and handed her an envelope.

Olivia stuck her hand under her hair and rubbed her neck.

Oh, boy. I owe you an apology, Vanessa.

"You shouldn't have spent so much money. That's a fortune."

"Jim said they were cutting back on how often and how many guests each employee can get in. So, I wanted to make up for it."

"You didn't have to do that. But thank you. You're the best."

As they hugged, Carmen joined them, her eyes soft, her smile sweet. "Hi, Vanessa."

Vanessa, her platinum spikes taller than the last time

Olivia had seen her, nodded and trekked back to the single dad where she resumed her flirting.

"I'm sorry. I don't understand why Vanessa is so rude to you."

"Not rude, not at all, *amiga*." Carmen's smile made it all the way to her eyes. "Say, Katherine wanted to know if you bought extra ice cream. Some of the boys are getting rowdy, and she thought that'd calm them down."

"Calm 'em? It'll give them more of a sugar rush."

"Well, by that time, they'll probably have gone home." Carmen's laugh tinkled merrily.

Carmen dished out more ice cream and cake while Katherine supervised more games. By the time every child had won a prize, the party started winding down. The guests repeated their birthday wishes to Zoe, said their good-byes, and went home.

Soon only the Delgados and Vanessa remained.

"Where's Frank?"

A cringe-worthy question if there ever was one. Vanessa helped Olivia package up the leftovers, stashing them in the refrigerator.

"I don't know." The ham platter needed Olivia's full attention.

"Why that…" Vanessa sputtered a few words that burned Olivia's ears, but she couldn't help agreeing with the senti-ment. Vanessa leaned against the sink, arms and ankles crossed. "What are you going to do about it?"

"Do?"

"You can't let him walk all over you. I understand why he didn't want you to go to San Francisco. But this? You lay down the law."

Wash the platter. Yes, the platter needed to be washed. Now. Olivia was unable to tell Vanessa she'd had the same thoughts.

Vanessa uncrossed her arms and slammed the heel of her

hand against the counter. "Really, Livie. Either that or just kick him out."

Belly quivering, Olivia squeezed her eyes shut. Why was Olivia shocked? She knew that would be Vanessa's advice. That was Vanessa. No nonsense. No grace.

"You know I can't do that, Van." She kept her voice low, otherwise she was sure Vanessa would hear it shake.

Vanessa paced the room. "And look where that's got you. I'm sorry. I know you sincerely hold these beliefs, but where do you draw the line?"

Yes. That was the question, wasn't it? Or was it?

"Would you please leave Olivia alone? You aren't helping."

Olivia and Vanessa spun around. Carmen had come in unnoticed.

"You too? I should've known. You two are hopeless." Vanessa didn't try to hide her exasperation.

"Not hopeless. Merely committed to Biblical values." Carmen may have spoken quietly, but she didn't waver from looking Vanessa right in the eyes.

"Ha! That's what I mean. Only fools believe some made-up God's gonna help you."

"Vanessa!" Katherine stood in the doorway. She seldom raised her voice, although this time she did not speak quietly. "You should not speak ill of something you seem to know nothing about. And especially not here. In this home."

Vanessa had the grace to redden under the reprimand of the older woman.

"Sorry, Olivia. I really do want the best for you." Vanessa patted Olivia on the arm, ignored Carmen, ducked her head at Katherine, then sped from the room. The front door clicked shut.

The three women stared at each other for a moment, then gave a collective sigh.

Katherine broke the silence. "I know you've been friends

with her for a long time, and you think you can be a positive influence. It pains me to say it, but I'm not so sure anymore."

"At least she had the decency to be embarrassed when you called her on it." Carmen, like Katherine, tried to be a peacemaker.

Olivia turned back to the ham platter. "Thanks for defending me, but Vanessa is still my friend."

Katherine and Carmen flanked Olivia and hugged her, while unshed tears clogged Olivia's throat.

"Of course, she is, dear. You're a loyal friend. I wouldn't have you any other way."

Carmen added an "Amen!"

"Well, let's move this love fest to the other room. There's a lot more clean up waiting."

Jorge and Carmen took down lights and the silken tent fabric, stuffing them back into bags. Zoe moved her birthday loot into her room, and Dylan, Gabe, and Arturo toted trash bags of wrapping paper and ribbon out to the garage. The house finally had some semblance of order, and the clean-up crew collapsed with a sigh of relief.

"I can't thank you all enough for pitching in."

Tsking and clucking noises murmured around the room, and the Delgados called it a night.

In the quiet, Olivia's mind returned to Frank. It was nearly eight o'clock and still no word from him. She didn't know whether to be worried or mad. He had missed all of Zoe's party, although technically it was still her birthday. For a few more hours anyway.

I suppose I should have tried calling him. But he should have been considerate enough to call her. But what if he can't? What if he had an accident? *I better try calling.*

Where was her cell phone? No idea. Not even the last time she'd seen it. She patted her body. Oh, no pockets. She rushed to the kitchen where she sometimes plugged it in. Not there.

The bedroom? She tripped toward her room and her bedside phone plug. *Ahh, there it is.*

She grabbed her phone. A voicemail notification from Frank. Two p.m.

"Olivia. You're probably busy with Zoe's party."

Naturally.

"Business went longer than expected. Be home tomorrow night. Tell Zoe happy birthday for me."

Anger returned. No, "I'm sorry." No, "I tried to get out of staying." Maybe Vanessa was right after all.

———

Words from Pastor David's sermon ran back and forth over the rocky desert floor of Olivia's mind, bumping and crashing, as she ferried Katherine and the kids home.

Frank hadn't returned from Las Vegas before church, and Olivia did not feel compelled to wait for him. In fact, maybe it had been better that way. Pastor David's preaching may have set Frank off, who probably would have thrown around ugly words.

What was the Lord trying to say to her this morning? Was He even talking to her?

Pastor David made a passing reference to David—the Biblical David, not himself—where David told his son Solomon to be courageous and do it. Somewhere in 1 Chronicles. She'd have to look it up when she got home.

If God was talking to her, what did He mean by "do it"? Do what? Leave Frank or stick by him? What was she to do? Sermons were supposed to clarify the scripture. Right? Not confuse you even more. Maybe this morning's sermon had nothing to do with her. That must be it.

Nevertheless, her stomach churned, and her lip became sore from being chewed as if it were lunch. Better get some real lunch.

They ate lunch without Frank. Even the kids agreed naps were in order. Also done without Frank.

Olivia's cell phone startled her out of sleep. Dozing. She was just dozing. A glance at the clock told her it was more than dozing. She'd been asleep for two hours.

"Hello, Olivia. This is Seth." Seth Cohen? As in Frank's administrative assistant? "I'm trying to get in touch with Frank. His cell phone goes direct to voicemail."

"Seth. Frank must still be on the road from Las Vegas."

"On the road?"

What about that statement didn't Seth get? Even half asleep, that should make sense.

"Yes, from Las Vegas."

"But everyone left Friday." Seth's tone was not hesitant. Definitive. Definitely definitive. Was there a word for that?

"What do you mean everyone left?" The conversation was going nowhere. She untangled herself from the comforter and jumped up.

Seth sighed into the phone. "Olivia. The team checked out of the hotel on Friday. We all came home." Definitive had turned to exasperation.

"No. He was driving home today." Exasperation was making the rounds. She paced with the phone tight against her ear.

"I saw Frank drive away from the hotel. With Ed Paisley. He told me he was looking forward to getting home."

Maybe Frank had been in an accident. No, the police would have called. What if his ID was lost and they didn't know who he was? No, they'd know by his car registration. Her mind flitted about looking for a likely place to land. Nothing made sense.

"Are you sure?" Seth had to be wrong.

He was sure.

"What about Ed?"

"Can't reach him either. And since he's divorced and lives alone, there is no one to call."

What if Frank did have another family stashed away? Maybe just a girlfriend. *Just?* At least Seth had confirmed he had gone to Las Vegas on business.

"Look, Olivia. I'm sure Frank's fine. I'll make a few more calls. But if he calls you or comes home, please let 'em know there's an emergency meeting scheduled for eight tomorrow. I'll be in touch if I learn anything."

The call disappeared from her screen. *No, Seth, don't hang up.* Her lifeline to Frank untethered.

Do it. *I don't know what that means!* Pastor David's and Seth's words jumbled in her head. Should she call the police? Would he be considered missing yet? Was he missing or just AWOL? She couldn't tell the kids or Katherine.

Olivia stopped pacing and slid her hand beneath her hair to rub the back of her neck. *Yikes!* And what were the kids doing while she slept and paced?

Late afternoon arrived, but not the man nor any word of him. Katherine and the children were sent off with the Delgados to the church family potluck and game night, Olivia pleading a headache to stay home. No lie. The headache beat arrhythmically behind her eyes.

She'd played it cool, so no one suspected, no one had asked where Frank was. Surely his own mother must have felt something was wrong.

The pacing continued. From the living room, across the entryway atrium to the family room. And back again. She stepped out the front door, her eyes searching, roaming the street up and down. Normally, he'd come from the north, but just in case, she didn't want to ignore the south tonight.

As she paced, she checked her phone. Over and over again. Seth had called back to ask if she'd heard anything. She hadn't.

And where was Ed? Were they going somewhere together?

If Frank had a tryst in mind, he certainly wouldn't have taken Ed. Would Ed have led Frank astray? Ed didn't have a family and sometimes played as hard as he worked. If Frank had a best friend, it was Ed. Frank liked to think of himself as independent and didn't need many friends. He had his game night buddies, but they really couldn't be considered friends. They didn't seem to call or come around at any other times. Of course, maybe for men it was different. Perhaps for men merely gathering for the season's game of choice qualified as friendship.

Ed was the trustworthy one. The one who called and came by the house, occasionally inviting Frank to a game or a visit to the shooting range.

None of his game night buddies, including Ed, called themselves Christians. No wonder he was drifting away. Was it merely drifting? Or was it worse than that?

If there had been an accident, who would the police have contacted about Ed?

Needing a new view, Olivia stared at the fireplace. The flames mesmerized but didn't warm.

The familiar thrum of an engine spun her around. Headlights flashed through the window. Olivia's chest heaved as the reality of his homecoming sunk in.

Oh, God. Thank you. Thank you.

She positioned herself in the family room doorway as Frank let himself in. "Frank! Where have you been? We've been worried sick."

He dropped his bag on the floor, shrugged out of his coat, and hung it in the closet. Had a tech master programmed him into slow motion? Frank finally looked at her, his brow furrowed, his face haggard. Could he have been drinking and been on a binge?

"Why? Told you I'd be home today." The weariness in his words matched the snail's pace of his movements. He picked up his bag and shuffled toward their bedroom.

Hysteria and indignation vied for space in her throat. She stuffed back the hysteria and allowed the ire residence. "Where have you been? You couldn't call?"

"I told you I would be home today." He spoke each word as if it were a sentence of its own. "It's still today. And I'm home." He tossed the bag to the bed and dropped next to it.

"Seth has been trying to reach you." She wanted to add, *Where have you been?* again, but knew even in his lethargy that it would send him over the edge. She settled for fisting her hands to her hips.

Frank unlaced one shoe and slid it off. Then the second shoe before he spoke again. "What did Seth want?"

"You have an eight o'clock meeting in the morning." Why did they talk about a stupid meeting? *Where have you been, Frank? Since Friday?*

Do it. Was this it? Was this the time?

"He said you left the hotel on Friday." She stepped back, pressing her elbows into her sides, and clutching her hands together in front of her.

Frank launched off the bed toward her, bellowing as he moved. "Don't you dare question me!" In one great leap, he reached her and grabbed her shoulders. "Don't you dare question me again. It's none of your business."

She'd been in this spot before. Head banging against the door as he shook her over and over again. Her teeth chattered, and she bit her tongue. Again. "St-Stop. Pl-please stop."

He threw her against the door again. This time he jammed his forearm against her neck. He cursed, the words burning her ears. The second time in recent days he'd cursed. The pressure increased, second by second. She could barely breathe.

With her free hand, she clawed the arm at her throat.

Frank drew his arm away from her throat and batted her hand away. He thumped her back against the door and released her.

Olivia crumpled to the floor like a Raggedy Ann.

Frank fell onto the bed, holding his head in both hands, folding his body into himself.

Great, gasping sobs wracked her. The ache in her throat and the pain in her heart threatened to overwhelm her. She bit back the bile, fearing anything she retched up would not get past her throat and drown her. Olivia didn't move from the spot on the floor, as if she were a dog curled at the foot of her master's bed.

None of this made sense. Would Frank have killed her? She didn't know. She only knew she couldn't take much more.

Chapter Fourteen

"Mommy! Can we go to Disneyland today? I need to use my new pass." Zoe waved her wrapped wrist in the air like a flag. "See? I'm all better."

"Please?" Dylan drew out the word so long, Olivia wondered how he could breathe.

"Sorry, guys. Not today. Maybe tomorrow." She hated to say no, but last night's incident…what a euphemism. Attack was a better word. The attack. Yes. She would have to admit it. The attack had drained her of everything. No energy. No hope. She withdrew the fruit and milk from the refrigerator and slammed the door.

Besides, Zoe was behind in schoolwork because of her wrist, and Olivia was behind in reviewing two hotel contracts for her clients.

She dealt with the whining and groaning, and then sent them off to get dressed for breakfast.

Katherine stirred the oatmeal on the stove. "I need to get home soon. I booked my return ticket for a week from tomorrow, the seventh. Easter prep at my church, you know."

Olivia felt her fortifications crumbling. Who would she have as a buffer with Katherine gone? Not that her presence had stopped Frank entirely, but perhaps it would have been worse without the probability of his mother's chastisement. Worse than almost being strangled? *Get real.*

"And, I really would like to go to Disneyland with the kids before I go."

Drat! Why hadn't she thought of that? She couldn't deprive Katherine of spending a day at Disneyland with her grandkids just because she was acting like a scared fool. Just get along. Remember? Oh, sure. And Frank would have to agree. How was that going to happen? He hadn't wanted Zoe with an injury risking Disneyland. He'd have to agree for his mother's sake, right?

"Of course. Of course. We'll go tomorrow. But we'll have to ask Frank first." Tension built in her head as she used her limited brain power to figure out how to get Frank to agree. To say nothing of sorting through tasks that must be done today to make Disneyland happen.

"I'll ask Frank. He wouldn't deny his dear ol' mother." Katherine looked at her with an expression Olivia couldn't decipher.

She hadn't asked Olivia anything about last night even though, without asking, Katherine had taken care of the kids' bedtime rituals. Olivia was certainly not going to bring it up.

"Katherine, could you supervise Zoe's math and reading? And help Dylan with his foam robot building? Sorry, it's a little messy with all those little parts, but he's having so much fun building. Anyway, that way I can be sure to get my client business done today."

Katherine clapped her hands together. "Oh, what fun! Start right after breakfast?"

Frank pushed to the back of her mind and a plan for the day in place, Olivia felt some of the tension release, and a small squirt of energy propelled her. She'll have to make do with that.

By late afternoon that small squirt had disappeared, and a

deadweight took its place. At least she'd checked off every task on this week's list and cleared her desk. With schoolwork complete, Katherine had herded the children to the family room to watch a video.

The TV droned softly in the family room as Olivia joined them. Katherine's snores droned a little louder. In repose, her face showed every minute of her years. Olivia was startled by the lines and sagging flesh unnoticed before. Was this the result of three weeks with her son and his family? Or were those life-earned features, hidden by the joy in her face when she was awake? Olivia wanted to make sure her family didn't add any more lines to that much-loved face.

When Olivia awoke with a start, the family room had grown dark. She'd slept? The front door clicked shut followed by the plunk to the floor of what must be a briefcase and the rustling of a coat. Frank was home. What would his mood be and what would happen now was anybody's guess. She didn't want to try.

Katherine sat up, stretched, and yawned. "My. That little nap felt good." She turned toward the entry way. "That you, Frank?"

"Of course, Mom. Who'd you think?" His voice was not unkind. Maybe a little flat. He appeared in the doorway, his charcoal-colored suit coat draped over his arm, and his red power tie already askew.

"I have a request, son." Katherine's sagging flesh and lines seemed to be replaced with an impish grin. "Disneyland. Tomorrow."

"I think that's an awesome idea. I'll even take the day off so the whole family can go."

Who was this man and what had he done with her husband?

Zoe and Dylan jumped up, all sleepiness gone, and fist bumped each other.

"Cool!"

"Oh, Daddy, thank you, thank you!" Zoe ran to her father and wrapped her arms around his waist. He stroked her hair.

"Yes, thank you, son." Katherine's face shone with triumph as she nodded at Olivia.

She tried to process what had happened, but Olivia's mind stalled. She couldn't get it into gear, much less figure out Frank's change.

"Mommy! Mommy! We're going to Disneyland tomorrow." Zoe ran to Olivia, jumped atop the arm of her chair, and then jettisoned herself onto Olivia's lap, injury to her wrist forgotten.

Olivia snuggled her daughter. She wouldn't try to figure it out. At least not now. She'd just be grateful. Yet a niggling doubt found a crack and wormed its way in.

———

It didn't matter that they lived only fifteen minutes from Disneyland. Between the long lines into the parking structure, security, waiting for the tram, then long lines at the ticket booth for Katherine's day ticket, an hour of their day was gone.

Fortunately, it hadn't worn away the sense of fun, even in Frank.

Although the kids had just been here a month ago, they bounced up and down as they went through the entrance turnstile and craned their necks at the iconic Disneyland logo and train station—for a few seconds at least.

Dylan spun to face the family. "Okay. We're burnin' daylight. Let's move it."

Everyone burst into laughter. Except Zoe of course. Her huff left little doubt she thought little brothers were a nuisance.

They made their way through the crowds, each family member voicing an opinion on how to attack the day.

"Might as well ride the train. It's right here."

"Churros! Can we have churros first?"

"I want to see the princesses in the castle."

Frank held up his hand. "First thing is coffee at the Market House where we can decide on a plan." He set off toward Main Street.

"But, Daddy, I don't want coffee." Zoe's nose wrinkled.

"You can have hot chocolate or a Frappuccino."

Katherine put her arm around Zoe. "Mmmm. Hot chocolate sounds delicious. What do you think?"

Zoe nodded a few times, the wrinkles disappearing from her nose.

"Yippee! Hot chocolate!" Dylan loved all things chocolate.

As they hurried under the train trestle and arrived at the Town Square, the majestic castle rising at the end of Main Street, Olivia became thirteen again.

Her Papa Adam and Mama DeeDee had brought her here for a vacation not long after they adopted her. The sights and sounds of the train, trolley car, and marching band traveled like the speed of light through her.

"Well, well, well, my girl. Here we are at the Happiest Place on Earth." Papa Hunter threw his arms wide and lifted his face. "And it's all ours for three days."

To think, she, Olivia, a small-town orphan child from New York made it to Disneyland. And to think her newly adoptive parents would bring her new best friend, Vanessa, with them? How did she get so lucky? As Mama DeeDee had explained, it wasn't luck. It was the grace of God. She'd still been trying to get used to her own newfound faith.

Olivia grasped Vanessa's hands and they squealed with delight.

Mama DeeDee put her ample arms around the giggly girls. "What shall we do first?"

"Teacups!" Olivia and Vanessa had rehearsed this and said it in unison.

"Teacups it is." Papa Adam set off with long strides. Hurry up or get left behind.

Olivia would not be left behind.

Now, visiting again as an adult, her memories would not be left behind either. Even so, she hadn't been this nostalgic when they visited a month ago. Adam and DeeDee had been on her mind a lot more lately. That must explain it.

Hot drinks in hand, they finally found a table large enough for the five of them and sat down to sip and strategize. They had learned on their last trip that you couldn't just follow the paths willy-nilly. They had to agree on the must-rides and figure out the best way to get them all in. Olivia had downloaded an app that helped them see the wait times so they could figure them into the plan.

Olivia held up her hand and waited for everyone to look at her. "I just have one request. The Teacups."

"Mommy, *you* want to go on the Teacups?" The incredulity on Dylan's face made her laugh.

"Seems kinda tame." Frank, the daredevil.

"You bet. My mom and dad brought me here just once on vacation from New York. We even got to stay at the Disneyland Hotel for three days, but my favorite was riding the Teacups."

"The Teacups it is then." Frank, the dove?

Today, anyway.

Their cups drained and their tactics formed, the troop set out.

Olivia received a lighter and lighter heart after each activity. This was the way families should be. Sure, it couldn't all be as fun as this, but why couldn't the camaraderie be present even at home? Everybody would have to cooperate. She was grateful Frank was on his best behavior today. In fact, he was acting like what a husband and father should. Why couldn't he act like this all the time?

And why can't you act like how you should all the time? You, hypocrite. If you'd only be a good wife, you could have more days like this.

The accusations began to fill her head. Wait! No. *Get behind me.* She would not listen. She would not allow this day to be ruined.

"Who's ready for dinner?" Olivia made a point to sound happy. She was happy.

"Hungry Bear!"

"Clarabelle's!"

"Let's see what Grandma would like. You kids can always choose when we come another day. Mom?" Frank, the thoughtful.

Wonder of wonders.

"Hmm. I think...Cafe Orleans?" Katherine looked around the circle.

Olivia willed Zoe and Dylan to not only agree but agree willingly. More wonders. They grinned and nodded.

Frank put his arm around Olivia's shoulders and pulled her close. She soaked up his strength and warmth. She'd be grateful for today, but, *Oh, Frank, can't it always be like this?*

The restaurant was crowded, but no one seemed to mind the wait.

"I want one of those benny yeahs."

Dylan was met with blank expressions.

Her son was always thinking about dessert. "Dylan, you mean beignets?"

"Yeah, that's what I said."

"Well, those are for dessert, but, yes, we can get some." The thought of the Mickey-shaped, warm, doughy treats covered in powdered sugar made Olivia's mouth water. They were definitely having beignets.

Plates of fragrant Monte Cristo sandwiches and macaroni and cheese crowded the table and silenced the hungry crew. Everyone tucked in with gusto.

Soon empty and half-empty plates littered the table, powdered sugar decorating it all, including the smiling lips.

"My, that was a fine dinner. Thank you, Dylan, for suggesting the beignets." Katherine swiped at her frosted lips.

"And, thank you, Grandma," Olivia said, looking pointedly at the others. "For treating us to that fine dinner."

Each got the hint and thanked Katherine.

"Stanfords! Imagine running into you." Vanessa's husband, Jim, appeared at their table side.

"Looks like you're working today." Olivia couldn't understand why Vanessa complained about her husband. He always seemed kind and friendly. But then Frank often seemed that way to others too.

"Yes, indeed. Glad Vanessa got you guys some passes. I may not be here much longer. Got offered a position at Epcot Center."

"Florida? You and Vanessa would be moving to Florida?"

"Maybe. We'll see. Haven't said yes yet."

"What does Vanessa think about this?" Olivia wanted to bite back her question. This could be a touchy subject.

"Well, I have a few weeks to think about it."

More than likely this would be a problem for Vanessa. She adored California, Orange County in particular. She hated humidity. Better pray for their decision.

"Better get back to work. Have a great day, Stanfords." With a wave, Jim continued on.

Frank stood up and pushed his arms through the straps of his backpack. "We need to hit the next couple of rides and then think of heading home."

Protests wiped some of Frank's good humor from his face. *No, Frank, don't ruin it now.* He must have heard her thoughts. His smile was weak, but it was a smile. His nod was met with squeals. Everyone jumped up ready to get to the next adventure.

"Backpacks, everyone." A mother's job was indeed never done.

Three hours later, they eased off Star Tours, looking a little bedraggled. They'd been at the park for ten hours. How could a five-year-old last this long? Olivia's feet ached. She couldn't imagine how Katherine was holding up. Even Zoe and Dylan seemed to be wilting.

"Katherine, how are you doing?"

Her usual well-coiffed hair flew about her head, and she walked slower than she had earlier in the day. Who wasn't?

"I'm fine. It's been a grand day. Right, kids?"

Zoe and Dylan just nodded. Dylan grabbed his grand-mother's hand and whispered, "I think I may be tired now."

Olivia's heart was full. What a wonderful day. Not marred by strife or bad temper. She had no idea that riding the Teacups would be such a joyful trip down memory lane. How she wanted this to be her family's reality. Togetherness. Frank acting like the man she thought she married.

Even with aching feet, she didn't want the day to end. It wasn't the day. It was the feeling. Love. Normalcy. It was as if slapping and near choking hadn't ever happened.

Chapter Fifteen

One good day. They'd had one good day. Well, two if you counted this day that had gone well until Frank arrived home from work.

Now he waved bank printouts in her face as she stood at the stove.

"Do you realize how much money you spent? I work hard for this money. You fritter it away." Frank's face was mottled. "And I don't want to think about how much we spent at Disneyland yesterday."

So Disneyland was her fault? And what about her income? She worked hard for it, too. She should be able to spend it. He wouldn't want to hear that.

"Frank, I only bought stuff for your mother's visit." The thoughts had been bold. The words soft.

"What were you furnishing? The White House?" His face was inches from hers. The volume of his voice many decibels above safety.

"Shh. Your mother will hear." Now she'd done it. Wouldn't she ever learn her lesson?

"I don't give a…" The curse words shot out of his mouth like a dragon's fiery breath.

Olivia covered her burning ears. As if that would put out the fire now burning in her chest.

He swatted her hands away from her ears. "You listen to me and listen good. You will not spend any more without my okay. Or I'll take your cards and checkbook away. You hear?"

She nodded her head as she worried that sore spot on her lip.

"Now I have to go figure out how to pay for all of this. I'll be in the family room *trying* to balance the check book." His voice was saturated with scorn. "Dinner better be soon."

Olivia remained at the stove, unmoving. He hadn't struck her. She was surprised he hadn't? Shouldn't she be surprised if he had? And yet here she was, not just surprised, but grateful. She shouldn't *have* to be grateful, because it shouldn't be a thing. Violence shouldn't be a thing in her life.

It doesn't have to be. You can just leave, you know.

Could she? Yes, why couldn't she? She didn't have to put up with this. She wouldn't know what to tell the children. Katherine. And money. She did well, but it was only a part-time job. Maybe she could make it into full time. But then, where would she go? Frank would never leave and let her stay in the house. He would never pay the household bills, and her earnings would never cover the cost.

Marriage is supposed to be forever. Your God won't like you leaving. And what about submitting to your husband?

How could the enemy of her soul argue out of both sides of his mouth? Did he have a mouth? Maybe not, but worse, he knew how to stick in a knife and twist it.

Which was right? Leaving Frank or staying and putting up with his antics? Were those her only choices? Maybe she could stay and assert her rights. Stand up to him and demand he admit he had a problem. Seek counseling.

She slumped forward, holding onto the counter for support. The vegetables she'd been sautéing had gone from caramelized to burned. She'd have to throw these out and start over. Olivia dumped the mess into the trash and reached for a bag of frozen mixed vegetables. These would have to do. She hoped Frank didn't see her wasting food. She'd really get slapped.

———

Olivia clutched her coffee mug as if it kept her from sliding over the cliff. A good day and then a bad day. What would today bring? The good day at Disneyland had been absolutely normal even by the average person's standard, as Olivia imagined normal folks behaved. Last night was misery. Frank had left for work this morning silently. What did that mean for this evening's mood?

Another careful sip of her favorite hazelnut brew. Here she was being grateful again that her neck wasn't sore. That her face was not stinging. Amid a second gentle sip, as if she expected to be wrong and he had throttled her again, Zoe and Dylan giggled with their grandmother in her bedroom. The day would have to start now.

She knew she should skedaddle to the family room before Katherine was overwhelmed by childish rowdiness, but the daddle was more like dawdle. Was skedawdle a word?

Hands flat on the table, she hoisted herself up and dawdled toward the noise.

Zoe and Dylan flanked their grandmother as they nestled together on her bed, while Katherine read to them.

"Mommy, we're reading *James and the Giant Peach*."

"You mean Gramma's reading. You're just listening." Zoe could be so imperious at times. Olivia would have to figure out a way to train her in humility.

"Yeah, well, you ain't readin' either."

"Aren't. Not ain't, Dylan."

She'd have to figure out a way to train both of them in a little more humility.

"I think your mom wants us to start schoolwork. We can read more of *James and the Giant Peach* later. Okay?" She hugged them and gently moved them off the bed.

Olivia instructed them to get dressed and make their beds first. They grumbled but headed to their rooms.

Katherine followed Olivia into the kitchen and came to stand next to her at the kitchen table. She laid her soft hand on Olivia's arm. "I know you don't want to, but I think we need to talk about Frank and what happened last weekend and yesterday."

Olivia fussed over the already-neat stacks on the kitchen table.

"Olivia? Dear?"

"It's okay. Really." She dipped her head to avoid her mother-in-law's gaze.

She turned Olivia to face her. Katherine barely came to her chin, having to lift Olivia's face only slightly to force her to look into her eyes.

"It is not okay. You and Frank need help. Talk to me."

Olivia took a shuddering breath and moved away from her mother-in-law. "There's nothing to talk about. I just overspent, and Frank was a little annoyed."

"A little annoyed?" Katherine's face was a perfect example of skepticism. "I'm not blind, Olivia. Or deaf."

Okay, so maybe her face was more than skeptical.

"Please. Don't go there. It won't do anyone any good." She kept her gaze on the school papers as she shuffled them some more.

"No, dear. You cannot avoid me. This." Katherine crossed her arms in front of her upper body. "You know—with all the yelling and slamming things, someone could call social services —or the police."

Olivia jerked her gaze back to Katherine's, and her mouth fell open.

"They wouldn't." Her voice was nothing but a croak.

Katherine's chest heaved with a sigh. "You must see the seriousness here. All of this is not good for the children."

Olivia sank into a chair and dropped her face into her hands.

Oh, Lord, who am I to be loyal to? What should I do?

Listen.

"We've talked a little about this before. But it has reached an inescapable level of seriousness. It is time, Olivia."

She moved her hands from her face and looked back at Katherine. Misery coursed through her body.

"O…okay. But…not now. Not here."

They agreed to finish schoolwork, and Carmen agreed to watch the kids that afternoon so the two of them could go on a shopping trip.

How ironic. Shopping. After Frank had forbidden her to shop. Well, they weren't really going shopping. They could still go to the mall. But it was hard to really talk in the middle of the crazed mall crowds. The beach? No, too far for today. And they'd done that. A park. She'd think of a good park that would get them in the outdoors, to talk amidst God's handiwork. At least the weather was good for it.

———

Rather than heading to a shopping mall, Olivia drove them to a Starbucks where they picked up venti Cafe Mochas before continuing to Santiago Oaks Regional Park. Olivia hoped the serene, rural nature of the park would make the telling and reception easier. The picnic areas and hiking trails could get crowded, but she doubted they'd be busy on a Thursday afternoon.

Houses and other buildings lined the suburban landscape of the road until they neared the park where the scenery morphed into woodsy rural. They pulled into a paved lot facing the historic orange grove in the distance.

"I am up for a short, flat hike. If they have one."

Olivia allowed the warmth of the sun to slowly fill her with resolve as the two strolled a path bordered by thick brush just beyond a wooden fence.

As they moved further into the woods, Katherine cleared her throat and spoke softly. "What is going on, dear? When we got home Sunday night, you were pale, and I could tell you'd been crying. And the last few days have been thick with it. Something happened."

And her throat still ached with the memory, if not the real physical after-effects. Katherine was his mother for Pete's sake. She would cover for him. No, she was the one who stepped between them before. Still, it would somehow be her fault, and Katherine would judge her as an unfit wife. She couldn't tell her everything.

"Frank's assistant said they all left Friday, but Frank wouldn't tell me where he'd been for two days. We argued." Olivia lifted her hair and rubbed the back of her neck.

"Surely, there's more to it than that. As I said, I'm not blind nor deaf."

The real words cowered in her throat. Yanking them out into the air would find her guilty, so she forced them down. Fake words would have to do. "He did say a few mean things to me." She looked off above the trees.

"Humph!"

Olivia realized they had stopped walking. Katherine stood with one eyebrow raised, her hands on her hips.

"What?" Defensiveness crept into her voice. "He did say mean things." Oh, she knew that's not what Katherine meant, yet she couldn't go where Katherine wanted her to go.

"No doubt." Katherine set out again, and Olivia followed.

Olivia's breathing became labored. It must be the uphill path. Or was it the guilt that pressed down on her? It wouldn't do any good to admit the physical part. There was nothing she could do about it. Even though Katherine brought it up, she surely wouldn't call social services or the police. Not on her own son. Maybe she could reason with her son, convince him what he was doing was wrong.

And he'd become a model husband, just like that?

Oh, yeah. Right.

No. She would just have to leave the slapping and choking part out. Calling the authorities would only make things worse. What would they do anyway? Slap his wrist? Then he would definitely lose it and do who knows what? She couldn't risk it. She just needed to get along. To keep the kids safe.

Olivia calmed her breathing. Yes, just get along. Keep everyone safe.

"Frank needs counseling." Katherine stopped walking again and put her hand on Olivia's arm.

Counseling. Olivia stared at her mother-in-law. "Counseling?" The word tasted foreign in her mouth. Could it be that simple?

"Yes. Perhaps with your pastor."

No, not simple at all. How was she to tell Katherine about Frank's tirade against Pastor David and the church? They had led Katherine to believe all was well on that score. She couldn't betray Frank. She couldn't betray herself. Revealing their lies, her lies, would make Katherine hate her. Olivia couldn't risk losing the one person's trust in all the world that she wanted.

"Umm. I don't think our pastor does that kind of counseling." Thank goodness that was true.

"Someone else at your church then."

"Our church's staff is really busy." Again, true. But not the whole truth. Olivia sought out the tops of the trees again. The sun dimmed, and the leaves seemed to no longer glisten.

"How about a counseling service?"

Bless her, oh Lord. She wasn't asking any questions that Olivia would have to answer with lies.

"Maybe. But I don't know of any." That was certainly the truth.

"I'm sure we can do some research and find something."

But who would convince Frank he should go? He would never listen to her. Would he listen to his mother?

A terror washed over her. If his mother spoke to him about it, he'd know Olivia had ratted on him. Her throat ached again as she thought about the outcome of that.

"Katherine. I don't know about all of this. Frank... wouldn't...listen to me."

"So, I'll talk to him." Katherine's voice was firm, firm as a mother disciplining her child.

Olivia began shaking. How could Katherine broach the subject without Frank thinking his wife was a tattletale? Frank respected his mother, but he didn't respect his wife one bit. He wouldn't harm his mother, but he wouldn't hesitate to take it out on Olivia.

"Olivia! Dear, you're shaking. Are you afraid?" Katherine took Olivia's hand.

Afraid? Why should she be afraid? Just because her husband had slapped her? Tried to choke her? Katherine didn't know that. And Olivia couldn't tell her. Even though she'd already guessed.

"Frank cannot go on talking to you that way. And being gone for two days without telling you? Missing Zoe's party. That's unacceptable. But there's no reason to be afraid."

Olivia didn't know what to say. She looked into Katherine's earnest expression and couldn't find an answer. She shrugged.

"Maybe."

Katherine linked arms with her. "Let's head home. It'll be all right. I promise."

She had no idea what she was promising.

Chapter Sixteen

Olivia didn't intend to eavesdrop. Early that evening she walked into the kitchen to check on the evening's dinner in the crockpot while Frank and his mother sat on the patio, their backs to the windows. The open windows.

"Counseling? I don't need counseling." Frank huffed as he spoke.

At the word counseling, Olivia's insides twisted. Frank was not only going to ignore his mother's advice; he was going to be really mad at Olivia now. Especially if he thought she had told his mother about the slapping or choking. Would he retaliate?

"I beg to differ with you." Katherine's voice was firm. "Getting angry. Shouting. Name-calling. Those are not good, normal behaviors. You need some sort of anger management classes."

Good one. Anger management was probably a more acceptable term than counseling. If only Frank would agree.

"Everybody gets angry." Frank crossed his arms over his chest and leaned away from Katherine.

Katherine leaned toward Frank, closing the space he had created. "Yes, of course they do, but it's how they handle it. It seems you aren't handling it well. Your family is suffering, son. You are suffering, even if you don't want to admit it."

Olivia stood away from the windows and quieted her breathing as silence lay over the patio. She could only see their heads and shoulders from her hiding place next to the pantry.

Somewhere down the street, a dog barked. Quiet again.

Frank cleared his throat. It was loud in the silence.

"I don't want my family to suffer."

Olivia almost missed his quiet admission.

"Of course you don't, son. That's why you need to try something."

"It's just I have these headaches."

No excuses, Frank! Own it.

"Then you need a checkup too."

Frank scrubbed his face from hairline to chin. He cleared his throat again. "Okay, sure. I can do that. But I don't know any place to get those classes."

A checkup? Is that just a delaying tactic? Maybe the headaches were just an excuse. She remembered the other night how he had curled up on the bed holding his head. Okay, maybe they were real.

"You or Olivia can do an internet search. Maybe ask around."

"No! No asking around. I'll Google it."

The Hallelujah Chorus played in Olivia's heart. Now if he'd just follow through.

"One more thing, son."

Frank sat up, his spine straight. Olivia couldn't see the expression on his face.

"How could you miss your daughter's birthday party? Where were you? Really." She was like a mother interrogating a teenaged son who had missed curfew.

"I stayed in Las Vegas. Couldn't drive because my head hurt so bad."

"I'm sorry. But couldn't you have called Olivia so we wouldn't worry?"

"I told her I would be home Sunday." His voice turned hard again.

Katherine reached out and laid her hand on him. Olivia couldn't see where.

"Frank. We know that you checked out of your hotel on Friday."

Oh, boy! Now Katherine had done it. He'll know Olivia blabbed about Seth's phone call. She didn't want to hear more. She wanted to flee the kitchen, but her feet had grown roots or something.

"And just *how* do you know that?" He bit off each word as he spoke.

"If that's a secret, you're in more trouble than I thought."

Frank harrumphed. "I suppose Seth or Ed told Olivia, and she told you. May have to fire Seth."

"No, you won't. This is important. Where were you?"

"If you must know, I checked into a different hotel so the company wouldn't know. I just couldn't drive. Ed was with me, but he had too much to drink the night before and was hung over. He couldn't drive either. So, we decided to stay until my headache was gone."

"Ohhh-kaay." Katherine sounded a little skeptical. "And it took you—and Ed—two nights to recover?"

Frank nodded.

"Why in heaven's name didn't you just call Olivia?" Katherine's voice was degenerating into exasperation. "Tell her the truth?"

"I don't have to explain my actions to her!"

The scorn and anger rose in Frank's response. *Katherine, quit while you're ahead!* Olivia wrapped her arms around her middle. This felt like someone probing a wound not quite healed. Each poke heightened the soreness.

"This is why you and your family are suffering. Olivia

loves you and needs to know you're safe. Jesus wants you to love your wife like He loves the church. Have you sought the Lord, prayed about what's going on in your life?"

"Okay! Okay! I get it." Frank shot up from his chair. Startled, Olivia moved closer to the hall door. "I'll make an appointment for a checkup and look for an anger management class. But I'm done with this conversation."

He turned away and headed for the sliding glass door. Olivia escaped to the other end of the house. The kids still played with the Lego racetrack in Dylan's room, so she huddled in her office where dusk was turning into night. The family room TV blared on with some sporting event. Olivia slipped out of her office and past the family room, her heart thumping like the Mariachi beat at the Delgados. The beat had somehow turned mournful.

Olivia flipped on the kitchen lights. Katherine remained seated on the patio.

"Katherine?" Olivia poked her head out of the open doorway. "Everything okay?"

"Mmmm." Katherine sighed. "He said he'd get a checkup for his headaches and look for an anger management class. The talk of counseling seemed to provoke him."

Katherine didn't know Olivia had heard their conversation. Should she tell her mother-in-law she eavesdropped?

Olivia stepped all of the way out onto the patio and stood in front of Katherine. "I...I heard most of your conversation. But I didn't mean to. I came into the kitchen to check on dinner. And, well, you were right here in front of the open windows." Like a child full of contrition confessing to her mother she ate the last cookie. She clasped her hands behind her back so Katherine couldn't see them shaking.

"Oh, well, then you heard his explanation for missing Zoe's birthday party?"

"I think he's mad about that." Was it really none of her business? Frank had to realize she needed to know he was safe.

And why wouldn't he want her to know about these headaches? Maybe she could help him. It didn't sound like he wanted her help.

And she doubted it was a coincidence that he bolted at the first mention of Jesus and prayer. Something's happened to his relationship with the Lord. What in the world was Frank thinking?

A mini stampede broke out in the kitchen. Zoe and Dylan, with King on their heels, herded themselves out onto the patio.

"When's dinner?"

"We're starving."

"Oh! The crockpot. Beef stew coming up."

The stainless-steel ladle clanged against the pot as Olivia spooned the savory smelling stew into earthenware bowls.

"Olivia!"

The stew missed the bowl and slopped onto the counter. Now her heart clanged. Olivia spun, holding the still dripping ladle in front of her like a weapon.

Frank stepped back from the gooey mess dripping onto the floor.

"What are you doing, woman? You're making a mess." He was beginning to have a permanent scowl on his forehead.

Olivia reluctantly withdrew the ladle from between them and put it back in the pot.

"Sorry."

Frank shook his head. The disgust was obvious, written across his wrinkled brow. "Don't dish any of that up for me. Going to Dave and Buster's."

How had she missed this was his guys' sports night? "Oh. I guess I forgot."

"Well, don't wait up."

Her heart rate began returning to normal as she heard the front door close and she sank onto a stool. He had been cool, but not belligerent. Maybe it was just putting off the inevitable, but she was relieved he was going out. Even a three-hour reprieve was welcome.

Really? What was that going to accomplish? Her body and brain fidgeted as she sat on the stool. Where could she go to hide? Had it been the right thing for Katherine to talk to him? Olivia knew she would never have been brave enough to talk to Frank like his mother had. But maybe she was going to need even more courage to withstand the fallout.

Lord, I can't do this! She had no courage. No place from which to gather it. God had the power to give her courage though, right?

Why would God bother with you, anyway?

Yeah, why should He? She was such a fool.

———

Why did it always seem like she was waiting for the next bad thing to happen? She felt like she was in a courtroom, like when she'd had jury duty. Frank swung from immediate sentencing to running out the door with an unspecified continuance. She preferred the former. Waiting was the worst. It gave her too much time for her mind to imagine a guillotine when the final sentence was really more like a temporary visit to the Salem stocks.

Olivia played Monopoly with the kids and Katherine for a while, but Zoe and Dylan complained when she didn't know it was her turn, or when she forgot to count the money as the banker.

She excused herself to get some work done at her desk, then stared at her computer screen until her eyes ached. Not even Facebook or Pinterest kept her focus. She banged her laptop shut. That was probably not good for the laptop. As she prepared to abandon her office, her cell phone chimed.

Ahh, a diversion. And Vanessa. That was even better.

"I'm so glad you called." Olivia leaned back in her leather desk chair.

"Why? Especially?" Did Vanessa's voice sound a little wary?

"Entertainment. Merely looking for entertainment tonight."

Vanessa's chuckle blasted in Olivia's ear. "I aim to please. Don't know how amusing I'll be though."

"Fortunately for you, it won't take much to amuse me tonight. But since you couldn't have known I'd want to be entertained, there must be some other reason you called."

"Jim said he ran into you guys at work. Glad you got to use the passes. Kids have a good time?"

"It was one of the best days we've had in a long time. I think it made Katherine's visit."

"Uh huh." Vanessa's voice faded out.

Olivia's senses came to full attention. Was Vanessa going to tell her they were moving to Florida? How would Olivia cope if her oldest friend moved three thousand miles away? Even though they had attended different colleges, the campuses weren't far from each other, close enough to visit on weekends. When Vanessa and Jim married and moved to Southern California, and Olivia and Frank moved to Philadelphia, Olivia practically had withdrawals. She was grateful when the Souls dropped Frank and he had to look for a different job. It took little prompting to get him to apply to companies in California. She'd been ever grateful both couples had landed in Orange County.

"Van?"

"Oh, yeah. Yeah. Sorry. Just thinking." It was not like Vanessa to hem and haw around. Something was definitely up. "I'm sure Jim told you about his Florida job offer."

The line went quiet.

"You still there, Van?"

"I told Jim I wouldn't move to Florida."

"Then he's not taking the job. Right?" Vanessa seemed to wear the pants in the relationship.

"Not exactly." Van cleared her throat. "He's going to Florida. I'm not."

"How will that work?"

"Obviously it won't. We're talking divorce."

Olivia gasped into the phone. This was not the kind of entertainment Olivia had been looking for.

"No. Vanessa, no!"

"Hey, no judging. And you can't save me. Even though you've been trying for nearly nineteen years. It is what it is."

There wasn't much to say to that. Olivia had indeed been trying to show her Jesus all these years.

Oh, Van. Why won't you listen and give your life to the Lord? She would never listen to Olivia's talk of salvation.

"I'm sorry, Van."

"Well, I'm not. We're way overdue. And no more lectures. From you." Her voice was hard.

They talked for a while, their words stiff. Zoe and Dylan started World War III. She hung up and went to negotiate.

There was something about someone else's divorce and a mini WWIII that at least kept her from worrying about Frank. As she sank onto the elephant, it hit her. Maybe she'd settled one WWIII only to be subjected to a bigger one when Frank got home.

Sometimes he didn't come home from his guys' night until after midnight. Perhaps he wouldn't come home until late, and there would be no discussion tonight. But there would be a discussion.

She laid her hand on her abdomen to quell the roiling in her gut. Yeah, like that was going to help.

Maybe Frank would voluntarily talk to her about anger management classes. If he only would. What if he didn't? She had to hold him accountable somehow. Maybe she could help him find a class. What about the checkup? Seth always made his medical appointments so that they fit in with his work schedule. How would she be sure that he actually made it to the doctor?

Her thoughts banged into each other like bumper cars, keeping her from following one logically. This was getting her nowhere. She bent to pick up the romance novel she'd been trying to read for weeks but retrieved her iPad and opened her Bible app instead. Better choice.

What were those verses in Chronicles the pastor had talked about? She poked her way through the various menus until she got to Chronicles. First or second book? *Second, she thought.* She skimmed the chapters looking for the verse that said, "Do it!"

"Therefore, your servant has found courage to pray before you." Not what she thought she was looking for, but she stopped and read on, anyway. "And you have promised this good thing to your servant."

Did God promise her this good thing? What was the good thing, anyway? And how did the servant find the courage to pray?

She read on looking for "Do it." Why that particular verse, she didn't know, but somehow it seemed important.

Aha. David told Solomon to be strong and do it. Twice. Of course, David was talking about building a house for the sanctuary. David also said to fear not, for God is with you.

Was God with her? Even though she wasn't building a sanctuary? Did it still apply to her? With all her heart, she hoped so.

Chapter Seventeen

"Frank. You're home." It was only nine. He never came home this early.

"Brilliant observation." He headed toward the kitchen.

Olivia heard Frank's and Katherine's voices, but not the words, coming from the kitchen.

Olivia felt her face redden, and her insides seemed to be connected directly to her face, for when she clenched her jaw, her insides tightened too.

I cannot put up with this, Lord.

She had no words, only inward groanings. She believed, at least hoped, the Lord knew the prayers of her heart. Yet she wasn't sure she knew what those were. Did she want to work this out with Frank? Did she want to stay married to this hurtful man?

No! No! No!

Her inner scream sent her scurrying toward her bedroom. As she arrived at the threshold of her sanctuary, she abruptly stopped.

Coward.

What am I doing? I can't just run away.

Not running away would be a small victory for herself. A small show of courage. Not much, but it was a start.

Olivia marched toward the kitchen, expecting to find Frank. Katherine was alone drinking her chai tea, the spicy aroma adorning the kitchen.

"He's in his man cave," Katherine said, nodding toward the garage. She stroked her hand across the table, wiping invisible crumbs. "You should go talk to him."

Beads of sweat formed on Olivia's upper lip, and she stood unmoving. The image of Daniel in the lion's den flitted across her mind. She shuddered.

"I can't do this."

"You can't. But Jesus can."

Olivia shook her head. "I dunno."

"The power that raised Jesus from the grave is the same power that will give you courage to face this."

"I've never been brave."

"Of course, you have. You've had many faces of courage. You were brave going from foster home to foster home. When you were adopted. You didn't know what your life was going to be like. But you stood up to it. When you went to college on your own. When Adam and DeeDee were killed. These are your many faces of courage. And there will be more in life. This is just one."

"Put on a face of courage?" It could be that simple?

"No, that would be superficial. Show the face of courage God has given you. Trust Jesus. Have faith. You already have had many opportunities for courage. Many times over. He will give you the power to show real courage. His courage. Show your face of courage."

Olivia stiff legged herself out the door toward the garage. She reached toward the door handle and recoiled as if the handle might be hot.

Just do it.

She snatched the door open and strode in. Frank looked

up from where he was tinkering with a piece of equipment on his workbench. He seemed startled.

"Frank."

"Olivia." He bent his head back to the workbench. "What do you want?"

Oh, maybe an explanation. Maybe an apology. Nothing important.

"What do I want?" She shrieked. Calm down. This wouldn't get them anywhere. Besides that's not bravery. More softly she said, "Where were you?"

"You know where I was."

"You missed Zoe's birthday party." Her voice dripped with accusation. Her fists clenched.

"Another brilliant observation."

Her jaw and insides still interconnected, because they tightened again as if in a vice.

"How dare you treat me this way."

Frank slammed the screwdriver to the bench and whirled on her.

"How dare me? How dare me? How dare you! You traitor." He leaned toward her, glaring.

Olivia reeled as if she'd been slapped.

"Me?" She squeaked. "What are you talking about?" But she knew. "We have to talk about this."

"*We* don't have to discuss anything. Now leave me alone."

"You still haven't explained why you were gone. Why you missed Zoe's party."

"I already told you. Again, we have nothing to discuss."

"Don't you think I deserve an explanation?"

Frank clenched his fists and, his jaw proceeding him, advanced toward her. She took another step back, but he kept coming.

"If you don't shut up, I swear!"

Finally, she stood her ground. "I will *not* shut up! A husband should tell his wife these things."

Spittle formed in the corners of his mouth. "And a wife should obey her husband. Respect him. Like the Bible says."

She hadn't thought her gut could clench any tighter. Olivia tried to speak, but, while her lips moved, no sound came out.

He raised his fist to her face. "You treat me right or there will be hell to pay."

The sneer on Frank's face followed her as she fled the garage. She made it as far as the patio doors where she leaned, rested her head, and allowed her shoulders to heave.

My God. My God.

When she heard the garage door open behind her, she stifled a sob and bolted toward the side gate. She kept going until she reached the shelter among the front atrium's greenery, collapsing onto the padded bench. But all she could see was her father leaning over her mother, shouting, his fist raised just like Frank's.

Oh, God. Oh, God. Where were you? Where are you?

Silence.

Maybe it was her fault.

Of course, it's your fault.

Olivia let the sobs take over until her chest ached and the black night surrounded her. Where was her courage? She believed Katherine, and she wanted to do better.

But the courage eluded her.

———

Sleep. There would be none for Olivia tonight after Frank's tirade. She clung to the edge of the mattress, away from him, her back stiff.

The scene replayed in her mind, over and over again— and then over again. Each time she promised herself she wouldn't think about it and tried to think of other things. Each time she pled with the Lord to remove it from her mind.

Yet, it returned as surely as the dawn. And that was coming all too quickly.

I want to love him, but right now, I am fighting hate in my heart. How do I become the kind of wife he wants? How do I find courage?

Her body may have been rigid, but her mind and soul squirmed. She knew what the Bible said about respecting your husband, but what did that mean? Did it mean she had to let him talk to her like she was flotsam? Besides, didn't the Bible also say he was supposed to love his wife? Was that love?

Frank was right. She was self-righteous, holier-than-thou. She needed to admit to him how much of a sinner she was. It was her fault.

Lord, help me to be a better wife. Try harder. Teach me to be more humble. Then he'll love me.

Olivia became conscious of light creeping into the room. She tried to remember what she'd just been praying. Apparently, she'd slept three hours, but it felt like no time at all. Frank's steady rumbling beside her indicated he was still asleep.

She shut her eyes trying to get back to that sweet oblivion. The light was stealing in through the shades, looting whatever the sand man had sprinkled over her just a few hours ago, leaving in its wake a steadily growing daybreak. Then it seemed as if a switch went on inside her mind, an "on" switch. Completely awake and alert, her adrenaline pumping, she knew it would be useless.

Easing to her feet, she tip-toed out of the room like an intruder sneaking out before the master of the house should waken and bodily throw her out.

In the kitchen she reached for the lights but stopped. She usually liked the room awash in bright lights, but this morning it seemed more appropriate to scuttle through the shadows like a mouse. She grabbed a K-cup, jammed it into the Keurig, and watched it sputter to life.

A bold Italian roast released its aroma and teased her.

When she was finally able to wrest the cup from the machine, she swilled a large quantity, burning her tongue and throat.

She gasped and dove for the refrigerator door, extracting ice and adding it with water into a nearby cup. The ice-cold water bunched up in her throat, but she gulped it anyway, and a lump expanded in her chest.

Why had she done that? She knew better. Or maybe she was stupid, just like Frank said.

Holding a hand over her chest while the mass receded, she sank onto a barstool and glared at the coffee cup as if commanding it to cool down. It wouldn't dare burn her again, so she took a tentative sip. The glare must have worked, and the liquid energizer now flowed easily down her throat.

"What are you doing up so early?" Olivia jumped at Frank's voice, causing another coffee disaster. Coffee spewed over the edge of the cup and splashed onto the counter.

"Oh, I'm-I'm sorry. I didn't hear you coming." Olivia grabbed the napkins and mopped up the brown rivers.

Frank's chuckle stopped Olivia mid-swipe. She looked up at him, opening her eyes wide. What? He's nice this morning?

"I guess I owe you an apology, babe. I don't know what comes over me. You do provoke me though." Frank slid his hand up and down her arm.

She shivered at this touch. Not in a good way.

"I'm s-sorry. I'll try to do better."

What was she saying? Olivia couldn't believe what was coming out of her mouth. It was Frank who hadn't bothered to come home. Who threatened her. She mentally shook her head. *No, he's right. I provoke him.*

"We just need to move on. Forget all this nonsense."

"Right." It was only a whisper.

"Now! How about some breakfast for your hard-working stud before he heads out to chase some paper?"

Olivia blinked. Stud? He'd never called himself that

before. Was that Las Vegas talking? Her mouth tasted like sludge.

She could only nod.

His breakfast consumed, Frank stood, throwing down his napkin. "The bacon could be a little crispier next time. And you know I like my eggs over easy. Not hard." With that, he strode out of the kitchen.

Olivia's fork clattered to her plate, her breakfast no longer appealing. She scraped the dishes into the sink, rinsed, and stacked them into the dishwasher. Picking up the bacon to save it for the kids, it crumbled at her touch. Wasn't that crisp?

Frank returned, dressed for the day, computer case dangling from his shoulder. He was breath-catching in his navy blue suit, snug across his broad shoulders, and baby blue shirt with the eye-popping red tie. She heard the word stud again. It didn't taste so bad in her mouth now.

"I want steak and potatoes for dinner. Be home at six."

Without a please, thank you, or goodbye, he was out the door.

Chapter Eighteen

After Frank left, Olivia collapsed into her desk chair and stared at the dark monitor.

What should she do now? How can she learn to be a better wife?

Lord, are you there?

My word is a lamp unto your feet.

She ran to her bedroom and grabbed her Bible, returning to her office to again sink into her desk chair. Her Bible fell open to John 1, so she read about Jesus, in Jerusalem for a feast of the Jews, walking among the sick at the pool of Bethesda, healing the man who had been ill for thirty-eight years.

Olivia didn't really believe in the open-and-point method of getting your answers from God, but she had thought something here would speak to her.

Lord, do I have to wait thirty-eight years for relief? She read back over the story and knew that Jesus walked through the crowd of sufferers and healed because He cared. Because He loved. He was with them. He would be with her.

She also knew that being with her, being her shield, didn't mean she would be free from difficult matters, free from suffering. *In this world, you will have tribulation*, but *behold, I am with you always, to the end of the age.*

Closing her Bible, Olivia realized she had started out by asking how to be a better wife but read about knowing the Lord was with her and would always be with her because he loved her. That was more important than the love she craved from Frank.

Where did that come from? She sat up straight, her Bible falling on the floor. She hadn't realized she was craving Frank's love. Of course, she knew Frank was being difficult, but didn't she know he loved her? She hadn't thought about it in that way.

No, actually, she rather thought he didn't love her anymore. Maybe if she would be a more loving wife, he would love her again.

You'll never be good enough for him to love you.

She covered her face in shame. *Lord, Lord.*

But I love you, Olivia.

The thoughts from the evil one fled. The war of words in her mind was won by the One who loved her. *Thank you, Jesus. Help me.*

A peace covered her like one of her Amish quilts. She thought she could get through this with Frank. If only Frank would turn to the Lord for help, it would be so much easier. But regardless, she would trust the Lord to teach her about loving him. He would see Jesus through her and realize all he was missing and draw closer to Him again. They would be a loving family again.

Olivia saw it all so clearly.

———

What she'd seen clearly that morning was a little hazy now just two hours later.

"But I provoke him."

Breakfast over, Katherine swept the kitchen floor, and Olivia scrubbed the stove top.

"No! No! That's what I used to think. It's just not true." Katherine leaned on the broom. "It is not your fault. You are not responsible for his actions."

Dark clouds gathered across the sky, the sun nowhere in sight.

"It is time to insist on Christian counseling, not just anger management." Katherine forced out each word slowly, quietly.

Dropping her head, Olivia whispered. "He'll never go for it."

"My dear—"

Olivia's head snapped up. "Do you think Frank's even saved?"

Katherine didn't often seem at a loss for words, but she stood there with her lips puckered, quiet. The question pressed like the fog outside, cloaking them in mystery.

Sensing Katherine's consternation, Olivia finally jumped in. "Oh, of course he is. I don't know why I said that."

The grayness outside continued to invade the kitchen putting everything in shadows. Olivia turned on as many lights as she could, trying to dispel the hostile gloom.

"Maybe not," Katherine whispered. "Every mother's nightmare is that her children are not saved."

Giggles and the pounding of little feet rescued them. Zoe and Dylan barreled into the room, dispensing smiles and hugs all around.

"Mommy, wanna hear a joke?" Dylan's smile was purely angelic. He didn't wait for an answer. "So, a man and a turkey walk into a bar—"

Olivia's head snapped up. What? "A bar? Dylan!" Where was this kid getting his material? What does a five-year-old know about a bar?

"It's okay, Mommy. Really. Just listen. A man and a turkey walk into a bar the night before Thanksgiving. The man asks the turkey if it wants anything to eat. The turkey says, 'No thanks. I'm watching my weight.' The man says, 'Are you sure? Not even the seed salad?' The turkey says, 'Nope. I'm stuffed.'" Dylan guffawed at his own joke.

Zoe groaned. "Dylan, really."

Olivia couldn't suppress her smile. This kid was one in a million. What would she do without his jokes and stories? Maybe she could do without bar jokes, but she loved him for his delight in entertaining them. The gold in Dylan's amber eyes always sparkled.

"Didja like that one, Gramma?"

Katherine grinned so wide Olivia almost missed the tears sparkling there. Grabbing Dylan, Katherine enveloped him in a fierce hug.

"Hey! I have an idea. I know it's kinda foggy out there, but how about I take Zoe and Dylan to Disneyland today?"

The room erupted in shouts and high-fives between Zoe and Dylan.

"Oh, can we, Mommy? Please?" Dylan clutched his mother's arm, pleading.

"Olivia, you take the day off. I'll take the kids. It's a good thing Frank gave me a key to his old Honda."

"Would...would that be okay with you two?"

Zoe looked skeptical, but Dylan bumped her arm, and they both nodded. Vigorously.

"Okay! It's settled then. You munchkins get dressed, and we'll be off. Can you put a few things in a backpack for them, dear?"

Katherine moved to leave but turned back toward Olivia. "You take some time for you today. No work. Okay?" She waited until Olivia nodded.

Wow. It was a good thing she had already blocked this day off as a vacation day with her clients. What would she do with an entire day free? She didn't know how to spend the day at home all on her own. A bubble bath sounded sublime. Or maybe she'd go out somewhere. Shopping? No, Frank wouldn't like that.

Vanessa. She really should take Vanessa to lunch and smooth things over from yesterday. Frank probably wouldn't like her spending money on lunch either, but this was important.

Oh, and she had to shop for steak and potatoes.

After a flurry of activity searching for coats, shoes, backpacks, the trio stood ready to make their great escape.

Olivia hugged Zoe and Dylan. "Got everything? Ok, then."

Just before Katherine opened the door, she held Olivia's gaze tight. "They'll be fine. You, too."

Alone in the house, Olivia wasn't sure what to do next. She was tempted to sit down at her desk, but she'd promised herself and Katherine no work today. She strolled through the house, tidying up. Mindless activity meant her mind was free to engage in reliving the last few days, worrying about Frank's current changeable attitudes, and what she was going to do about it all.

Katherine was right. *Frank's the problem. He needs help. But where to get it?* Pastor David was definitely not an option after Frank's argument with him. Pastor Mark would be a good counselor, but would Frank think Pastor Mark was still a little too close? Maybe an outsider that they didn't know could be more objective? Would Frank consent to go at all?

She would just have to insist. Anger management was one thing. But counseling? Be brave. Show that face of courage and have faith Jesus will give her the strength she needed.

But the thought of standing up to Frank still terrified her. Olivia would much rather just let things go on the way they were than force another confrontation. Her childhood self learned speaking out resulted in pain, physical and mental. Look how last night turned out.

Her breathing constricted and hands clammy just at the

thought of forcing the issue again, Olivia tried to push it all away, to think about something else. She felt like a mouse caught in a trap, one end of her body squeezed so she couldn't breathe, the other end flailing with no hope.

Her mind refused to let her out of the trap. Her thoughts continued to writhe under the necessity of standing up to Frank.

Collapsing on the elephant, Olivia curled herself into a fetal position, her eyes squeezed so tight her forehead began to ache.

I can't do this.

When the pounding became too fierce, Olivia opened her eyes and forced her brow to relax. Family photos nestled on the bookcase stood in her line of vision. Zoe and Dylan. Dressed in Christmas finery. Being silly on the beach. Proudly sitting astride motorcycles at the races.

I have to do this. Protect them.

Lord, please give me the courage. Your Word says you have not given us a spirit of fear but power and love and self-control. *Give me your power to do what is right.* Out of love. To protect Zoe and Dylan.

As she lay there, Olivia expected, hoped, courage would begin coursing through her veins, that she would somehow feel like Wonder Woman. Or at least Wonder Girl. Was there a Wonder Girl? When she realized she felt no discernible difference, she sat up and slapped herself mentally.

Get up! Do something. Act like you're brave, then maybe you will be.

She didn't know what that meant, but she decided to at least do something with her day. But what? She had fences to mend with Vanessa. She'd start there.

Extracting her cell phone from her pocket, she figured she'd better go for it before the mouse trap asphyxiated her. Olivia thumbed on her phone and clicked on Vanessa's phone number.

At first Vanessa seemed reluctant, but Olivia lured her

with lunch at one of her favorite restaurants, Gulliver's. No fast food today. Vanessa's only requirement was they meet in an hour because she had a client meeting. No long soak in the tub for her. At least not this morning. Maybe this afternoon.

Olivia rushed through her shower, giving her hair a quick blow-dry, and slapping a tiny bit of make-up on so she didn't scare anyone. Standing in front of the closet, she questioned herself over why she thought choosing just the right outfit was important. Olivia didn't have an answer, but she carefully selected a red, Friday-casual jacket and matching skirt, pairing it with her favorite white silky tank top. Heels today, yes, heels. And accessories.

Why a power suit? Certainly not to impress Vanessa. They'd been friends for so long that Vanessa didn't need impressing. Maybe to impress herself. Give herself some of that power she was looking for.

Checking herself in the mirror, she saw a beautiful suit, but a pale face that nearly faded into the background. The lack of make-up clashed with the power suit. She'd have to be five minutes late.

She flew back to the lighted mirror to bring the face up to the standard of the suit. Mission accomplished and another check in the full-length mirror. She felt empowered. At least a little.

Chapter Nineteen

Minutes later, Olivia drummed her fingers on the steering wheel, wishing she could use the carpool lane. She had forgotten to check her phone's GPS traffic, and the 55 Freeway was backed up for miles. Olivia sputtered. Oh, well, it wouldn't have mattered. There really wasn't any faster way to get to the restaurant next to the John Wayne Airport. Surface streets would be more annoying with all their red lights and stop signs.

Her car may have been idling in traffic, but her mind was not. She tried to think of some way to share Jesus with Vanessa again. That divorce was not the answer. To convince her she should go to Florida with Jim.

Was she being a hypocrite thinking divorce was not the answer for Vanessa, but maybe it was for herself? She didn't really want to think of divorce for either of them. At least Jim wasn't abusive. Was he? You never knew. Would anyone outside of their home—Carmen and Jorge, for instance—think Frank was abusive?

Abusive. The word was foreign. She hadn't used the term in relation to Frank before.

Finally. Traffic opened up, and she made it to the 405

Freeway and the McArthur ramp. Close to the freeway, the restaurant, a red-brick building reminiscent of eighteenth-century England, came into view within moments.

Olivia knew Vanessa would order the famous prime rib. She always ordered the prime rib.

The interior was a little dark coming in out of the bright light and into the dim ambient lighting. Olivia admired the wood-beam ceilings, wood paneling, and upholstered chairs. She enjoyed teasing Vanessa about how much she loved a restaurant with a decidedly senior atmosphere when she was usually all about the hipster vibe. Olivia appreciated variety, old-world, modern, hipster, whatever.

Olivia was directed to a smaller dining room called Jonathan's study. Vanessa waved to her from a table by the fireplace, her spiky, platinum hair contrasted against the paneled walls and old-English paintings.

Vanessa remained seated, so Olivia bent to hug her stiff frame, then took the seat across from her.

"I'm so glad you were available today—"

"Who'd turn down Gulliver's prime rib?"

Olivia looked around at the aging, but beautiful clientele around her. "Tell me again why you like this restaurant? I mean I know the prime rib is great, but how do you even know about it?"

"When I was a kid, my grandparents took me on vacation every summer to visit Disneyland. They died before you moved next door." She shrugged. "Anyway, we always ate here."

"I remember now. That's why you knew your way around Disneyland that time. And you liked prime rib as a kid?"

"Always." Vanessa took a sip of her cocktail, then held the glass up as if in a salute. "Drink? Of course not. What was I thinking?"

Was there an edge to Vanessa's remark? Olivia wasn't sure, but she could feel her own body tensing. *Forget it. It didn't matter.*

"I would like some iced tea."

A waitress dressed in a peasant costume approached the table. Olivia ordered her tea, and as the waitress began to walk away, Vanessa said a little insistently, "We'll order now. Two prime rib lunches."

Olivia had planned to order the salmon but shrugged it off. It didn't matter. Vanessa ordered another drink.

While they waited for their lunch, they engaged in small talk about their mutual business concerns, and Vanessa complained about her husband. Olivia steeled herself against the comments about Frank that she was sure was coming, but Vanessa seemed to be interested in only talking about herself.

Fragrant platters of steaming beef and piquant German potato salad arrived, and Olivia found herself glad Vanessa had ordered her the prime rib. They stayed quiet for the first couple of minutes, tucking into their meal.

Vanessa began to raise her empty glass toward the server, but as she looked at Olivia, she set her glass back down on the table.

"Oh, all right. I won't have another."

"I didn't say anything!"

"It was that look."

"Honestly, Van. I did not. But—"

"Yeah, just as I thought."

Exasperated, Olivia put her fork down and sat back. "Well, you have to admit, three cocktails before you get in the car is dangerous."

"I hate it when you do that holier-than-thou routine. I can take care of myself. Even after a few drinks. How's that working for you with Frank?"

Olivia was stunned into silence, so stunned even her thoughts remained silent.

Vanessa snickered. "Thought so."

It must be the drinks talking. How many had she had before Olivia arrived? She realized Vanessa had said "a few drinks." Vanessa had never spoken to her with such ridicule before, even at Zoe's party, and there was still a tenseness from yesterday's conversation.

Pushing her plate away, her appetite gone, heat began to crawl up Olivia's spine like fire in dry brush. Words finally made their way back to her brain, but Olivia knew those words would not be helpful, and she bit them back. They would certainly not be said in love.

For years, Olivia spoke the gospel sparingly, so as not to beat her over the head, instead she tried to live her life before Vanessa so she would see the love of Jesus. Perhaps she had made a mistake.

"If you weren't such a goody-two shoes, you'd kick that jerk out. I just kicked my jerk out!"

Olivia hadn't thought she could be anymore stunned with this conversation. No wonder Vanessa was drinking and surly. And why she was so strident yesterday.

She reached over and caressed Vanessa's forearm. "Oh, honey, I'm so sorry."

Vanessa shook off Olivia's hand. "Don't feel sorry for me. Feel sorry for yourself. Until you find the gumption to stand up."

"Well, I *am* sorry for you. But you are right about one thing. I need to stand up for myself. I won't kick him out, but I'll insist on counseling. Maybe you and Jim can get counseling."

Vanessa's coarse laugh reverberated throughout the dining room, and the other diners glanced up. "Not on your life!"

The fire now banked in her spine, Olivia mourned for her friend's marriage and her soul.

"Is it okay if I pray for you?" She expected more scoffing and was surprised by Vanessa's response.

"Why not? It can't hurt." Vanessa stood, and threw her napkin on her plate. "I gotta get outta here."

"Can I call you tomorrow?"

"Afraid I'm gonna do myself in?"

"Oh, Van."

"Don't worry. I wouldn't let a little thing like this get me down. Not for long anyway."

Vanessa strode surprisingly steadily out of the restaurant.

Prime rib juices congealed as Olivia stared at her plate. When she told Vanessa she needed to stand up for herself and insist on counseling, she surprised herself. She'd been thinking those words—telling them to herself over and over again, but she hadn't been able to say them out loud before.

Saying them out loud and doing them are two different matters.

That was true. But she *would* do it. She straightened her shoulders and stood up.

"Check, miss?"

She'd forgotten the check. It's a good thing she'd planned to treat Vanessa today. Olivia sat down again to wait for the check.

What a waste.

She wasn't sure if she was thinking about their uneaten lunches, her day of relaxing, or Vanessa's marriage.

Freeway congestion was even worse on her drive home, and the tension began to build. She *would* talk to Frank when he got home. Katherine and the children would be gone until late, so it was the perfect opportunity. The Lord would have to give her the words, because she didn't have them.

Oddly enough, Vanessa's attitude had given Olivia a small boost of courage. She didn't want to end up like Vanessa— alone, bitter, and hard. Running from the Lord. And definitely not downing cocktails at lunch time.

Finally freed from freeway traffic, Olivia sped toward home. That bubble bath sounded better and better. She looked at the dashboard clock. Only 3:30. Plenty of time for a nice long soak.

She pulled into her driveway and was about to get out

when the image of steak and mashed potatoes flashed on to the screen of her mind.

Oh, no! The grocery store.

She slammed the door and gunned the engine in exasperation. Why couldn't Frank be satisfied with what they had on hand? Yet she knew the advantage of giving her husband a good meal before any discussion. Visions of a bubble bath began to fade away as fast as popping bubbles.

Chapter Twenty

Later that evening the dinner conversation, starting out benign and boring, had lapsed into silence. Olivia had greeted Frank when he got home with such high hopes of what the evening would hold—a discussion of his actions, her demand for counseling, and, of course, Frank's ready agreement. But his amiability threw her back into keep-the-peace mode. Don't rock the boat when there was no storm. She wanted to enjoy the peace.

Yet she knew a storm was always one drop of rain away. One wrong word. One hint of indigestion.

Olivia's gut burned with disappointment in herself. She knew they had to talk, but she also knew it would not be the optimistic version she had envisioned.

"Leave the kitchen for tomorrow. Watch TV with me."

Must you always command? While she inwardly rebelled, she knew sitting with him would give her an opportunity to redeem herself and the discussion.

Frank had settled into his favorite recliner, so she chose the recliner's twin next to him. She preferred her padded armchair across the room or the elephant. It was not as cozy and intimate as if sitting together on the elephant, but this would have to do.

Images of dead bodies on morgue tables lingered on the TV screen. She wasn't a fan of crime investigation shows, so she didn't know which one he was watching, nor did she care.

When a commercial comes on. Maybe that wasn't the best strategy. He'd be distracted when the program resumed. Could she ask him to turn off the TV? No, that would just irritate him and set the wrong tone.

It always seemed as if her mind was at war with itself, battling over what was the best thing to do. She was decisive in her job, always knowing what was right for her clients. Knowing how to ask for and get contract concessions. In control. Why was she so out of control when it came to Frank?

Well, her clients didn't beat her up mentally.

Their first ten years, well, really only eight, seemed picture-perfect. After Frank was cut by the Soul, they moved to California, where Dylan was born two years after Zoe. They were involved in their mega-church enough to be on talking terms with many of the thousand members. Frank excelled in his career as a production manager and later a vice president, and Olivia had successfully begun her own business from home and launched into homeschooling, with Frank's okay, if not with his involvement.

What happened between years eight and ten? She could now see the subtle shift changes, beginning with him complaining how much time she spent working to his interacting less and less with the kids, even to complaining to her about their normal, child-like behavior. He went to church less and less frequently, and his recent demand about Bible study in their home left her adrift in a sea of confusion.

And she hadn't foreseen the protection of the early years would turn into control. Worse, he was becoming mean. She could no longer afford to be tossed about by the storm. She had to grab on to something.

Lord, I don't know what else to do, so I'm trying to hold on to You. Except her heart told her to trust in the Lord not because she didn't know what else to do, but because it was the first, most important thing to do.

Forgive me, Lord. You are in control. Show me what to do.

More dead people on morgue slabs flashed across the TV screen. She tried to avert her eyes.

Tom Jones belting out *She's a Lady* from her cell phone saved her from the morgue scenes. She gratefully grabbed her phone. "It's your mom and the kids!"

When their phones connected, Olivia's screen lit up with their smiling faces.

"Hi, Mommy." "Hello, dear," with the chaos from Disneyland in the background, they chattered over each other, waving their hands in front of Katherine's cell phone screen.

Olivia chuckled. "You having a good time?"

More chatter came describing their latest ride experience, then Katherine shushed them. "Just wanted to see if it was okay if we stayed until closing? That's nine."

Frank leaned over to get into the picture. "You sure they're not driving you crazy? Maybe you should come home."

"I'd really like to stay for the parade and all. We're fine."

"Well…"

"Please, Frank. Your mom leaves in a couple of days."

"Oh. All right. But you kids mind your grandma. And be quiet when you come home."

Olivia sputtered quietly at the last admonition but smiled and waved into the camera. "Have fun. Love you guys." The gathering noise around them cut off their goodbyes, and the screen went blank.

Back in his chair, Frank flipped through channels with the remote. *The dead people must be all hacked up. Thank goodness.*

"I—"

"Get me some ice cream, will ya?"

More commands. What happened to please and thank you?

Olivia dished up a bowl of his favorite butter pecan and presented it to him.

"What's this?"

"You asked for ice cream."

"I wanted the moose tracks."

She grabbed the bowl from him.

"Hey! Watch the attitude!"

When she returned with the bowl of moose tracks ice cream, she gathered her courage as she handed it to him.

"We need to talk." A headache pinched her forehead, but she plowed on. "About how you treat me and the kids—"

"It's the only way I can get your attention." He kept his eyes going back and forth from the TV screen to his ice cream.

"Yelling at me? Calling me names? Ordering me around?"

"That's your job. Bible says you are to respect your husband. Be my helpmeet. Yet you continually squander my hard-earned money. Spend more time with your *clients* than with me." His voice began to take on that hard edge.

A voice in her head began to sneer. *What kind of wife are you?*

She collapsed onto the elephant, her head in her hands, guilt eating her from the inside out.

Frank turned off the TV and rose. He thrust the empty ice cream bowl at her. "We're done here."

Wait! How did this become about me? Isn't this about him? What gives him the right to treat me this way?

How can a wife respect a man who ridicules and shouts? Ignores his kids most of the time? Threatens. Doesn't come home for his child's birthday? Then won't talk about it?

Are you to respect his conduct? Or his office of husband? The thought pushed her back in the chair. Olivia ran that thought through her mind, over and over again.

Lord, I need help.

She'd had such high hopes for their talk. Look where her so-called face of courage got her. Nowhere.

———

What started out as a fun family day at the park with the Delgados the following Sunday turned ugly with Frank berating Dylan for whining over baseball. Zoe and Dylan had moped the rest of the evening and willingly allowed themselves to be bedded down early for the night. Olivia fussed over Dylan's covers and sat next to him on the bed. She stroked the back of his hand.

"Sweetie, I'm so sorry about what happened at the park. I think Daddy was just tired. Just like you." She hated making excuses for Frank.

"I know, Mommy."

"You know he still loves you, right?"

"I know, Mommy." His yawn nearly swallowed his words. "I'm tired."

Olivia held back a sigh and patted his hand. She tucked it under the covers. "Okay. Goodnight, sweetie."

King snuggled on the bed next to Dylan. She really should make King go to his own bed in the laundry room, but Dylan already had his arm draped over his furry friend. She turned his dual lamp from bright to night light and pulled his door closed.

She turned toward the family room. After two steps, she stopped and walked back toward her room. Three times she headed toward the confrontation, then away from it. At this rate, she'd wear a path in the carpet. Exasperated at herself, she started toward Frank one more time.

Frank's and Katherine's voices now mingled. Hers still soft. His a little less so. Katherine had to be challenging him. Good, she wouldn't have to do it.

Oh, you coward. Don't let Katherine tackle this. Not by herself at least. She could not allow Frank to berate her children. What would he do next? Strike them?

Olivia set her jaw and marched into the action.

Katherine looked up as Olivia entered. "Oh, good. Olivia."

Frank turned his glare from his mother to his wife but remained silent.

"I was just telling Frank that he must get a handle on his anger. And that perhaps anger management classes was a good place to start."

Finally, it was in the open. Olivia wouldn't have to explain to Frank how she knew about his mother's suggestion.

"And what do *you* say?" Frank's question ended in a growl.

Olivia swiped a hand down her thigh. "I-I think that's a... good suggestion."

"I tell you, it's these headaches!"

"Get that checkup I told you to. But I think you should also try the anger management classes."

Frank's nostrils flared. He jumped up and paced in front of the fireplace.

"I don't need anger classes." He tangled his hands in his dark curls.

"B-But Dylan is just a little boy. He was tired. How you handled it wasn't right." Olivia sat on the other end of the couch, as far away as possible from where Frank walked. Her boldness went only so far.

"Well." He sputtered. "He needed to man up."

"Frank! He's five-years-old. Not a man." She must feel safer than she thought from this distance.

"Son, once you start talking that way, the next step is harm."

His face turned ashen as he stared at them. Different emotions played over his face. Was he getting it?

Oh, Lord, please let him get it.

"Okay. Okay." He slumped in his chair.

"Olivia, can you help Frank get an appointment for a checkup and then search for anger management classes?"

"Seth sets up all of my doctor appointments. He knows my schedule better than Olivia."

"And can Seth set up some sort of anger management classes for you?"

"No! I'll do it myself. I can use a computer, you know." His voice alternated between hard and resigned.

She wanted to be relieved. She wanted to jump for joy. But he had agreed before. What about his headaches? They seemed real, but did they have any bearing on his bad behavior?

Why couldn't life ever be simple?

Chapter Twenty-One

"I wish you didn't have to leave tomorrow."

"I know, dear. I wish I didn't either, but I committed to projects for Easter services." Katherine folded and inserted her blouses into packing cubes.

"Even after they fired you?"

"They didn't fire me. It was a mutual decision."

"Humph." Olivia crossed her arms over her chest. She pouted like a child, and she didn't care. How would she get along without Katherine? Especially now that Frank said he would take steps. Would he, without his mother to prod him on?

"I'll keep in close touch with Frank. Encourage him to follow through. I think he realizes he has a problem now."

Does he? Olivia wasn't too sure. What if he was just being agreeable to put his mother off? Olivia visualized Frank coming after her when Katherine was gone.

And Katherine didn't know the worst of what her son had done. She didn't know about the slapping and near choking. The watermelon seed in the pit of her stomach grew into an entire watermelon.

Olivia inserted Katherine's shoes into special shoe bags

and placed them inside her suitcase. "Did you get your dresses out of the dryer?"

"Oh, no. Thank you for reminding me." Katherine tossed the shirt she was folding onto the bed.

"I'll get 'em."

On her way to the laundry room, Olivia checked on Zoe and Dylan who, a bit subdued today, lay inert on the couch, a four-legged pacifier lying between them. She faulted the hiking, baseball, and abundance of food yesterday. They always overdid it when given half a chance. Lots of *whams* and *zaps* emanated from the TV as they watched the latest Pixar video. Olivia declared today a non-school and non-workday in honor of Katherine's last day. Truthfully, Olivia wasn't up to either activity, although she was going to pay for putting off both. The kids would have to play catch-up in their school-work, and she would have to work extra hours later in the week to take care of her clients.

And Vanessa. She needed to follow up with Vanessa. On the one hand, Olivia couldn't understand how Vanessa could contemplate divorce, but then, if Frank didn't straighten up, was that something she'd have to consider? She just couldn't. Once Katherine left, she'd suggest lunch with Vanessa again.

Satisfied Zoe and Dylan were well occupied, Olivia retrieved Katherine's clothing from the dryer. The lavender fabric sheets infused the laundry room, and as she fingered the silky fabric, her thoughts eased. How strange that lavender and silk were so calming. She imagined throwing herself into a giant laundry basket of lavender and silk. Throw in a little cashmere. Heavenly.

She slammed the dryer door. *Enough of that, Olivia.* Too much fantasizing only left one disappointed.

Katherine's suitcase threatened to gush over the sides, and she hadn't packed her nightclothes or toiletries. How would she get it all in one suitcase?

"You're never going to get everything in one bag. Why

don't you take one of ours? You haven't committed to just one yet. Right?"

"Oh, no! I haven't checked in yet!"

Another suitcase brought out and filled, her boarding pass printed, and they declared the packing done for now. Time for lunchtime.

Olivia and Katherine worked side-by-side, pulling deli meats, cheeses, and condiments from the refrigerator. Bread from the panty. Olivia extracted a tomato from the countertop basket and grabbed a cutting board and knife to slice the tomato.

"Ow!" Olivia sucked on her bleeding finger for a moment, then clamped the cut with her other hand. Tears gathered then gushed.

"Oh, dear. That must really hurt. I am so sorry." Katherine put her arm around Olivia's shoulders and squeezed.

"N-no. It doesn't hurt. It's just that…" The sobs cut off the rest of her words, and she turned into Katherine's embrace.

Katherine patted her back.

She gulped back the sobs and pulled away. The kids should not walk in on this. "I'm sorry. I just wish you didn't have to leave."

"Everything will be fine. I promise."

Fine? No, they wouldn't be fine. She loved Katherine, but if Olivia had one complaint, this was it. Katherine was just too optimistic. No, too trusting. Pretty good record. Only one fault. If only Olivia could say the same about herself.

Besides, Katherine didn't have the whole story. And Olivia was still not going to spill it. Katherine might not believe it, anyway. Frank said it was her own fault. Was it? She had a whole boatload of faults.

Olivia sniffed and wiped her eyes and cheeks. *Get it together!*

She washed her hands, applied a band aid, and they went back to preparing the sandwiches.

Clanging from the entryway announced someone at the door.

Olivia wiped her hands on a towel. "Who would that be?" She opened the door to a uniformed FedEx guy who thrust an electronic pad at her, indicating the need for a signature. Duly signed for, a large envelope was handed over.

"Katherine, it's for you."

"What?" Katherine took the envelope, and after looking it over, laid it aside. "I think I forgot to tell him I was coming home tomorrow."

"Who?"

"Just my financial advisor. These could have waited until I got back to New York."

"What is it? Sorry, none of my business." Olivia stacked two large and two small sandwiches on plates along with cut apples and carrots, plus chips.

"Nonsense. Merely papers needing my signature for some financial changes I'm making." Katherine placed the laden paper plates on the kitchen table. The colorful lunch on plain white plates livened the white tabletop. "Shall I go get Zoe and Dylan?"

At her nod, Katherine left Olivia alone. She didn't want to be left alone with her thoughts or, well, anything. What financial changes was she making? Katherine hadn't elaborated, and it really wasn't any of Olivia's business, so she wouldn't ask.

A throbbing finger distracted her from her thoughts. She was almost grateful for it.

The kids chattered between bites of turkey and carrots. Sometimes they managed to talk around whatever was in their mouths.

"Hey, let's chew our food first, and let your grandmother eat in a little peace and quiet."

Katherine smiled at the two across from her who appeared to have chipmunk-stuffed cheeks. "You know I don't mind the chatter. But maybe you should chew first. Don't want anybody choking."

Taking advantage of the momentary silence, Olivia broached another subject. "Katherine, remember when you first got out here, and we went to the beach, and you said you would like to live out here? Well, why don't you?" She was out of breath by the time she arrived at the end.

"Why don't I what, dear?" Her brow crinkled.

"Move. Here. To Orange County. You could see the kids more often. Go to Disneyland with us." She was begging. Did she sound as desperate as she felt? She just couldn't be left to face Frank alone.

"As wonderful as that sounds, I don't think so. I've lived in the same township, the same house all my married life. It's where Frank was born. And even though..." she glanced at Zoe and Dylan, "things...were not perfect when Isaac died, it is still the house we lived in together. I'm just too old, dear. You understand."

Why would Katherine want to uproot herself from everything she's ever known to move here? Just because her daughter-in-law was a coward.

"Of course. I was just dreaming. All right, kiddos, time to take a little rest. Bodies sacked out on the bed. Books encouraged, but optional."

"But, mom, I was hoping we could play games with Gramma." Zoe seldom wanted to give up her reading time.

"Yeah. Me too." Dylan on the other hand often had a hard time deciding whether he wanted to read or play with his racetrack. The racetrack usually won. Unless there was a game to play.

"How about we play right after you take a rest? The sooner you go rest, the sooner we can play." Katherine had a knack for getting the kids to follow the plan.

Olivia and Katherine picked up the remains of lunch, working quietly.

A cell phone played "Rock of Ages." It was definitely not Olivia's phone. She'd never heard Katherine's phone ring the entire three weeks she'd been with them. And just how had the decidedly non-technical Katherine figured out how to add a ring tone?

"Excuse me, dear." Katherine tugged her phone from her pocket. "Hello? Hal? How are you? Oh, no. I'm so sorry." Katherine hurried out of the kitchen, her phone pressed to her ear.

Hal? Who was Hal? The name sounded familiar, but she couldn't place it. She had more to worry about than who her mother-in-law was talking to on the phone. Not that she didn't care, but really, it wasn't her business.

Maybe she could still talk Katherine into moving. Maybe she just needed to get used to it. After all it was a new idea. *Stop! She's not going to uproot her life for you.*

She wiped the counters and the table. Could she wipe Frank clean? Herself? No, that was Jesus' job. He had wiped her clean, hadn't he? Why did it seem like her sin just hung around like a swarm of flies?

"Good thing I'm going home tomorrow." Katherine bustled back into the room. "That was Hal. You remember my oldest and dearest friend, Reggie? Regina. You met her and Hal when Frank brought you out before the wedding. Reggie has MS, and Hal is beside himself taking care of her. The MS is getting worse. Their only child died five years ago. He's alone, and he needs help." Katherine collapsed into the kitchen chair, her breathing hard after the long explanation.

Olivia made soothing noises. She was beside herself caring for Frank. She needed Katherine's help too, and so did Frank. Would Katherine remember to check up on him from three thousand miles away? How would she ever talk Katherine into moving here with her friend sick?

The self-centeredness of her thoughts choked her. How selfish could one be?

Somewhat calmed, Katherine continued. "Hal and Reggie were my only support when Isaac died and when we found out about the other family. Hal took care of all the legal matters, too. I owe them so much." A little sob hitched her breathing. "I don't know what I'll do without them."

That swarm of flies got thicker.

Shame bowed her head. "Katherine, I really am sorry about your friends."

Although with her head bowed and couldn't see Katherine, she sensed Katherine watched her. Oh, she must have really disappointed Katherine now. She groaned inwardly.

"What's going on?"

Maybe she had groaned out loud.

"It can't be just that I'm leaving." Her voice was always gentle.

Yes, it could. She looked up.

"I don't think I'm strong enough to handle all of this, whatever this is, with Frank."

"That's the thing. You don't have to handle it by yourself. It's in the hands of God the Father, in the name of the Son Jesus, and the Holy Spirit dwelling here with you." Katherine patted the general area of where Olivia's heart beat a wild tune. "All you have to do is trust."

That's all. Just trust. And how do you do that?

"I don't know…"

"Have faith, Olivia. Faith."

"That's just it. I don't! Not enough anyway." Olivia's voice became strident.

"You know as well as I do that the Bible says we only need faith the size of a mustard seed. If you feel like you don't even have that, ask for it. He's a good God and wants to give you all the good gifts. Faith is a good gift. Just take courage and do it."

There was that phrase again. Take courage and do it.

Maybe that was what the Lord had been telling her through the pastor's sermon. Courage. Ask for faith. Do it.

Katherine wrapped her in a bear hug, so tight Olivia was astounded at her strength. "I have a few things to do, and then the kids will probably be ready to play games." She kissed Olivia's cheek and went out, leaving Olivia alone.

Olivia stood at the kitchen window seeing nothing outside but her lack of faith. She mentally lifted her hands into the air, pleading with God for just a mustard seed of faith. Funny, but as she imagined those hands in the air in supplication, she saw bootstraps clutched there. She wasn't even sure what boot-straps were. But somehow, they were important.

Lord, help me be strong enough to hang on for that seed of faith. Help my unbelief.

———

Frank again commissioned Olivia to take his mother to the airport. He said his goodbyes and promised to follow through that morning.

This time the kids accompanied them to the airport. Giggles and tears punctuated the adventure, and sometimes the tears fell from Zoe and Dylan. Between the last wave before Katherine disappeared through security and their arrival back home in Villa Park, only sniffles broke the silence.

Seemingly void of welcome, the house offered only more silence. Zoe and Dylan threw themselves on the elephant, slumping on opposite ends, a slobbering fur ball edging between them.

Olivia's heart twinged for them and herself. "How about a video?" She always defaulted to videos. There must be alter-natives, but if so, she couldn't think of any at the moment.

"Naw. Don't want a video." Dylan flopped on his stomach, burying his face in King's black coat.

Zoe sat up. "Can we invite Gabe and Artie over? Or go to

their house? We haven't played with them much while Gramma was here." Her face lit with eagerness.

Dylan turned over and now the two of them had hope written all over their faces.

"Sorry. Carmen already told me they had doctor appointments all day today."

Deflated, they both resumed the posture of a teddy bear void of its stuffing.

As much as she wanted to join them on the couch, it wouldn't do. Action was needed. One giant clap of her hands should do it. They barely flinched.

She slapped her hands together again and raised her voice. "All right, team! It's either help me in the kitchen making dinner or go out back and play."

Only groans met her decree. "Make up your mind right now."

They scurried toward the kitchen, but she was pretty sure they didn't plan to stop there. Not today. They often liked to help her in the kitchen, especially Zoe. But they needed to jump and run, not putter about the kitchen. And they knew it.

Sure enough. When Olivia got to the kitchen, Zoe already pumped her feet on a swing, and Dylan jumped on the trampoline. Not with much speed. If they swung and jumped any slower, they'd being going backward. But it was something.

Olivia opened the refrigerator, hoping dinner lurked somewhere inside. Maybe the pantry. Colorful labels on cans and packages stared back at her but offered no clue that led to dinner. She slammed the pantry door.

To-go menus flashed from the hanging cubby on the wall. She flipped through pristine brochures heralding pizza, Chinese, Jewish deli sandwiches, and one declared you could have it all with one phone call. Olivia was a little skeptical over a name like GrubHub. Grub. Really?

As she glanced out the window to check on the kids, her conscience pricked. She wouldn't let the kids slide into inactivity, yet she thought she could give up and order take out? She shoved the menus back in their resting place and opened the pantry again. Pasta and canned sauce. That was the limit of her conscience today.

Her phone pinged an incoming text.

Katherine?

TAKING OFF IN 5. LOVE YOU.

She texted? Their technology must have finally rubbed off.

LOVE YOU, TOO. PRAYING FOR A SAFE FLIGHT.

Olivia hit send and pushed up her sleeves, ready to face making dinner when she'd rather be face down on the couch like Dylan had been.

The western sun glowed into the kitchen as she worked. It wouldn't be sunset for some time, but she called the kids in. Time to give them a break.

"Before you ask, yes, you can go watch a video."

Dylan threw his arms around her middle. "Thanks, Mommy! I love you."

As she turned toward the stove, the digital numbers on the clock meant Frank would be home soon. She dragged a palm down her jeans. Why did she sweat just because Frank was coming home? How she hated sweat.

She could do this. Olivia imagined Frank being sweetly apologetic for his past behaviors and declaring his commitment to going to the doctor and anger management classes. She imagined a return to the happy family they once had.

And when was that? Maybe the first few years of marriage. After he retired from the Soul and they moved to California, life had begun to change. She just hadn't noticed it creeping up on them. The unkind word here. The bad word there. Questioning her about a purchase one month. Ignoring the checkbook the next. Wanting to know where she was every minute for a week. Then lacking any interest.

Maybe life never was perfect. Maybe it never would be. But it could get better. Right? She had to believe it. Trust. She asked for more faith. He was a good God who gave good gifts. Her mother-in-law said so.

The front door whooshed open and closed with a loud click. She stiffened, but then willed her body to relax. At least he didn't slam the door.

The evening edged toward night, and Olivia edged toward an explosion of nerves. Putting the kids to bed was a study in patience. Theirs, not hers. When she could stand it no longer, she escaped to the patio. She set her coffee mug on a side table and wiped the dirt and grime off her bright green Adirondack chair, hoping in the semi-gloom she'd gotten the worst of it.

Nothing can be done about it now.

She sat down gingerly, the chill of the paint and wood seeping through her jeans. Mug cradled in both hands, she blew across the surface of the hot coffee. She didn't need a lip or tongue blister. Somewhere along sip four or five, she stopped and stared into the coffee. Usually, the robustness of the dark roast aroma was part of her experience. She didn't want to say the most enjoyable part, because she loved the taste of her coffee. The taste was almost an obsession.

If she had any sense, she'd march right in and get a commitment out of Frank. If she really had any sense, she'd take the kids and get outta dodge. He'd been exceptionally quiet tonight. He hadn't asked about his mother, the kids. She shivered at the lack of knowing Frank's state of mind.

Frank, what is your problem? Did she dare bring up the subjects of a medical appointment or anger management?

The sliding glass door *shooshed* open, and Frank stepped out onto the patio. Olivia pulled her sweater tighter. He sat down in his companion chair, a neon orange.

Olivia stopped herself from telling him the chair was probably dirty. Why open herself up to a tirade that she should have cleaned it in anticipation that he would want to sit there?

Cola was his beverage of choice, and he sipped from the familiar red and white can.

A couple of night birds twittered a lullaby. An open window next door revealed the ten-year-old trying to get Alexa to respond, but his lisp somehow messed with Alexa's understanding, so the command was repeated several times before he gave up.

Say something. Where does one start a conversation with a schizophrenic? Wait. Was that Frank's problem? No, just a figure of speech.

Clunk. Frank set the can down on the fluorescent yellow table between them. At least the patio was cheerful.

"Olivia. We need to talk."

Duh, brilliant observation. She sounded like Frank now. Her conscience pricked at the sarcasm in her thoughts. She apologized silently. To the Lord and to Frank.

She sucked in a breath. "Uh huh."

"Look. I don't know what's wrong with me. Don't even know if anything is wrong."

He doesn't know if anything is wrong? Gotta be kidding here.

"But I made an appointment today with the doctor for a checkup. And I will ask him about a source for anger management classes." Frank picked up his can and took a long swig of the cola.

A breath mixed with hope bottled up in her chest. Was this her answer to prayer? She wanted it to be. Oh, how she wanted it.

"No comment?" His voice was brittle.

"Th-That's wonderful news. When is your doctor's appointment?"

Frank slammed his hand against the chair's armrest. "Already doubting me?"

Olivia drew as far away in her chair as she could get. "Of…of course not." Yeah, now that he mentioned it.

"Just don't you worry about it. But if you must know, it's

next Wednesday afternoon. The twelfth." He took another long swig and tossed the can toward the trash barrel. A rimshot. Football wasn't his only prowess. "It's time for bed."

Frank stood and arched his back, then stretched to the right and left. "Coming?"

"Yes, dear. Right behind you."

Yes, she wanted to be behind him, to hope. But the conversation held so many mixed messages, she had whiplash. Is it about trust, Lord? Of course, it is. *Brilliant observation, Olivia.* She really had to stop the sarcasm, even in her own head.

"Babe?" He still stood in the open doorway, the kitchen light framing his head.

No. Definitely no halo. But she dutifully followed her husband. To where, she didn't know.

Chapter Twenty-Two

"Yeah, doc says I'm healthy as an ox."

It had been a gloriously sunshiny Good Friday, and now they sat together that evening as a family at the Orange Hills Mining Company Restaurant high on a hill. Orange County spread out before them below, the lights of the cities twinkling here, glowing there.

The only thing that would have made it better was attending a Good Friday service, but Frank had promised them full involvement with Easter morning services. She allowed joy and contentment with that.

"Daddy, how healthy is an ox? Do you know what you call a sleeping bull?" Dylan looked at each person expectantly, but only got shaking heads for a response. "A bull-dozer! Get it? A bull-dozer!" Dylan guffawed.

Frank tittered, and Zoe groaned. As usual.

"Good one, sweetie." Where did that boy get his jokes? She could understand if he went off to school each day with thirty other kids, but he didn't. Their attendance at home-school co-op groups had even been limited lately.

Back to Frank's doctor's report. "What else did the doctor

say, anything?" Olivia looked at Frank, who was busy cutting his steak. "Frank?"

"I'm healthy. No worries."

"What about the headaches?"

Frank slammed his fork and steak knife to the table. Zoe and Dylan jumped. "I. Am. Fine." He stared at her for a moment, then resumed cutting.

That apparently was all he was going to say on the subject, but there must have been more to the results. Olivia concentrated on her salmon.

Why did she have to push? They'd been having such a nice dinner. Why did she have to trade open communication for peace? Dare she ask about the anger management classes?

The waitperson approached the table to refill their water glasses. "Everything okay here?"

Not even. She smiled at the young blond man who didn't look over sixteen. "Yes. Thank you very much."

"Bring us more bread."

Frank could have at least said please and thank you.

The young man brought more bread. Frank grunted his thanks. He tore off a piece of bread and popped it in his mouth.

"Who wants a surprise?" The irritation on Frank's face was replaced by little-boy glee.

"Yes, Daddy. Please." The ever-polite Zoe, unless it was toward her brother, stopped eating, fork in the air.

"What is it? What is it?" The not-as-polite Dylan talked around a mouthful of mashed potatoes and bounced in his seat.

Oh, no. What now? Frank's surprise could be anything. And past history had proven it to be so. Olivia put her fork down in, what? Anticipation? Dread?

"How would you squirts like to take a vacation? A real honest-to-goodness vacation?" His look around the table included Olivia.

Their last vacation ended in disaster with Frank working all the time only to be interrupted by an invasion of rats. Frank had borrowed a Big Bear mountain cabin from an employee who had insisted he had checked out the cabin the week before, and there had been no rats. If only Frank had been willing to spend the money to rent a cabin from a reliable source. Olivia was sure Frank had badgered a reluctant employee into loaning them the cabin. Did that employee lose his job over it? Probably, knowing Frank.

"Are you ready? We're going to Catalina!"

Zoe and Dylan responded with blank stares.

"What's Catalina?"

"Where's Catalina?"

"Catalina is an island. We get to take a boat."

The mention of a boat turned into grins from the kids. But Olivia's insides quivered at the thought of a boat. It wasn't that she was afraid of boats. She'd been on many as a teenager and had been a passable seaman. She wasn't worried they would sink like Adam and DeeDee had, but the memories, even though she hadn't been there, left her anxious.

"Oh, wow. Catalina on a boat. Won't that be fun?" She couldn't let Frank or the kids think she was afraid, because she wasn't. Just keep saying it often enough and it would have to be true.

"What's the matter with going to Catalina? I thought you'd be thrilled to get a vacation."

She should have sounded more excited. "No. I think it's great. We'll love it." Was that enthusiastic enough? "When are we going?"

"We leave on the twenty-fourth and will stay five whole days. In a nice little hotel. Play on the beach. Take boat tours. I hear they even have a jeep tour that takes you on inland back roads."

"Ohhh, I wanna go in the jeep." Dylan was getting excited enough for the two of them. "What'll we see?"

"Oh, wild animals. Maybe even buffalo."

The kids' eyes widened at that.

"The twenty-fourth? That's in only ten days." How would she get them all organized, her business caught up, so quickly? "Why so soon?"

"And why not? You're so hard to please, Olivia."

Hard to please? He sprang a sudden vacation on her without consulting her, without regard to her business, or the kids' schooling. Schooling that they were still behind in. And he knew—or at least knew at one time—about her aversion to boats since her adoptive parents' death.

"Besides that's when Mr. Bascomb, one of our biggest clients, will be stopping in Catalina. So, I had to take advantage of that."

Clanking dishes and the chatter of fellow diners receded into the background. So that's what this vacation meant. Business again. He called this an honest-to-goodness vacation?

"I know what you're thinking. But I'll meet with Mr. Bascomb the first day, then he's leaving, and we'll have the next four days all to ourselves." His expression was hard and allowed for no arguments.

She nodded, smiling weakly, she was sure. "Ok." It was thoughtful of him to include the family. He didn't have to do that. She would make the best of it. No, not just make the best of it, but expect it would be a good time. She read somewhere when we expect good, we're more likely to get it. When we expect bad, we're more likely to get that. Actually, it was a matter of trust, a matter of faith in the one who gives good gifts.

Now, with videos playing and headsets on the kids, the interior of the car was quiet.

Frank reached over and grasped Olivia's hand. The gesture was so rare these days that it startled her, but she recovered quickly. At least she hoped so. She squeezed his hand.

Frank glanced at the kids in his rearview mirror. "I didn't want to talk about this in front of the kids." His eyes sliced back to the rearview mirror again. "Found a referral to one of those classes. One's scheduled for next week."

Her belly fluttered as she gently bit her lip. God was indeed the giver of good gifts. Was this the more faith she asked for? The result of trusting Him? Having the faith of a mustard seed?

You don't buy this for a minute, do you? He's lying to you. What didn't she buy? Who did the enemy mean? God or Frank? She threw her shoulder back against the seat as if shrugging off unwanted attention. Which she was. She would not doubt God.

But a seed of doubt had been planted.

———

Easter Sunday had been a glorious day. A stirring church service, time with their church family, and best of all, Frank was at least physically present. Olivia wasn't sure he was always mentally engaged, but for now she'd take his physical presence. The Lord could use that, right?

Katherine had called and, from the conversation Olivia could hear on this end, Frank assured his mother that he had an anger management class scheduled the following Wednesday.

And today was that day.

Frank was due home from work any minute. Olivia had fussed around all afternoon, moving in high speed from one task to another as if she could push the clock faster.

But now that the time had actually arrived, she repeatedly twisted her hair up, repositioning the clasp. She wished she could anticipate his mood, but she'd never been able to do that. And how was she, or even Frank, to know in advance how it would go?

When high on a hopeful attitude, she imagined he'd come home humble and cured. A different person. The old Frank. Then a reality TV show script booted out the fantasy island script. He wouldn't be changed in one session. Would he?

Of course not, but he could be happy and encouraged about what he'd learned. That would at least be something to look forward to. And maybe with each session he'd come home happier.

Olivia jumped out of her imaginings to realize Frank was home, talking to Zoe and Dylan in the family room. How had she not heard him come in? Stay calm, stay focused on cooking dinner. Don't make a big deal out of it.

But it was a big deal.

Dinner was ready to serve, and Frank still hadn't wandered into the kitchen. She washed her hands and dried them on the taxi-cab yellow hand towel as she went in search of Frank.

He was no longer in the family room with the kids, so she continued on to their bedroom. She stopped at the threshold. Frank lay back on the bed, his arm shielding his face. Fidgeting at the door, Olivia ran her hand down her jeans.

"Frank?" She said it so quietly she didn't know whether he could hear her, but she waited a moment. "Frank?" A little louder.

"What?" His voice was muffled from behind his arm.

"You okay? Dinner's ready." She stayed where she was at the doorway.

"Yeah. Be there in a minute." Still behind his arm.

"You sure?" *Shut up, Olivia.*

"I told you I'd be there in a minute." His voice was louder and harder from behind his forearm shield.

Olivia retreated from the doorway, calling the kids to dinner as she went.

Not a good sign.

She desperately longed for him to talk to her about the

class. More importantly, a burning intensity inside her needed to know Frank—life—would get better.

But there was no answer just now.

There was no answer during their quiet dinner or during his TV time.

As they slipped into bed, she could stand it no more. She knew better, but she asked anyway.

"Frank? How did your class go today?" She couldn't bring herself to say anger management class for fear it would set him off. It seemed so value laden.

"Fine." He picked up a prescription bottle from the bedside table, shook a couple of pills from it, and gulped them down with the water from the bottle next to his side of the bed. And with that, he flipped off the bedside lamp. Frank turned his back to her and slipped further under the comforter.

He hadn't had a headache since he'd been to the doctor. At least as far as she knew. She battled her twin worries. The return of his headaches, that is if they had ever been gone. And the other twin. The anguish of not discovering how his class went.

It wasn't as if he'd make a 180-degree turn in one class. Still, she had to know something. But it wouldn't be tonight.

———

Catalina was a glorious God send. The crossing on the Catalina Express had proven uneventful and the Portofino Hotel quaint and comfortable. Situated on Crescent Avenue, the main street running along the harbor, the location allowed them to see the water and boats from their room.

The first two days the family explored downtown Avalon and lounged on the beach despite of the lower-than-expected temperatures.

Mr. Bascomb had put off his meeting with Frank for some unknown reason until tonight.

Olivia and the children wandered toward their hotel, the shop lights coming on as the dusk grew and the lights of the boats in the bay glowed. Up ahead, beyond their hotel, the iconic, rotund Casino held court over the landscape.

Avalon had little to offer children after dark. As they strolled, Zoe pulled her jacket closer around her. Time to get out of the chill.

The hotel's front doorway led past the glass door of the postage-stamp lobby on the right, and into a narrow passage that ended in a small, only slightly larger-than-postage-stamp, atrium. Stairs to all the upper floors shot up from the atrium. The lack of elevators had disconcerted her for a few moments when they arrived, but Frank lugged the bags up three flights of steps with ease and good humor.

Who was this man and what had he done with the man she'd been living with these last two years? She wasn't complaining. Really.

Could one anger management session change her husband so much? Or was something else at work?

Now, as she and the children drew opposite the lobby, Olivia glanced over. Frank's assistant Seth stood at the front desk, apparently talking to someone there. He turned toward them, hesitated for a moment, then gave Olivia a quick wave.

"Hello, Seth. I didn't know you were here, too." In fact, she was quite surprised. What was he doing here, and why hadn't Frank mentioned it?

"Oh, well. I just arrived. Had to bring Frank a package for his meeting. Pick up some signed papers from Frank." Seth fidgeted with his glasses, adjusting and re-adjusting them.

"He already went to meet Mr. Bascomb. Do you need to know where they're meeting?"

Seth assured her he'd already been there and delivered the package.

"Seth, I want to thank you for helping Frank get his doctor's appointment. It's so much easier since you know his schedule."

Zoe and Dylan ran up and down the first few steps. Better they expend their energy now before they got cooped up in the hotel room for the night.

"You're welcome, of course." He had a curious expression on his face. "But I haven't arranged for a medical appointment in a long time."

Curious indeed.

"You...you're sure? Not in the last month?"

He shook his head. "I'm going to treat myself to a good dinner, then turn in. My boat back is early tomorrow. No sightseeing for me." He chuckled, gave a two-finger salute, and went out to the sidewalk.

What did that mean? Frank had lied to her, of course. The question was, what did he lie about? Maybe he lied about Seth making the appointment but made the appointment himself. No, he distinctly said Seth made the appointment. Besides, why would he lie about that? It was clear he had lied about being at the doctor. Period.

Olivia herded the children up the staircase and into their room. It was a cozy mini-suite, and right now the pillows mounding on the king-sized bed looked pretty inviting.

"Can we turn on the fire?" Dylan stood in front of the fireplace, his hands on his hips. Just like his father. Better not become a liar, too.

"Good idea, sweetie." Olivia knelt near the fireplace and turned on the gas key. It sputtered, popped, and then the flames reached up around the fake logs.

"Can we have hot chocolate?" Zoe called from the bathroom.

"How did you know I brought hot chocolate?"

Zoe came out of the bathroom. "I peeked." She giggled behind her hand.

"Mommy, you sure King's okay at that boarding place?"

"They're taking good care of him. I promise." Olivia ruffled Dylan's hair.

Clad in warm pajamas, holding warm, chocolaty-fragrant mugs, the three of them cuddled on the pull-out sofa. The fireplace was decorative, but the warmth was about as fake as the fireplace. All show and no delivery.

The children began to nod. She was thankful she had pulled the bed out of the sofa before they settled in. Now she slid off of the bed, retrieved their mugs, and tucked them down under the blanket.

Beyond the balcony window, the water continued to shimmer in the moonlight. She hated to shut out the view, but it was cold. She glared at the traitorous fireplace. Maybe she should turn on the heater.

Instead, she dimmed all the lights except the one next to her bed and nestled under the heavy ivory-colored comforter. She reached for her iPad and tapped her way to her digital Bible. She'd been trying to read through the Bible in a year with a plan that started on January 1. The reading plan on her screen accused her of neglect, showing she was only on February 5, somewhere in the middle of Exodus. Olivia began to nod over the details of Israelites' house of worship. She turned the device and the lamp off and slid further under the covers. How could she be so sleepy at 9:30? Probably self-defense, so she didn't have to confront her husband tonight.

Chapter Twenty-Three

The wind whipped their hair into a frenzy as they bounced along the dirt roads of Catalina's interior in an open Hummer. The guide stopped every few minutes to explain the terrain, the history, and any animals they spotted. But none of this was conducive to confronting Frank.

Conditions had not been favorable since she'd talked to Seth two days ago. And tomorrow they headed home. Yesterday they had ogled schools of fish from a partially submerged boat fitted with windows and then skimmed across the water of the Catalina Channel in a high-speed inflatable boat to and from the tiny village of Two Harbors at the Isthmus.

Now Olivia held her rebellious hair away from her face as they bumped along the road in a Hummer.

"Buffalo!" Zoe's squeal was loud even with the wind trying to drown her out.

"Actually, bison." The guide pointed toward six or so large, shaggy animals peacefully grazing on the hill. "In 1924, approximately fourteen bison were brought to the island for the filming of a movie. They never actually appeared in the movie but were left here when the movie people went home.

Now the Catalina Conservancy maintains care of the animals."

Zoe and Dylan stared open-mouthed at the 1,800-pound mammals.

The guide continued. "Because this island is not their native home, these animals have had to adapt to a far different eco-system. They have necessarily become quite resilient. In 2016, bison became the national mammal of the United States. A fitting symbol of the American people, a resilient people."

Now it was Olivia's turn to stare. At least mentally. Maybe she could learn from these bison. Could she become resilient, adapting to her eco-system? The bison had to adapt to survive, because they had no choice. Did she have a choice? Maybe she could choose to adapt or get out. No. There had to be another way.

Frank sat next to the driver, chatting and rattling along with him all the way back to Avalon. Olivia felt the rattle in her bones even as she climbed down from the Hummer. Ah, terra firma. She was even happier to be on firm ground now than when they'd disembarked from their various boat trips. Either the land tour had been particularly jarring, or she'd gotten used to boats.

No doubt Seth's revelation rattled her thoughts.

Dylan bounced up and down on the pavement. "That was so cool! What's next?"

How could the kid be revved up after all of that? Olivia longed for the plush bed waiting for her in their hotel room.

Frank mimicked Dylan's bounce. "I know. Let's go tour the Casino. Then it'll be dinnertime."

Dylan's quirked eyebrow seemed to doubt such a tour would be fun.

"That's the big round building with all the flags, right?" Zoe at least sounded enthusiastic.

Olivia sided with Dylan. Not that she didn't want to tour

the famous Catalina Casino, but a nap was all the excitement she wanted right now.

"All right. All right. The Casino it is." Frank clapped his hands with way too much glee.

So much for that nap.

A casino with no gambling. Interesting. The large ballroom, with its broad wooden dance floor, was elegant and worth the price of the tour. The dance floor was on the second story, and they stepped out onto a balcony looking back toward downtown Avalon and the Bay. The view of the bay full of brightly colored boats and the curving shoreline was worth missing her nap.

Dylan had chosen the lunch venue, so Frank gave Zoe the opportunity to pick a restaurant for dinner.

"I choose...The Avalon Grille. And I'd like steak, please."

"Awww. I wanted pizza."

Olivia took Dylan's hand as they crossed the street. "Why didn't you choose pizza for lunch then?"

"Because I wanted a hamburger for lunch, silly." Yes, of course, it made perfect sense.

The hanger steak and garlic fries with aioli reached perfection. Her children maintained perfect behavior. And so did her husband.

So, what was wrong with her? She couldn't shake the feeling her husband's perfect behavior was instead a perfect lie.

───

"Daddy, that was so much fun. When can we go to Catalina again?" Zoe had prattled on about Catalina the entire boat and car ride home, and even now at home and unpacking.

"Yeah. I wanna go on a Hummer ride again and see the bison." Dylan wrestled with the over-exuberant King who apparently wanted to make up for lost time.

"What? Oh, we'll have to see."

The minute they'd walked in the door and dropped their bags, Frank parked himself in front of his laptop. Olivia was sure that family was now relegated to the real estate in the back of his mind, and she doubted they occupied very much of it.

"Let your father work. Get unpacked. And don't forget. Your dirty clothes go in the hamper, not on the floor."

The kids moved in slow motion toward their rooms, and while she wanted to berate them, she wasn't moving much faster.

Give 'em a break.

She threw Frank's bag on the bed and unzipped it. With two fingers, and an overwhelming desire to hold her nose, she removed his dirty socks and underwear, consigning them to the bottom of the hamper. You'd think she'd be used to the smell of dirty clothes after ten years of marriage. Maybe her attitude influenced her nose.

Suit jacket still smelled clean. Maybe he hadn't even worn it. Yes, he had worn it to meet Mr. Bascomb. Dry clean pile. She plunged her hand into each outside pocket. The inside pocket revealed a couple of receipts, one from Steve's Steakhouse where he and Mr. Bascomb had had dinner. The second receipt was for a purchase from his gym. Odd place for that receipt. Why wasn't it in his gym bag?

Olivia peered at the worn paper trying to decipher what he had purchased. Workout shorts, tee-shirt, socks, towel. Why would he purchase those instead of wearing what he already had? All purchased very recently. Her eyes fell on the date and she squinted to read the smeared ink. April 19. 2 p.m.

Why did that date seem familiar? And he was usually at work on a Wednesday at 2 p.m.

Suitcases emptied, she shoved them back in the closet and figured it was time to check on the kids' progress.

"We're all done! See! And I put my clothes inna hamper."

Dylan swept his arm toward the hamper in a Vanna White gesture. They were almost inside.

"Okay, sport. Zoe?"

Zoe's hamper lid on the other hand was neatly closed. No errant sweatshirt sleeves or pant legs.

"Can we watch a video now?"

With much more speed than on the way into their rooms, they scampered out toward the family room.

Time to check her business calendar. See what she had to catch up with on Monday, maybe over the weekend if she found a minute or two. That would all depend on Frank. Was he going to ignore the family and concentrate on business? Or would they be able to extend their vacation spirit through the weekend?

Olivia traced all the red lines on her business wall calendar from the past week's due dates that had been postponed because of their vacation to the red arrows on the following week. All appeared in order. Maybe she ought to get rid of the paper calendar and just use the digital calendars that resided on her phone, her laptop, and her iPad. But there was something about a large paper calendar that was so satisfying. As long as she didn't forget to manually sync the paper and digital versions. Occasional mess ups happened, but why change now? She patted the wall calendar.

April 19. It alone had black ink, standing out where the following weeks had been bled all over in red ink. Frank. Class. 3 p.m. How could he buy gym clothes at 2 p.m. and be at his class clear across the county at 3?

She plopped into her office chair and stared at the calendar as if it would answer her question. Frank? No doctor's appointment? No anger management class? She shook her head. But if he hadn't gone to a class, how was it that he'd been acting so much better? Maybe there was some other explanation. Maybe he changed dates and hadn't told her. Could be.

Olivia's stomach tightened. She wanted to believe that, but something still didn't add up.

She had to confront him. Okay, maybe not *confront*. Maybe just talk calmly. Yeah, that would be better. Whether it was confront or talk calmly, it required the same dose of courage. Where would that come from? *Faith. Trust.*

Inhaling deeply and lifting her chin, she set out for the family room.

Frank was asleep in his recliner and the kids slept, occupying opposite ends of the elephant. King snored from his spot on the rug. Animated animals ran across the TV screen talking to each other in squeaky voices. The scene deflated her bravery like a balloon with a slow leak.

Had she missed the faith and trust? Was she stupid to think God was behind her? Shuffling away from the family room, every deep breath increased the frustration in her chest. What if she couldn't muster the courage again?

Get a grip, Olivia. Her family was safe at home, peacefully napping. She could do this. Just later.

Concentrating on dinner might help. The kitchen was pristine. Not a dirty dish, eating implement, or crumb in sight. She hated to dirty a clean kitchen. She was in luck. The refrigerator had been cleaned out before vacation and now stood pretty barren. Unless you counted all of the jars of pickles, olives, jam, and mayo. Hard to make dinner out of that. She fared no better in the pantry.

Ahh, the takeout menus called to her again. This time she answered. Besides, Dylan never got the pizza he wanted on Catalina. And for the sake of a clean kitchen. If she was going to throw their healthy eating out the window—maybe that had already been done on vacation—she'd do it up big. She ordered an extra-large deep dish with everything. Without the anchovies, thank you very much. Delivery in an hour.

What would she do with that hour? How long would the nappers be out? Normally, she would take advantage and nap, too. But she was too antsy to sleep. Across the kitchen, the laundry room threw guilt signals at her. Duck and get out of the line-of-sight fast.

She wasn't usually so lazy. Was she?

Back in the family room, everyone still sacked out, she sat down in her armchair across from her husband whose scruffy style was turning into the Rip Van Winkle look. He was still handsome. No grey in that jet-black hair.

He twitched and groaned, mumbling something indistinguishable. Still asleep, he rubbed his temple and squinted.

What's wrong, Frank? If only he would talk to her.

Zoe was still curled up on her end, and Dylan now sprawled out, arm and leg drooping off the couch while King lay nearby. Her heart filled with gratitude for these two gifts from God.

The expansive windows behind Frank looked out on their greening front lawn, now in shadows as the sun was beginning its descent.

Olivia was tired of being in the shadows. Of Frank being in a different sort of shadow. It felt like she'd been crying for help, and she wasn't heard. *Are you there, Lord?* She just wasn't sure *anymore*.

A pricking in her heart led her eyes to her Bible. The real, leather-covered, tissue-weight pages one and the digital one on her iPad, stacked together on the marble side table. She sought the comfort of holding that volume she'd cherished for almost twenty years. It was the first Bible she ever had, given to her by DeeDee, her spiritual mentor. She'd acquired a few others over the years, but she always went back to this one.

Olivia picked it up, opening to the inscription. "To my beloved daughter, Olivia. May the Word of God be your constant companion. Love, Mom." She ran her fingers over the "beloved daughter" and "Love, Mom." Not, adopted daughter. Not, adopted mom. *Lord, why did you take them too soon?*

Her devotional had used a verse from Philippians 4, so she opened to there.

"The Lord is at hand...do not be anxious...Let your requests be known...the peace of God...guard your hearts and mind."

The Lord is at hand. The peace of God. Was this really His message to her? Yes, she knew it had been written by Paul to the church at Philippi. But all Scripture is worthwhile. It must have some application to her.

"Whatever is true, honorable, just, pure, lovely, commendable... Practice these things...the God of peace will be with you."

She nestled further into her chair and a peace settled into her mind.

The doorbell bonged and jerked her awake, her Bible still in her lap. She'd fallen asleep? The doorbell pealed again. Pizza! The family room stirred to life as she ran toward the front door and their dinner.

"Mommy! Pizza? Whoopee!" Dylan was right behind her.

Long after the remnants were disposed of and the kids tucked into bed, the aromas of oregano, cheese, and tomatoes lingered. Frank watched an old movie with lots of explosions and car crashes. Olivia remained content to sit in the same room reading her romance novel. For now.

Chapter Twenty-Four

At the end of each page read, or almost read, the sight of Frank massaging his temples distracted Olivia more and more. No way was he okay. There was definitely something wrong. And she had to find out what was going on.

She squirmed in her chair. Where was the courage she dredged up earlier? And the peace? It had definitely deserted her. How to get both back? She recited every Bible verse she had ever memorized. At least she tried. Hummed a few choruses.

Frank leaned forward, planted his elbows on his knees, and cradled his head in his hands. He let out a low moan.

Olivia came to kneel at his side, laying her hand on his forearm. "Frank, what is it? Are you having headaches again?"

"I'm okay. Leave me alone." He didn't bother to look at her.

"But you're obviously in pain."

His moan turned into a growl.

"You never went to the doctor, did you?" The words hardly out, she covered her mouth with her hand. Betrayed by her own sharp tongue. What was the matter with her?

"You're questioning me?"

He swung his arm until it connected with her head and shoved her into the coffee table. The corner bit into her back before she slid down sprawling onto the floor.

"I'm the head of this house, and it's your job to be an obedient wife." He bellowed as he jumped from the chair, his feet landing next to hers. Frank lifted his booted foot and brought it down with force onto her bare one.

Olivia screamed.

"Shut up, woman. Remember that next time you think about questioning me."

"Mommy! Mommy! What's going on?" Zoe and Dylan stumbled through the doorway, stopping just inside the room. They clutched each other: their eyes shiny with tears.

King trotted over to Olivia and licked her toes, adding a little whine.

"Get out, you two! Go back to bed!" Frank's voice was hard, brooking no resistance.

"It's okay. Mommy just stumbled. Go back to bed. I'll come in and tuck you in again in a minute. Take King with you." That is, if she could walk. Olivia's tightened jaw ached in concert with her foot, and her heaving chest played a dirge.

Olivia whimpered as quietly as possible, but her mind railed and shrieked. This was it. She couldn't allow it to go on. What would be next? Him hurting one of the kids? That could not happen. She'd take the kids and get out. No! She'd make him get out.

At their father's command, Zoe and Dylan hightailed it out of the room, King trailing behind. Frank stared down at her, dark emotions playing over his face. He collapsed in the chair and put his head in his hands again. Maybe it was the pain in his head that altered his facial expression.

Bouncing between rage at his violence toward her and sympathy for his pain, Olivia's mind was torn. Maybe it wasn't his fault. Maybe it was the pain that caused the violence. And she couldn't forget she had provoked him. She knew better than to question him. Especially when she knew he suffered from a headache. What was the matter with her?

Wait. What was the matter with Frank? Yes, he had headaches. But surely others with pain as severe didn't dole out punishment like Frank. The pain didn't justify his actions. Did it?

She tried to avoid his attention by silently crab-walking away. There was no way out of the room but within his line of sight. *Keep your head down, Frank. Keep your head down.* She grabbed onto the sofa table and hoisted herself to an upright position. Gingerly she tested the throbbing foot and found she could just stand on it. Just. She hobbled away inch by inch, willing Frank to not look up, swallowing a gasp with each step.

Dylan's room was empty. The three of them huddled on Zoe's bed. Olivia took a deep breath and walked as normally as possible to join them.

"You hurt your foot?" A wide-eyed Zoe made room for her on the bed.

Guess her attempt to walk without a limp didn't make the grade.

"I'll be okay. Dylan, time for your own room and back to sleep now."

His eyes filled with tears again. "Can I please stay with Zoe? She said I could. And King?"

Olivia looked into their puffy faces. "Sure. Okay. Just for tonight." She grabbed them both in a mama bear hug. "I love you, guys." She patted King's head.

"D-does Daddy still love us?" Dylan's chin quivered.

"He loves you very much. Now, there's nothing to worry about. G'night."

They scooted under Zoe's quilt, and Olivia smoothed it over them. She kissed all four cheeks and then forced herself out of the room. How she wanted to crawl in with them. She wanted someone to kiss her cheeks and reassure her there was nothing to worry about.

Why hadn't the Lord taken care of her? Prevented Frank from this mayhem? Was he too busy somewhere else? Didn't she have enough faith? Enough trust? Maybe she just wasn't worth his attention.

I knitted you in your mother's womb. I have loved you with an everlasting love. You will have trouble in this world.

Was that the voice of the Lord? No audible voice. But words from Bible verses swirled in her head. Was that how God talked to you?

Lord, what do I do? She couldn't let Frank hurt her again. Or the kids. How could she leave him? She didn't have enough money. Very little money was in her control. Even her commissions from her job went into their joint bank account.

Without a doubt, she knew Frank had not been to an anger management class. Should she demand he skip that now and go right to counseling? If he hadn't gone to one of those classes, what made her think he'd go to counseling?

Threaten to report him to the police. *Oh, God, no!* She couldn't do that. Everyone would find out, and Katherine would take his side. No, she knew better than that.

Olivia hesitated to go to her own room. If she slept in her own bed, she would have to look at Frank when he came in. And be near him. She couldn't do that. Not tonight. Could she ever?

Instead, she went into the guest room. She lugged her aching body and throbbing foot onto the bed, dragging the extra quilt from the end of the bed over herself fully clothed.

She had to do something. But she couldn't think anymore tonight.

———

Woosh. Thump. Thump.

The water rushed into the washing machine, and the newly washed tennis shoes tumbled in the dryer. It was Saturday, chore day, and Olivia could no longer ignore the mountains of dirty laundry they'd amassed on vacation. She chose to ignore her aching foot that dragged as she went back and forth adding the appropriate garments to the separate piles of blacks, whites, and colors.

Where was Frank now? It seemed as if she was spending an awful lot of time lately worrying about where Frank was. When she emerged from the guest room a few hours earlier, Frank was not in their bedroom, although the rumpled bed revealed Frank had slept there. And the absence of his red Corvette in the driveway confirmed he was nowhere in the house.

Zoe and Dylan had eaten their breakfast quietly and continually glanced at her when they thought she wasn't looking. Carmen's phone call asking if the children could come play livened everyone up considerably. She shouldn't be relieved the children visited the neighbors, so she didn't have to pretend everything was okay. But she was.

She had to think. Think about what to do about Frank, the kids. Katherine. Should she tell Katherine?

Her thoughts circled in her mind like a dog circling to find his comfortable resting position. But she found no rest, no spot of comfort. No decisions. Heck, she couldn't even come up with decent alternatives.

If there was any positive result of her lack of decision making, it was the laundry and a clean house. She stood back and admired the neat piles of towels she'd just stacked in the linen closet. The heavenly scent of lavender fabric softener mingled with the clean citrus aromas of her bathroom cleaners.

At least there was something positive in her world today.

Behind her was the sound of a loud throat clearing. She spun around. Frank stood in the bedroom door, clothing rumpled and askew, his face haggard. His fashionable scruffy look had degenerated into a shaggy homeless look.

Olivia stepped back on her bad foot and winced as she bumped into the bathroom sink. It took every fiber of resolve to not slam and lock the bathroom door.

"Livie?" Frank's voice came out in a raspy whisper, his eyes wide and haunted. He held out a hand toward her.

What was she to do with that hand? Take it? Smack it away? She did nothing.

"Livie, please. I am so sorry. I...don't even know how to tell you how sorry I am." He lowered his hand.

Olivia tried to answer, but no words would come. Instead, she inched her way out of the bathroom, sidled toward the bed, and lowered herself. All the while Frank stared at her dragging foot and the little that remained of his already pale coloring drained away.

"I did that?" Frank rushed toward her.

She reared back on the bed steeling herself against his next physical assault.

He dropped on the floor next to her and buried his head in her lap. Between the sobs consuming his entire body, he managed to say, "I'm sorry. I'm sorry."

Sorry had been part of his making-up routine before, but he'd never cried. A few tears, maybe. Nothing like this.

What was this all about? Her brain, already stymied into inactivity, was paralyzed. Olivia looked at the hulk of the man with his head in her lap and couldn't reconcile that it was her husband. The man she loved and feared.

Her emotions puddled on the floor next to her broken husband, and she threw her arms around his head and shoulders. Olivia's sobs mingling with his, and they rocked back and forth in unison. Finally, no sobs apparently left, Frank crawled up on the bed, and the two of them lay cradled together.

"Frank, something has to change. It has to change now."

"I know. I know. I promise I'll really go to the doctor. And those anger management classes."

"I think we should consider counseling." Olivia held her breath as she uttered the word counseling. Would it set him off?

"Yeah. Okay. Whatever you say."

"Really?" Had she just heard him right? He was agreeing to counseling. Just like that? Was this another one of his half-hearted agreements?

"I love you and the kids. I don't want us to live like this."

Heart singing, cautiously this time, she prayed. For him. Their marriage. Their family.

She had no idea how long they lay there, but suddenly was startled awake by the kids stampeding in through the front door.

"Olivia? You here? Got some pretty wound up kids for you." Carmen's musical laugh floated down the hall.

"Be right there."

Frank stirred beside her as she untangled herself.

She got up, ran her hands through her hair, and looked at her face in her vanity mirror. Not too bad, considering. She wiped her face with a tissue and went to find Carmen and the kids.

She felt lighter than she had in a long time. If only it would last.

Chapter Twenty-Five

The steamy water enveloped her, relaxing her knotted muscles.

There had to be a solution for Frank. Saturday night's meltdown showed there was hope, in spite of the internet words she'd read that said no counseling would help an abuser. If not, what then? You can't trust everything on the internet. What—or who—could she trust? She wanted to trust she would not need to call the police or leave Frank. She would not be able to do either.

Some help here, Lord?

She washed her hair, soaped herself up, and rinsed. As she grasped the shut-off knobs, she thought of her OBGYN's reminder. It had been a while since she did a breast self-exam. Olivia rubbed and prodded her right side and moved on to her left.

What was that? She hesitated a moment, then went back over the spot. Again. And again.

Surely, that was nothing. Just some tissue. Her scalp prickled as unease coursed through her body. *Stop, Olivia! Don't borrow trouble. You have enough trouble already. It's probably nothing.* But she prodded again. Both sides, testing the differences.

She sank against the shower wall, the water still beating down on her. *What if this is cancer? What if they can't cut it out?* Dozens of what ifs crashed through her brain like old cars at a destruction derby.

Dim voices from the other side of the bathroom door finally reached her consciousness. The kids already greeted the day with enthusiasm, and it was Monday morning. Time to get the day and week started.

How could she face the kids and act like everything was okay? She had just reached a tiny point of optimism about Frank and her marriage, and now...this. Whatever this was. The Lord would be with her. Trust. Faith. But did that mean he would prevent this from being cancer?

Please, Lord, don't let this be cancer.

Persistent knocking and little voices pierced her inward groanings.

"Mom...Mommy. We're hungry. You coming out soon?" Zoe's usually tender voice was becoming a little shrill in her pleas.

"Mommmmmmmyyyy." Dylan added his two cents.

Olivia snapped to and shut the water off. "Out in a minute. Why don't you two set the table, and I'll be there?"

Zoe and Dylan mumbled something, and then all was quiet on the other side of the door.

She had to get it together so she could get through the day. But something had to be done. Another task. Another mountain. Making a doctor's appointment had to be first on her list. After breakfast.

All morning her cell phone acted like a lighthouse, a beacon seeking her.

I'll call later.

Now the children sat at a small table in her office. The setup allowed them to work on projects together or each on their own while she worked. After showing the children what schoolwork they needed to do and how to do it, Olivia swiveled her desk chair toward her desk ready to work. She turned her cell phone screen-side down, but then for good measure, stuck it between the file folders neatly aligned in her horizontal trays.

I'll call later.

To keep her mind from wandering dark alleys, she would review the hotel contracts for her biggest client. As she pulled the folders from the tray, her phone became entangled with the paperwork, and landed with a thud squarely in front of her, screen-side up. *No!* No need to call the doctor. This is nothing. Just her imagination running amok. She shoved the phone further under the pile of folders and set to work. But her fingers came back to the lump in her breast. Maybe this time it would be gone.

She felt for it again. Still there.

Wash. Rinse. Repeat.

If she wasn't thinking about the lump, she was worrying about Frank. She needed to call a counseling center.

Tomorrow. I'll call tomorrow.

———

Two days of walking through life on automatic torture, and she'd met her limit. Enough.

Olivia called the doctor's office and croaked as she tried to talk. "I've found a lump in my breast." *I can't believe I'm saying this.* It can't be true. It's nothing.

"Olivia, I'm sorry. The doctor's out of town, and I only have Wednesday a week from today at 1 p.m. Will that work for you?"

Next week? Seven days? And how long will it take to find out? Her head was woozy with questions.

"It's probably nothing. Thirty-one is far too young for breast cancer."

"Yes, that's fine. Thank you."

Despair began to settle around her heart as she sat immobile in her desk chair. How could this even be a thing? She was perfectly healthy. She ate well and exercised. Okay, maybe she hadn't been to the gym much lately. She vowed to get back to the gym right away. *As if that's going to change whatever is already happening in your body. Stupid!*

What would she do if this was cancer? Maybe it was just a small lump that could be cut out. But what if it was more? What if she had to have everything cut off? What was it called? Mastectomy. She shuddered at the word. Chemo? Would she need chemo? She'd heard so many horror stories about the terrible side effects. Being so sick you couldn't move. Losing your hair.

What if she had no options? What if they told her there was no hope?

Oh, Lord. Help! My kids need me. Even Frank needs me. Especially now, when he needed so much help.

Stop borrowing trouble. This may mean nothing. Didn't the nurse tell her she was too young for breast cancer?

The Lord will never leave you nor forsake you…He is your strength in time of trouble . . . The Lord will fight for you. Olivia tried to let the words of Scripture soothe her aching heart, but it was so hard!

Are you sure He's really there? Are you sure He hasn't already forsaken you? Left you to face this alone? Olivia recognized the enemy's saber rattling, but her armor must be tarnished, because she wasn't doing battle very well.

Frank! She hadn't mentioned the lump yet. Should she tell him? Should she ask him to go to the doctor with her? She hated to have him worry if it was nothing. No need to say anything if it was nothing. Plenty of time later if it was something.

That would mean keeping the lump secret, going to the doctor alone. Getting the news alone. Did she want that? Could she handle it?

As her thoughts bombarded her, nausea snuck in and gathered speed like a downhill snowball. But this snowball was moving up, up into her throat. Olivia wrapped her arms around herself and gulped it back. *It's not really nausea. I'm just imagining it. Except this is a good imitation!*

Olivia bolted for the bathroom.

Insides cleaned out, she rinsed her mouth and washed her face. *Oh, God. Oh, God. Oh, God. Help!*

"Mom! We're home!"

"Mommy, where are you?"

Home already? Zoe and Dylan had spent the morning on a field trip to the Bowers Museum with Carmen and her kids.

Buck up, Olivia. No time to wallow. The kids need you.

Oh, Lord, yes, they need me. Please.

The three of them settled in the family room with books. Dylan concentrated on an easy reader, and Zoe was reading another Nancy Drew. It tickled Olivia that Zoe loved the same books she had loved as a child. The same books her birth mother had loved. Many details of Olivia's birth mother were lost to her, but because books had been such a bond between them, Nancy Drew was not one of the lost memories.

Olivia read over and over again the same page in the same romance novel she'd been trying to read for a week. Usually when she read a book the house could burn down. Maybe she should switch to a Stephen King novel. They usually held her riveted. Would anything hold her attention again? She just needed to get past this.

Talk about functioning on automatic. She managed to put herself on autopilot and ride through the rest of the day until the kids and Frank slept. Every time she looked at Frank to tell him, she couldn't find the words. Tomorrow. Surely tomorrow will be soon enough.

Now that the house was dark and silent as a graveyard—Olivia recoiled. Graveyard. *Good one, Olivia.* There was the ticking of the old clock in the living room. Her only company.

No one was there to interrupt her thoughts, her questions, her fears, her rants.

Gotta get some sleep. She slipped into bed, then tried every sleeping position she could think of. Her body hopelessly wanted sleep. Her mind wanted peace. But she got neither. She prayed.

Lord, help me. I can't do this without you.

What kind of tests will I have to have?

Your peace, Lord, your peace.

How will the kids cope with whatever happens?

For every sentence she prayed, her mind wandered off to the situation.

Worried her tossing and turning would wake Frank, Olivia slid out of bed and headed to her office. As she sat in front of her computer, she decided it was time to quit just asking questions and acquire some information.

Olivia followed link after link, learning things she didn't want to know, seeing photos she didn't want to see. Disturbing images of ugly and misshapen breasts. Shots of mutilated chests, scars that looked like stitches on a baseball. Grotesque. So disturbing, she wanted to vomit.

Yet she kept searching. Reading. She had no idea there could be so many reasons for a lump. That at least was sort of encouraging. How many forms of breast cancer existed?

As she read, some words seemed familiar, but she couldn't figure out why. She'd never had any reason to read about cancer, especially breast cancer, before. The thought niggled at the back of her brain until she had to banish it.

Banishing the cancer thoughts was easier than not feeling for the lump. Again. And again.

Chapter Twenty-Six

Irvine Spectrum mall goers hurried or strolled the sidewalks as if life was normal. Of course, life was normal for them.

Olivia had walked out of the Irvine medical building into sunlight so bright she had to blink a dozen times. The blinking may have also had something to do with the post-visit instructions in her hand that set a biopsy in another seven days.

While home was usually her place of refuge, today she couldn't face it. If she went home, she'd have to pick up the kids from Carmen's. What would she do without Carmen? She had been available to watch the kids over and over in recent weeks. No questions asked.

That was the other problem. When she did get to the Delgados', Carmen would know something was wrong. Carmen had probably sensed over the last few weeks that the atmosphere in the Stanford house was terribly tense—to say the least. But like a good friend, she hadn't pried. There was no way she could tell Carmen before she told Frank.

How was she going to do that? Frank had been mellow, but he hadn't asked her if anything was wrong the past week. A week in which Olivia thought she was watching a Zombie Apocalypse movie. Except she was the zombie.

Frank had allowed Olivia to make a doctor's appointment for him, but it wasn't until next week, the day before her biopsy. What timing.

The crowds jostled her. Who would have thought so many people shopped on a Wednesday morning? The diminutive clock tower ahead chimed out the noon hour. Lunchtime. Nearby office workers and women with too much time on their hands swarmed into the restaurants. Should she find a restaurant? No matter how busy, they would have a seat for one, surely. Could she find a quiet eatery? Quiet would allow her too much time to think about the doctor's words. "We definitely need to have this biopsied."

Her purse clutched to her side, she finally found a clear path and a fast food store that didn't have lines spilling out the door. Olivia looked over the menu at the back of the counter.

Nausea welled up in her throat. She ran out the door and frantically looked for a restroom. This wasn't going to wait. Olivia turned into a secluded corner that gratefully had a brick-lined planter.

She found a tissue in her purse to wipe her mouth and sank onto the narrow bricks, keeping her back to the crowds.

"You okay, miss?" A young security guard stepped around in front of her.

Please don't let him see the putrid stuff that I spewed into the planter. But he glanced in that direction. How humiliating.

"I'm fine. Thank you." Olivia stood and scurried away as fast as she could. Would he think she was guilty of something? That is, something more than barfing her guts out in a public place? Was that littering? Her mind screamed, *Who cares!*

Four store fronts later, she found a Tender Greens restaurant across from a seating area with umbrella-covered tables. She bought a Sprite and grabbed a table just as it was being vacated. As she sipped on the straw, the cool bubbly liquid slid down her throat. She hoped it would as easily slide into her stomach without repercussions.

If she'd thought Frank's problems kept her unstrung, her thoughts of cancer jacked up the stress levels to the heavens. The heavens. Had she been praying about this? Was there anybody up there who was listening? In her heart, she knew someone was listening, someone who cared. But something was scrambling the signals between her head and her heart.

Olivia crossed her arms in front of her on the table and put her head down. She didn't really know how to pray right now. Silent groanings would have to do.

She would have to tell Frank right away. But how? He had his own problems. At least she'd seen a confirmation letter from a counseling center, proving he was headed for a session next week. The kind of mood he'd be in would have to determine whether she told him about the biopsy tonight.

Wouldn't tomorrow be soon enough?

The clock tower striking the one o'clock hour penetrated her thoughts. Whether she wanted to or not, she needed to pick up Zoe and Dylan and go home. When Olivia leaned heavily on the table to stand up, it tipped, and she scrambled to recover her balance.

"You sure you're okay, miss?"

Oh, great. The same juvenile security guard. He was sure to think she was drunk or something.

She smiled her thanks and once again trotted off as fast as she dared toward the parking structure. After five minutes, she skidded to a stop. Where had she parked? Was this the right parking structure? The Spectrum could be really confusing at the best of times. This was not the best of times.

Was that area across the street familiar? Of course it was. All of it was familiar. She'd been here dozens of times. A rising panic shoved her breathing into overdrive. Hand on her diaphragm, she forced herself to breathe in and out slowly. Olivia crossed the street and walked toward a sign that looked familiar. Maybe. Yes! This was the right structure, the right elevator.

At last she slid into her Honda CRV with a sigh and laid her head back on the headrest. A sudden urge to get home gripped her.

———

In spite of all the upheaval, she calmed down the minute she arrived home with the kids. Her conscience nagged at her for not getting out of the car at Carmen's, but she just couldn't face her right now. Olivia would have had to tell her about the lump and the biopsy, but she owed it to Frank to tell him first.

How in the world would she do that?

"Hey, guys. You all played out? Wanna play UNO?"

Dinner was in the slow-cooker, and she needed something to occupy her. Spending time with her children, who she had shuffled off to Carmen's way too much lately, was the best way to keep her mind off weightier matters.

Twenty minutes into the game, Zoe leaned over the cards, covering them with her crossed arms. "Mommy! Dylan's cheating."

"Am not! You're just mad cuz I'm winning." Dylan tried to shove her arms off the cards.

"Hey, don't touch me."

Zoe and Dylan glared at each other.

"Okay, kids. If we can't play nice, we stop playing. Dylan, are you cheating?"

Dylan dropped his chin, then looked up through his impossibly long lashes. "A little." His voice quivered with the admission.

"See! I tol' you!" Indignation and triumph vied for dominance.

"Hmm. How can you cheat only a little?"

"I only got rid of one extra card. Only one." Now he was hopeful as he looked up.

"That's still cheating, Dylan. You know cheating is wrong. Tell her you're sorry. And, Zoe, you re-shuffle and deal again."

"Sorry."

"Humph." Zoe wasn't being very forgiving.

"Zoe?"

"Okay, okay. You're forgiven."

"Any more cheating or arguing and we'll stop."

The game resumed, although not without some exasperated sighs.

Buzzing in the kitchen stopped Olivia mid-play.

"Ah, the chili's done. Sorry, guys. Mommy has to go finish dinner."

"Can we still play without you?"

Olivia nodded. "Daddy will be home any minute. Then you'll need to put it away."

Daddy. The game and the kids' wrangling had efficiently kept her from thinking about the talk she needed to have with Frank tonight. At least it wasn't to confront him for a change. It hadn't completely kept her from thinking about the lump. The biopsy.

The kids finally in bed, Olivia found Frank propped up on bed pillows reading a business journal. *Oh, God, how do I tell him this?* How will he react? She wished she could be sure of his support. She couldn't handle this knowledge alone any longer. Olivia gnawed on her lower lip.

"Frank?"

His eyes flicked to her and back to his magazine. "Yeah?"

"Frank—"

"For Pete's sake. What is it?" At least he put the magazine down and looked at her.

"I, uh—Oh, God, Frank! I have a lump." She collapsed on the bed, tears soaking her cheeks again.

Frank's trim eyebrows shot up and his square jaw hung slack. Absolute stillness for a moment, then a whispered "You're sure?"

"Of course, I'm sure I have a lump. In my breast. I went to the doctor today and I have to have a biopsy next week." She held her breath, waiting, hoping he would take her in his arms and comfort her.

He sat straight up and narrowed his eyes at her. "What? You didn't tell me this before? Why?"

Olivia turned her face away from him. Was he concerned about her or was he concerned she'd kept something from him? "I didn't want to worry you." She kept her face averted so he wouldn't guess the truth in her eyes—that she was afraid, afraid of the test results and afraid of his reaction.

The bed rustled behind her. She felt Frank on his knees behind her, then his arms encircling her. He laid his cheek on top of her head.

"Oh, Livie, I'm so sorry. But why didn't you tell me? I could have gone with you today."

She sagged against Frank's chest in relief. *Thank you, oh, thank you, Lord.* It felt so good to share the burden. Frank would be there for her. And, she realized anew that the Lord would be there for her, too. Frank continued to hold her as they fell on the bed together.

Even as Frank held her, her mind whirled. She was so afraid. Afraid of the as of yet unknown diagnosis, afraid it was cancer, of the pain that could come, afraid of dying. How could she leave Zoe and Dylan? What would they do without her?

Stop! You don't even know if you have cancer.

She tried telling herself that over and over again.

It wasn't working.

Chapter Twenty-Seven

Waiting for Frank and the kids to come home from the community carnival, Olivia stood staring at her wall calendar. Three days since the biopsy. How long? How long would she have to wait? Since today was Saturday, most likely she wouldn't hear anything until Monday.

I can do this. I can't do this!

She'd already made it through ten days of agony. Mother's Day had been double torture. Frank, with the kids' help, had lavished her with gifts, brunch out, a free day to do what she wanted. They suggested a mani-pedi at the spa, but she'd elected to spend it with the three of them at the movies. Maybe that had been a mistake. The darkness of the theater allowed too much time to think.

Well, that was behind her now. Two more days and she should find out. She couldn't wait much longer.

Her cell phone chimed on the desk in front of her. Unknown caller.

She thumbed on the answer button.

"Olivia, the biopsy reveals...I'm sorry. You have breast cancer." Cold, dispassionate words. *I'm sorry.* Really? Where was the doctor's horror? Her cry of pain? Her pity?

Buried in the noise of the doctor's words lurked labels and information she probably should be hearing, learning. Something about type and possible stage. None of it made sense.

"We will have the oncologist's office call you to set up an appointment."

"Wh—What'll happen now?" Could the doctor understand her through her stammering?

"When you meet with the oncologist, she'll go over your options with you."

Olivia became a puddle on the floor. She lay there for a time, her mind not processing. Without getting up, she brought the phone to her face and stared at the screen. Had she just had that conversation?

No, no. It must be my imagination.

This can't be happening. She tapped into her phone and opened her recent calls screen. There it was. The unknown call. The call that was now known, yet still unknown.

The wail grabbed the bottom of her gut and yanked it up toward her throat. She snatched a pillow off the side chair at her desk and smashed it against her face just in time to push the wail and her gut back down. Without an escape route, the wail blasted within her head over and over again.

Photos from her internet search burst through her mind. Pictures of women with freakish, scarred chests, bald heads, gaunt faces. She squeezed her eyes shut tight, trying to banish the images from her memory, but they refused to leave her.

She was going to die. The certainty of it delivered a Sunday punch. Who will take care of Zoe and Dylan when she was gone? How will Frank manage two children on his own? He couldn't even manage them well when she was here.

Her mind was suddenly no longer certain of anything. Was she going to die? She turned her face from the Lord, because He was the one who knew the answer. And she didn't really want to know. Not knowing would somehow mean it wouldn't happen.

Olivia's mind went wild with questions that seemed to have no answers. Why? Why is this happening? *Maybe I haven't been eating healthy enough. I shouldn't have been so lazy about going to the gym.*

Was this a punishment? A punishment for not being a good wife? For not praying more? Olivia sucked in a breath and started choking. Why? *Why me?*

Olivia felt her body being sucked down into a swamp where despair resided. What was it that Christian sunk into in *Pilgrim's Progress?* The Slough of Despond? She was too weary to fight anymore. She let it drag her down until she didn't have to think any more.

Voices from the living room drifted down the hall. She realized she was curled up on her bed. How had she gotten here?

Frank and the kids were home from the carnival. Olivia had been surprised when Frank agreed to take the kids, particularly without her. Was this a sign the counseling was helping Frank?

Olivia hurried to the bathroom to wash her face and brush her hair. She removed the blonde strands her brush hoarded, put the brush away, and watched the wad of hair as it floated toward the trashcan. *Will I still have hair to brush? What will Frank think if I'm bald from chemo?* It wasn't certain she'd have to have chemo. Hopefully she wouldn't.

She slathered foundation around her eyes and over her nose, trying to conceal her sob fest.

Zoe and Dylan bounced, alive with carnival game stories, fueled by the sugary treats she was sure Frank had allowed them. It wasn't often they got out with their father, so she overlooked the indulgence.

"Mommy, do you have a cold?" Zoe was too observant sometimes.

"Must be why I have a headache." She ignored Frank's quizzical expression. "Did you guys have any real food?"

"Do hot dogs count?" Frank grinned, and Olivia recognized the boyishness she fell in love with.

Why can't he be like this all the time? Things had been better lately, but she ached for their dating months and their first years of marriage. Frank had been so loving and easy-going, bringing her flowers, supportive when she had a melt-down over her past. And church. He had been the one to involve them with the congregation and in church whenever the doors opened.

What happened after those first years? Zoe was born, and he started working as the project manager of the electronics firm. Gradually he began criticizing how she handled the baby, how she spent too much time with church activities. He said she was neglecting him. So many times, she had backed away from a church activity because he objected. It was about that time that Frank spent less and less time comforting her when the dark thoughts of her past overtook her, more often telling her to "get over it." But he had purchased her dream house after Dylan was born. That showed he loved her, right?

Cancer. The word slammed into her brain. Thoughts of the past had no room now. Only her future. What was her future? Surely Frank would stand by her through this. He said he would. The thought that maybe he wouldn't terrified her.

Frank and the kids roughhoused for a few minutes until he suddenly stopped and announced gruffly, "Bedtime. To your rooms."

Seemingly unaware of their father's edict, Zoe and Dylan kept going. His shout of "Stop! Get to your rooms!" froze them in place as if they played the child's game of statues. "Go!"

Crestfallen, they scurried away.

"Frank." Her voice was barely a whisper, and he apparently didn't hear her since he headed to the kitchen.

Olivia followed him.

"I know I shouldn't be. But I'm hungry. Must be all those

sweets and not a real meal." He stuck his head in the refrigerator. "I could use a steak. Aha! Leftover roast beef."

"It's cancer." She spoke a little louder this time. "Breast cancer." As if he couldn't figure out that it was breast cancer. She clutched the counter and fell onto the barstool.

Frank's face blanched. Then disbelief took over his features. "No. It can't be."

She thought she was all cried out, but a sob hitched in her throat.

"No. I'm so sorry, babe." Frank crossed to her in one stride and hugged her so tight she didn't think she could breathe. "What did they say? What happens now?"

"An appointment with an oncologist." Hiccups punctuated her words. "Don't know when yet."

"We'll get through this. We will. I promise." He hugged her tighter, if that was possible. "We have to tell the kids. Don't we?"

"R-right now we don't know what we're dealing with. Could be a simple lumpectomy. After the oncology appointment will be soon enough." The word oncology left the taste of bile in her throat. How was it even possible she had to use that word?

Please let it be a simple lumpectomy. Were lumpectomies simple?

If there was anything positive here, it was she felt more loved than she had in a very long time. Scared, yes, but loved and hopeful. Perhaps the Lord had allowed all of Frank's issues to come to a head to prepare them for this moment. And all the other moments in the coming months.

———

Although the tinted windows of the exam room reduced the heat and glare, they still allowed Olivia to watch the people below scurrying into the buildings of the hospital campus trying to avoid the temperatures of the May heat wave.

The gynecologist referred Olivia to City of Hope for treatment, and fortunately City of Hope and the insurance company approved the request. The oncologist had delivered her recommendations kindly and gently, yet the words exploded in her mind as she imagined a grenade would feel like. Double mastectomy, chemotherapy, radiation. Reconstruction down the line—far down the line—if all went well.

She and Frank now waited for the doctor to return with the forms.

What had the doctor asked about whether there was a history of breast cancer in her family? They wanted to test for some kind of gene? Her brain was so foggy with information she couldn't process it all. Must ask her more about that.

Olivia searched her mind, impatient that she couldn't remember why the words "family history" should have any meaning, frustrated that she couldn't retrieve the information.

At least the prognosis was positive. Possible full recovery. If you could count losing parts of your body as full recovery. It was better than losing your entire body to death. Wasn't it?

Olivia's mind tried to follow the timeline the doctor mentioned. It stretched for months. It sounded like forever. How will she make it through all of it? Who will help with the kids? Frank still had to go to work. What about her job? Her income was extra money, but that extra money would be needed to help pay the medical bills now. She was under no illusion this was going to be cheap, even with good medical insurance.

Now her hands began to tremble in her lap, and Frank reached over and wrapped his beefy fingers around hers. It felt so good to have Frank, strong and sturdy, beside her.

She didn't seem to be the only one afraid. Frank had recently started re-attending church but had chosen not to attend Sunday church services since the diagnosis. She wanted to ask him why, but those kinds of conversations did not go well. Even after several counseling sessions. *Don't rock the boat!*

Even with Frank beside her, she could not stop the trembling. She'd never had surgery before. Even so, a double mastectomy sounded like a lot of pain, pain that she could not begin to imagine. How would she withstand it? What if she died during surgery? Should she get her legal papers in order? Yes, she should do that anyway. Should she plan her funeral? She didn't want Frank to have to worry about that, too.

Oh, Lord. Oh, Lord! I can't do this!

The Psalm she had read yesterday came out in a silent cry, *Why do you hide your face from me?*

Do not be anxious about anything.

She knew she wasn't supposed to be anxious. Was that it? The Lord wasn't answering because she was so anxious, so afraid? Not enough faith. Could she be forgiven of her anxiety, her fears?

Give me the faith I need. Courage. *You know I've never been good about being brave.*

Dr. Martin entered the exam room, her feet whispering across the tile. "Olivia, I know you're anxious."

Could the doctor read her mind? All the way from the other room? Everyone she saw was anxious.

"Please try to be as calm as you can. Take this information home to read." She handed a sheaf of papers to Olivia. "Frank, read them with Olivia, discuss, and when you come in next week, I'll answer any questions. By then we should have a surgery date. Do you have any questions right now?"

Olivia clutched the pages. "Double mastectomy? Are… Are you sure that's necessary?"

"Even without having your genes tested yet, I believe it is in your best interest. Of course, you have the final decision."

"What was it you said about the breast cancer gene?"

"We should test you for a gene called *BRCA*. *BRCA* stands for breast cancer susceptibility gene. It's supposed to protect you from getting cancer, but when there has been a mutation in the genes, it can lead to cancer."

"How does that happen?"

"It's usually inherited." Dr. Martin flipped through some pages in her chart. "How in the world…? How could this be? I don't see anything here about your mother's history. Has your mother had cancer?"

"I…I'm not sure. She died when I was nine. But not from cancer."

"What did she die from?"

Olivia cringed. She hated answering this question. The answer made her feel dirty somehow, as if when the doctor heard how her mother died, she'd think less of Olivia. So worthless coming from a woman whose husband beat her to death.

You are not worthless. You were created in the image of God, and though you are a sinner, your sins have been forgiven. You are a new crea-ture. How could you be worthless when I love you so much?

Raising her head, Olivia looked into the doctor's eyes and told her.

Dr. Martin's features softened. "I see. And you don't know if she ever had cancer before she died or had the *BRCA* gene?"

"Babe, wait. Remember the papers you found when Zoe had her accident? Weren't they some of your mother's medical records?"

"You're right! I found some papers a few months ago. I think it may have said something about her being diagnosed with breast cancer, but, but, my brain is just too—"

"Do you think you can find those papers again? Email them to me?"

Olivia nodded. The remembering had collided with all of today's details, leaving her unable to say more. Unable to think anymore. Only questions. So many questions.

Images of disfigured, grotesque chests played in her mind

like a computer in a bad loop. She wished she hadn't done that research, because she couldn't unsee the photos.

Her mind and the images skidded to a stop. *Forget what you're going to look like!* How will she get through the pain? She'd never had major surgery before. Nothing to measure this by. Okay, she'd given birth twice, but she'd had a fairly easy time of it. Compared to the stories of her friends.

She could depend on Frank. Right? What about Katherine? They would have to tell Katherine. Maybe she could come out to help. When Katherine left, she'd gone to help her friends, but surely, the couple had recovered after two months. Frank and Katherine will be with her.

And the kids? How would they tell the kids?

Frank took Olivia's arm and raised her to a standing position with him. He extended his hand toward the doctor, and they shook hands. "Thank you, Dr. Martin. It is a little much for us right now." Frank cleared his throat.

Olivia nodded.

When they reached the first floor, the hospital doors glided open, and Olivia and Frank stepped out to receive a heat blast seemingly straight from an oven. City of Hope lay nestled just below the San Gabriel Mountains where the heat bumped up against the rocky formations settling over the area like a tea cozy, trapping heat.

Frank handed the valet their parking ticket. "Good thing we parked here. I'm not sure I could make it all the way to the parking lot in this heat."

Olivia stared at him. He didn't think *he* could make it? *Which one of us has the cancer?* She shrugged. *Just a slip of the tongue.*

The 210 and 57 freeway traffic was bumper to bumper, even though it was only two in the afternoon. The SUV's AC worked like a champ, but the sun coming in Olivia's side window hammered at her. She awoke only when they pulled into their driveway.

Villa Park temperatures were only slightly cooler than City of Hope's, but grateful for that small difference, she stepped out of the vehicle. "I'm going to take a nap."

"What about the kids?"

"Let them stay at Carmen's for another hour or so. Then you can go get them." Olivia unlocked the front door before turning to him.

Frank had moved toward his Stingray. "Uh, I was going to head to the office for a while."

"Frank." Olivia barely kept the whine out of her voice. "It's Friday of Memorial Day weekend. No one else will be there."

He made no reply, just stared at her. He was going to drive all the way back to Pasadena? Now? They'd just come from that area. Pasadena was another ten miles past City of Hope, but in this traffic that meant another hour once he made it as far as Duarte again.

"Sure, you do that." So much for strong and steady.

Chapter Twenty-Eight

Frank hadn't made it home from his jaunt to the office until ten the previous night. He was somber but not morose this morning. Maybe that was his way of coping. It didn't matter that she'd had to cope alone. With the kids. Alone.

It had to be done today. They agreed to have the talk with Zoe and Dylan. The big C talk, right after breakfast. Olivia hurried through cleaning up the kitchen. It was the best way to clear her mind, gather her strength.

"The kids and I are waiting for you." Frank called to her from the family room.

Frank sat up straight in his recliner. Zoe sat primly on the elephant. Dylan sprawled with King on the floor.

Frank frowned, his eye jumping with a tic. Dylan looked expectant. As if he had no inkling of what was to come. And why should he? On the other hand, Zoe's face was pale. Her chocolate eyes wide. More perceptive than her brother, perhaps she'd sensed something amiss.

Frank cleared his throat. She and Frank had agreed he would do the basic telling. She'd add whatever details she thought appropriate, depending on their reaction.

"Kids, we have something important to talk to you about.

But first we want you to know we love you." Frank stopped and cleared his throat again.

"And remember Jesus loves you." Olivia felt compelled to add.

"Yes, well. Your mommy has something called cancer. Do you know what that is?" Olivia couldn't read their expressions.

"All you need to know is that it is a disease. You can't catch it. Your mom will need to have an operation or two. And then, everything will be okay. See?"

Tears welled in Zoe's eyes. "But I remember Pastor Mark's mom died of cancer last year. I remember because we made a card for her funeral. Mommy! Are you going to die?"

Dylan came to sit on the elephant between her and Zoe. His lower lip trembled.

"There's no reason to think I'm going to die." She reached out, trying to catch both of them in an embrace. Had she just lied to them? Absolutely not. There was no reason to think that. Then why was she thinking about it? All the time.

"Really?" Zoe sounded skeptical.

"I promise." Frank said it with such conviction.

Frank, you can't promise that! But Zoe and Dylan visibly relaxed. Oh, Lord. *Make it true.*

"You're gonna have a opration? Will it hurt?"

"Yes, I will be having surgery soon. The doctors will give me lots of medicine so it won't hurt. I'm going to need you two to be really helpful while I'm in the hospital and when I get home."

"When, Mommy?" Zoe got up and perched on the elephant's arm.

"Soon. But I don't know the date yet."

"We promise to tell you when we find out." Frank was so good at promises. Would he be able to keep them?

Dylan pressed closer. "Where will we be when you're gettin' your opration? Will we be able to come see you in the hospital?"

"We haven't worked all that out yet. But you will be in good hands."

"Auntie Carmen's?"

"We haven't told Auntie Carmen yet. So, can you keep this a secret until we tell her and Uncle Jorge?"

They both nodded.

"What about Gramma? Maybe she could come stay with us."

"Maybe. Daddy and I are going to call Grandma later today."

That went as well as could be expected. One nasty task checked off their list. How many more to go?

Chapter Twenty-Nine

"It's true." The telling took its toll, and now she could only whisper in response to Katherine's astonished words.

"Oh, my sweet thing. I am so, so sorry. When is your surgery?"

"Waiting for the date. But soon, I hope." Olivia swiped her damp palm down her jeans. "Do…do you think you could come out for the surgery?"

Katherine was quiet on the other end.

"Katherine?"

"I don't know. Reggie's been given only a few months to live. Hal is also declining. Mostly, I think, at the thought of losing Reggie. I have even had to move in with them to help. There is just no one else."

In spite of it being a sunny afternoon—at least it had been when she sat down to call Katherine—the world outside her bedroom window dimmed. The light inside the bedroom dimmed, too. She blinked rapidly. Now it was a little brighter, but her stomach dropped down into her toes.

"Olivia, dear. You know I would come if I could. I just don't see how I can leave Hal and Reggie. They were the only thing keeping me alive when Isaac died. Frank will be by your side. He is doing better, right?"

Olivia heard tears anointing Katherine's words.

"Of course."

"And Carmen. Have you told Carmen? I know she will help you." Katherine's tears turned to pleading.

"Of course."

Give Katherine something. She was in her own pain right now.

"It'll be fine, Katherine. I'm sure Carmen will help out. Maybe even Vanessa."

Vanessa? Not likely. They had only spoken once since their scene in the restaurant, and, while Vanessa had apologized, she hadn't been in touch since. Did she still harbor anger at Olivia? Would she come help?

It didn't matter. She wasn't going to go begging other people to drop their lives to help her. It wasn't fair to them. Besides, why would they want to? It would be a high price for their friendship. Olivia had lost friends over much less trivial matters.

They spoke for another few minutes, Katherine asking more questions about the treatment and prognosis. Questions Olivia didn't really have the answers to. With promises of more frequent phone calls with updates, they said their goodbyes.

In the backyard, King's low barks mingled with Zoe and Dylan's squeals. Frank's deep voice telling them to shush. Not to disturb their mother.

So, it starts. How will the kids cope if they have to tiptoe around their mother's illness?

I have cancer.

Somewhere she'd read a breast cancer survivor's experience. She had said she didn't have cancer. Cancer had her. She covered her ears. No! No! No!

Olivia grabbed the arms of her chair as if the chair could

somehow keep her from falling. She only let go when her fingers began to cramp. She closed her eyes and rested her head on the back of the chair.

Sleep. She wanted to go to sleep and not wake up until this whole thing was over. Maybe she was already asleep, and this was a terrible dream. A nightmare.

Olivia crawled onto her bed. She'd go to sleep and wake up from the nightmare. Wouldn't she?

Panting for breath, she woke up from the sleep that was supposed to have freed her from the nightmare. Instead, in her sleep, the nightmare had become more horrifying. No one came to help her. She walked around, her chest naked, scarred. People jeered at her. And the pain. Unbearable pain.

Wakefulness hadn't rid her of pain. Her chest felt heavy and the pain pulsed. Was she having a heart attack? The more she tried to regulate her breathing to ease the pain, the more she hyperventilated. Was this a panic attack? What does one do with a panic attack? She couldn't think.

Olivia forced herself to lie still and allow her breathing to regulate itself. Finally, feeling more or less normal, she looked at her bedside clock. Four in the afternoon. She could no longer hear Frank or the kids. Actually, the yard and house vied for the title of most silent.

Sitting up slowly, just in case, she tried to attune her ears to sounds, any sounds. The soft tick-ticking of the living room clock. Where was everyone?

Exploring the empty house gave her no clues, but her Honda was gone out of the driveway. Where could they have gone? Frank could have at least told her they were leaving. No, she had been asleep. A note, at least.

Olivia quickened her steps back into the kitchen. She hadn't looked at their usual spot for notes. Next to the hanging bins on the white fabric board was a note.

"Taking the kids to the movies. Hope you got some rest. Be back about 6. Bringing home pizza."

Pizza again. Was this their destiny? To become sick to death of pizza in the next few months? Zoe and Dylan will be glad of that.

An hour and a half alone. To kill. She could go back to sleep, but she shuddered at the thought of the nightmare playing again. Reading Christian romance or Stephen King novels was usually her go-to form of relaxation and utterly focused entertainment. The thought of reading about someone else's starry, gooey, perfect romance or being scared out of her wits was not appealing right now.

Work. She needed to get her files straightened and figure out what she would do with them while she was unable to work. This would take her mind off…things.

She stared at the file folders neatly resting in their appropriate trays. Taking a deep breath, she turned a switch in her mind, and pulled a stack out of the tray toward her. The most pressing accounts. She reviewed each file, writing reminders on Post-it notes, and sticking them to the file folder, and then adding similar notes to a project list beside her.

Every file folder had been reviewed. Every folder returned to its proper place, and the project list was placed front and center on her desk. Work was a good drug sometimes.

Shouldn't you have been praying? Why weren't you praying? Not working.

The thoughts stung. She was a terrible Christian, allowing work to take the place of praying.

He wouldn't have listened to you, anyway. Worthless pursuit. He doesn't care about you.

Ah, her enemy had gotten her attention with the truth, and mixed it with a lie. She was astonished that she was lucid enough to realize that.

Yes, God loved her. He would listen. But how would He answer her? She could pray for a miraculous healing. Sometimes He answered that way. But the large numbers of people dying from cancer, other diseases, and accidents dispelled the idea she could expect He would heal her. Still.

He would be there for her though, right? Yes, He said in his Word that He would be with her always. Through everything.

Some thought He didn't give his people more than they could handle. She didn't believe that. She believed that He did stay with them through whatever it was, and that He handled it for them. At least she used to believe that. Or so she thought. Did she still believe it?

Through Frank's angry fits and fists, she had wondered. That seemed like child's play compared to cancer.

Olivia laid her head on her arms, covering the project list. She allowed her thoughts, troubled though they were, to fly heavenward.

Giggling and the smell of pizza brought her out of her prayer thoughts. A tentative peace had settled over her. Now her family was home.

I am forgiven. I am redeemed. I am a royal daughter of The King. Thank you, Lord.

———

The Delgados' patio, although now they called it an outdoor living space, had been completely transformed between their anniversary party in March and today, Memorial Day.

Olivia was stunned by the wow factor. The patio had a cantilevered roof with an opening that allowed the tanning enthusiasts to get their tans. And the pool. Carmen said it was a negative-edge pool, whatever the heck that was, but it was definitely jaw-dropping. And costly, she was sure. She'd always wanted a pool in their yard. Not something this modern or expensive. But Frank wouldn't hear of it. Too big an expense and too much danger to the children, he said. He wasn't about to be irresponsible.

Modern outdoor couches surrounded a gray-stone and stainless-steel fire pit. Facing the seating area was a triple-sectioned outdoor kitchen with stainless steel counters, sink, cabinets, even a mini-refrigerator, an oven, and barbecue.

The Stanfords and Carmen, along with a couple of other mutual friends, gathered on the muted grey cushions of the outdoor couches while Jorge stood at the barbecue.

Olivia had been surprised when Frank agreed to attend the Memorial Day barbecue. In reality, the Delgados were more Olivia's friends than Frank's, even though they were neighbors. Frank preferred hanging out with his Thursday night sports buddies.

To Frank's credit, he had been catering to Olivia's needs and wishes since her doctor's appointment on Friday. The idea of major surgery, chemo, and most likely radiation seemed to have sobered him. She didn't know how much credit to give his two counseling appointments, particularly when he chose not to discuss them with her. Olivia would have been suspicious about Frank falling into his old ways and lying about going, except for the little tidbits he held out to her. Tidbits about the doctor, his office, the staff, but seldom about the sessions themselves.

Now Frank seemed to be enjoying gabbing about the baseball season with Jorge and their other friends in attendance. The kids splashed and squealed in the pool. The other mom sat at the end of the pool, keeping a keen eye on her preschoolers and the bigger kids.

Carmen and Olivia talked about this and that, but sometimes Olivia lost the thread.

"*Chica*? You okay?"

Olivia drew her eyes away from the pool, that she'd only been staring at, not really seeing. Carmen looked at her with brows furrowed.

"Can we talk later? After everyone else goes home?" Olivia lifted her hair and rubbed her neck.

232 SUSAN K. BEATTY

"Sure."

"Steaks will be off in five. Carmen, my darling, my Spanish rose, everything else ready?" Jorge chuckled, seemingly at his plethora of endearments.

Carmen's chuckle matched Jorge's. "Yes, my darling, my handsome conquistador, my prince charming." Her next chuckle sounded a great deal like "ha-ha-did-ya-one-better."

Why was it so easy for some people to love and show their love? Even if it turned a little gooey? And so hard for others? Olivia admired the Delgados easy teasing that was done so obviously out of love. She gazed at Frank animatedly talking to the men. He was as handsome, if not more so, than Jorge. And he looked a little more Hispanic with his abundance of black hair than Jorge, even though Katherine assured her there was no Latino DNA in their genes. Olivia loved Frank's strong manly face and physique. How he kept up his physical fitness training with his schedule was always a mystery to her. But since leaving football nine years ago, he seemed determined to not let it go to flab.

"Everyone! Come grab a steak before everything gets cold." Jorge set a platter of hickory goodness on the table, already laden with every type of side dish one could think of.

New lighting automatically came on adding a glow to the outdoor living room. Mountains of food had been consumed, dishes done, and the others had gone home. Carmen sent the kids to play in Gabe or Artie's bedroom.

"Now, *chica*—"

"Olivia! It's time to go home." Frank stood tapping his foot and rubbing his temple in sync.

"Frank, do you mind if Olivia and kids stay a little longer? There's something I want to talk to her about." Carmen's dimples deepened.

"Yeah. Okay. My head hurts, so I'm going home. Don't be too late, Olivia. Got an early day tomorrow." Frank didn't wait for any comment, no goodbye, no thanks for the dinner. He merely strode out the side gate.

Olivia held back a sigh. She would not take that as a bad omen but take it at face value. Yes, that was better. Best.

"He going to be okay?"

"Carmen, I do need to talk to you."

Carmen wrapped her arm around Olivia and led her inside to a corner of their living room with its beamed ceiling and wood paneling. They sat on the plush upholstered furniture.

Her story spilled out as Carmen's expression turned from concern to thunderstruck. Olivia held back her tears until Carmen's flowed freely. Two hot messes.

"Oh, Livie!" Carmen wiped her face with a tissue. "I am here to help in whatever way you need. Of course, the children will stay with us while you are in the hospital. Longer if needed. Oh, what about Katherine? She is certainly coming to help."

"Katherine is tied up with her dying friends."

Carmen's jaw dropped for a moment, then she snapped her mouth shut.

"Don't you worry. I'm right here." There was a little huff in her words. "After surgery, the kids can stay here. Or I can come to your house and watch them and take care of you."

"Thank you. Let's see how it goes. I'd like it to be as normal as possible for the kids."

"And, Frank? How's he taking this?" She grasped Olivia's hand and squeezed it.

What does Carmen know? Olivia had never shared anything about what was happening in their home. Nothing about the angry outbursts, the violence, the headaches, or the counseling. Yet, Carmen seemed to know something.

"Good. He's being very supportive." She prayed that would continue to be true.

Carmen sighed. Was it with relief? "I'm glad. Will he stay home with you after the surgery?"

"Plans to."

"And don't you worry about their schoolwork. They'll just work alongside Gabe and Artie. Oh, hey! I just remembered your mom's medical records you found the day of Zoe's accident. Didn't it say she'd been diagnosed with breast cancer?"

The memory she couldn't quite bring up in the doctor's office flooded her mind. Now she remembered. Frank and the doctor had talked about it. Where had she put her mother's papers? She needed to scan them and email them to Dr. Martin.

"What about Lance? Dr. Gordon?"

"What about him?" Why was she bringing him up?

"He's a doctor at City of Hope. Remember? Maybe he could help."

"Dr. Martin seems to have it all in hand." Dr. Gordon gave Olivia chills. And not in a good way.

"Okay, but if you need someone, I'm sure he'd be an advocate there for you."

"I'll keep that in mind." She would not call Dr. Gordon. She didn't know why, but she wouldn't.

They talked a little longer about possible child and patient care scenarios, food trains, and potential surgery dates.

Her cell phone dinged. A text from Frank. YOU COMING HOME SOON?

She had no emotional or physical energy left to talk about the situation, a situation unimaginable a couple of months ago.

———

Talking to Carmen about the cancer quieted Olivia's heart, and she'd been able to sleep a few hours, but by four in the morning, she was wide awake. Rather than let her mind's gymnastics weary her further, she got out of bed and headed to the kitchen to make coffee.

She sat in front of the cold fireplace with her steaming cup cradled in both hands and resting against her chest, the warmth comforting. Only every few minutes did she remember the coffee was there to drink. Each time she took a sip and then replaced the mug against her heart.

The quiet of the early morning was usually Olivia's favorite time of day, the stillness soothing. Today there was little solace, the silence only allowing for her mind to continue the exhausting tumbles and vaults.

Today should be the day. The day to get a surgery date. *Lord, please let it be soon.* The waiting had to be worse than the surgery. It needed to be over with. Except that was only the beginning.

Olivia's head jerked up with a start as warmth spread across her T-shirt. She jumped up from her armchair, yanking the coffee-sogged shirt away from her body. Nodding off didn't seem possible, but it was the only explanation for the spill. A glance at the clock confirmed her theory.

Time to start breakfast for Frank.

Now all she wanted was to sleep. *Why couldn't I have been sleepy at night, when one is supposed to be sleeping? Why wait until now?*

Frank came to the kitchen doorway. "My breakfast ready? It's late."

Olivia wasn't too tired to notice an edge had returned to Frank's tone.

"Why haven't you been taking care of yourself?"

Olivia slowly turned to gape at her husband. "What?"

"That must be why you've got cancer. You've allowed yourself to get worn down. Why didn't you eat right? Go to the gym?"

Another gut punch followed by an uppercut to her jaw. *Where did that come from?*

"Are you serious?" Olivia couldn't admit she'd had some of these thoughts herself, but that Frank was so…accusatory.

"Well, you must have done something to bring this on."

Had she brought this on herself? Could she have done something to avoid it?

Oh, Lord Jesus! Why?

"Forget breakfast. I'll be late tonight. Gotta make up for the long weekend." Without a by-your-leave, he went toward the front door, slamming it behind him.

Long weekend? He'd worked—or so he said—for hours Friday evening after the doctor's appointment.

"That must be why you have cancer." The words echoed off the walls of her mind. She mentally tried to shake them out. Dr. Martin said there was nothing she had done. Frank had heard her. *Then why, Frank? Why say these horrible things?*

The eggs in the frying pan, forgotten, turned extra crispy. Turning off the stove, she realized she still wore a damp, coffee-soaked tee-shirt. She stepped over to the laundry room, hoping to find clean tee-shirts waiting to be put away. Success. She exchanged the dirty one for a lavender-scented one and headed to the patio.

Should have made a new cup of coffee. She could go back. The beckoning of her Adirondack chair won. She barely had the energy to sit down, much less go back in to put a K-cup in the machine. Yeah, that was too much work.

May gray had invited itself in, although it wasn't chilly. The birds still chirped. The hummingbird still sought out the feeder. She admired the colorful stripes below the wings that flapped with all of its heart. Hadn't Frank told her a hummingbird's heartbeat seventy times a second? Odd pieces of trivia that one remembered. How many beats to her heart? She wasn't even sure it was still beating. Frank may have punched it to death with his accusations.

Her backside began to ache from sitting on the wooden seat. She looked at her cell phone screen to see the time. It was still only seven a.m. Only. She'd already been up for hours. Maybe she had time to call Vanessa before Zoe and Dylan got up. She gauged she had half an hour knowing that yesterday wore them out. Otherwise they would be up already.

Before she could think better of it, Olivia tapped on Vanessa's name on her Favorites screen.

"Hello, Livie." Vanessa's voice was strangely soft rather than her usual forceful tone.

"Everything okay, Van?"

"Why not? What's up with you?"

Vanessa sounded troubled. Should Olivia bother her with her problems? Vanessa wasn't sharing with her, but she had to get this off her chest. Yuck, bad choice of words.

Olivia barreled ahead and told Vanessa about her breast cancer.

Vanessa gasped and let out a slew of expletives. "Sorry. But I just can't believe it. At least you'll get a free boob job out of it."

Olivia flinched, biting her lower lip. She couldn't decide whether she was more hurt or insulted. What did Vanessa mean? That Olivia needed a boob job, that her breasts were somehow disappointing? Not good enough? She tried to give Vanessa a little leeway. How could she know a mastectomy resembled an amputation? But Olivia heard, "Go ahead, get your arm chopped off. At least you get a new mechanical arm." She'd rather keep her own, thank you very much.

Just laugh. Just laugh. *Vanessa's only trying to make you feel better.* "Gotta look on the bright side, huh?"

"Say, have you looked into juicing or going organic? I heard cancer patients have had amazing results."

Et tu, Brute? Vanessa must also presume she'd been doing something wrong. Otherwise, why would she suggest such "cures"?

"I'll think about that."

Vanessa asked Olivia specific cancer and surgery questions. *Why must people ask such personal questions?* At least they seemed personal.

Stop, Olivia! Friends were naturally concerned. Of course, they'd want to know. She tried to be grateful for her friend's questions. They confirmed she at least had friends.

"Do you want me to take over your clients? Temporarily, of course."

They'd heard of some agents who had "helped out," then talked the client into staying with them after the first agent came back to work. Pirating was frowned upon.

"Thank you. That would be helpful. I'll let you know when my surgery date is. I'm hoping to hear today."

"Whatever else you need, I'm here for you."

"Van, what's going on? Tell me."

"You don't want to hear it."

"Tell me."

"Jim's gone to Florida. I...I think I made a mistake." Vanessa's voice hitched.

"It's not too late. Go to him."

Vanessa laughed sharply. "He's settled in. He doesn't need me."

Olivia spent the next five minutes trying to convince her it wasn't too late. She would have kept on her, but she heard the kids rousting around in the kitchen.

"I gotta go, but just think about it. And I'll call you when I know my surgery date."

It felt good to think about someone else's problems for even a few minutes. She mentally slapped her forehead. She hadn't said one word about the Lord. About seeking Him through her troubles.

You're such an idiot sometimes.

Zoe's voice became a little commanding. Olivia better go rescue Dylan from little miss bossy.

Chapter Thirty

After six weeks of waiting, every one of Olivia's nerves stood on end. The household AC was cranked up so high her iced tea glass really didn't need ice to stay cold. In spite of the AC, the July heat wave caused sweat to drip down Olivia's back. Or was it the outside or the inside stress?

Six weeks of waiting, imagining, worrying. Talking to her new breast cancer friends on Facebook. Acquiring facts she needed to know. Reading stories that broke her heart.

At least the waiting was almost over.

She packed a few necessary toiletries in her hospital bag. Clothes. A front buttoning shirt to come home in. Someone in her breast cancer Facebook group advised buttons, because she wouldn't be able to raise her arms after the surgery. Smart thinking.

Sweatpants. Would they be too warm? They would be comfortable, at least. Underwear. She grabbed a bra and was about to stuff it in the bag when she froze, staring at the suddenly foreign object.

Not going to need this. Probably not for a long time. It could be a year before she had reconstructive surgery. Olivia stuffed the offensive garment back in the drawer and slammed it shut.

Toothbrush. Won't they give her toothbrush and toothpaste? No, she preferred her own, so she put them in the hospital bag.

Olivia ran a trembling hand through her hair. She wanted this day to be over with, yet she wanted it to go on forever, so she didn't have to go through the surgery.

You can't have it both ways, Olivia. This day will end. Tomorrow will arrive.

The sweat overpowered her. Time to take a shower and change into fresh clothes.

Cool water flowed over her, bringing her back to life. She stepped out of the shower and toweled herself dry.

She slipped into capris, but lingered in front of the mirror, her chest exposed. She'd been avoiding the mirror for weeks now, but she stopped to examine herself. It would not look like this the next time she looked in the mirror. Yet, she even now couldn't see her real self. All she saw were the images of scarred, wounded chests that she'd viewed on the internet and couldn't get out of her mind. Photos of women post-surgery —flat but bumpy from scars. Gashes where the breasts should have been.

Being petite, she'd never been big busted. But she still looked like a woman. How was she going to look flat chested? How scarred would she be?

And she remembered the photos of tattooed chests, often colorful, elaborate. She'd never been interested in tattoos like some of her friends. Would she want them now? No, she definitely wanted reconstruction.

Olivia turned abruptly from the mirror, grabbed her T-shirt and jammed it on over her head. She was sick. Sick of looking at herself. Sick of the idea of a double mastectomy. Sick of the idea of breast cancer. Sick.

Oh, Lord! Help me!

Hold it together. Hold it together. She hadn't cried in weeks. *Don't start now.* Too late. Tears coursed down her face and dripped from her nose and chin. Olivia grabbed the marble sink for support, her throat aching from the sob she held back.

I'm going to be so ugly!

In the bedroom, her phone started ringing with Katherine's ringtone. Swiping the wetness from her cheeks, she knew she needed something to stop her dripping nose.

Where were those tissues? She needed to pick up the call before it went to voicemail. Using her fingers to pinch the end of her nose, she then wiped them on her clean shirt. Somewhere she had more clean T-shirts.

"Katherine. Hi."

Sniffles greeted her.

"Katherine? You okay?"

"Oh, my sweet girl. I am so very sorry I can't be there. Can you ever forgive me?" She cried softly.

"There is nothing to forgive. How are Hal and Reggie?"

"Not good. Not good. But I called to see how you were."

"I'm fine." But a sob that she'd been stuffing down escaped. "No! I can't do this!"

"No, you can't." Katherine had stopped crying and her voice was strong and clear.

What?

"But Jesus can. Remember, I told you the power of Jesus' resurrection is the same power He will use to help you face this with courage."

The face of courage.

"I don't know if I have enough faith."

"Ask Him for it. He loves you and since He is the giver of good gifts, He wants to give you the gift of faith and courage."

"Yes, the face of courage."

"That's right. You've shown many faces of courage before. You can do it again."

Peace like a light shawl settled across her shoulders. She'd been looking for the full-length mantle, but she was grateful for this. It was a start.

Promising Katherine to have Frank call her as soon as the surgery was over, she said goodbye, and, remembering her T-shirt turned tissue, went to her closet to exchange it for a clean one.

As Olivia emerged from her closet, shouting and banging erupted from another part of the house. What now? Olivia rushed toward the clamor. Where was Frank?

The middle of the family room was a tangle of little arms and legs.

"Ow! Dylan, that hurt!"

And apparently fists.

Olivia stamped her foot. Good one. Who's the parent here? *Certainly not you.*

"Zoe and Dylan! Stop right now." Her shrieking brought the brawl to a standstill. "What's the matter with you two today?"

Heads bowed, Zoe and Dylan stood in front of her looking as forlorn as she'd ever seen them.

"Mom, are you going to the hospital now?"

"When are ya comin' home?"

Olivia's eyes and nose stung as she realized they just acted out of their own fear. She knelt and grabbed them in a tight embrace.

"I'm so sorry. Sorry for yelling at you. Yes, I'm going to the hospital after we take you to Auntie Carmen's. In a few minutes. I may be home in a day or two. It just depends."

Dylan's face was a soggy mess, and Zoe sniffed back her own tears.

"Do you have your overnight bags packed? Your back-packs with schoolwork?"

Dylan wiped his nose on his sleeve and nodded.

"Yes, Mommy." Zoe's breathing hitched from holding

back the tears. "Will Daddy call us at Auntie Carmen's when the operation is over?"

"Absolutely."

"Promise, Mommy?"

"Yes, of course."

Frank better follow through with the promise.

They sat on the floor in one big pile, sniffling and hugging.

Frank banged in through the front door and halted as he saw them all tangled together. "You kids got your bags? Let's go." His voice was anything but gentle.

Give him a break. He was stressed, too.

"Your bag ready, Livie? In the bedroom?"

At her nod, he went to the bedroom and returned before she could stand up.

"Okay, everybody out and into the SUV." Now Frank barked.

"I'll be right out." As the other three went out the door, Olivia walked through the house one more time, making sure all was secure. The dryer was off, and the patio and atrium security lights were on.

Everything would be different when she came home.

She switched on the entryway and front atrium security lights and locked the front door.

As Frank pulled out of their own driveway and before he could pull into the Delgados' driveway, Olivia saw Carmen and the boys waiting on the front porch. Jorge was probably at work.

Zoe and Dylan got out of the vehicle in slow motion. Usually they flew out of the car in anticipation of playing with Gabe and Artie. Today was definitely not the same. Only King bounded out.

"Let's go, kids. I gotta get mommy to the hospital."

Olivia and Carmen hugged.

"Thank you for taking the dog, too."

"I'm praying for you, *chica*."

Olivia nodded her thanks and pulled Zoe and Dylan into another fierce hug. As she released them, Carmen stepped up and put her arms around the children.

"They'll be fine. I'm praying for you," she whispered.

"Olivia. We'll be late."

Leaving her children, even in the care of such a trusted friend like Carmen, tested her. Another face of courage.

———

Nurses and technicians came and went from her hospital room. It seemed like each time they entered, someone attached a tube or machine to Olivia. Each time they'd ask her name and birthdate, then looked at her wristband to see if she was telling the truth.

The faded blue geometric patterns of her hospital gown did little to raise her spirits. It was just a gown. Not a fashion show. But anything to keep her mind off what was happening.

Frank sat by her side and allowed her to hold his hand, even though she often squeezed his fingers so tight she must be cutting off the circulation. Just like when she was giving childbirth. Also, all too often, she felt him squirming in his chair. Who could blame him? It was one of those plastic hospital chairs not known for comfort.

One technician, Rob, she thought, checked her breathing. "Your breathing is too rapid, and you're going to hyperventilate. What I want you to do is concentrate on breathing in and out slowly. Can you do that?"

Instantly, her breaths came more rapidly. She recognized a panic attack coming on.

"Not the direction I wanted, Olivia. Breathe in, breathe out. Slowly. Okay, that's better."

Her breathing eased, and she lay her head back, trying not to think about any of what was happening. Rob left but was soon replaced by another.

"Olivia." The RN who had introduced herself as Lacey stood at her side. "I'm going to put something to relax you in your IV. You'll get a little drowsy, but you won't go to sleep for a while."

She'd gladly go to sleep. It would keep her mind from racing with thoughts of the surgery. What would it be like? Really, she didn't care what the surgery was going to be like. It was the post-surgery that concerned her. How bad was it going to hurt? How soon could she go home?

The surgeon, Dr. Bruce, barreled into the room. "Good morning, Olivia."

Frank popped up from his seat, almost standing at attention. "Do you need me to leave the room, doctor?"

He acted like he couldn't wait to get out of there, and Olivia couldn't blame him. She couldn't wait to get out of there either.

"No. No. Have a seat." Dr. Bruce had a fringe of graying hair and a soft, kindly face. "Are you all ready, Olivia? Do you have any questions?"

Yes, a million. "No. I don't think so, Doctor. Except. Remind me how long this is going to take?"

"Anywhere from two to four hours. It depends on what we find, whether we have to take out lymph-nodes, and how many."

Did her face pale as much as Frank's? She nodded at the doctor. "Thank you."

"You're welcome. They will be coming to get you shortly. You'll be under anesthesia the next time I see you, so the next time you see me will be when you wake up in recovery." Dr. Bruce patted her hand, shook Frank's, and just as briskly as he had entered, strode out of her room.

The room had no windows. What was it like outside right now? She wished she was out there, even though she knew the temperature was well over a hundred degrees. Anywhere but here. Any temperature but this cold. She shivered.

Her mind started to return to what it would be like when she came out of the anesthesia, but then slowly she thought of how nice Dr. Bruce was. And even more slowly, she wondered what Zoe and Dylan were doing. Her mind pretty much came to a grinding halt. Ahh, this must be what Nurse Lacey meant by relaxed. She turned to Frank and tried to smile. Her facial muscles must have been too relaxed.

Frank gave her a small smile and patted her hand. He stood, arched his back, then paced. It's a good thing she was relaxed, or the pacing would have sent her to the ceiling.

"Okay, Olivia. You ready? It's time to go." Rob was back with friends.

"Bye, babe. I'll see you when you wake up." Frank kissed her cheek and shot out of the room.

Yeah, can't blame him.

Rob pushed the bed while the others moved the machinery.

Olivia closed her eyes and prayed.

Chapter Thirty-One

What was that brightness poking at her closed eyelids? She needed to find the switch. She had to open her eyes first, but they were too heavy. Turn it off!

A sort of semi-consciousness finally turned on in Olivia's brain. She was in the hospital. Had she had surgery? It seemed like only moments ago they'd wheeled her in. Maybe she hadn't gone to sleep yet! Were they going to cut her while she was awake?

She tried to stir but a heavy weight pressed on her chest. Were they holding her down?

Blinking once, then twice, she closed her eyes. She was too tired.

Full consciousness stabbed her, and she was wholly awake, her eyes wide open and staring at the white lights overhead. She turned her head to the right. Machines and tubes. To the left. Machines and tubes. Back to the white lights above.

Apparently, she had lived through surgery. That was a good thing. Had they cut her breasts off? Cut out the cancer?

She raised her hand, weighted down with tubes, to her chest. Fabric. Must be a hospital gown. Padding underneath. Bandages.

"Olivia. I see you're awake." The nurse looked at the array of monitors flashing and adjusted the pulse monitor on her finger. "Pulse good. Everything went well. The surgeon will be in shortly, then you'll be moved to a room in an hour or so. I'll tell your husband you're awake." Her rubber-soled shoes squeaked as she left the room.

Her eyelids had a mind of their own, so they dropped again until she felt a hand on her arm.

"Olivia? How are ya feeling?" Frank's voice sounded flat even through her anesthetic haze.

Like I've been run over by a bus. "O-okay-I guess." She hesitated. "No, not okay. Can't move. Afraid if I do move, it'll hurt."

Frank tried to make soothing noises, but they came out sounding like a hen clucking.

"Did you call your mom and Carmen? Let 'em know I'm still alive?" Her eyes just wouldn't stay open.

"Yeah. Yeah. Course. Everybody sends their love."

Could Frank have said that with any less enthusiasm? Maybe it was the anesthesia impairing her hearing.

A noise at the door forced her eyes open. A doctor bustled in and stood on the side of the bed opposite Frank. Dr. Bruce. He nodded at Frank.

"As I told your husband earlier, you did just great. Everything went as planned. We performed a double mastectomy. Removed the sentinel and surrounding nodes from your left side. The side where the cancer was. It looks like we got everything with clear margins. Of course, we've sent it off to pathology to be sure."

Frank looked ashen. All they needed was for him to faint.

Dr. Bruce continued. "They will take you to a room shortly. You have pain medication dripping directly through the IV. Nurses will explain how to control the pain. I will check in on you again later tonight." He patted her arm, nodded again at Frank, and hurried out.

A different nurse came in. A look-alike for Carmen's mother. "Hello, Olivia. I'm Ereselda." Except, unlike Ramona, Ereselda spoke perfect English. "I'm going to check your bandages. Sir, would you mind stepping out?"

Frank looked like his hair was on fire as he ran from the room. Guess he didn't mind stepping out.

Ereselda continued to speak in soft, soothing tones as she lifted the blanket and untied her gown. She moved her gown down and patted here and there, tugged ever so gently, and re-covered Olivia. "We'll start getting you ready to move. Go ahead and get some more sleep. Do you want me to send in your husband?"

Had the nurse picked up on the fact that maybe Frank wasn't ready to be in the room yet? Or Olivia might not want Frank in the room? Olivia moved her head from side to side and closed her eyes.

Opening her eyes again, the machines and the tubes remained the same, but the room looked somehow different. She must have slept while they moved her. Frank was slumped in a chair by the window, snoring softly.

The heaviness in her chest had increased and pain consumed her. Had they told her how to control the pain? She couldn't remember. There must be a call button somewhere. Sliding her hand around on the bed, she found no remote. Her breathing became rapid as she searched more quickly.

Don't panic.

Too late.

"Frank?" Her voice sounded hoarse. "Frank?" Could he hear her? "Frank!"

"What?" He jumped to her side. "What's the matter?"

"I need a nurse. Find the call button."

The next few hours meant anxious pain, calls to the nurse, and restless sleep. Ereselda and other nurses came and went. Frank wandered away, came back, then slept in the chair, then wandered away again.

The pain never wandered away, only became a little duller.

Chapter Thirty-Two

Why do hospital staff always tell you to get some sleep, and then do everything to interrupt it? Between the pain and the nurses coming and going, it seemed to Olivia she hadn't slept at all.

Grayness shrouded the room, although behind the sun-blocking blinds, it was bright as blazes. At least that's what the television news said. Sterile air, lacking in any distinguishing odors, tickled her nose until she wanted to gag.

An attendant crept into the room with her breakfast tray, placing it gently on the bedside table. After she left the room, Olivia lifted a lid to find indescribable mush. Cream of wheat maybe? Cold toast, a thin slice of cantaloupe, and weak coffee rounded out her first-meal feast. She didn't know how good she'd had it when the room just smelled sterile.

Olivia pushed the tray away, pushed the button on her pain monitor, and lowered the head of her bed.

She felt herself nodding off, just as Dr. Bruce bustled in.

"Good morning, Olivia!"

No cheerfulness, please.

"How did you sleep?" His voice may have been cheerful, but his face was sterner this morning.

Maybe if she closed her eyes and pretended to sleep, he'd go away.

"All right, Olivia. I need to look at your surgical site."

No luck. He wasn't going away.

He gently removed the bandages and made non-committal noises.

"Have you looked at your chest yet? No? Then I want you to look now."

What? No! She shook her head violently.

"It's important to get it over with. Won't be easier later."

There was no way. It was too soon. Lord, please!

Her pulse sped up, and with it fear and anger reached every cell of her body. Why was he so insistent?

"Olivia." Dr. Bruce's kindly tone had turned insistent.

As if she had no control, she looked down. She thought, even through her fear, she knew what to expect. Nothing could have prepared her. Bile crept up her throat as she looked at the angry red gashes. Drain tubes, filled with an ugly, red liquid, sprouted from her chest.

Her chest. No, this was not her. This was someone, something else. Something mutilated, offensive.

"There now. You've gotten it over with. You'll feel better now." The doctor re-bandaged the obnoxious sight.

Feel better? Not even. An ache in her chest that had nothing to do with its exterior condition overwhelmed her. She would never be whole or pretty again. Yes, she would hopefully have reconstructive surgery, but it wouldn't be the same.

How could the doctor have done this to her? Made her look? So soon? Feel better? What does a man know about having your breasts hacked off?

"Everything looks as it should. You're doing great." Dr. Bruce patted her arm and left the room.

Olivia turned her head away and ran straight into a cage

with bars of sadness, and a metal door clanged behind her. Her tears, however, would not be kept hostage.

———

Balloons, crepe paper, and welcome home signs festooned the front of their house as Frank pulled the vehicle into the driveway. Carmen, Jorge, all of the kids, and even Vanessa congregated, cheering her homecoming.

Emotions welled up as she waited for Frank to help her from the CRV. With his help, she slid slowly out onto the concrete and inched her way toward the party.

"Mommy! Mommy! Welcome home!" Zoe and Dylan ran toward her, but when their father held out his arm, skidded to a stop.

"Remember, Mommy just had surgery. That means the upper part of her body is very…sore. You know what it's like when you get an ouchy? Well, Mommy's one big ouchy. So be careful." He withdrew the barrier he'd created.

The children hesitated to move.

Olivia made sure to smile really wide. "It's okay. You can hug me on the side for now. Just be really careful." She struggled to extend her right arm as best she could, but she was limited by the weakness and pain it caused.

The children nodded and sidled up to her slowly.

"How do you feel, Mommy?"

"We have presents for you."

"And we helped make you lunch."

Emotions continued to bubble over. She gave thanks for the gift of life, another day to be with her children.

But I'm oh so tired.

"Let's get your mom into the house, kiddos. It looks like she needs to sit down." Bless Carmen's heart, she always knew what Olivia needed.

All four children began to hop around in excitement.

"C'mon Mommy, we've got a surprise for you, a big surprise." Zoe was so excited her words ran together.

They led her slowly into the house and toward the family room.

"I think I need to go to bed, kids."

"Wait, you have to see this."

What's this? Stopping at the threshold of the family room, she stared at a large brown reclining chair that hadn't been there before surgery.

"Surprise!" The crowd erupted in unison.

"See? You don't hafta go to bed. It's a special chair."

"It's a special chair."

"I don't understand. Where'd this come from?" Should she mention the brown chair and the big gray elephant clashed? And, how through the post-operative brain fog, could she even have had that thought?

Vanessa stood next to the recliner and punched a button. The back reared up while the front looked like it was kneeling. "It's a mechanical recliner. All you have to do is stand against the chair and push a button. The chair sits you down. Reverse to stand up."

"Try it, Mommy! It's fun!" Dylan hopped from foot to foot.

Olivia backed up to the chair.

"Ready?" At Olivia's nod, Vanessa pushed the button again. "Just push this button and it will take you down."

The mechanical recliner eased her to a sitting position.

"B-but where'd it come from? Who bought it?" Olivia frowned, trying to reason it without much luck.

"It's on loan from a ministry to post-mastectomy patients."

Carmen jumped in. "Vanessa arranged for it. They dropped it off this morning. You get to use it during your recovery, then they come and pick it up for someone else to use."

Olivia relaxed as best she could against the brown,

corduroy-like material. She never dreamed such a chair existed, much less that someone would loan her one. The color no longer mattered.

———

Before Zoe and Dylan had gone to sleep that evening, they prepared her bed. Quilt turned down, pillows propped up. Pride for helping care for her shown on their faces.

Now alone, the pillows mocked her. Incisions and drains meant she couldn't lie down flat. How was she to sleep sitting up all night? It was one thing in a hospital bed, but another here at home. Well, the pain may keep her up anyhow.

Olivia absently fingered the edge of her post-mastectomy camisole. Her fingers traced the tubes snaking under the garment and ending in the roo pocket at her waist. She removed one of the hollow rubber balls. The body fluid, her blood, a disturbingly bright red, oozed into the ball.

This was flowing out of her body, and it curdled her stomach.

A nearly full ball meant it was time to drain. Olivia moved into the bathroom and stood before the mirror. She unbuttoned the camisole and freed the tubes. Time and space seemed suspended as she froze before her own image.

How was she to do this when she couldn't move her arms very far? She couldn't. She would have to call Frank for help.

He answered her call and silently fumbled through the procedure.

Tears of embarrassment chased down her face, threatening to soak the bandages on her deformed chest.

Chapter Thirty-Three

Usually, the sight of a sizzling steak or someone enjoying an ice cream cone on TV teased Olivia's salivary glands. Conquering the nausea from her first chemo treatment four days ago was still a work in progress, and now the sight only provoked her insides to well up into a ten-foot wave. Olivia wished she could throw the remote through the TV screen. It was a good thing she didn't have the strength.

Instead, she squeezed her eyes shut willing the wave to ebb back out to sea.

She'd made it through surgery five weeks ago and lived through the pain and indignity of the aftermath. Now a new agony.

China and silverware clanked in the kitchen as she assumed Carmen was making lunch. The thought brought another wave.

"How are you doing, Livie? What can I make you for lunch?" Carmen came to sit on her haunches next to where Olivia sprawled on the elephant.

For all the jokes about the big old gray couch, and now that the special reclining chair had been picked up, it was the perfect place to rest now that her chest was healed enough to lie somewhat horizontally. If you called being propped up by a half a dozen pillows horizontal. Lying flat still pulled at her wounds.

"Nothing. Thank you."

"You need to eat."

"Just talking about it makes me sick. Sorry."

"No, I'm sorry. I wish you could eat something."

"Frank barbecued steaks yesterday and mine tasted like a trash can." Olivia tried to sit up, but the semi-healed scars on her chest pulled if she moved a certain way.

Carmen put her arm and shoulder under Olivia's and steadied her as she rose to a sitting position. Olivia remained immobile for a few moments to gauge whether the change in position brought on a tsunami of nausea.

Her stomach settled, so she leaned her head back on the couch.

"Thanks. Thank you for everything. What would I…we… have done without you these past few weeks? You're the best." Olivia patted Carmen's knee that parked next to her own.

"Always here for you, *chica*." As she stood, Carmen's knee popped, and she groaned. "I must be getting old. The knees are just not cooperative these days."

"Thought you were going to have surgery on that knee." Olivia gave her the ol' stink eye.

Carmen looked away. "Soon. Soon."

Olivia brought her head up off the couch as quickly as she could without completely disturbing her equilibrium, sucking in a breath as she did so. "Carmen! Did you postpone surgery because of me?"

"Even if you don't want lunch, the kids do. I think I'll make grilled cheese sandwiches. Zoe and Dylan still like grilled cheese, right? And tomato soup?" Carmen continued to prattle as she walked away.

Olivia let her head fall back. Instead of nausea, guilt

washed over her. Poor Carmen suffering from that bad knee because of her.

The sympathy flashed and died. It was just a knee. She would not have her breasts chopped off. She would not be scarred for life.

Feeling sorry for yourself, are we? How selfish! How shameful! After everything Carmen's done for you.

Now the groaning wasn't from nausea but self-flagellation.

Zoe, Dylan, Gabe, and Artie stampeded into the kitchen from the backyard making a racket that Olivia heard from her spot on the couch.

"Ssh. Settle down, gang. Lunch in a few minutes. Why don't you kids go say hello, quietly, to Olivia? She's resting in the family room."

Eight little feet tiptoed up beside her.

"Mommy. How you feeling?" Zoe's face was crunched into a permanent frown these days.

Olivia took her hand. "I'm okay, sweetie. What have you kids been up to?"

Dylan's frown had matched Zoe's but now his face transformed into a dazzling grin. "We built a fort. Outta the boxes Uncle Jorge gave Gabe and Artie."

"Not a fort. A playhouse." Zoe put her hand on her hip in indignation.

"A fort!" Three little boy voices said in unison.

Zoe's frown was now a look of disgust. Outvoted. "Oh, okay. A fort. Sheesh."

Olivia laughed as much as she dared. Except for the pain it created in her wounded chest, it felt wonderful to laugh. She'd been doing so little of that lately.

"Auntie Olivia?" Seven-year-old Gabe's pillowy cheeks resembled his mother's, but his eyes were worried. "Are we making too much noise?"

"You're doing just fine, Gabe. But thank you for asking." Olivia smiled at Gabe hoping to ease his sensitive soul.

Artie was nine and took on the older sibling role with gusto, rather like Zoe did. "I'll make sure they be quiet, Auntie Olivia. You just rest." Artie stuck out his hand as if to pat her on the arm, but withdrew it quickly, looking embarrassed.

"Ahh. Thank you. You're so sweet. I'm just going to lie down now. I bet your lunch is ready." As much as she loved the four musketeers, the exchange had worn her out. She eased herself onto her back, sighing with the effort.

The front door slammed, startling Olivia awake. She thought the kids promised to be quiet. She opened one eye to see that the light filtering in through the window was dimmer. Must be late afternoon. Had she slept that long?

Something heavy dropped onto the tiled entryway.

"Hello? What's going on?" She wasn't sure if her voice could carry as far as the entryway, although it was just around the corner.

"It's just me." How could those few words from Frank convey such meaning?

A meaning Olivia couldn't quite figure out.

Frank came into the family room with his own frown plastered on his face. Did everyone have to go around frowning? She supposed they were no worse than her own. Something needed to be done about that.

That saying, "If momma ain't happy, ain't nobody happy," ran through her head. The converse was true. She had to at least act happier. From her supine position, Olivia smiled up at her husband. He didn't return it.

"Where are Carmen and the kids?" Frank fisted his hips.

"Don't know. Just woke up. Can you help me? I need to go into the bathroom." She rolled to her side, and Frank lifted her to a standing position.

He stepped back to give her room to walk toward the powder room off the entryway. A little unsteady from having lain so long, Olivia thrust out her arm to grab Frank for support. He froze for a moment, then led her out and to the right, stopping in front of the powder room.

"You okay now? I thought I'd better go let Carmen and the kids know I was home."

She nodded, and he rushed toward the kitchen. She shut herself in the little room plastered with the signs Olivia had painstakingly painted not long after they moved in. While she did her business, she read each plaque. "Family." "Every day's a beach day." "God is love." Smudged and dirty after four years, the plaques probably needed replacing. Finding the joy to make new ones was not even in her peripheral vision right now. But a new beach print was crossed off her list. Every day was not a beach day.

Oddly, she felt energized by the time she emerged from the powder room. Frank and Carmen's voices came from the kitchen, so she turned right toward them. Under her own power for a change.

Somber faces looked up at her.

"What's going on? Something up?" Olivia hoped not. She couldn't take a new crisis.

"Just getting ready to gather the kids and head over to my house." Carmen seldom kept herself to one sentence. And she didn't usually avoid eye contact.

Frank helped herd the kids in from the yard. "Zoe and Dylan, you're going to Carmen's to spend the night. Go put your pajamas and toothbrushes in your backpacks. She said you could pack your swimsuits, too. Quickly now."

What? This hadn't been part of today's plan. Had it? It happened regularly enough, but why tonight? What had she forgotten? Or was it that Carmen or Frank thought she needed more rest?

"Enchiladas are in the oven. Done in five minutes. Frank, don't forget. Like you did last time. You don't want to eat dry, burned cheese again. Livie, call me if you need anything." This time, for a few seconds, Carmen's gaze locked onto hers with a laser-like intensity. Then she moved to the front door where the kids soon assembled.

Occupying the entry with them was a very large suitcase. New. Where did that come from?

Zoe and Dylan gave gentle hugs around her waist, avoiding her chest.

"Be good, kids. We'll see you in the morning."

"Kids, got all your stuff? Carmen, can you handle everything?" Frank opened the front door for them.

Zoe and Dylan scrambled out.

Carmen stood opposite Frank in the doorway, her eyes never leaving his. "Of course, I can. Can you?" She turned on her heel and fast-walked after the children.

What did that mean? Olivia looked at Frank with raised eyebrows, but he didn't bother to look at her as he closed the door.

"We need to talk." His tone was hollow, and, without looking at her, he went into the family room and dropped into his recliner.

She guessed he meant her to follow. Something was coming, and now her gut roiled for a different reason. Had they fired him? No, impossible. Was he sick too? He didn't act sick. But neither had she. Whatever it was, meeting it head on gave her another chance to show a face of courage. *Right.*

Frank fidgeted while she perched on the edge of the couch in spite of the discomfort it caused her scarred chest. He took the remote and clicked off the television. This must be serious.

Silence lay over the room like a heavy blanket.

Frank cleared his throat. "Olivia, I can't do this anymore."

"What do you mean?"

He waved his arm toward her and then around the room. "None of this. This is not what I signed up for. I can't handle you, your cancer, the kids, the house. None of it."

"What do you mean?" She needed to figure out a more original line.

"And I can't handle pretending anymore."

"What do you mean?"

"I'm leaving." Short and to the point.

Olivia couldn't think of anything but, "What do you mean?"

"I'm moving out. I don't want a divorce. Not yet, anyway." Frank's voice was quiet, but it held no softness.

In fact, it fueled a sucker punch to Olivia's gut. She worked her mouth, trying to say something, but no sound came out.

"I'm leaving tonight. I'll be back to pick up more of my things in a few days."

He couldn't handle her cancer.

Oh, Lord. Frank's leaving me because of my cancer?

"Can't handle pretending? What does that mean?" Funny, she zeroed in on that.

"Who believes that Christian nonsense? Never have. Not even as a kid."

"N-never? But you're a PK." Olivia's head felt as if a tornado was inside, demanding out.

"That was just to get you. You were hot. Then."

Meaning now that I have no breasts, merely huge, ugly gashes, I'm not.

A sickening anger welled up inside, joining the whirlwind, looking for an escape.

"I don't want to deal with your Christianity, your cancer. I didn't sign up for this."

"So you said."

"I'll continue to pay the bills. For as long as I can, anyway."

"What do you mean?" There she went again.

"Supporting two households will be difficult."

Indeed. "But that's your choice, Frank."

"Like I said, I'll do the best I can for as long as I can."

"Then what?" Would she and the children be homeless?

He shrugged, then stood. "I'm going to start packing." Frank went to the entryway and wheeled the black monster of a bag to the bedroom.

Out on the street? With cancer? Who would take care of Zoe and Dylan when she couldn't? She had twelve more weeks of chemo. Then radiation. Every inch of her body was numb. Including her mind. She could no longer think coherent thoughts, see, hear. Except a roaring in her ears. The tornado.

Darkness overtook the room, but Olivia ignored it.

She didn't know how long she sat there, but an acrid smell floated through the hall. The enchiladas! Why wasn't Frank watching the dinner? Oh, because he was done. Done with it all.

The tornado, the anger, disappeared. In its place a new feeling, an iciness seeped to her core.

Ignoring the gloom that engulfed her and the house, she shuffled to the kitchen, snapped on the night light, and turned off the oven. She peeked inside at the dry enchiladas and the cheese burned on the bottom. Waving a hand before her nose, she slammed the oven door and returned to the family room. Good thing she wasn't hungry.

A light flashed. Olivia blinked as Frank stood before her.

"Why are you sitting in the dark?" His tone declared her stupid.

She figured he didn't need or want an answer. He was done.

He dragged the behemoth of a suitcase and a smaller bag. "Seth will pick up the big case. It won't fit in the Stingray. Don't worry. I'll just leave it in the front atrium."

How thoughtful of him.

He looked at her for a moment. No regrets took over his features, only relief. "Goodbye, Olivia. I'll be in touch." He trundled the bags to the front door and was gone. Two minutes later, the Stingray roared out of the driveway.

At least it saved her from throwing him out.

———

The darkness deepened, broken only by the lamp Frank turned on hours ago and the night light in the kitchen. It didn't matter.

A tapping on the front door startled her. She glanced at the cell phone clutched in her palm. Nine o'clock. When did she grab her phone? Who was she going to call? She had no idea.

Another tap and the door creaked open.

"Olivia? You awake? It's me. Carmen."

Carmen was like a sister, one she never had. Vanessa, too. But was she ready to talk about this, even to a sister?

Wait! Did she know? Is this what the two of them were talking about? Why she gave him a look? Oh, Lord, no!

Her beautiful sister/friend paused in the doorway, curls flying around her head. Funny Olivia noticed her hair amidst a crisis. Maybe not so funny. Hair was on her mind a lot these days. If not for long on her head.

"Livie? What's going on? I see Frank's car is gone. Talk to me?" She sidled over to the elephant and sank into it. Watching.

Olivia swallowed. "What did Frank tell you?"

"Just he had to leave and you might be alone tonight. All night. I don't mind looking in on you, but, really, that seems pretty rude of him. To be away. Right now—"

"He's left me."

"What do you mean?" Carmen stole her line.

"He's done being married, being a father, being a cancer caregiver. Being a Christian. Except he said he never really was." Done being the husband of a wife whose chest looked like Jack the Ripper's handiwork. But she couldn't say it out loud.

"He, he left? For good? Why that, that…" She sputtered. "He just pretended to be a Christian all these years? Why?"

"Apparently so I would marry him."

"Why that, that…" Carmen was having trouble coming up with new lines, too.

"Explains why last winter he decided everyone at church was a hypocrite, and he forbade me to hold Bible study here. He was done already."

Carmen cradled Olivia's hand. "I am soooo sorry. What now? I mean, of course, we'll be here for you. Continue doing everything we've been doing. More even. But what about financial support? Is he filing for divorce? The medical bills?"

The medical bills. Something else to worry over.

Olivia sighed. "I don't know. I can't think about any of that right now. But…What do I say to the kids? I assume he hasn't told them."

"I doubt it. They're both as happy as clams. The coward." Carmen said the last through gritted teeth. "Did you suspect?"

A few images rolled around in her mind's eye. "I could see he found it difficult to help me. Especially when I first came home after my surgery. Frank couldn't wait for you to come over to take his place. H—He hasn't touched me since before the surgery."

"Well, no. He wouldn't ask *that* of you."

"I didn't mean *that*. The only time he physically touches me is when he has to help me. They're not caresses."

Yes, she should have realized, but she thought it was merely his way of being sensitive to her physical limitations and maybe afraid of hurting her if he touched her in the wrong place. So much for that idea.

"Have you told Katherine?" She nodded toward the phone in Olivia's hand.

Olivia stared at the object gripped in her fist. As if she hadn't known it was there. Well, she hadn't a few minutes ago. "I don't think so."

"You don't think so?"

"No. I haven't." How could she tell Katherine her son was a jerk, a coward? That she was so abhorrent to look at that he needed to escape.

The icy coldness was beginning to thaw, melting from the mounting anger.

"I'll go get my nightgown and come back to stay with you." She stood.

"No. I'll be okay."

"But—"

"No. I need to be alone tonight. Decide how to tell the kids. Tell Katherine. But thank you." Olivia looked up at Carmen, pleading with her eyes for her to understand.

"Of course, *chica*. I'm only a phone call away. If you want Jorge for anything, we're here. Don't worry about Zoe and Dylan. We love them like our own." Carmen leaned over and squeezed her hand. "We love you, too. Everything will be all right." Carmen slipped out, clicking the front door closed.

Chapter Thirty-Four

Lamps shining gently, Olivia's bedroom glowed with a homey, intimate, even romantic ambiance. Forget the romantic. That hadn't been true for a long time. And would never be true again. But she was glad she had redecorated the bedroom before her surgery. If she was going to be captive here, she wanted it cozy.

Gauzy curtains billowed over the roman shades, softening their hard edges. Frank had not appreciated the curtains. Too girly. Yep. That was kind of the point. Dozens of pillows, small and large, piled at the head of the bed. He definitely had no patience with the pillows.

Her small slipper chair had been replaced with an oversized, padded armchair that took up too much real estate in the room, causing Frank to nick his shin every time he tried to get to the closet. That was no longer a problem.

Olivia stood in the middle of the bedroom, appreciating the desired effect of her redecorating, peace and calm. Something sorely needed since Frank left a few hours ago. She just hadn't had the energy to move from the family room.

After Carmen left, Olivia allowed the anger to at least fuel her with enough pep to escape to her prison cell turned haven. She breathed in and out slowly.

Ten o'clock was too late to call Katherine three time zones away. Just as well. Olivia still had no idea how to break the news to her. Maybe Frank called her? That would have been too thoughtful. Responsible.

Time to put on a clean nightgown and try to sleep. Avoiding all mirrors, she exchanged the more utilitarian one she wore for lying in the family room for her favorite, most feminine, but modest, gown. The silk glided over her body.

What wonders surrounding yourself with beauty did for your soul. How glad she was to have read that book about homemaking and beauty by Edith Schaeffer when she was first married and re-read before her surgery. It gave her the courage to make the changes to her environment.

Olivia prepared the essential oils diffuser with lavender and other relaxing oils. Immediately the diffuser's contents swirled up into the air, spreading its healing mist.

In the middle of washing her face, she stopped. How is it that she could be thinking of beauty when her world had fallen apart? Again. She held the warm cloth to her face, inhaling the rose scent of her face wash. She patted her face dry.

Should she take the Ativan to help her sleep? Stories of how addicting it could be kept her to taking it only when absolutely necessary. Even when she thought she needed it. It was hard to keep it to a minimum because it helped with her nausea and anxiety too. She needed it tonight. But maybe that was exactly when she shouldn't take it. Olivia picked up the bottle and took the recommended dosage.

Hopefully she wouldn't regret it.

Rearranging the pillows and comforter, she held a pillow against her chest and eased herself into bed, propping herself up against the nest she'd created.

She willed the anger to go away. She demanded the rage to disappear. Where was her courage?

Lord, where is my courage?

It's okay to grieve, my love.

Holding the pillow more tightly, she allowed the sobs the freedom to escape, taking the grief with them.

This too was a face of courage, right?

———

The Ativan had not done its job well. Olivia awoke and lay immobile in her bed. Where was the smell of brewing coffee? The rustling of little feet? There was nothing.

Self-pity threatened to overwhelm her. Olivia forced herself out of bed before the woe-is-me turned her into a petrified lump. It helped that her bodily purposes hadn't ceased to function and propelled her, slowly, from bed.

Afterward, she eased herself into her armchair, holding her phone in her hand. Time to get the call to Katherine over with and move on with her day. A day filled with the more difficult task of telling the children.

Katherine picked up the phone immediately and prattled on for a moment.

She hated to be rude and interrupt. "Katherine. I need to tell you something. Something hard. Unless you've already heard from Frank."

"Frank? No. What's wrong? Is Frank all right?" Worry infused the tone of her voice.

Olivia related to her mother-in-law what her son had done, trying to keep it neutral. But how could one do that when the jerk deserted his children and sick wife?

"Katherine? You still there?"

"I'm here." It was barely a whisper. "But I do not even know what to say. I am so sorry my son has taken this turn for the worse. I thought the counseling had helped. But how can counseling help when he has renounced his faith? I guess, as he said, he never really had it."

There was little left to say. Olivia would just make soothing noises and hang up. But Katherine apparently had more to say.

"How will you get along? Who's going to be with you?"

"Carmen. She already said she and Jorge would help. Staying with me as much as I need. The kids stayed with them last night."

"Oh, no! How are the kids doing?"

"They're doing fine." Olivia knew that Katherine was really asking how the news was affecting them, but she sidestepped that for the moment.

"You know I would be there if I could." Katherine let out a sigh bigger than her five-feet-zero. "Reggie has lived so much longer than they thought, but she is back in the hospital with very little time left. Hal is inconsolable. I don't expect him to last much beyond Reggie."

Now Olivia did make those soothing I'm-sorry-type noises.

"My dear girl, when they both pass, I'll be out there quick as a wink. Not that I want to hurry their passing."

"Of course. I understand." The courage she'd used to call Katherine was beginning to wane. Tears clogged the back of her throat. She would not cry. Yet.

"Olivia. Olivia. You just go ahead and cry. Sometimes we need to do that."

"It's...I don't know how to move forward. I can't find that courage anymore."

"Jesus hasn't changed. Like He did for Simon Peter, He can pray for your faith to increase."

"But the more I find faith and courage, the more I fail." Her breath shuddered with tampered down tears.

"Peter certainly failed right after that. Three times. Before the rooster crowed."

"I know. I know. But Peter was…Peter. Why should the Lord listen to me? Sometimes I'm not sure He is."

"God formed your every part. Remember? If He formed you, He cares about you. He cares about the sparrows. The lilies of the field. You are His creation. He cared so much for you that He died on the cross for you. His scars were all for you." Katherine's every word was filled with intensity.

Scars. Scars like her own? Even though she stepped a mile around every mirror in the house, she knew exactly what her chest, her scars looked like. Her mind's eye saw them as new and raw. Jesus' had been much worse than that. The pain. She remembered her pain, but her Lord and Savior's had to be a million times worse, especially as He hung on the cross for her. For her.

Gratitude anew welled up in Olivia's soul. *Thank you, Lord. Please pray for my faith.* She continued to pray for courage and thankfulness for Katherine.

"You are forgiven. You are redeemed. You are the royal daughter of the King." Katherine said the words softly, almost a whisper.

"I…I…tend to forget. Will try to remember. Always. Thank you, Katherine."

Olivia thumbed her phone off and continued to sit immobile. But this was a good stillness. She prayed, praying more deeply than she could every remember praying.

When she finally opened her eyes, she knew they had to be wide open. Definitely spiritually. But physically, too. She allowed herself a smile and was sure the joy within must be shining on her face.

You think this momentary little joy fest is going to last? You'll be doubting again in no time.

Probably. But at least she knew the road back.

Chapter Thirty-Five

How do you describe the smell and feel of the chemo room? It was Olivia's second visit and she still couldn't put her finger on it. But one thing was for sure. It was distinct.

She tried to block it out by sleeping through as much of it as possible. But her eyes blinked open.

"How ya doin', *chica*?" Carmen smiled, but it didn't carry to her eyes. Was she worried?

"Okay. Just a little sleepy from the meds. This is the easy part." Olivia closed her eyes again.

"As if any of this could be easy for you."

"Hmm. Yes. But the real *fun* comes later." She smiled, but kept her eyes closed. Yeah, the fun of the nausea, no energy, no hair.

Someone at a breast cancer support site recommended she shave her head before it started falling out in clumps. Less traumatic that way.

She remembered Carmen's reaction when Olivia asked her after her first chemo what she thought of a head shaving party.

Carmen's eyes had gone wide. "A what?"

After Olivia's explanation, Carmen gave a wary smile. "If that's what you want to do, that's what we'll do."

So Carmen and Vanessa planned to make a head shaving party into an event with food and drink. And laughter. Lots of laughter.

Still hours to go on this chemo round, she needed to sleep while she could, in between nurses checking the IV line for progress.

Speak of the devil.

Her nurse bustled in, flicked the line with her finger, checked the bag for the volume level. "Okay. The last one coming soon."

Olivia's nod was all the response she could manage as her eyelids fell.

Ah, come on, folks. Let me sleep. She came awake as the rustling and chatter grew.

"Okay, Olivia. You're about finished here. You can get ready to go."

What? That was the first time she'd slept through changing the chemo meds.

"Hungry?" Carmen stood close by as Olivia got off the bed.

"Actually. I am. A little."

"Coffee cart, cafeteria, or cafe?"

They made their way to the first floor. It wasn't really a coffee cart. Starbucks and City of Hope had converted the coffee cart to a full-blown Starbucks store.

Olivia chose a loaded caramel macchiato and yogurt. She could afford the extra calories, if not the sugar, since her weight was dropping.

"So when should we have this head shaving party?" Carmen sipped her own decadent Frappuccino and chewed on a scone with gusto.

They discussed possibilities and stood to leave when *She's a*

Lady played from Olivia's phone. "Katherine. I better take this."

"I hope you are finished with chemo for the day, dear. You doing okay? Carmen with you?"

"Yes. Yes, and yes. How are you?"

"Hal passed away this morning. Totally unexpected. I was sure Reggie was going first."

"Oh, no. I'm so sorry. How is Reggie taking it?"

"Not well, of course. And the doctor had downgraded her to just days. This may push it faster." Katherine cleared her throat. "I've been thinking about selling my house and moving to California. I know you've been struggling with how to keep the house since that beastly son of mine is providing less money than he promised. I don't think I can buy the mortgage out. It's pretty high, but I could buy something a little smaller that we could all move into. What do you think?"

Conflicting thoughts and emotions battled in her head. She was sorry about Hal and Reggie, but she would love to have Katherine in California. But move? Live together? Katherine had always been easy to live with short term. How would it be long term? In a smaller house. The kids would love it, of course.

Olivia had gone through so much of her trust fund already trying to keep up with the medical bills that it would not cover paying off the mortgage. This would certainly be an answer.

Her heart cried over the probability of losing her dream home. But it was just a house. The Lord would provide another roof over their heads. It looked like he was going to do it through Katherine.

"Oops. I have to go. Reggie needs me. Talk later." The phone clicked off.

Olivia told Carmen about Hal, Reggie, and Katherine's offer.

"Wow. How generous of her." Carmen's chestnut brown

eyes opened wide. "That would mean you wouldn't live down the street from me anymore! I won't like that. The kids won't like that." She let out a *humph!* "Sorry. Being selfish here. Of course, that would be a perfect answer." Carmen chattered until they reached the valet parking lot.

They kept the conversation to lighter topics as they drove back to Orange County. Olivia's mind churned with possibilities and decisions. Perhaps the doctors would be wrong about how long Reggie lived. It would take Katherine a while to sell her house, buy something else here, pack, and move. Besides, she didn't have the energy to pack and move. Not anytime soon.

———

October in Southern California showed only little change from summer to fall, and even though Olivia had lived here for nearly five years, those subtle changes still eluded her.

She walked briskly through her neighborhood, hoping to get in some exercise before she was down after her fourth chemo later in the morning. In spite of the year-round green weeping fig trees spilling shade in many spots, the sun remained blistering. Olivia tilted the water bottle to her mouth. Only a quarter of a mile and she was already parched.

Darn the heat wave. Where was the crisp fall air of her childhood? That was Buffalo, New York, and this was Orange County, California. Sure, she'd take the summer-like conditions in October over the winter snow. But, really. Did it have to be 80 degrees at eight in the morning with 95 predicted for the high? She guessed she should be grateful it wasn't 100 degrees.

She would try to think about something else. The problem with that was her thoughts naturally turned to her chemo. Only halfway through her chemo treatments and she was a hot mess. Today, that was literal.

She'd been such a hot mess that Dylan's birthday had barely been acknowledged, at least to her way of thinking. Katherine had made a cake, bought gifts, and generally made it as festive as she could. With no help from Olivia.

Without wanting to, she patted the scarf that covered her smooth head. Olivia was glad she'd shaved it right after her second chemo. Should have done it before chemo, but it was done now. So much for hoping she wouldn't lose her hair at all.

But you couldn't preempt losing your eyelashes by shaving. She supposed one could shave off eyebrows, but she'd hoped they wouldn't also disappear. She was wrong. Again.

Another long gulp of water. Her steps slowed.

Gotta get around the block. At least do one mile.

Why hadn't she used her gym membership and gotten fit? Before the breast cancer diagnosis? What a fool to think she had all the time in the world and could just say, "I'll start next month." Now it was too late. Cancer patient friends on Facebook assured her she'd be able to start working out after chemo. That would be a priority to help in her recovery.

Nine weeks, three chemo treatments down and even though the nausea and bone-crushing exhaustion laid her low, she was determined to be strong. At least in her mind.

More faith, please, Lord.

Walking, especially on chemo days, helped her stay strong throughout the day. Mentally as well as physically.

The faster she could get through these treatments, the better. She wanted to be done in plenty of time to enjoy Christmas, especially since she would have to go through Thanksgiving this way. At least the closest chemo was two weeks before the holiday. Usually during the last week of the three-week rotation, she felt almost human. One week in every three.

Staggering, she made it back to her front door. Her front door. How long would it be hers? Frank was not paying the mortgage as he promised. Not giving her much money at all. Thank the Lord for Katherine.

Katherine's house was on the market, and she'd arrived just last week to stay with Olivia and the kids until a plan could be decided.

The cool entry atrium felt like an oasis after her walk. What a temperature merry-go-round. Heat wave outside, cool at home, and always freezing in the chemo room regardless of the outside temperatures.

"Oh, my dear. Are you okay? Are you sure you should have taken a walk in this heat?" Katherine wiped her hands on a dishtowel as she came from the kitchen to greet Olivia.

"It helps me get through the chemo. It is hot out there, though. Going to shower and change. Carmen will pick me up in half an hour."

By the time they reached City of Hope, Olivia was agitated. Traffic did that to her these days. And she wasn't even driving. Then the wait to check-in, have her blood drawn, and be called back to the chemo room raised the tension.

What was the matter with her? There was always a wait. Why should she be anxious today?

Carmen squeezed Olivia's hand. "Been meaning to ask you if you would be willing to talk to Jorge's cousin. She was just diagnosed with breast cancer and is totally freaking out. She needs some help. Would you mind talking to her? You have had such a calm spirit through all of this."

Olivia stared at her. What on earth was Carmen saying? A calm spirit? She had no idea.

"I'm not much at talking to people. You know, counseling kind of stuff."

"Look at the great work you were doing with the homeless ministry."

"I just did paperwork."

"Moira told me how you personally guided those new

families through their applications. She can't stop singing your praises."

Olivia massaged her temples, then slouched in her chair to rest her head against the wall.

"I'm sorry, *chica*. I shouldn't have brought this up right now." Carmen squeezed Olivia's hand again.

"I—I'll try."

"Stanford?" A nurse approached her.

Thank goodness. Olivia stood up.

"I'm sorry, but your white blood cell count is too low for us to do chemo today. We need to get your white blood cell count up. An injection of Neulasta® should help. Pick up the prescription at the pharmacy before you leave. It's an injection that you can administer yourself or have someone do for you. We've rescheduled you for next Tuesday, and hopefully your count will have improved."

Her body sagged. A self-injection? A delay?

No way could she inject herself. Hopefully Katherine or Carmen would do it for her. Otherwise she'd be out of luck.

Plus, she was all psyched up for today's chemo. And a delay would throw everything off. Now she'd have chemo the week before Thanksgiving. Not enough time for a decent recovery.

And what if her count wasn't up next week? Would she have to have chemo two days before Thanksgiving?

No. No. No.

Carmen put her arm through hers and led her away. "It's okay. There's always next week. Let's go pick up your injection stuff. I can help you with it. Unless you'd rather have Katherine."

Can't this be over? She wanted to close her eyes, go to sleep, and wake up after the whole nightmare was over. But what if she didn't wake up? What if they hadn't found all the cancer during surgery? And the chemo didn't get it all? With their father out of their lives more and more, her kids needed her. She couldn't just die.

How could she help anyone else? She'd agreed too quickly. But she had agreed.

At least she'd have another week of being relatively nausea-free. She kept telling herself that all the way home.

———

Katherine's words, spoken kindly, still felt like a hot poker to the soul, reminiscent of the pain of the injection Katherine had given her last night.

"I…I know we should put the house up for sale, Katherine, but—"

"It will be hard. I know. I felt the same way about putting my house on the market. But I don't see an alternative."

How could Olivia be so stupid? Here she was complaining about losing her house of four years, and Katherine was sacrificing her home of thirty-five years. Just so she could come help Olivia. She swallowed hard, and then hugged Katherine as gently as possible to protect her chest.

"I am so sorry. How selfish of me. I should have thought about how hard it was for you."

They stood there for a few seconds, giving each other support. Katherine patted Olivia's back and moved away.

"It's what families do."

Frank should be here. Then Katherine wouldn't have to be giving up her home. It was Frank's childhood home, too. What would Frank say? Olivia doubted he'd care, considering how much he hated his father. But what about their own home? Would he be upset if she put it on the market? Really, he'd have no choice unless he started paying the mortgage. Delaying any longer and the choice would be snatched from them. The house ripped away in foreclosure.

How could Frank have stopped paying the mortgage

months ago, keeping it from her? Of course, he wasn't just keeping that from her. He was keeping quiet about everything by not calling, not coming by to see the kids even.

Katherine had wanted to buy the mortgage, but it was just too big. It would have taken every dime of her sale and then some.

Selling her home. Chemo. Was there any good news anywhere?

Yes, God loves you. Has a plan for you. Faith. Trust.

"Maybe we could use my week off from chemo to get the house on the market?" Could she trust the chemo delay as God's provision?

"It will probably take longer than a week to get it on the market. We have to find a real estate agent, and he or she will probably want to stage the place for a better sale. I had to do that with my house."

Swiping a sweaty palm down her jean-clad leg, Olivia nodded. How would they get the place staged while she was pinned to the couch after chemo? How about the packing? It would take longer than a one-week delay in her chemo treatment. *And please, God, no more delays.*

She edged her shoulders back. "Then let's get started. We have a couple of good real estate agents in our church. Let me see which one Carmen recommends."

"Do you want me to talk to Frank, dear? I would kind of like to give him a piece of my mind." Katherine set her mouth in a grim line.

Would Olivia be a coward to let Katherine talk to Frank? Probably.

"You can give 'em that piece later. I better talk to him." Olivia hoped she'd made the right choice. She would have to find her face of courage.

Frank had been indifferent about selling the house. Olivia was lucky she'd been able to keep him on the phone for two minutes. He was definitely done with everything to do with her and the kids. Her heart broke for Zoe and Dylan, who hadn't seen their father since Labor Day weekend when he came to pack up more of his belongings.

Her next two phone calls produced more satisfying results. Carmen gave her the name and number of a real estate agent, and her phone call with Sheena Wilson was like a balm to Olivia's soul. Sheena reassured Olivia all would be well without overwhelming her with details, and that she'd come to the house tomorrow.

"Katherine!" Was that hopefulness in her voice as Olivia called out for her? "Our new real estate agent will be here in the morning."

She may be feeling better than if she'd had chemo yesterday, but the day had exhausted her, and it was time to rest.

Chapter Thirty-Six

Olivia opened the front door and had to look up quite a distance to meet Sheena Wilson's coal-black eyes. Her build could have been that of a football player if she'd been a "he."

Olivia stepped back slightly from the imposing woman on her doorstep. Sheena gave her the whitest smile she'd ever seen, set against skin that was like the finest ebony.

Belying her size, Sheena's voice was soft and caressing. "Olivia, I am so pleased to finally meet you. Carmen has told me how wonderful you are." She extended a warm, soft grip.

Katherine joining them, Olivia and Sheena wandered about the house discussing how best to showcase it for sale.

"I have already put together some comps, and after seeing your lovely home, this is the price I recommend we start with." Sheena showed them a sheet with some calculations and a dollar figure ringed in red.

"You think we can get that?" Olivia felt her eyes open wide.

"It's just a starting point, of course."

"And you have to split the proceeds with Frank." Katherine brought her back to reality.

"And as much as I hate to say it, the market isn't that great right now. But we know we can trust God to be in it. Right?" Sheena gave them another dazzling smile. "Now, let's make a list of everything we need to do to showcase your house."

They sat at the white kitchen table and discussed the ever-growing list.

"Mommy, what are you doing?" Zoe stood next to Olivia, and Dylan was right behind Zoe.

"Oh, talking about some things we're going to do to the house."

"Why? You're just going to sell it. Why do anything to it?" Zoe had a sour expression.

How in the world did Zoe know that? Olivia had been so careful not to talk about it in front of her.

"Sell the house? Doesn't that mean we live somewhere else? We won't live down the street from Gabe and Artie?" Dylan's voice became whinier the more he spoke. "I don't wanna move!"

Olivia's chest ached, not from her scars, but from the wounds Dylan in his own grief was adding. She gathered them in her arms.

"I know. Mommy wishes we didn't have to move, too. But Mommy and Grandma only have so much money to use for our expenses."

"But will we be homeless?" Zoe's face had gone white.

"No. No. I promise we won't be homeless." Olivia gulped back tears. She had no idea they'd worry about being home-less. A year ago, they drove past the homeless shelter by the Santa Ana Riverbed, and stared aghast at the hundreds of ragged tents and what appeared to be junk everywhere. She didn't realize they remembered that and equated it with their situation.

Zoe sighed. "Okay. I guess moving to a different house is better than living in a tent."

Tears filled Dylan's eyes. "But what about Gabe and Artie?"

"You'll still spend a lot of time at their house while I'm having chemo and radiation. I promise."

Dylan sniffed and nodded his okay.

"Zoe and Dylan, why don't you come with Grandma and we'll start a game in the family room. What should we play?" Katherine maneuvered the kids out the door as Zoe and Dylan argued over what game to play.

"Sorry about that." Olivia gave Sheena a rueful smile.

Sheena covered Olivia's hand with her own. "Don't you worry. About anything. I'm here to make it all easier. Right? I'll get this written up tonight. Then how about I pick you all up tomorrow and we'll go looking for your new home?"

This was real now. Selling and moving was going to be harder than Olivia thought. One half of her mind screamed its rebellion at selling. The other half calmly accepted the fact. But she couldn't be double-minded. She had to trust the Lord, in faith, completely, and that He had sent Sheena to make it a little bit easier.

Thank you, Lord, for what you are going to do.

Help my unbelief.

———

Fatigue dragged at Olivia's bones. Even if the smell of Katherine cooking bacon wasn't already turning her stomach, the chemo sores in her mouth would make eating it almost impossible. And still two chemo sessions to go.

She eased into sweats. Jeans, her normal uniform of choice, had become too much trouble to get on. Even the thirty seconds it took to put the sweats on was enough to put her back in bed. Instead, she collapsed onto her easy chair. The pale green with bright splashes of red hibiscus usually cheered her, but today the upholstery flowers became just something to sit on.

Where are you, Frank? And why couldn't you stay? He didn't love her. That's why. She got that. But why? Why didn't he love her?

Because you are unlovable. Worthless.

No! God loves me. He created me. I am worth His dying on the cross for me.

If that's true—no, it is true. Then what's wrong with Frank?

She knew from Frank's assistant, Seth, that his headaches grew more frequent. Olivia was grateful for Seth, who risked his job to answer her questions—when she was brave enough to call and inquire.

Seth had told her Frank was seeing a doctor and on more medications. So why wasn't he better? Couldn't these drugs make him realize he was needed at home? Not just by her, but by his children? Maybe there was no drug that could do that.

Her mind latched on to another thought. Did she really want Frank to come home? Did she love him? She wasn't sure anymore. As the doubt coiled around her heart, for a moment she stopped breathing.

But God's Word didn't say you could divorce your spouse if you stopped loving him. Or even if he stopped loving you. Frank said when he left, he didn't want a divorce—yet. Did he want one now?

The fatigue pressed harder. Better get up now or she was liable to be rooted with the upholstery flowers. She slid to the edge of the chair and slowly stood. Pulling her T-shirt toward her, she slid it on over her head, snubbing the irritating prosthetic. All accomplished in slow motion.

———

Olivia stared at her cell phone. Sheena had hung up after gushing with what she considered to be good news. They had a buyer. But for a far lower price than they had hoped.

Katherine stood next to Olivia on the patio while Zoe and

Dylan played on the jungle gym, trying to collect the last rays of November afternoon sun before it set.

"Was that Sheena?" Katherine's voice was hopeful.

Three weeks with no offers. At least until today.

"Thirty-thousand less than the asking price."

"You don't have to accept it, right?"

"Sheena suggests otherwise."

Katherine thumped into one of the Adirondack chairs. Olivia eased into the other one.

Happy squeals from the children tore at Olivia's heart. They had made an offer on a condo with a patio but no back-yard. Yes, there was a common playground, but Olivia knew the kids would miss their own jungle gym and playhouse. She'd miss her gazebo.

"Sheena will be here in the morning for me to sign the papers. The buyer asked for a thirty-day escrow."

"What? We can't have you out of here in thirty days. We've barely begun to pack. And Thanksgiving's coming up." Katherine's voice grew more and more indignant.

"And I have two more chemo sessions to go." Olivia's throat clogged with emotion.

Lord, I can't do this!

"The escrow won't be closed on our condo that soon."

Olivia sat up straight. "We'll counteroffer. I was so dumb-struck, it didn't occur to me to tell Sheena to do that. Calling her back now!"

———

"I thought your unusual Eichler home would bring more, but I think the uniqueness of the home combined with the current economy became a liability. I'm sorry. But the good news is the buyers have agreed to a forty-five-day escrow and raised their offer by $10,000 to make that happen. They are moving in from out of state and are in a bit of a hurry." Sheena fiddled with her pen as she sat behind her glass and chrome desk across from Olivia and Katherine. "And the sellers of your condo have agreed to let you move in as a rental if that escrow isn't closed."

"I knew the Lord would provide a solution." Katherine's diminutive form looked large on the spindly chrome chairs she and Olivia perched on. The rest of the modern furnishings complimented Sheena's desk.

Relieved the buyers had accepted their counteroffer that was a counteroffer of their counteroffer, Olivia still had difficulty escaping the mental fog that had her bound since they had agreed to sell the house. It had taken days to come to an agreement with the buyers.

And the last chemo was tomorrow.

Even with fifteen more days to pack, moving wasn't going to be easy.

Olivia took the pen Sheena offered and signed the papers, wishing Frank hadn't relinquished his power of attorney to her. But he'd given up helping her carry the load months ago.

———

That evening she explained to the kids the house was sold and dried their tears as she put them to bed. Katherine had retreated to her room. Now it was her turn.

Olivia stepped into the shower with the water running as hot as she could stand it. She lifted her face up to allow the force of the power spray to beat against her.

Lord, they've taken my breasts, my hair, and now my house. What else must I give up?

Tears mingled with the shower spray to run down her face, her neck, her flat chest.

Her mind screamed "No!" so loudly in her head she almost thought she'd yelled it out loud. But no one came running to find out what was the matter. She sank to the shower floor and huddled there until the water ran cold and she began to shiver.

Stop it, Olivia! God's got this. And He's got you.

She almost believed herself.

Olivia turned the knobs off and stepped out into the steamy bathroom. She wrapped herself in her baby pink extra-large bath sheet.

No more pity parties. God's got a plan.

He had to. Besides, she had to get strong for chemo tomorrow.

Chapter Thirty-Seven

The whirlwind of the last three weeks had drained her. Chemo, Thanksgiving, packing. Chemo had kept her from much of the packing, and Katherine had been nursing back pain. Zoe and Dylan, usually so well behaved, had acted out their fears by resisting every directive. Or it seemed like it.

At least today was her last chemo. She would get her strength back. And lose the nausea. The mouth sores would heal. She might even be able to enjoy Christmas.

After a few hiccups at the beginning, the escrow now moved along smoothly.

Count your blessings.

But all she could count right now were her thorns. Frank continued to be no help. Chemo. Moving from her beloved home.

Olivia moved toward her bedroom door. *This must be what a slug's pace is like.* Her cell phone rang, and she realized she'd left it on her bedside table.

Giddyap, slug, before it goes to voicemail.

City of Hope.

She answered around the lump of dread in her throat.

"Olivia? I'm sorry, but we will have to postpone today's

chemo. Your drugs didn't arrive. I've re-scheduled you to next Tuesday. Same time. Take the opportunity to relax. See you next week."

Seriously? Her last chemo. Postponed. Relax?

I can't even.

Her body twitched and then shook, throwing her back into the chair. The smooth upholstery had all at once become like burlap, causing her to jump up again, as if her entire body itched.

"Olivia? I'm ready to take the kids to Carmen's." Katherine called from the doorway. "What's the matter?"

Olivia could barely unclench her teeth to talk. "Chemo postponed. Can you believe it? They don't have my drugs. How could a place as big and as organized—supposedly—not have my drugs?" She paced in a rage-fueled frenzy, her fatigue forgotten.

"You must be terribly disappointed, dear. I'm so sorry." One look at Katherine's face displaying lines she didn't have two months ago and her eyes shiny with tears made Olivia collapse again, this time on her bed.

The delay put her last chemo a week before Christmas. Her Thanksgiving had been one horrible bite of turkey, one horrible day on the couch due to the last delay. Now it looked like it was destined to be repeated for Christmas. Would this never end?

"I'll go get the kids settled." Katherine walked slowly down the hall.

Get over yourself, Olivia. Poor Katherine was feeling the stress, too. In her head, she heard Katherine's words again from weeks ago about putting on her face of courage. Faith. Trusting God, no matter the circumstances. Thanking Him, regardless.

I'll try, Lord. That's as much faith and courage as I can screw up right now.

Why did she take one step forward, only to take two backward? She should be better at this by now.

Katherine's phone rang faintly from the family room.

"Good news, bad news, dear. Sheena just called me because she couldn't get you. Escrow on this house is set to close on December 26 now. Escrow on the new condo can close on December 27. But then we have to be packed and ready to move two days after Christmas."

"That assumes no more problems." Olivia sat up and smoothed her T-shirt, careful not to go near her chest.

"Yes, indeed." Katherine sighed. "I know we thought we could pack this up ourselves. I cannot believe we even entertained that idea. I'm going to call the moving company and add their packing to our contract."

"But that's so expensive!"

Katherine raised her hand, palm outward. The universal stop sign. "It's done. We can't worry about this too."

Once again Olivia looked into the lines on Katherine's face. There she went again, thinking only of herself. No way would Olivia be much help with packing. That would leave it all to Katherine. Of course, she couldn't handle it all. The packing cost would eat into their down payment on the condo, but that's the way it had to be.

I am forgiven. I am redeemed. I am a royal daughter of the King.

———

Seventy-nine degrees and sunny in December? *Olivia, you're not in Buffalo anymore.*

With the scorpions of frustration and sadness nipping at her heels while she moped about the house, and the glorious weather outside beckoning, how could she not make a run for it? Besides, the kids were at Carmen's and Katherine was packing her bedroom.

Olivia pointed her CRV—how soon would this money hog have to go?—toward the Brea Mall and some retail therapy. She'd never believed in retail therapy before, and truth be told, today would only be window shopping. Real retail therapy was out of her budget.

Even on a Wednesday morning the mall was overrun with parents and grandparents looking for the perfect Christmas gifts and teens—why weren't they in school?—hanging out. Olivia wove in and out of the crowd, trying not to get jostled. So much for that. Store windows held merchandise she couldn't afford, not only in cost, but the space it would take up in moving boxes. Every two minutes a Kiosk vendor accosted her, asking if he could just ask her one question or give her a sample. No thanks!

What was she? A ball in a pinball machine?

Maybe this had been a bad idea. Here she was inside when it was so glorious outside. Torturing herself with crowds and material things she wasn't going to buy.

Coffee. At least she could stop at Starbucks for a latte.

Tapping her foot as she waited last in a line ten bodies long, thoughts of the chemo delay added another ten bodies to the line in front of her. Or so it seemed. Time to bail. Did she really need coffee this bad? She looked at the line behind her. At least six more people had joined the queue. Wait. Only five people stood in front of her now. She'd invested too much time to give up.

"Mommy, look at that lady. She's bald!"

A child somewhere behind her whispered in his outside voice, and Olivia's shoulders hunched.

"Shh."

Olivia tried to look straight ahead so as not to embarrass the mom further. The middle-aged man in front of her turned around, looked her up and down, and stared at her head. He didn't even seem embarrassed. Two teens sitting at a bistro table to her right stared and snickered.

Yes, I'm bald! Okay? She wanted to shout out loud but knew she couldn't. She wanted to run but knew she wouldn't.

"Isn't she beautiful, son?" A masculine voice to her left asked softly.

"Yeah, beyoutifool," a little boy whispered back.

Olivia allowed herself to look toward the man and his son, who smiled at her. She smiled her thanks, and the little boy waved.

Her heart a little lighter, she finally ordered and grabbed her coffee. It was time to get out of here.

As she slid into her vehicle, her cell phone beeped. Marissa Cinzano, Breast Cancer Support, appeared on her screen.

"So glad I caught you, Olivia. I just wanted to remind you about the group gathering today. Can you make it?" Marissa's voice bubbled, like a newly uncorked bottle of champagne. Or so Olivia thought. She'd never really had much champagne.

Why not? It was safer than the mall.

Getting out of the mall was another matter. A long SUV hovered near the back bumper of her car so close she could barely back out. Other cars driven by cranky shoppers circling to find the best—or any—parking spot, cut her off, honked, and generally created mayhem.

Olivia gripped the steering wheel. This was too much. She was just going to head home. But once out of the parking lot and onto to Birch Street, she realized she was about to drive by the community center.

Okay. Okay. Must be some kind of sign.

Not that she believed in signs, but it was not a coincidence that she chose to go to the Brea Mall. Right next to the support group meeting location.

She made a U-turn and slipped into the center's parking lot.

The community center was still a foreign country to her, having been here only twice before. Scattered around the large conference table were women, mainly alone, but a few clusters of two or three seemed to know one another. Middle-age described the majority of the attendees. Several could even be called elderly, sixties at least. Some heads were bald, some with peach fuzz, some with scarves or obvious wigs. A couple of full heads of hair stood out. Were they passed the baldness or just getting started?

A petite red-head, freckles playing tag across her cheeks, bounced up to Olivia.

"Olivia? I'm so glad you could come. Thought I'd just take a chance and give you a call. Come in. Come in."

Marissa took her by the arm and led her to the nearest full head of hair. "Olivia, I'd like you to meet Isobel. This is Isobel's first time. Excuse me, won't you?" With that, Marissa skipped off to another new arrival. Yes, she definitely skipped.

Olivia swallowed her temptation to run. Isobel looked to be in her early forties. What would they have in common? Besides cancer. "Hello, Isobel. Welcome. This is only my third time here, so I'm sort of a newbie, too."

Isobel sighed, her dark brown eyes looking suspiciously moist. "But you're obviously further along in your treatment." Her voice not unkind, but her eyes flicked to Olivia's head.

"Almost finished with chemo. You?"

"Surgery next week. Do you mind me asking something?"

"S-sure."

"Do you—do you—oh, shoot. Do people stare at your baldness?" Isobel's pecan-colored face became pink.

"If you only knew." Olivia grimaced and related the mall scenario only an hour earlier. Maybe she shouldn't have shared that. Poor Isobel looked as if she would faint.

"Oh, my, I'm so sorry. I shouldn't have asked." Pink was becoming red. "It's just that my hair is my best feature." Isobel caressed her dark brown mane. "What will I do when it falls out?"

Olivia's heart beat with Isobel's. "First, there's no guarantee you'll lose your hair. But I do understand—"

"Just don't say, 'It's just hair. It'll grow back!'" Isobel's voice grew shrill.

"Wouldn't ever say that. Hair means so much to us as women—"

Marissa called their attention to the front, so they sat down together.

Women shared and asked questions while Marissa moderated and added thoughts from her own experience as a breast cancer thriver, as Marissa liked to call it rather than survivor. They were invited to visit the adjoining prosthetic/wig room or the make-up salon, where one could receive a free makeover with free makeup.

The meeting over, the women dispersed, and without checking out the other rooms, Olivia promised to keep in touch with Isobel.

"Thank you, Olivia, for talking with Isobel. She was a hot mess at first. She looked so much better when she left." Marissa's green eyes danced as she spoke. "You'll come back, won't you? You have a way with others."

Olivia gave a non-committal answer and bolted.

Would she come back? She had to admit she felt better. Maybe she should have taken advantage of the makeover. Maybe next time. If there was a next time. Her heart gladdened at the thought she may have helped Isobel. Still.

If only she really could help Isobel and others.

Baring her soul was like tearing a scab off before its time. No, that took more courage than she could muster.

———

Taking advantage of the unwelcome lull between chemo sessions, Olivia cleaned out the kitchen cupboards preparing for the movers to pack. She supervised Zoe and Dylan sorting and discarding toys. It was more like a treasure hunt, unearthing old toys that became new again, toys that needed to be played with. Katherine tackled the bathrooms.

Olivia rubbed the back of her neck and shuffled to the

elephant. No more! *Oh stop whining and groaning.* She flopped down anyway.

As she picked up her iPad to check Facebook, her phone rang announcing Sheena, the Wonder Woman of real estate.

"Olivia, I know you are busy with chemo and packing…to move into your fabulous new condo…" Sheena's voice trailed off for a moment. "I have a friend who has just been diagnosed with breast cancer. A very, very frightened friend. Would you mind talking to her, answer her questions? I know it's an imposition right now. But I'd be thankful."

The more she resisted, the more she felt nudged—pushed —from behind into helping others. And the more she helped others, the harder the push.

Guess the Lord wanted her to help.

Even as she agreed to talk with Sheena's friend, her gut clenched. Why was this so hard?

You're such a coward! Remember who has the power here.

I am forgiven. I am redeemed. I am the royal daughter of the King.

———

Miracle of miracles! The tune from Mom DeeDee's favorite movie *Fiddler on the Roof* ran through her mind over and over. She and DeeDee had watched the classic movie together at least once a year during Olivia's teens.

But she wasn't thinking of the love between a newly engaged couple, but the love of her Father in heaven who had brought her through her last chemo treatment. She didn't doubt that the next few weeks as she recovered would be difficult. Through it all, He would help her recover her strength, a healthy mouth, and hair.

Hair. How long would it take to regrow her hair?

Olivia knew He would not forsake her now.

Miracle of miracles!

Balloons and signs held by Katherine, Carmen, and a

couple of nurses crowded the narrow hallway outside the glass door of her treatment room. Her peeps—she smiled to think of them as her peeps—tried to be subdued so as not to disturb the other patients still receiving chemo, some of whom slept. Yet the silent excitement was as palpable as fireworks.

Olivia could not hold back the smile or the tears as she thanked them. She took her little happy dance on the road, circulating around the treatment rooms. She'd gotten to know a few of the patients whose rotations coincided occasionally with hers. The awake patients received a goodbye and encouraging words. Hey, if she could make it through, so could they.

Hey! Look at me! I can help others. Even in this small way. Her heart settled into a sweet spot.

Riding away from City of Hope was like shedding a bad dream from her memory. It didn't matter that she'd be back sometime next month for radiation. That was a different dream.

Even if she hadn't been in Carmen's luxurious Escalade, she'd feel like she was riding on air. She began to nod.

Squeals brought Olivia awake. Outside of the vehicle's window, Zoe and Dylan hopped from foot to foot. Chaperoned by Jorge, who had volunteered to stay home from work and watch the kids so Carmen and Katherine could be with her. The group was rounded out by Gabe and Artie, with more balloons and signs.

"You're our superhero!"

"Welcome home, Mommy!" Zoe squealed and Dylan laughed.

Olivia poured out of the vehicle and hugged everyone.

Inside the house, the dining room table was covered with Olivia's favorite dishes. Creamy potato soup. Buttered noodles. No marinara sauce that would provoke her mouth sores. Vanilla pudding.

Carbs. Carbs. Carbs.

Where was the protein? The vegetables?

It didn't matter. They had been so sweet to fix soft comfort food that she loved. It didn't matter because she would be able to eat none of it. Even now, as she surveyed the table, her stomach roiled. She looked at each dish with envy, imagining how wonderful it must taste. How she wished she could eat it all. She needed the calories.

"You all go ahead and eat." She smiled her thanks. "I need to lie down first."

The elephant never looked better. She eased herself down onto the softness and sighed. Everyone must have realized how much she needed rest because no one followed her.

Someone had lit the lights on the Christmas tree, the only nod to the season in the house. It didn't seem logical to decorate while in the middle—well, the beginning—of packing. The kids had insisted on at least a tree, a real one. Olivia could not deny them.

Now the lights sparkled and added a comfort to the room and to her soul.

She would close her eyes for just a little while.

Chapter Thirty-Eight

Thumping marching bands and gorgeous flower-bedecked floats inched their way down Colorado Boulevard. Olivia, Katherine, and the kids sat warm and comfortably as they watched the televised Rose Parade replay in their new condo's family room. King cozied up to Dylan. He had seldom left Dylan's side since the move.

A new year. A new home. Chemo complete. The prospects should be encouraging. But Olivia felt a heaviness.

Christmas had come and gone with little fanfare. Katherine tried to make it festive for the children but moving three days after Christmas didn't allow for any decorating other than the small tree. They declined Carmen's invitation to spend Christmas Day with the Delgados, because it was too hard to get up off the couch, physically and emotionally. Katherine saw to it they all had presents, a festive dinner, and carols.

As the next horse-riding team came into view, Olivia swallowed her post-Christmas guilt and her eyes flicked away from the parade. White flat walls. No gorgeous, grand stone fireplace. No built-in bookcases. They had been fortunate that the elephant had fit in the family room, but it left little space for anything else. The dining room table on the end near the open kitchen. One additional easy chair. Hers. Frank had finally taken his favorite recliner.

Katherine's antique mirror graced the front entryway. Across the entryway, the small living room held only a few pieces from her old living room.

At least they each had their own bedroom. A tiny bedroom would be her office whenever she felt up to working again.

She'd tried to give the master suite to Katherine, but she wouldn't hear of it. At least it had a large closet. Nothing like her walk-in at home. And she still had her own en suite bathroom.

Two stories would take some getting used to. Even the staircase was plain Jane.

It was all so boring. Maybe it was because unpacked boxes were still the major decorative touches. Once they got rid of those and really decorated, it would look more like a home. But her home was back in Villa Park. Not here in Yorba Linda.

Get over it, Olivia! It was just a house. This was now her house—well, condo. Her family was here, all together, minus one, of course. Frank would never be here, would he? But it would still be their home now. It would just take a little time.

And a lot of prayer.

She tried not to be bitter over the loss, praying for forgiveness, a change of attitude, trust, and faith.

Changing positions in her easy chair reminded her how much the move had sapped her of any new strength she had gained since her last chemo. She couldn't lift. Having her lymph nodes removed meant her arm had a limited range of motion, making the move more difficult. Such a pitiful figure she was.

Now Zoe and Dylan greeted Katherine with squeals of delight as she brought in mugs of hot chocolate. "Do you need anything else, dear?" Katherine asked as she handed Olivia a steaming, fragrant mug.

"I'm good. Thanks." She took a tentative sip. Ahhh. The drink of the Mayans. A few weeks ago, just the thought of hot chocolate would have nauseated her. Thank the Lord for chocolate.

"Mommy, look at the superheroes on that float! Can we go sometime?" Dylan's face was lit from within and a whipped cream mustache sprouted from his upper lip.

Her strength may be pitiful, but she was still blessed from the Lord. The hardest part was over, at least that's what she was being told. Radiation and reconstruction still to go.

Radiation. What would that be like? Couldn't be as bad as chemo at least. Sometimes she still felt like she was scrabbling up Mount Everest barefoot, but she'd come through so much in such a short time.

Katherine drained her cup of hot chocolate. "I'll go put the prime rib in the oven. Zoe, would you like to help?"

"Can I?" Zoe shot toward the kitchen.

"Hey, I wanna help." Dylan, followed closely by King, raced to catch up with his sister.

Talking about prime rib made her hungry. Another miracle. *Thank you, Lord. For each new day. For another day to live.* For helping her adjust to her new normal—a healthy, new normal.

Olivia pushed radiation and reconstruction to the back of her mind. She would celebrate the new year.

———

City of Hope had become her second home. It was more familiar to her than their new condo.

Olivia turned into the complex and headed straight to the valet parking. What a God-send valet parking was. For three dollars, you could pull up right out front, and let the valet park your car so you could get right to the business of poisoning your body to get rid of the cancer.

Well, she was done with chemo. Now she'd be burning her flesh in radiation. Not today, though. She only had to see Dr. Martin, her oncologist, and meet her radiation oncologist, a Dr. Gordon, who would outline her radiation treatment.

A little independence was welcome, and it felt good to drive herself for a change. She was forever grateful to Katherine for moving to Orange County and rescuing them from apartment living by buying a condo for the four of them. But it was hard to get used to smaller quarters. And she'd never lived with Katherine before. A month or so as a visitor in Olivia's home was certainly different than living long-term in the condo partially owned by Katherine.

Not that Katherine hadn't made it clear that it was Olivia's home as much as it was hers. And Katherine had Olivia listed on the deed. The sale of Olivia's house had contributed to the mortgage after all. Yes, it belonged to both of them.

Oh, yes, driving alone definitely felt good today.

Checked in, she was then directed to the proper floor and waiting room. How long would she have to wait today? She settled in with her book, the latest by one of her favorite authors, Rachel Hauck.

"Olivia Stanford." The nurse called her, and she hadn't even completed the first chapter. How many more chapters in her breast cancer saga?

"Hello, Dr. Martin." Olivia's middle-aged oncologist, with a face reminiscent of Julia Roberts, had become as close to her as Carmen. Almost. But so very different.

Dr. Martin asked all the usual probing doctor questions, then moved on to the next step. "Dr. Gordon, your radiation oncologist, will meet us here momentarily, and discuss your further treatments. From what he and I discussed, I will probably follow-up with you in about six weeks, but, as always, if

you have any questions or concerns, get in touch." Someone
tapped on the door. "Come in. Oh, here is Dr. Gordon now."

Olivia almost choked on her own saliva. The silver-haired
fox, as he was known among the church singles, Dr. Lance
Gordon, stood before her.

Dr. Gordon held out his hand. "Hello, Olivia. I had hoped
to see you at church and let you know I'd be working on your
treatment, but we never seemed to connect."

She shook his hand, his slender fingers strong. "Dr.
Gordon."

"I forgot you two know each other. Well, then, Olivia, you
are in good hands. I'll be in touch." Dr. Martin smiled her
Julia Roberts' smile and slipped out.

He sat on a wheeled stool across from her and looked at
her intently. "How have you been? Really? I have been
praying for you ever since I heard Frank left. I'm so sorry."

Stammering her thanks, Olivia folded her arms over her
stomach to keep it from twitching at this development. She
wasn't sure she was okay with having Lance as her doctor. On
the other hand, it wasn't like they were close friends. They'd
met only four or five times, usually at the Delgados' or church.
But something about him set her on edge.

He sat quietly for a moment.

That steel-gray-eyed stare made her squirm. Now she
remembered. One of the things that unnerved her about him
was how much the color of his eyes matched Frank's. In actu-
ality, Frank's were gray-blue, Dr. Gordon's gray. Of course,
they were nothing alike. The men or their eyes.

"Olivia, are you okay with me being your radiation oncologist? You look a little unsettled."

Yuh think? *No. I'm not okay with this.* "Of course. I've heard
you are a very capable doctor."

He described the future, what to expect, when to expect it,
and how long the process would take. Radiation five days a
week for five weeks.

"Today I will examine you and mark the areas for treatment."

Shock was not strong enough to describe the sensation she felt when he said "examine" her. She sat up, her spine military straight. There is no way she was going to let this man examine her scarred, ugly chest.

He's a doctor, for heaven's sake. And she didn't really know him. He was pretty much a stranger. But the tittering at church about him—shame on you, ladies!—calling him the silver-fox, strategizing who could get him to ask who out first. Shameful behavior. She had never participated, for one, because she had never really considered herself single. Yes, Frank was gone. In fact, she hadn't seen him in four months. Only spoke to him about the sale and closing of the house. But she wasn't free.

And now this man was going to be her doctor?

She took a deep breath. "I have to admit it might be a little awkward at first. But one thing about having breast cancer, you learn fast that no modesty is allowed. I'll deal with it."

Beautiful speech. Too bad she would be tested on whether she believed it.

"Good. Let's prepare you for radiation treatments. Here's a gown. I'll give you a few minutes."

Wow, that test came fast. Now she knew one thing for sure. She didn't believe one word of her speech.

With shaking fingers, she undressed and put on the gown. She would get through this. Olivia perched atop the exam table. All too fast the tap came at the door, and Doctor Gordon entered.

A half an hour later, she couldn't get out of that building fast enough. She handed her parking ticket to the valet and tapped her foot as she waited.

It wasn't that bad. Yeah, who's kidding who. It was mortifying. Her nose stung with unshed tears. *No, not here.* Instead, she focused on The Wishing Tree in the parklike area across the circle, the tree where patients and family members hung paper symbols of their wishes and prayers to be freed of this horrible disease.

She'd made it through a double mastectomy, through chemo, through her husband deserting her, through losing her home. She could make it through being examined by the silver fox. An opportunity to show a face of courage.

Actually, she just had.

———

Although it had only been a week since she first met with Dr. Gordon and three days since she started radiation, it seemed like forever.

I don't think I can do this!

Five weeks times five days a week. Twenty-five radiation treatments. And only three days down. How was she going to do twenty-two more? The road ahead looked like a stretch through the flat California desert toward Las Vegas. No end in sight.

Olivia sat in City of Hope's parking lot and rested her forehead against the car's steering wheel. *I can't do it!* It didn't matter that she'd survived a double mastectomy and chemo. She was done. Done. Just like Frank. She gritted her teeth. The drive from Yorba Linda to Duarte every stinking day! It was only thirty miles according to Google maps, but in driving time? More like an hour. Each way.

The indignity of Lance seeing her scars. He wouldn't be judging. He did this every day. Right?

Where's your courage? Where?

Oh, Lord, I don't know.

Marissa. Breast cancer support group. Maybe she could find some courage there. Olivia glanced at the clock. With some traffic luck, she hoped to be only a little late.

Scree! Oh, great. She forgot the engine was already running. Hopefully that didn't ruin the starter. She snapped on her seat belt and threw the car into reverse.

Somehow the traffic to Brea was light. It was never light. *Thank you, Jesus.* Olivia pulled into the building's parking lot just as the meeting hour began.

Marissa's short red curls bobbed as she bounced on her toes near the end of the conference table. How was it that anyone could be that bubbly? Especially a breast cancer survivor—thriver. Maybe that made the difference. Thinking of yourself as a thriver, not just a survivor.

Olivia squirmed as the whining ricocheted around the table. *Please, ladies, can we get to something positive?* She had enough of her own negativity. *How do I survive four and a half more weeks of radiation? Then, reconstruction?*

Finally, Marissa took control and began driving the discussion. "Something that helped me, and it still does five years later as I experience other challenges and even with a metastatic diagnosis, is trying to be positive. I know that may not even seem possible to you right now. For me, it was realizing how I had taken life for granted. Now I am grateful for every single day I have. I don't have children, never been married, but I am thankful for the time I have with my aging parents. Thankful they haven't had to bury their only child yet."

Tiny rays of gratitude touched Olivia's heart.

But as Marissa dismissed the meeting, and Olivia approached the glass doors, the tiny rays evaporated. The sun outside the doors shone, so why did it feel dark?

"Olivia?" Marissa stood beside her. "Are you okay? Is there something I can do?"

Can you erase the last few months? Or can you at least magically give me the courage I need to get through the next year?

"How can I get through this? Survive, much less thrive? I've been praying, but I'm not sure my prayers are getting through the ceiling."

Marissa's eyes took on a new sheen, and she led them back to the conference table. "I am so happy you mentioned praying. That's the only way I made it through my cancer. I want to be sensitive and not assume, but are you a Christian?"

Ahhh, that's why Olivia felt a connection. "Yes. I kind of thought maybe you were, too."

"So, tell me why you think your prayers aren't getting through?"

How to explain? Olivia rubbed her hands together. "I have never been brave."

"Never?"

Okay, maybe she had been a few times. She sat up a little straighter.

"Olivia, what do you think being brave has to do with your prayers being heard?"

"How can I have faith if I don't have courage?"

"Faith is a gift of God. You can't manufacture it. The Lord will always grant faith when you ask for it because He's said He will give us whatever we ask in His name. Assuming it's within His will, of course. And I'm sure God wants to give you faith. God has not given us a spirit of fear. The opposite of fear is courage. In that faith, you can ask for courage."

"I make a few small steps towards asking for and getting a little courage—sometimes—and then it seems I become afraid and lose ground again."

"We have an enemy that delights in slinging his arrows at us, don't we? So, to be strong, we're told to put on the whole armor of God. To take our stand against the evil one."

"But how do I *do* that?"

"Someone told me once that the chief piece of armor is the breastplate of righteousness. God is the truly righteous one, and when we live each day in obedience to Him, His righteousness produces in us a practical, daily righteousness. And when you have on your 'good-news shoes,' when you have trusted God for salvation, there is a peace with God that is your sure foundation to stand firm in His strength."

Is that what Katherine meant by showing a face of courage? "My mother-in-law told me courage comes from faith and grit, and when we rely on that faith and in the Lord's strength, we act strong, with grit, showing a face of courage."

"Yes! That's right. I like that image. Grab your faith and grit and show that face of courage." Marissa hugged Olivia so gently Olivia didn't even have to protect her radiation-seared chest.

Chapter Thirty-Nine

Olivia lay back on a well-padded recliner on Carmen's patio. Her face to the sun, her eyes closed, as Carmen bustled around offering snacks and drinks.

This is why Olivia loved California. Seventy-five degrees and sunny in January. Her first week of radiation complete, she relaxed, her chest not uncomfortable as long as she kept herself covered. She had no intention of slipping on a swimsuit, much less a bikini, anyway.

Katherine kept a close watch on Zoe and Dylan as they splashed about the heated pool with Gabe and Artie. The way the young foursome had greeted each other, they acted as if they'd been apart for a year rather than a week. They were used to trotting down the street any time they wanted to see each other. Since the move, and with Olivia's radiation, it took a little more effort to get them together.

She felt the chair next to her move and opened her eyes.

Carmen patted her arm. "How are you? Don't lie. I'll know." Carmen's smile puffed out her already round cheeks.

"Me, lie? To you?" Olivia chuckled. "I'm feeling pretty well, actually. Last week I didn't think I'd make it through the first week of radiation, but it's not too bad. If you don't count the daily drive, of course."

"You go in the morning, right? Home by noon?"

Olivia's forehead grew tight. Her eyebrows must be all puckered. She drew her sunglasses down and looked over the top of the rims at Carmen. "Why?"

"I have an idea."

"Uh oh."

"Now just listen. As long as you're feeling okay, and you're all moved in, how about helping out again with the homeless ministry?" Carmen leaned toward Olivia.

"Oh, I don't know if I'm ready for anything yet." Olivia shoved her sunglasses back up where they belonged.

"We're having a team meeting tomorrow. You could just come, see what we're thinking about, and see if there's something you'd feel comfortable doing. No commitment. And your experience would help at the planning meeting even if you don't want to continue."

"You remember I only did the paperwork, the ordering, and other stuff like that, right?"

"That's exactly what we're going to need!" Carmen sat back, satisfaction written across her face.

"Tomorrow?"

"Yes. Since it's Martin Luther King Day, everyone is off work. 2 p.m. here. Okay?" Swallowing a sigh, Olivia nodded.

———

Pulling up to Carmen's house the next afternoon, Olivia marveled at the number of cars. She had no idea there were going to be so many people. Maybe they didn't need her after all. She almost had herself convinced to pull away from the curb, when someone knocked on the passenger window.

"Dr. Gordon!" Olivia pushed the automatic control to lower the window. She'd seen him in the office only three hours ago. And he'd seen her. Funny how it didn't bother her —much—in the treatment room, but now she squirmed at the thought.

"Remember. Call me Lance, away from the hospital. You're coming in, aren't you?" Dr. Gordon—Lance—smiled, his silver hair glinting in the sunlight.

"Yeah. Well. Of course." Now she was caught. She closed the window and dragged herself from the car. "I didn't know you were going to be here...Lance."

This was her home away from home, so Olivia walked in without knocking, Lance just behind her. The living room was abuzz, ice tinkled in glasses, and someone laughed loudly.

"Sounds like a party. Shall we join them?" Lance lightly touched her back, and they moved toward the hubbub.

As light as it was, his touch felt as if it seared her back. She forced herself not to squirm.

"Olivia! Lance! You're here. Good!" Carmen's long curls billowed about her head, her curls frizzing in the seventy-six percent humidity.

The fuzz on Olivia's head stayed right where it was.

Carmen clapped and brought the meeting to order.

How Olivia became a permanent part of the team, and with Lance as a partner, she couldn't remember. The humidity must have addled her brain. Now she and Lance were tasked to work on coming up with a new purchasing plan to acquire supplies and making deals with local hotels and motels, but within the new, limited budget.

Nevertheless, she and Lance made plans to have lunch the next day after her radiation treatment. It would save both of them a trip.

Olivia shuddered as she thought about it. How was she going to make the transition from patient to teammate within an hour?

Each Tuesday for the past three weeks, Olivia and Lance met in the City of Hope café after her treatment. Each week it became easier for Olivia to go from patient to colleague with Lance. He was gracious, listened to her ideas, and praised her for what she'd accomplished, finding suppliers the preceding week. Olivia appreciated that Lance made time in his busy schedule to keep up his end of the team arrangement, convincing hotels and motels to work with them.

Now sweat dribbled down her back despite the car's air conditioning blasting against her face. Seventy-nine degrees in February was maybe just a little too much. The radiated site on her chest was tight and sore as she drove home from the treatment, and the A/C didn't seem to be helping. She tried to shrug it off and be thankful that she only had one more week of radiation.

She could do this!

The garage door rumbled as it rolled back on its tracks. Olivia pulled her white SUV into the garage, thankful for the cool darkness. She pushed the button to close the big door, and it rumbled again, hitting the end of the track with a clang.

As she stuck one leg out of the open car door, her cell phone beeped.

Lance's voice crooned into her ear. "Are you home safely? You looked a little worn out when you left today."

Thanks, Lance, you know how to make a girl feel good. Wait. He's your doctor. He is here to heal you, not make you feel good about yourself.

She continued to straddle the threshold of the open car door, half in and half out, while she answered him.

"I'm fine. Are you just calling to tell me I look a wreck?" She added a chuckle so he wouldn't take offense.

"I'm sorry. That didn't come out the way I intended. I'm actually calling to see if you were free for dinner tonight." Lance lowered his voice. "Or tomorrow night."

Dinner? Was he asking her on a date? No. She was still

married, even if Frank hadn't talked to her since the house sale closed. *How do you ask a man if he was inviting you on a date?*

Olivia stumbled over some unintelligible words before she could stop herself. She finally clamped her mouth shut to halt the babble. A silence stretched to several seconds.

Lance broke the stalemate. "I have a few new resources I'd like to go over with you."

Ah, okay. Not a date. How stupid of her to think that it was.

"Yes, of course." Her voice came out a little hoarse. "Let me check with my mother-in-law to see which night works best for her. Call you back in a few minutes?"

After he assured her that was fine, she said goodbye, thumbed off the phone, and grabbed her purse. As she stepped out of the car, her mind couldn't let go of why this discussion couldn't wait until next Tuesday.

Chapter Forty

Lance's BMW carried them through the hills of Laguna, the moon bright through the sunroof. *Should that be moonroof?* Olivia was more relaxed now that radiation was over. They had met for dinner two weeks in a row, supposedly to discuss the homeless ministry, but she couldn't actually remember the subject coming up either time.

How had he convinced her to go out to dinner tonight? She remembered him telling her no one should stay home alone on Valentine's Day. Didn't she tell him she wouldn't be alone? Not with two children and a mother-in-law. But somehow, he had convinced her she shouldn't let him be alone.

It was true she felt more comfortable in Lance's presence after working with him the last few weeks. So, she'd said yes, but she wouldn't... couldn't...call it a date.

It seemed disloyal. She wasn't really free, was she? Frank continued to say he wasn't going to ask for a divorce—at least that's what he'd said two months ago, the last time they'd talked. Why not, she didn't understand. She was certainly not asking for one, because she believed the Lord didn't want them to divorce. Would they ever be a married couple again? She doubted it.

In the meantime, Lance, for the most part, was good company. It gave her a chance to stretch her brain when they discussed the ministry, and he treated her like a woman. If she thought too hard about it, the fact that he'd seen her chest, scars and all, during her radiation appointment just last week, made her cringe.

Olivia had felt guilty when he first arrived to pick her up. But as the evening progressed, and Lance's warmth held a proper distance, she relaxed and enjoyed herself. They were just two new friends enjoying each other's company. Had he leaned too close toward intimacy, she would have called it a night.

The prime rib dinner had been excellent. How wonderful she could delight in good food again. Riding through the beautiful hills lulled her into a further sated condition.

She turned in her seat to better view his profile—a strong jaw and that beautiful head of silver hair. He had a kind face. Why had she been wary of him?

"Olivia, you should get involved in the new children's program. As a housewife and mother, you'd do better working with children."

Startled by this sudden topic, she didn't respond. Did he think her only experience in life was with her own children? Didn't he know she had, until cancer, a thriving business—with adults as clients? A college degree?

It didn't help that he spoke with a firmness that grated on her nerves, spawning a renewed uneasiness. Was this why she'd been cautious?

"I know the homeless ministry is important. Which is why I've given it my time. But I'm also heading up a team to put together a new program for children. It isn't really my area of expertise, being single and no children, but all the other deacons were busy with other projects." He took a breath. "I think you'd be better used with the children."

"You know I have my own business as a rep in the meeting

industry, right?" Her words came out stiff. "And I'm only working on the homeless ministry to lend my past experience as a favor to Carmen."

"Well, of course. Complete your commitment. As will I."

He ignored her statement about her own business. How did he know what she'd be better at? *It's not like they'd been friends that long, for Pete's sake.* Not that caring for her own children wasn't vital or that the children's department was less important. But she had other skills, talents, that she could use. Right?

"I may not have time. My breast cancer support group leader has asked me to help her." She worked hard at keeping the edge out of her voice.

She had no idea whether she'd have the guts to open herself up to the support group enough to be a leader. Potential or no potential. It came down to whether she had the courage to share her experience.

"Don't you think it's too soon? You're not ready."

"What are you talking about?"

"You need time to heal, physically and mentally."

"I've never been in a better place mentally or spiritually—"

"Trust me. I don't think you're ready. Remember, I see a lot of breast cancer patients."

The lights from the approaching cars on the four-lane highway glared at her. She had to blink and look away.

How dare he assume she was or wasn't ready for anything! If she wanted someone to tell her what to do, she could just call Frank.

Maybe with his medical and cancer experience Lance had a point. Yet, the back of her neck quivered.

Lance pulled into a parking spot in front of her Yorba Linda condo. It wasn't her dream home, the one she had left behind, thanks to Frank, but it was comfortable, perhaps a little cozier than she liked.

Katherine had left on the living room light for her, and it shone like a beacon calling her in.

With his arm on the back of her seat, Lance leaned toward her, his mouth slightly open. "I really enjoy spending time with you, Olivia. You are an incredible woman." He leaned closer.

She hoped it was to say something more, not try to kiss her. She had to admit, two hours ago, it might have been tempting. Not now.

But she wasn't taking any chances.

Olivia slid out of the car, saying over her shoulder, "Thank you so much, Doctor Gordon. Lance. Dinner and Laguna was such a treat."

The driver door slammed, and Lance ran to her side of the car. He took her arm and walked her up the sidewalk. "These last couple of weeks have been wonderful for me. I hope for you, too." His arm moved to her shoulders.

Despite her irritation at his bossiness and the fact she was still married, a craving rose up in her soul to be loved and desired by someone. Frank hadn't filled that spot long before he abandoned her.

Lance was a great guy, and he could take care of her on so many levels.

What are you thinking, Olivia? How could she have let her mind go there?

It was wrong. *Forgive me, Lord.*

Wriggling away as discreetly as possible, she stepped up her pace. "It has been very enjoyable. Thank you. Now I really need to get in and see that my kids are okay. Good night."

"But—"

Olivia didn't know what Lance was about to say, but she didn't want him to say it. He was charming, and she was beginning to like him despite his highhandedness and his recent attempt at romance. He wasn't like Frank. But she didn't want, couldn't have, a relationship, not yet. Maybe never.

———

"Katherine? I'm home." She dropped her purse on the entry table and her house key in the bowl beside it.

The mahogany and marble-topped table was Katherine's. Not Olivia's style, but she didn't really mind. It had been quite a trick getting two households of furniture combined, edited out, and into the small condo.

"Have a good time?" Katherine was in her bathrobe with a cup of something that smelled like cinnamon. She held the cup toward Olivia. "Like some apple pie tea? It's herbal. No caffeine."

"I can get it." She hung up her sweater in the coat closet and turned into the kitchen. It was really called a great room, one big room for the family room and kitchen.

"Did you have a good time?" Katherine had followed her across the room and sat down at the table. King followed and lay at her feet.

"Oh, sure. Lance knows how to buy a great dinner and show you the sights from his lovely BMW."

"That does not sound complimentary to Lance."

"He really is very nice." Besides, how could she talk about her almost feelings for another man in front of her husband's mother? Especially when she was still married to the husband? "He wants me to join the children's department at church. And doesn't think I should spend more time at the breast cancer support group. He says I'm not ready." The microwave turntable spun her cup of water around.

Katherine harrumphed. "Professional or personal opinion?"

"I assume a professional one. I told him I was more than ready, but maybe I should heed his advice. For a while anyway." Because maybe she wasn't really ready emotionally, and it had nothing to do with the cancer.

"Are you going to see him again, dear?"

"It's nice to have someone who treats me like a woman. Take me out to dinner—" The dinging of the microwave indicated her water was hot. Not a proper tea, but at ten o'clock at night, microwave tea would do.

"You don't want to lead him on." Katherine's tone was soft. "There is just something about him."

Although she had from time to time thought the same about him, hearing Katherine voice the same suspicion got her back up a little.

"Why? What's the matter with Lance?"

"I don't know, but you shouldn't let him tell you what to do."

"I *have* learned a thing or two about that." She hadn't meant to sound sharp, but Katherine's eyes widened in what Olivia assumed was surprise at her tone. "Sorry. I just meant, I agree. He isn't really like that. Besides. I'm still married to Frank, and this was not a date."

Katherine nodded. "The kids and I put on a video, ate popcorn. They went to bed a little bit ago, and they fell asleep the minute their heads hit the pillow. They are out."

"Thank you for watching them. It means a lot to me and them—"

Why was the front doorbell ringing at ten o'clock at night?

Lance. *If he's back, I'll give him a piece of my mind.*

Olivia yanked the front door wide. She stepped back nearly crashing into King whose sharp barks cut through the night.

What were two very large, uniformed officers doing on her doorstep?

"Olivia Stanford? Mrs. Frank Stanford?"

Her gaze cut back and forth between the two officers. The burliest spoke again, repeating the questions.

"Y-yes. What's going on?"

"I'm County Deputy Sheriff Mackay, and this is my partner Deputy Sheriff Nguyen. May we come in?"

County sheriffs?

"Ma'am?"

Clutching King's collar, she moved aside, and the two officers stepped into her entryway, filling every square inch of the floor and air space.

"Shall we sit down, ma'am?" Officer Nguyen's voice was gentle in spite of the fact he was the largest Vietnamese man she had ever seen.

Olivia sat next to Katherine on the elephant and introduced her to the officers.

"Mother-in-law? Then you're Frank Stanford's mother?"

"Mrs. Stanford—and Mrs. Stanford—I'm sorry to have to tell you Frank Stanford was found this morning in his Pasadena condo unresponsive and has died."

Olivia must not have heard right. "No! You—you must be wrong. Have the wrong Frank Stanford."

"No, ma'am. I'm sorry."

Katherine reached for Olivia's hand. Both trembled.

"H—how did he die?"

"I can only say it appears to be an overdose. The Pasadena Police Department will need you to come in tomorrow morning to identify the body and answer a few questions."

Why were there two police officers in her house? What were they saying? Died? Overdose?

Now Katherine grabbed both of Olivia's hands in hers.

The officers spoke several more sentences, but Olivia could make none of it out. They stood and, shepherded by King, moved to the entryway.

"Here is my card and the information for the Pasadena Police Department." He laid cards on the entry table. "Will you be all right?" He looked from one to the other and back again.

Olivia only nodded.

As the front door closed behind the unwanted messengers, Olivia and Katherine wrapped their arms around each other and allowed the tears to flow.

An earthquake, too? Must be, otherwise why did she feel as if she were falling? She slid to the floor, taking Katherine with her.

Midnight? Her eyes and mind refocused as she looked at the only familiar object in the room. Her antique clock. She glanced at Katherine, who still stared into space; her face a wet mess. Had the two of them really not moved for two hours?

Lord, I don't understand. Why? Why?

And what was she doing out with another man while her husband lay dead? The officer hadn't said so—he said overdose—but had Frank done it on purpose?

How would she tell the children? Children. Olivia gasped, not able to get another breath for a moment. What if it was suicide? Her birth father and now her husband? *Was it her fault? Was she somehow to blame?*

Twenty-two years later, and she was still processing what her father's suicide had done to her soul, her spirit. Now how was she to help her own children navigate this truth?

Stop, Olivia. It may have been accidental. Had to be.

———

Amidst the anxiety of each difficult event of her life, Olivia had never thought of the events with a descriptive word attached. Not even when she was diagnosed with breast cancer and advised to have a double mastectomy.

Frank's death was like a high-intensity lamp shining on an

open dictionary, a long slender finger jabbing at the word. *Yeah.* That's it. That's you. *Tragic.*

Lord, I know I'm not guaranteed a tranquil life, but how can one person suffer so many tragedies? Every time she thought she found that face of courage, a new disaster hit her like a freight train whose engineer was late for dinner. Hadn't she learned her lesson yet? Whatever the lesson was. Olivia wasn't sure she ever knew.

Get over yourself, Olivia. All of these tragedies may have happened to you, but they weren't really about you. Do you think your parents' deaths were about you? They're the ones who died. Frank is the one who died. It wasn't about his mother either. Ultimately, it was between Frank and God.

Had Frank taken his own life? Or was it an accidental overdose? Had he made things right with God? Was he saved at the end?

At the thought that Frank may not have gone to heaven, a sickness wrenched inside her belly and her soul.

She now sat alone in her bedroom, unable to move for the questions careening like bumper cars in her mind. She had retreated to the darkness of her bedroom seeking solace, but the bedroom was not yet familiar enough—still too new. At least the furniture was the same. But as she sat in the over-stuffed chair, the normally comfortable and cozy was rendered as uncomfortable as a spindly, ladder-back.

Not exactly a balm for the fatigue and burning from radiation.

Yesterday Olivia and Katherine had identified Frank's body, answering the detective's questions. It would be some time, due to the investigation, before Frank would be released for burial. Today they had visited Frank's office to clear out his personal effects. Seth offered to clear out Frank's Pasadena condo, put it all in storage, and send her an inventory. After she decided if she wanted to keep anything, he would take care of an estate sale.

What had possessed her to read Job this week? Yeah, wasn't she like Job? Wanting to tear her robe in grief? She didn't have real hair yet, so didn't have to shave her head.

City of Hope was near Pasadena so it only made sense—really?—to keep her appointment with the plastic surgeon and visit the police on the same day, making the day even longer.

Today they had met with Frank's attorney to review his will. Not that there would be much money after paying off Frank's condo mortgage. A mortgage that was already in arrears. Fortunately, Frank's boss had offered to purchase Frank's Stingray, so at least that debt would be paid off with a little left over. Some insurance money would come to her. Not a tremendous amount, after funeral expenses, but it was still a little something.

Was this all her fault? If she'd been a good wife, she could have made a difference. Couldn't she? Why couldn't she keep him at home?

Looking for some answers as to how the overdose could have happened, she'd spoken to Frank's doctor, Dr. Strong. It took all of her powers of persuasion to get him to reveal Frank's condition and medication. Speaking in generalities, he explained about patients with head injuries, particularly football injuries, like Frank. The concussions left them with headaches, depression, unexpected rages, paranoia, and a need to control others because they felt out of control. And often suicidal tendencies.

Olivia now recognized all these things in Frank. It explained so much. Why hadn't she talked to Frank's doctor sooner? Could she have found a way to help?

Dr. Strong wouldn't commit to whether he thought Frank capable of suicide but said the medication—a benzodiazapene—could have been combined with Percocet to result in an overdose. The doctor had refused a prescription for the latter and cautioned Frank about using the two together. He expressed his condolences.

Had Frank obtained Percocet from somewhere? Taken it on purpose?

Swirling thoughts caused Olivia's chest to ache below the radiation burn with an emptiness that brought her head to her knees as a low keening slipped from her throat. She fell to the floor on her hands and knees then crawled to her bed, scaling it like a mountain. By the time she lay on top, her body curled tightly in spite of her tender chest, the wailing had grown louder. She jammed a pillow up to her mouth.

Mustn't let anyone hear her. Katherine had her own grief, and the children still wallowed in shock, a shock that would be broken wide open hearing their mother wailing like a banshee.

Everything before the brief years with the Hunters and all of the years after were shrouded in gray.

Now images pierced the fog. Images of Frank slapping, controlling. Rages that, having been spent, sent him to his bed. Rages she now knew were caused by his head injury induced migraines.

Snatches of dialog replayed in her head. "I can't handle this." "I'm done." "You were hot. Then."

Frank, I'm sorry! I did love you. Still do. In spite of it all. So sorry.

Lord, forgive me for not being the wife I should have been. Not loving him more.

Sounds, sights, thoughts warred within her. She prayed for relief.

Watch and hope for the Lord.

How, Lord?

Gratitude.

Gratitude? Lord, what is there to be thankful for?

Memories now slid back past the last two difficult years and showed up at the years of their courtship, wedding, and first eight years of marriage. Those years played like good theater in front of her mind's eye. Years of love, happiness, and a new, little family.

Her life *had* exhibited a glow in the center of all that gray. Yes, some things to be grateful for.

In that moment, she recalled that after Job tore his clothes and shaved his head he did not sin or blame God. He chose to praise God.

I choose gratitude. I choose praise, Lord.

The pain remained, but the goodness of God surrounded and overwhelmed the pain, comforting her.

Moments of praise like this would probably come and go as she worked through her grief, yet she would grab every moment and hold it tight. Could she strive to praise God through it all, even though she wouldn't succeed every time?

I am forgiven. I am redeemed. I am a royal daughter of the King.

The music from "Glorious Day" suffused her soul.

———

How could the dawn test her resolve to praise God so soon?

The next morning, in search of her early morning coffee ritual, Olivia started past Katherine's door, but soft sobs froze her in place. Her own grief had pushed aside thoughts of Katherine's. Olivia's husband was gone, but so was Katherine's son, a bond just as strong. Stronger?

How would she feel if it were Dylan? Katherine had lost a husband and a son. She had lost two fathers and a husband.

Enough of this head game of one-upmanship. She castigated herself, asked for forgiveness, and tapped on Katherine's door. Hoping she heard," Come in," she pushed open the door.

Katherine lay in bed, covers to her chin, trembling, her face red and blotched.

Olivia ran to her and knelt by her side.

"I'm so sorry you have to go through this. I am so sorry." Olivia stifled her own tears.

Katherine mopped her cheeks with the back of her hand

and then pushed herself up. Olivia adjusted the pillows behind her.

"No mother should have to live beyond her child. A husband is one thing."

Olivia stiffened. Had Katherine dismissed Olivia's loss?

Through new sobs, Katherine said, "Losing Isaac was bad enough. I'm not sure I can bear losing Frank."

Zoe and Dylan burst into the room, and horror contorted their features at the sight of their grandmother and mother in tears. They threw themselves on the bed between the adults, buried their heads in welcoming flesh, and bawled. King inserted himself into the mix.

They remained in the huddle until Olivia's legs went to sleep and she had to stand. The spell broken, Katherine again wiped her cheeks and spoke.

"It's okay to cry, kids. We're all sad. Let's remember too that Jesus loves us. Remember your Sunday School lessons? He cares for us and understands our sadness. He's sad too."

Zoe hiccupped. "Is Daddy in heaven?"

"Oh, yes, he is! Your daddy is not sad anymore. We can be happy about that."

Could Katherine's words be true? She wasn't sure.

"Doesn't he miss us?" Dylan's voice squeaked.

"Of course."

"But wouldn't he be sad? Like us because we miss him?"

Dylan had Katherine there.

"I think it's different in heaven, Dylan. Your daddy knows he'll see you in heaven, so there's no need for sadness. Time isn't the same. In the blink of heaven's eye, we'll all be together again in heaven."

Her mother-in-law's halo glowed brighter. Olivia couldn't have found such encouraging assurances.

Lord, for Katherine's and the children's sake, let that be true. She needed it to be true for herself, too.

Chapter Forty-One

After Frank's funeral, Olivia, Katherine, Carmen, and Vanessa sat in the Villa Event Center at a round banquet table sipping champagne. Guilt pummeled Olivia's heart. Champagne seemed so...so...festive. As if they were celebrating. Not mourning and closing out Frank's memorial reception.

The banquet room was almost empty of guests, but the overwhelming mixture of scents from the hyacinth, freesia, and rose floral displays transported from the cemetery permeated the room. In the background, quiet sounds of hymns accompanied the tinkle of glasses and silverware being cleared from the tables.

Whether the children should attend the ceremony or not had been a matter of much discussion. Olivia and Katherine believed Zoe and Dylan needed to be at their father's service. They all agreed Gabe and Artie didn't.

Jorge had taken Zoe and Dylan with him to pick up Gabe and Artie at their *abuela's* after the reception, taking the four kids back to the Delgados'. He wanted the "girls" to have some time together. If only for an hour.

Lance huddled with the Pastors David and Mark next to

the still loaded buffet table. The center had provided twice the amount of food she'd ordered. Or so it looked from the leftovers.

Giggling from the other side of the table ended her reverie. Carmen and Vanessa held their heads close. Giggling? What was up with them? They rarely got along. Not for Carmen's lack of trying.

Lance appeared at Olivia's side. "Can I talk to you for a minute?" He pointed to a corner of the room with his chin.

She followed him to the designated spot.

"Again, I want to say how sorry I am for your loss." Lance drew her into a tight hug. "Although you no longer lived together, I'm sure this can't be easy."

Olivia made grateful noises but extricated herself from his arms.

He cleared his throat. "I hope this isn't too bold or improper—" Lance looked aside and stroked the hair at the nape of his neck. "Would you go to dinner and a concert with me next Friday?"

Bold? Improper? At her husband's funeral?

"Lance, I don't know." She shifted away, but Lance held her back.

"Just think about it. It's time to start living again. I'll call you in a few days. I realize you need time...to...time. I'll call you." Lance strode to the exit, then turned and waved.

The pastors collected their wives and voiced their condolences and their goodbyes.

Olivia dropped onto a folding seat.

"What was that all about?" Katherine sipped her champagne. "With Lance."

Olivia shook her head and took a sip from her own champagne flute.

"Girl, we need to go have fun. We haven't had a night out in ages." Vanessa's bigger-than-life voice boomed in the nearly empty room.

"Vanessa, dear. I'm not sure that is entirely appropriate." Her mother-in-law was one of the few people she knew who reprimanded kindly.

"What?" Vanessa feigned shock. "Me, be inappropriate?" She grabbed Katherine's hand and squeezed it. "I don't want to be inappropriate, Katherine, really I don't. I'm worried about my friend. You, too, of course."

"Well, I for one, agree with Vanessa." Carmen agreeing with Vanessa? Unheard of.

"After the long wait to get the coroner's ruling and the release, *chica*, you do need a night out."

"What do you mean? Lance just asked me out."

The other three women straightened, eyes wide.

"You didn't?" Katherine sounded bothered.

"With the silver fox? Why not?" How had Vanessa heard about the silver fox? As a non-believer, she had never even attended their church.

Carmen's face flushed a rosy pink.

"Carmen!" Olivia shook her finger at her.

Everyone burst into laughter. Oh, it felt so good to laugh, and laugh with her favorite people. But she couldn't shake the guilt. Here she was laughing and drinking champagne while her husband was dead and buried.

"Seriously, though." Vanessa wasn't going to leave this alone.

"I still agree with Vanessa." Carmen looked at each of the women in turn. "What? I do."

Only Katherine didn't laugh.

"Maybe I will." Olivia wasn't sure what she was agreeing to, so she raised her glass. "But now. A toast. To Frank, my first love. The father of my two sweet children. He seemed to have so little peace in the past few years. May he rest in peace now."

But did he rest in peace? Did he die without being saved?

She had to wipe that possibility from her mind, even as she wiped away unshed tears.

Faith. Courage, my beloved.

Chapter Forty-Two

Light rain and fog outside Olivia's bedroom window made her shiver. She twisted her robe tighter around her body to ward off the early morning chill seeping through the windowpane.

In the week since Frank's funeral, she had comforted her children's grief daily and consoled her bereaved mother-in-law. What had she done for her own heartache? She realized with a start that she felt nothing. No grief. No heartache. What was wrong with her? Was she in denial? She honestly didn't think so.

It was as if a finite amount of grief had been deposited in her account, and now it was all used up. Balance zero. Was that normal?

Olivia shook her head to rid herself of the internal scrutiny. She turned away from the window and plodded to her bathroom. It was time to think about her future. As she showered and dressed, she encouraged her mind to seek and examine her limited options.

They would need income despite the small amount left from Frank's insurance and Katherine's contribution. She'd taken a leave of absence from her job at the meeting procurement company. Did she want to resume that work? She couldn't think of anything else that would pay as well and that she would enjoy. Besides, looking for something new could take a long time. Meanwhile, Vanessa had been keeping her clients happy.

What about ministry? She had stepped back from the homeless committee after Frank's death. Did she want to help again? She would definitely not be joining the children's work.

Then there was Lance. He had been upset when she wouldn't accept his invitation for dinner and a concert. Repeatedly. And he was again unhappy that she wouldn't join the children's program team. If she rejoined the homeless ministry team, she'd surely be working with Lance again. She would be okay with that. But a date? She liked him, but she didn't think she was ready for romance.

And what about her breast cancer support group? She missed attending the last couple of months. Why hadn't she gone a few days ago? It hadn't seemed fair to Zoe and Dylan to leave them, even for the evening.

She needed to begin teaching the children again. She'd let their education slide since Frank's death to give them time to heal. Getting back into a routine would help all of them.

Not only was it time to resurrect routines, it was also time to get back into the world. She stared at her face in the bathroom mirror for a moment, then stroked foundation onto her face and added a little mascara and lipstick. Her gazed moved to her head. It was growing back, still blonde, but an inch of hair didn't need a comb.

She slipped her arms into her favorite blue cardigan and headed out of her bedroom, adjusting herself to a fresh attitude with which to face a new day and new world. It helped that the house was quiet, with everyone else still asleep.

Coffee was her first order of business. As she waited for the Keurig to drip the fragrant brew into her mug, she placed a banana muffin on a plate and grabbed a napkin. Once the sputtering ended, Olivia withdrew the mug and took the bounty to her office.

Office was not really descriptive of the tiny bedroom she'd commandeered when they had moved in. None of the condo's bedrooms were large, but this one by far was the smallest. It had one tiny window and just enough room for a small desk with return, a tall filing cabinet, and a squat storage chest with her printer on top. Not even room for a bookcase. She'd have to arrange for shelves to be hung on the wall. Packed boxes occupied the little remaining floor space that blocked access to her desk.

On the desk's return was a file box with folders containing her client information. She hip-bumped the boxes on the floor over far enough to set her breakfast on the desk and sit in her office chair.

Everything felt unfamiliar. She quickly ate the pastry and gulped her brew. The quicker she got her desk organized, the sooner she'd feel back in action.

Vanessa had been handling her clients long enough.

Olivia spent the rest of the day unpacking, and finally the room resembled her office.

She wasn't quite ready to face everyone at church, so she, Katherine, and the kids watched a church service on Christian TV. After a Sunday dinner of Parisian roast chicken, the aroma of lemons and thyme lingered while they played board games.

Even Zoe and Dylan seemed more peaceful by bedtime.

———

The next morning Zoe and Dylan fidgeted at the kitchen table, math papers strewn in front of them.

"Come on, guys. I know it's been a while, and I promise you don't have to do a lot of schoolwork today, but we have to start somewhere." Olivia tried to keep the frustration out of her voice.

"Aww, Mom. Why do we hafta do schoolwork?" Dylan did not try to keep his frustration out.

"Yeah, Mom. Can't we just read or something?" Zoe chimed in. At least she spoke calmly.

"You can read after you do math. And Grandma promised to watch a video with you after that."

"Whadda you gonna do? Aren't you gonna watch, too?" Dylan spun his pencil on top of his math page.

"I have to work today. Just like you have schoolwork, I have to do business." Olivia tapped Dylan's papers with her fingernail.

Zoe's shoulders slumped as she expelled a sigh. "Okay. What video are we going to watch?"

"You and Grandma can decide."

"Hey, Mom! You wanna hear my new joke?" Dylan wiggled his eyebrows at her.

She tapped his pages again. "After schoolwork."

Dylan wrinkled his nose but stopped twirling his pencil. He bent over the page.

Getting back into the groove of schooling wasn't going to be easy.

Then, she never thought it was going to be.

———

Finally, as the kids, Katherine, and King settled in front of a video, Olivia moved toward her office wondering if King recognized the dogs in the video as his kin.

She positioned herself at her desk, ready to chat with Vanessa. The desk looked almost as it had before the move, and without thinking, she reached for her red business phone that was not there, but still packed away. The red landline phone—the gift from her husband—and her husband all resided in the past.

Slipping her cell phone from the pocket of her jeans, she filed the memories away.

"Well, Livie. Girl! So glad to hear your voice. How the dickens are you?" Vanessa's voice was as loud as always.

Olivia assured Vanessa she was fine. Vanessa assured Olivia she was fine. Neither were really fine. Jim was now living in Florida. Vanessa in California. Olivia's husband was dead.

"So how are my clients?" Olivia adopted a business tone, a cue to Vanessa to do the same.

"Ah, you must be ready to work again."

Vanessa brought her up to date and promised to email her updated digital files, then drop by in the next couple of days with a box of physical records.

"Van, I am so grateful for you keeping up with my clients. I wouldn't have trusted anyone else."

"Sure. Sure. Hey, I have an idea—" Already Vanessa had an idea.

"Uh oh."

"You're getting back to work just at the right time. The semi-annual rep conference is next week in Dallas. The company is introducing some changes in protocols that you'll need to know about, and it'll be a good shot in the arm."

"Next week? In Dallas? Airfare will be outrageous."

"You can use my air miles, and we can room together. It's the Dallas Gaylord, you know. My treat. You can't say no."

Life always moved faster with Vanessa. Yes, it would be helpful for her job. And spending time with Vanessa would be fun. Heaven knew she could use some of that. But leave her children?

What should I do, Lord?

Trust.

Yeah, but what does that mean?

"Let me talk to Katherine. See what she says about watching the kids."

"Sure. Sure. But don't take too long. Okay, girl?"

Olivia assured her she'd call Vanessa back by the end of the evening. They said their goodbyes and clicked off.

What in the world would Katherine say? She wasn't overly fond of Vanessa, but Katherine was a reasonable woman who loved her daughter-in-law and wanted the best for her.

And what would the kids say?

"My, that's very generous of Vanessa." Katherine removed her reading glasses and gave Olivia her full attention. "It sounds like it would be good for your job."

"But do you think I should go? What about the kids?" Olivia squirmed in her armchair.

"They'll adjust."

"It's not too soon?"

"How do you define too soon? It's been three and a half weeks since his passing—" Katherine's voice hitched at the word passing. "And how many months since they'd even seen him? You wanted to get back to work."

"Maybe I should wait until after my reconstruction."

"That's what? Four months away?" Katherine softened her voice. "You need the stability of work now. I can take care of the kids. Teach them."

"I have no doubt about that." Olivia hoisted herself from the depths of her chair. Her body was almost back to normal. Well, if you didn't count the flat chest and stubble on her head. Both would be rectified in the next few months.

Yikes. She hadn't thought about going to the conference with so little hair. Maybe it would grow fast between now and next week.

Olivia patted her mother-in-law's shoulder. "Okay. I guess I'll go. Thank you, Katherine. I can always count on you."

———

With an "Enjoy your stay at the Gaylord Texan," the hotel clerk handed Olivia a hotel map and a small folder containing her room key. Olivia thanked the smiling woman and moved away from the expansive front desk.

Which direction did she say? I had no idea this hotel would be so huge!

Olivia stood in a long hallway-like area that extended for, it seemed, miles. She glanced at the map in her hand. She juggled the handles of her suitcase, briefcase, and the papers. In order to consult the map, she'd have to put everything down.

How hard can it be to find my way without the map?

She headed to a wood and stone archway and found a cozy, but large, lobby complete with a blazing fireplace and large leather chairs. Beyond was an atrium. Olivia pushed her rolling cases in front of her, the wheels rumbling in the grooves between stone tiles.

Stepping into the atrium was like entering an outdoor plaza and garden. There was a bridge spanning a small stream, trees, and fountains, all adorned with twinkle lights. The atrium, whose roof was made of some sort of clear material, soared toward the dark sky. Buildings, rising to meet the edge of the roof, walled in the courtyard. Balconies and windows on ten levels ran along the facades.

She gazed around, spotting ground level entrances in many places around the plaza.

No wonder they provided a map. Should've listened when the clerk gave me directions.

A stone bench to her right convinced her she'd be wise to sit and look at the map. She parked her cases next to the bench and plopped down on the cold stone that quickly seeped its chill through dress slacks.

"Livie! Why are you sitting here?" Vanessa barreled toward her, long arms spread wide to embrace her.

"You didn't have any trouble finding your way around?" Olivia's travel fatigue wormed its way into her tone.

"The conference last June was at the Gaylord Nashville. Layout's pretty much the same. Oh, I'm sorry. You weren't able to come to that one." Vanessa grabbed the handles of Olivia's roller bags and tossed her silvery-spiked head. "Let's get you settled."

Vanessa set off at a power walk, while Olivia adjusted to catch up.

Many twists and turns later, Vanessa held a key card in front of the sensor and then swung the door wide.

Olivia bit back an appreciative gasp. "You got a suite?"

They walked into a living room complete with a leather couch and velour-side chairs, and a modern dining room table. One wall, sporting a large TV screen, ended at a pair of glass French doors. Through the doors, a king-sized bed dominated the bedroom.

"This is your bedroom, Livie. I have an adjoining bedroom. Right through that door." She pointed to the other side of the living area.

Olivia walked over to look into Vanessa's room. "Why didn't you take the suite's bedroom? I can take this one. Besides, this must have cost you a fortune."

"I had points to spend. You keep this room." Vanessa called from the bedroom where she'd deposited Olivia's cases. "I was on my way to get a drink. Let's go. You can unpack later." She grasped Olivia's arm and marched her out the door.

So much for getting settled.

———

The next day was a bustle of activity. Keynote addresses, workshops, networking with other representatives, and a meeting with their manager. To say nothing of two sumptuous banquet meals.

Vanessa guided Olivia to an after-dinner reception in one of the hotel's restaurants. They stood in the doorway as Vanessa surveyed the room.

"Van. I don't really want to go to this. Anyway, it's been a long day." Olivia stroked the bare nape of her neck and turned to walk away, but Vanessa grabbed her arm.

"No. Please come in for a little while. This is where a bunch of the vendors will be, and it's always a good idea to make some connections. For your clients, you know." She led Olivia to a table crowded with men in business suits with ties askew.

Music thumped in the background, but at least it was quiet enough to talk over.

Introductions were made, and the two women were invited to sit. Olivia found herself seated next to a dark-haired man, with dark eyes, and a black suit. He smiled broadly, his white teeth flashing against a tanned complexion.

"Hi! I'm Hi."

High? Great. Just what I need.

Olivia's face must have shown concern.

Hi continued quickly. "Short for Hiram. I know. I know. Who in this day and age names their poor kid Hiram?" His voice was smooth with a hint of amusement.

"Ah." Olivia said with some relief. "I'm Olivia."

"Glad to meet you, Olivia. I'm from L.A. You?"

"Orange County. California. Not Florida. Are you here as a venue rep?"

He nodded, and his dark hair flopped over his forehead. He swept his well-manicured fingers through the wayward hank, shoving it back. "Beverly Hills Events Center. You?"

"I'm an account sales rep with PeterJohns."

"Ah, our hosts. Worked for the PeterJohns company long?"

A waitperson who looked like he should be retired set a

tall glass of ice and a clear liquid with a twist of lime in front of Olivia.

"I didn't order anything." She hoped her face looked apologetic.

"That young lady ordered it for you." He nodded toward Vanessa. "Pellegrino with a twist. I hope that's satisfactory."

"Oh, yes. Thank you." Olivia gratefully sipped the sparkling water.

Hi sipped something amber from a short glass. Olivia thought it smelled like whiskey. At least what she thought whiskey would smell like. She fingered the large platinum hoops dangling almost to her shoulders. Why had she given in to Vanessa when she insisted on loaning them to her? Olivia would have felt more like herself with her own small diamond studs.

Conversations around them buzzed while she and Hi talked about the business, his manner attentive, his words articulate. Olivia relaxed. After a time, she discreetly yawned to relieve the tightness in her cheeks. They hurt from smiling. Hi had barely glanced at her one-inch hair do. He probably thought she was trying to fit in with Vanessa's short style.

She looked up and caught Vanessa's eye. Vanessa winked at her and turned back to the older gentleman she'd been talking with.

Ugh.

Olivia covered her mouth with her hand as if it would cover the pain that began in the back of her throat brought on by a sense of guilt. *Was she somehow being disloyal? But he's so nice. And attractive. Why not just relax and enjoy talking to a man about business?*

"Married?" He raised his eyebrows at her.

Great. Personal questions now. "Widow. You?"

"Mmm. Not at the moment." He flashed his dazzling grin at her.

Meaning he was separated, divorced, or lying.

"I have two children. Six and nine—on Sunday. Dylan and Zoe. Do you have any children?" The subject of children should put him off.

"No. Never had the privilege. Marriage didn't last long enough."

The same waitperson delivered another glass of the amber liquid and set it in front of Hi, who nodded his thanks.

"Perhaps you'd like to come and take a tour of our facilities? Have lunch?"

Well, children hadn't put him off. Maybe he's just thinking of business after all.

"Sure. If I can fit it in. I'm just getting back to work after a leave of absence. A lot to catch up with." Drat. Now he'd probably ask her why she'd taken a leave of absence. She didn't want to talk about her cancer. "I should probably say goodnight. I still haven't recovered from my flight." She fiddled with the hoops again.

"I understand. Here's my card." He withdrew a card from his jacket pocket and handed it to her.

Olivia took it and slipped it into her handbag. She looked up to Hi's questioning face. "Oh. My card." She felt herself blushing. "I haven't had time to get new ones made, but here's my old one. The PeterJohns' contact number and email address are still the same."

She rose and caught Vanessa's eye again.

"I'm going to hang out here awhile, Livie. Sweet dreams."

Olivia stared at Vanessa a moment. Why was she staying when her expression looked as if she'd rather be anywhere else?

"It was nice talking with you, Hi. Good night." Olivia tucked her handbag under her arm as she turned to leave.

"I enjoyed meeting you. Our paths will probably cross again during the conference. But if not, I'll give you a call and try to set up that lunch date."

Date? Hopefully, he was using the word generically. But

what if he wasn't? Was she ready for that? She hadn't been ready for it with Lance.

———

Over the next two days, she and Hi ran into each other more times than Olivia thought reasonable. She may not have spent much time in the company of other men except Lance since she and Frank had been married, but she was pretty sure she could tell when one was interested in her.

Here was an attractive man, presumably successful, who treated her as a desirable female despite her lack of hair. Of course, he didn't know her chest was fake. And she wasn't about to let him find out, no matter how tempting such attentions were to a lonely woman. She had rebuffed him as kindly as possible.

The conference behind them, she and Vanessa now passed through the airport security and settled at their gate with two hours until boarding.

Olivia sagged against the vinyl airport seat, fatigue setting in. Beside her, Vanessa did the same, her face drooping in weariness. Or so Olivia assumed. Even last night, Vanessa had been subdued as they readied for bed.

Her companion sighed and fidgeted.

"Tired or is something wrong?" Olivia tried to catch her gaze.

Vanessa was quiet for a moment. Then she twisted in her seat to look fully at Olivia.

"I think I've made a mistake." The volume of her voice was much lower than usual.

Olivia cocked her head to the side and waited.

"Can you believe it? I miss Jim." She crossed her arms. "I'm at such a loss. Do you think he'd still want me to move to Florida?"

Olivia had never heard her express doubt about a decision

before. Once Vanessa had made up her mind, it would not be dislodged. She was like a tsunami. Unstoppable.

"Without question. You two need to be together. Call him and tell him you're coming to Florida." Olivia's spirit cheered as she thought about her oldest friend finally doing the right thing.

"Really think so?" Her friend's puckered face did not look convinced.

"You may not want to hear this, but the Lord…and the natural order of things…wants husbands and wives together." If only Frank had believed that. "And I'm sure he loves you and will welcome you back. And the Lord loves you."

"How can He love me?" Vanessa's voice was laced with dejection.

"He created you. Died for you, for your sins. He wants to give you the gift of eternal life, if you'll just admit you are lost because you need the Lord—not just because you want your husband back. Accept the gift, allow Him to give you the faith to walk a new path with Him as Your Lord and Savior."

"It's that easy?" No skepticism lurked in Vanessa's words, only a genuine need to know.

"Not easy—simple. But, make no mistake, it doesn't mean you're free from bad things happening to you or that you won't be tempted to stray. And since His plan is for married couples to remain married, He'll be with you through that, too."

"Then why did He let Frank leave you? Die?"

How many times had Olivia asked herself the same question?

Olivia took a deep breath. "I don't know. Honestly, I've asked myself that too, but through it all, I know God loves me and will work it all out for my good. Somehow. I can't see it now, and maybe never will. But I believe God's Word, so I know it's true."

Would Vanessa get it? Would the fact that Olivia couldn't

give a better answer turn this new inquiring Vanessa away? Was she finally standing on the threshold after twenty years? Olivia had shared the gospel with her since they were neighbors in junior high.

Lord, please let this be real. Use my feeble words to reach her.

Vanessa asked more questions, and Olivia answered, praying the answers were right.

What was behind Vanessa's wide-eyed gaze?

Vanessa nodded. "Okay."

"Okay? Okay, what?"

"I want to become a Christian. I don't want to live like this anymore. And I want my husband back." Her best friend's eyes shone with tears. Vanessa never cried.

Olivia could barely breathe, but she grasped Vanessa's hands.

"You can pray right now. Admit your need for salvation and ask Him to be your Lord and Savior. He will be faithful to accept you into His family." Olivia expected Vanessa to balk. Admitting her need and praying in an airport would take courage.

But she didn't hesitate. Aloud Vanessa repented and gave her heart to the Lord.

Olivia's was filled with such joy, it tried to beat its way out of her chest.

The two women cried, laughed, and cried some more.

"You should call Jim. Tell him about your new faith. He's a good man, but he, too, needs Jesus." She squeezed Vanessa's hands. "How long would it take you to pack and move?"

Vanessa jumped up and faced Olivia. A vein pulsed in her jaw. "I'm going to exchange this ticket for a ticket to Orlando. Would you mind picking up my suitcases at John Wayne? I'll arrange to have them picked up and forwarded." Despite the twitch, Vanessa's face glowed all the way up to her platinum spikes.

"When you make up your mind, you don't waste any time,

do you?" Olivia wasn't sure just catching a plane was her wisest course of action, but she wasn't going to dissuade her either. Olivia jumped up and threw her arms around her friend. "I'll miss you. But you go, girl."

They hugged again, and with a wave, Vanessa strode off.

She dropped back into her chair. Olivia prayed Vanessa's heart was genuine and that she'd find Jim waiting for her with open arms. But first, her impetuous friend had to get to the ticket counter in time.

As Olivia pulled out her iPad to check her email while she waited, her mouth went dry. What if Jim didn't want Vanessa there? She shook her head. No, Jim was the steady one. One of the good guys.

Chapter Forty-Three

Zoe's birthday party was in full swing when she arrived home that evening. Katherine had outdone herself to make it special.

The next day Olivia basked in the afterglow of Vanessa's decision, in the love of her children, and the care of her mother-in-law. Her heart hadn't been this light since before... well, she couldn't remember. She even proclaimed, since it was Easter week, a vacation from schoolwork. They all agreed to celebrate Vanessa's decision with a trip to Disneyland the following day.

After spending Wednesday recovering from Disneyland's crowds, on Thursday Olivia forced herself to work on her post-conference tasks. Katherine and the children went to the Discovery Museum for its latest exhibit. Legos?

As she sorted through her notes and business cards, Hi's card surfaced. She stared at his photo on the card, running the options through her mind. She pressed her lips together and put his card at the bottom of the stack.

No. Can't go there. Not even for business.

Four hours of phone calls and emails put a crick in her neck and a pain in her backside. A walk to get her limbs moving was in order. She pushed away from her desk and lumbered upstairs to her bedroom. She slipped on her running shoes, shoes she never actually ran in, and grabbed her phone.

Aromatic pepper trees, with their lacy leaves, swayed gently in the spring breeze. The sun caressed the top of her head and her shoulders as she followed the sidewalks that wound through her condominium community.

She had waded through paperwork and tasks, now she grappled with the thoughts jumbled in her head. She had dismissed Hi and any personal or business connections. She just couldn't take the chance of being wooed into a personal bond that might develop through a business relationship.

Lance wasn't an option either.

Why do I need a man? I had the courage to face Frank's abuse, deal with my cancer. Now, I need to find out who I am. If I can stand on my own two feet.

Romance was not on the agenda…was it?

She shook her head, hoping the breeze would clear her mind. She had to face the future and figure out what that looked like first.

Courage.

With each step, she examined a facet of her life.

Work. She'd continue with her job. Homeschooling. Thanks to Katherine, she could continue working and home-schooling Zoe and Dylan.

Ministry. The homeless ministry was a worthy endeavor, but she no longer felt a passion for the work. Okay, she'd continue through the quarter, but she would have to let Carmen know she wanted to pursue other ministry opportunities. Marissa, her breast cancer support group leader, had called the day before with an invitation to be her assistant. Could she open herself up to do that? Baring her heart and soul did not come easy.

Lord, what should I do?

She was so deep in thought she almost missed a little bird standing sentinel on a neighbor's gate. The bird, mostly gray with blue-tipped feathers, didn't seem worried that a human lurked nearby. He watched her, then tossed his little head at her as if to say, "Come on. You can do it," and flew off.

Laughing at her fanciful thoughts, she continued home. She still didn't know what to do about the support group, but at least she'd made a few decisions. Her mind circled again to Hi and Lance. Maybe her decisions weren't as firm as she thought.

———

Guilt punished Olivia as her chest tightened. She knew she should have gone to church. Today she'd deprived her kids and Katherine of worshipping the Lord on Easter Sunday. What was the matter with her?

It's just too hard, Lord. Too hard. Please forgive me.

Courage, my beloved.

At least the four of them had read Scripture together and listened to praise music in the morning. They were on their way to Carmen's for Easter dinner. She cringed at the scolding she was going to get from her best friend.

The cloudy, cool day didn't brighten her spirits.

When they turned onto their old street, her spirits sank further.

"Mommy, look! There's our house." Dylan voice was quiet. "Do you think it's sad without us?"

"Silly. Houses don't have feelings." Zoe was ever the practical one. "Wonder who lives there now?"

"I bet it is too sad." Dylan's voice was shaky with unshed tears.

"We're sad—a little—aren't we?" Olivia broke in to forestall a sibling battle. "But we have a beautiful new home. And we get to come see our old house when we visit our friends. Let's remember to thank Jesus for the good."

Sniffling came in response to her words, from Dylan and even Zoe as Olivia parked the SUV near the Delgados'.

Gabe and Artie greeted them at the door, bouncing in excitement. Carmen, with her smiling face, joined the greetings. They made their way to the great room that was both kitchen and family room. There Jorge's sturdy, former-military posture was evident as he directed Carmen's mother and sisters in food prep.

The family greeted their visitors with shouts of welcome, then resumed talking over each other and laughing. Knives clicked on cutting boards, and pots and pans clanked. Olivia's gloominess parted, and the sun peeked through.

She and Katherine pitched in with the preparation. No easy task with six women and one man in the kitchen. Olivia could see why the Delgados lived in a house with a kitchen that took up half of the home's first floor. Unusual for a Craftsman home.

Busy cooks produced a feast of rich roasted lamb, sweet brown sugar and ham, and cheesy potatoes.

Olivia wiped down the butcher-block counters and enjoyed their well-worn smoothness. She dried her hands on a nubby terry cloth towel damp from use. She leaned over and withdrew a clean one from the drawer. As she straightened, a silvery-haired head across the room drew her like a beacon.

Why hadn't Carmen told her she'd invited Lance? Would it have made a difference in her decision to attend? She sighed. Probably not. She didn't want to let her insecurity with him interfere with spending time with Carmen's family, who had become like her own.

Lance strode across the room, and the scent of his musky cologne warred with the rosemary on the lamb.

"Olivia, I'm so glad to see you. I missed you at the homeless ministry meetings. Are you all right?" Those gray-blue eyes softened as he spoke to her.

"I'm good. Thanks. I've been out of town for a business conference. Gotta get back into the swing of things, you know." She hoped she'd kept her voice light.

"Take a seat, everyone! Time to eat." Jorge's deep voice carried across the loud chatter.

Carmen had added extensions to her dining room table and placed a small folding table at one end to accommodate the crowd that filled the eighteen dining room chairs. The kids occupied another table in a far corner. Both tables declared the season with early spring flowers and pastel plates and napkins.

Quiet lasted only long enough for Jorge's heartfelt blessing, and then the chatter erupted again as the platter and bowl passing began.

Olivia wasn't surprised to find herself seated next to Lance. *Who arranged that? Lance or Carmen? Pretty sure it wasn't Carmen.* But the talk was amiable as they discussed his upcoming travels, the homeless ministry, and her future reconstructive surgery.

During a conversation lull, Carmen, across from Olivia, interjected, "Will you come to the homeless ministry meeting this week? The next two Thursday evenings will be crucial to finalizing the plans. Pastor has asked us to make the announcements at church on April 15. Two weeks from today."

Before Olivia could reply, Carmen's oldest sister Angela muttered just loud enough for their end of the table to hear. "There she goes again working for free. She should get a real job. One that pays real money. Oh, wait. She only knows how to shoot guns."

"That was good enough for you when I rescued Tia Graviella. I thought we were past this." Carmen's voice was low.

Olivia remembered the story Carmen had told her of traveling to Mexico City, even though she was frightened out of her wits, to help their great aunt. Using her military gun expertise to foil a gang, she saved her aunt from a robbery. But shame on Angela for bringing that up after all these years.

Angela shrugged but didn't say anything. The dinner guests around them returned to their conversation, and Carmen turned back to Olivia with a shrug of her own.

Lance leaned forward. "Yes, please do come. We'd like to hear the history of some past decisions that only you can provide."

Olivia looked from Lance to Carmen. Apparently, she was attending the committee meetings.

———

The next two weeks caught Olivia up in a whirlwind of activity, as if she were in the vortex of a cyclone. The conference had more than jump-started her business, and clients were demanding her full attention. It was all she and Katherine could do to keep Zoe and Dylan on track with their schoolwork.

Her reconstructive surgery was only three months away, with a plastic surgeon's appointment taking up nearly an entire day. And that didn't include the thinking time she had to put into making decisions about the surgery.

Had she really considered that she could handle both the breast cancer support group and the homeless ministry meetings? At least it was the end of the two weeks now, and she was done with that ministry. And hopefully there would be no more excuses to see Lance.

It was Saturday, and she intended to relax. The temperatures had been up and down, but today was warm and sunny, perfect deck weather with a good book. She placed her coffee and Kindle on the side table and fell into her Adirondack chair.

"Olivia, dear. The kids and I thought we'd go to the park. I know your week was so busy, so I thought you'd prefer to stay home. Am I right?" Katherine spoke softly and gently touched Olivia's shoulder.

What would she do without her mother-in-law? Really, she was the only mother she'd had for years.

"You are not wrong." Olivia grasped Katherine's hand and squeezed it.

"You just relax, and I'll go wear the kids out." She turned to leave, then looked back at Olivia. "Church tomorrow? Do you feel up to it?"

The guilt overwhelmed her again. "Yes. Probably."

Katherine smiled and nodded, seemingly without judgment before she made her way through the doorway into the house.

Funny how guilt sapped one's energy, the ability to relax. She left her Kindle on the table and lifted her face to the sun with her eyes closed, her coffee also forgotten. The gentle breeze softly brushed her cheek.

Lord, forgive me for not making church a priority. I know busyness with activities, even if they're for the church, is no excuse. Is grief?

Truth be told, she didn't feel like she was mourning any longer. Hadn't for a long time. Maybe that was what opened the door to guilt. Shouldn't she be mourning?

Lord, I need to face whatever I'm feeling. My decisions for the future. But I don't know how.

Courage, my beloved.

She alternated between prayer and silent meditation, waiting expectantly for the Lord.

The strident ringing of her cell phone jerked her out of whatever state she'd fallen into. She regretfully reached for her phone, thumbed it on without looking at the screen, and spoke.

"Olivia? Is that you? It's Lance." His voice was buttery warm.

And despite her recent thoughts to the contrary, she was glad to hear from him. After the usual pleasantries, Lance asked if she was busy late in the afternoon the next day.

Why was he asking? "Did I forget some homeless ministry business?"

He hesitated. "I have something I'd like to talk over with you. Not ministry business."

"Oh? What would that be?"

"I'd really rather talk to you about it in person."

What in the world? Was he going to try to talk her into the children's ministry again? He had said it wasn't business. So, what could it be? She thought the polite thing to do was give him a hearing.

"Four, okay? At my house. I need to make an early night of it. I'll have another big business day on Monday." *As if a radiation oncologist wouldn't have a busy day. Sheesh, Olivia.*

"I had hoped to take you out to dinner."

"As tempting as that is, I better say no."

Lance hesitated again. "Four o'clock at your house it is then."

Olivia thanked him and they said their good-byes. She punched her phone off, and let it drop into her lap. *What was that all about? What does he want now? Why do I feel so uneasy?*

The deck no longer seemed the sanctuary she had started out with. Rays from the sun still beat down on her head, but now she no longer felt their warmth. The wind was more like a slap in the face.

Chapter Forty-Four

The last notes of the praise song faded away as Olivia moved out of the sanctuary into the foyer. Katherine, Zoe, and Dylan waited outside the glass doors with Carmen, Artie, and Gabe.

For six weeks after Frank's memorial service, she'd avoided attending church. Even skipping Easter. It was just too hard. Despite the joy from Vanessa's salvation and her reunion with Jim.

This morning she had continued to argue with herself. With the guilt. But something prodded her to action, and now unexpected joy bubbled up. How did Pastor David know the right verses, the life lessons to present today? How did the worship team know the songs that would soothe her? *Okay, it was the Holy Spirit.*

She praised the Lord as joy worked its way around her heart. Not that the tough times were over. Far from it. She knew grief, or the guilt-ridden lack thereof, wasn't dispatched that quickly, to say nothing of the reconstructive surgery ahead. And there was no guarantee she was cured for all time. But, for now, she chose joy.

Someone called to her as she started to open the outside glass door.

"Olivia!" Pastor David's secretary barreled toward her. "Pastor was wondering if you could wait a few minutes and talk with him in his office?"

Why would the pastor ask to talk to her? Was he going to grill her about why she hadn't been to church since Frank's funeral? No, he wasn't like that. Was he?

She nodded.

"He's meeting with the Sunday School Superintendent right now, so could you wait about ten minutes then meet him in his office?"

The seventy-something woman seldom smiled. Was that what thirty years of widowhood did to a woman? Olivia shuddered. She nodded again and offered what she hoped was an encouraging smile. The secretary's lips twitched. Was that her version of a smile?

Joining her family and the Delgados outside, she was bathed in April's Orange County sunshine. She lifted her face for the full dose of vitamin D. The sun's rays must have been a tonic for the kids, too, because Zoe and Dylan ran in circles with the Delgado kids. They seldom played so freely these days.

But also amidst the joy of the day, her heart ached that her children had to go through losing their father. Her own ache's history went back twenty-two years to her birth father's death —a self-inflicted gunshot wound. So far, she'd been able to avoid any mention of suicide regarding Frank. No child should have to live with that. While she had her own doubts, she accepted that Frank's was ruled an accidental death. Her children must never think of it as anything else.

"Oh, Olivia. It's so good to have you here today." Carmen's smile was like warm chocolate.

Vitamin D and chocolate. Good combination.

"Thank you again for talking to Jorge's cousin. She's still scared but talking to you helped her so much. She feels she knows what to expect now, and you're her hero. And Sheena says you had the same effect on her friend. Wow! Look how the Lord's using you—"

Katherine's soft squeal interrupted Carmen's non-stop chatter. "You found the courage to put yourself out there? Congratulations. See. And you found the courage to attend your work conference last month. Another face of your courage."

"Don't know about that. But I'm glad I was able to give them a little help." Olivia's upper lip perspired as she remembered how hard it was to share her story. *It'll be easier next time.* Why did she think there'd be a next time? No, she didn't want to open herself up that way again. It hurt too much. But, then again, she had spoken a few times at the breast cancer support group meeting. *Huh.* What did that mean? Should she accept Marissa's invitation to assist with the group?

"Katherine, Pastor asked me to stay a few minutes to talk about something. Mind waiting around with the kids?"

Before Katherine could respond, Carmen jumped in. "Katherine, why don't you and the kids come home with us? We can have lunch when Olivia gets there. Some of my family will be there, too."

"I don't mind, Olivia, and the kids will love it. They've missed Artie and Gabe since the move. Of course, it's up to you, dear."

Olivia looked sideways at Carmen. "No menudo."

"Just spaghetti."

Olivia and Carmen laughed together while Katherine looked at them with one eyebrow raised.

"Sounds great. Won't be able to stay too long. Lance is coming over."

The rising wind whipped Katherine's and Carmen's hair into a frenzy. Olivia rubbed her hand over the soft cap of one-inch hair growth. How soon would hers be back to normal? Would it be normal? Changed? Gray? Curly?

Squeals erupted from the kids.

"I'll go check on them." Katherine pushed her hair behind an ear and strode off.

Show off. She grinned behind Katherine's back.

Carmen linked arms with Olivia. "So. What's up with Lance?"

"Not sure. Oh, I'm sure it's some business or another."

"Not a date then?"

"No. No...Although, he chooses great places for dinner. And he likes to talk about art, and history, and travel. He's travelled all over the world. We don't always talk about the ministry though."

"Sounds like you'd like it to be a date."

Olivia took a breath. "He can be a little bossy."

Carmen withdrew her arm from Olivia's and frowned. "You've been there. Done that."

"Well, I'm not dating him."

"Humph!"

"What?" Olivia frowned back. Carmen seldom poked her nose in, yet never had she said so much in so few words. "Really. It's fine. Really. We are just co-workers. Friends."

"Olivia!" Pastor's secretary called out as if Olivia were a delinquent student. "Pastor's waiting."

"Yes. Coming."

Olivia hurried inside.

———

The church, housed in an industrial building, took a bit of getting used to for Olivia. Her idea of a church included the requisite spire and organ, but she loved this pastor and congregation regardless of the form the building took.

An industrial-strength door stood ajar and was noted only with a simple plaque that said Pastor David Wu. She knocked.

He invited her in and asked her to leave the door open.

Rubbing her palm down her jeans, Olivia perched on the

edge of the wooden armchair facing the pastor. The pastor sat at his captain's desk with the obligatory over-stuffed bookshelves towering behind. He leaned forward, clasping his hands on the leather blotter.

"You look like you're coping well with all the changes in your life. Of course, sometimes looks can be deceiving." He leaned further toward her.

"I...I think I'm coming along." She shared the joy she'd found in the service and Vanessa's decision.

"What a praise! Sounds like you're in a good place to talk about why I asked you to come in. We've several breast cancer patients in the congregation. A couple of them asked if the church would sponsor a Bible study specifically for them. The elders agreed. The ladies also asked if you would lead the study."

Olivia wasn't sure if she was breathing. She must be because she squeaked out, "Me?" *No! Not me. I can't.* "I don't know if I can do it."

"Carmen told me how you counseled her cousin, and Sheena told me that you spoke with her friend. You clearly have the compassion. And from the Bible studies we used to have at your house and our chats during your treatments, I know you have the Bible knowledge."

"They talked to you about that?" She knew she sounded indignant but couldn't help it. Were they gossiping about her? She rubbed her bare neck.

"They sang your praises to my wife, who told me, because I asked her opinion about you leading the Bible study. And then, yes, I asked them directly." Pastor's brows furrowed. "I'm sorry. I didn't mean to offend you."

Heat crept up Olivia's neck. "Just surprised." Suck it up. Time to be honest. "Sometimes—most times—it's not easy for me to talk, to share personal stuff. You know, one on one or in small groups with strangers."

Pastor David's rugged face softened. "Brave of you to have

done so then. Perhaps you can take those brave experiences and build on them to work with these women? They will become friends, I'm sure."

The denim on her thighs would be worn through at this rate. "Well—"

"Would you pray about it? If the Lord leads you to do this, he will equip you. Perhaps the Lord used your previous experiences to prepare you?"

"Pray. Yes, I can pray about it." Wasn't that about the same thing as saying yes? Had she agreed?

"Know that I will give you all the help you need. If you decide the Lord is calling you." The pastor stood up and came around the desk but kept his distance. "Take your time."

The pastor followed her out into the hall and extended his hand. When she put her hand out, he gently squeezed it with both of his.

———

As usual, raucous laughter and good-natured ribbing filled the Delgado house. It made it easier for Olivia to sit quietly without engaging too often.

Could she lead this Bible study? Of course not. Ridiculous idea. *What if God wants me to do it?* Her mind recoiled at the thought. But it would be a way to give back to the Lord for all He had done. She liked helping others. In theory at least. What if she failed? Disappointed Pastor David and the elders. And the group.

And what about the breast cancer support group? Could she, should she, do both? Or one or the other?

Pray. She said she would pray. So, amidst the chaos of the Delgados', Olivia lifted her thoughts to the Lord.

"Olivia? *Chica*? You okay? You're awfully quiet." Carmen was suddenly at Olivia's side. "What's up? What did Pastor David want?"

"You know, I need to get the kids home. Lance will be coming by soon. Thank you for everything."

Carmen raised an eyebrow. "Sure. Anytime. Why don't you let Katherine and the kids stay? We'll bring them home."

Ugh. She hated evading Carmen's questions, but no way could she talk about this yet. Guilt niggled at her. She didn't want Carmen to talk her into it.

"Sure. Thank you."

———

The sun had moved slightly toward the horizon as Lance's car pulled up to the curb outside her window. She stopped in front of the entryway mirror to...what?...fix her hair? Hah! Instead, she concentrated on the mascara that smeared under her eyes because she had so few eyelashes, and the ones that bothered to show up were far too short. Maybe she should get eyelash extensions. Was that too...too...well, she didn't know too what, but it was too something. Had to be. Forget the mascara. Eyeliner. Lots of eyeliner.

She straightened the silky folds of her skirt. It had been time to get out of her jeans and into something more feminine.

Why did she feel the need to be more feminine for Lance today?

The doorbell rang, and she turned to open the door.

Lance stood to his full height, a grin taking up all the real estate on his face, and at least three dozen roses—red—clutched in his hands.

"How beautiful, Lance. Thank you." Olivia took the roses and allowed the thick scent to go to her head. She led Lance to the kitchen to find a vase. "Tea or coffee?"

Olivia arranged the roses in the vase then prepared the coffee and a plate of cookies. Lance stood quietly as she worked.

Her neck prickled.

"Deck okay?" At Lance's nod, she led him out the French doors to the deck. The wind had died down to a soft breeze that tinkled the wind chimes. She set the coffee tray on the slated table between her familiar Adirondack chairs. She sat in her bright green one and Lance sat in the neon orange one. Frank's chair. She squirmed at the thought.

Olivia handed Lance a cup of coffee, the rich aroma mingling with the scent of star jasmine vines climbing the deck. "You're quiet tonight, Lance. Everything okay?"

"I was going to say the same about you." He sipped his coffee, peering at her over the rim.

She didn't take a sip, instead she looked down into the dark liquid as if it had the power to make decisions for her.

"Actually. Well. Just a bit on my mind—"

"I'm a good listener."

Could she tell Lance? Just go for it already.

Olivia explained how she'd talked with the two women and the other support group ladies, and what Pastor David had asked her to do. "I don't know if I have what it takes—"

"Olivia." Lance squatted in front of her and took her hands in his smooth ones. "If you'll let me, you don't have to do that."

Her mind raced. What was he talking about?

"I want to marry you. Maybe it's a little too early, but I wanted my intentions known." His gaze searched hers.

Was he looking for an answer there?

For the second time today, she wasn't sure she was breathing.

Marry? They hadn't even dated. Not really. They were just friends, co-workers, doctor and patient.

A warmth flooded her. It felt like Carmen's warm chocolate smile. Didn't they say eating chocolate felt like being in love? Was she in love?

She'd only been a widow for eight weeks, although Frank

had been pretty much out of her life for eight months. Could she think about marriage so soon? It would be wonderful not to be alone, to be cared for, accepted scars and all, a father for her children. Marrying Lance would free Katherine up. She could get her life back.

What would it be like to be married to a doctor? Certainly, she wouldn't have any more money problems. But did she love Lance?

A picture of the unsmiling church secretary, thirty years a widow, flashed in front of her. Then, just as quickly, Katherine's life and character in widowhood came to her mind, standing in contrast to the church secretary's. No dour face for Katherine. And it wasn't just her face. That could be faked. Katherine's conduct radiated joy.

"Marry? I…I'm…I don't know—"

"You don't have to say yes right now. But I wanted you to know how I feel. If we got married, you wouldn't have time to lead the Bible study or the breast cancer support group. Besides, you shouldn't do it now. It's too soon, and you're not equipped."

Shouldn't do it? Not equipped?

"But Pastor David told me if God called me to it, He would equip me. Don't you believe that?"

"In general. But I don't think God's calling you to do this. Either one." Lance returned to his chair but leaned over the wooden arms separating them. "It's not good timing for you. That's why I dropped the idea of you in the new children's program."

He dropped the idea? As she recalled, she was the one who declined.

"Besides," Lance resumed his argument, "I would like us to get married and travel. I have a lot of vacation time, and I'm getting itchy feet. And you've told me how much you would like to travel."

Olivia had dreamed of traveling her entire life. Europe, Asia. Norway. She really wanted to see Norway.

Olivia leaned towards him and smelled the coffee on his breath. "And my kids?" She whispered.

"Of course, we can take them with us. Most of the time. We'd want a honeymoon trip alone, of course." Lance's smile was beguiling, but there was still something in those gray-blue eyes that reminded her of Frank.

She sat back, distancing herself from him. "Are you saying you wouldn't *let* me do the Bible study if we got married?"

Lance moved further away now, too. It was as if they danced a weird dance. Forward. Back. Forward. Back. The music was sluggish. Like Chopin's Funeral March. Olivia shuddered at the thought of a funeral.

"Well..." He tugged at his shirt sleeve. "I wouldn't go so far as to say I wouldn't *let* you."

A chill wind swept across the deck and her spine as the sun lowered toward the horizon, preparing to bid them good night. Olivia picked up the coffee tray and wordlessly led them into the house. Setting the tray down as they walked through the kitchen, she continued toward the front door, Lance's footfalls on the carpet behind her.

When she reached the front door, she placed her hand on the knob, and turned toward Lance.

"You have been very special to me. I wouldn't have made it through radiation and Frank's death without your support. But, no, I can't marry you—"

"But—"

She put a hand on his arm. "Lance, I don't want to hurt you, but I don't want to get married for security, to travel, or anything else but for love. And I'm not ready for that right now."

He opened his mouth to say something, but Olivia withdrew her hand from his arm and put her hand palm out to stop him.

"I believe God is leading me to do this Bible study and the support group, and He will give me everything I need to do them both. It scares the heck out of me. But I have to do it."

Was the panic welling up inside of her because she had made the wrong decision about Lance or at the thought of really taking on the Bible study as well as the support group? She swallowed the panic.

I am forgiven. I am redeemed. I am a royal daughter of the King. I will put on the full armor of God.

Olivia stood on her toes to peck his cheek and then opened the door. "The Lord bless and keep you."

Funny thing. Lance looked resigned, but not heartbroken. He returned the blessing as Olivia ushered him out.

She closed the door, and turning her back, sagged against the solid wood.

The entryway mirror came into focus. As she looked into the image of her face, she stood tall and straightened her shoulders.

She saw a face of courage.

The End

Author's Note

God promises us He will use all things for good.

My inspiration for writing *Faces of Courage* and the Faces of Courage series came from my daughter Melanie's battle with breast cancer. Her courage in dealing with not one, but three, breast cancer episodes, the second placing her in the stage IV metastatic category, of which there is no cure, has been amazing. (Her father calls her his hero.)

Also, her courage through faith and grit inspired my author tagline "Courage at the intersection of faith and grit."

Melanie has been my expert resource on what breast cancer patients face before, after, and during treatment. She and I wanted this book to be authentic, which also means it may be a bit grim in the details.

This also applies to the subject of domestic abuse. It, too, may be difficult in its uncomfortable specifics. My daughter did not face this issue (Praise God!), so my expert resources came from a lot of research and reading. The character's domestic abuse situation was her necessary training grounds in courage so that by the time she confronted her cancer diagnosis, her courage muscles had already begun to form.

The setting is Orange County, California, where I live. All

locations are real. Olivia's home is one of the famous Eichler-style homes in Orange County and Northern California. I based the details on a compilation from research, as is the Delgado craftsman home, which abound in our area.

After the novel was finished, I realized how often Olivia and friends ate! Food is an important part of our lives, not only for nourishment, but for comfort and fellowship.

Any errors you may find relating to breast cancer, domestic abuse, or the setting are purely my own, and I apologize.

Melanie and I are grateful to our Savior for showing us that this novel and the associated series may be one good thing that could come from her situation. We pray that if you have not faced cancer (or domestic abuse), you will have a better understanding of what others endure. If you have been in these situations, I pray you can find comfort and encouragement here.

I also pray that whatever trials you face, you are emboldened to find courage at the intersection of faith and grit.

Acknowledgments

While writing a book may seem solitary to the author at the time, in reality, she never does it alone. It takes a crowd. And I am so grateful for everyone in "my crowd."

Most of the acknowledgements that I've read in Christian fiction begin with the crowd and finish with the one, most important person to thank. I'm bucking the system and starting with the One.

First, to my Lord Jesus Christ, who saved me, changed my life in so many ways, and granted me fulfillment of this life-long dream, I thank you and praise your name.

My husband, a person who normally doesn't read fiction, but who nevertheless reads my books and whose encouragement and teasing motivates me through this journey. I love you.

To my children and their spouses, thank you for loving me and being my family. Special thanks to my daughter Melanie, whose personal breast cancer experience has been used by God in many ways, including being my expert consultant on living with cancer. I love you all.

And unmeasurable thanks:

To my publisher Celebrate Lit and Sandy Barela for

taking on this newbie and leading me through the twists and turns of publishing and marketing.

To the many other fabulous mentors in addition to Sandy Barela, who have been praying for me and walking beside me, teaching, training, encouraging: Chautona Having; my Serious Scribblers critique group (Cathleen Armstrong, Nancy Brashear, and Kathleen Robison); my prayer team (Denise Bates, Anita Cole, Sharyn Dike, Randi Flynn, Rebecca Kocsis, Sharon Snook, and Susan K. Stewart); my fellow ACFW-OC members; my WordGirls Group (particularly its knowledgeable and kind leader Kathy Carlton Willis); and Kathy Ide, who encouraged me while we worked on writers conferences together. And the fabulous women's fiction authors, Cynthia Ruchti and Ginny Yttrup, who taught me through workshops, newsletters, and their Facebook groups. (When I grow up, I want to be like Cynthia and Ginny.)

To my first writing mentors, my high school English teacher Mr. Leo Schwartz and author Cecil Murphey. Each of these men had a profound impact on my life and my writing with their encouragement.to write.

To my editors who have shown me how to make the story stronger, how to polish the prose, and generally made this a much better book: Chautona Having and Denise Barela along with her Celebrate Lit editing team. And to my Serious Scribblers critique group members, past and present, whose comments have made a huge difference in my writing since 2016.

And to all the writers who invested their time in teaching at writers conferences such as Mount Hermon and the SoCal Christian Writers' Conference.

With a grateful heart,
Susan K. Beatty

About the Author

Susan K. Beatty is passionate about finding courage through faith and grit, particularly through the trials of breast cancer. Her daughter is a metastatic breast cancer thriver and has been an inspiration for her writing. Susan retired from a full-time job in 2017 and is now pursuing a novel-writing career. Her first novel, *Faces of Courage*, is in revision. Susan is the author of *An Introduction to Home Education* manual, was the assistant director of the SoCal Christian Writers' Conference, and is the president of her local ACFW-OC Chapter. She is a professional writer/journalist. Susan is proof you can begin a writing career after age seventy.

[f] facebook.com/SusanKBeattyAuthor

[BB] bookbub.com/authors/susan-k-beatty

[o] instagram.com/susankbeattyauthor

Also by Susan K. Beatty

Faces of Courage Series

House of Courage: A Faces of Courage Novelette

Isobel's Mission of Courage: A Faces of Courage Novelette

Courage for Your Everyday Life: A Faces of Courage Flash Fiction Devotional

A Wedding Miracle

A FACES OF COURAGE SHORT STORY

SUSAN K. BEATTY

Chapter One

Carmen's hair billowed about her head as the doors of the Princessa del Mar Resort swooshed open. Juggling her purse, her cell phone, and a fistful of papers, she stepped across the threshold wishing she had a free hand to tame her curly masses, getting curlier every moment from the nearby ocean air.

How had she been put in charge of organizing Beatriz's wedding? She got that their mother was getting on in years and didn't feel capable, but Angela was the oldest sister and a Type A personality who wanted to take charge of everything.

Carmen preferred not to be in charge. At least when it came to a family event. Sure, she was competent enough to organize a wedding, perhaps more than proficient. Although her army career was all about weaponry, she had managed teaching and class schedules. And sure, she'd spent the last few years concentrating on being a wife and mother, but she had proven herself at their great aunt's in Mexico City. Hadn't she?

So why was Angela suddenly too busy? Another merger was just another merger. Nothing new. She even got the fact that during the wedding planning, Beatriz's vice president chores would be curtailed, and as president, Angela would have to take up her slack. But that hadn't slowed her bossy big sister before.

Being second in the sibling birth line, Beatriz was almost as bossy as Angela. Together the two of them were a force and more than Carmen wanted to fight against.

So here she was at the wedding venue compelled to deal with the chaos. Angela's last words gutted her: "There was just no one else to ask." What a vote of confidence. And if she didn't get it right, she knew they would blame her.

"Carmen Delgado? Hello, I'm Fiona Hanlon, catering and sales."

Fiona extended a hand as Carmen surveyed the hotel rep's short, sandy-blonde hair. Maybe she should get a pixie cut like this young woman's.

"Yes. Hello." Carmen juggled the items in her arms and shook Fiona's hand. "Sorry for the change in coordinators at the last minute."

"No worries. We can get you caught up to speed in no time." Fiona's generous-lipped smile was tinged with pale pink lipstick and seemed genuine. "This way to my office, and we'll tackle those challenges, too."

Although Carmen knew that's why she was here, she cringed at Fiona's use of the word "challenges." Might as well just call them what they were, problems. And what kind of problems would she have to tackle?

Carmen followed Fiona into a large room with a sea of cubicles. The sales and catering rep offered her a chair in a neatly organized space that barely had room for a desk and accompanying chair, much less the guest chair that Carmen lowered herself into. She guessed Fiona was using the term office loosely.

She followed Fiona's explanation of the wedding plans for the first fifteen minutes. Maybe this wasn't going to be so bad after all.

"The schedule conflict is beyond our control—"

"What? What schedule conflict?" Had she missed something?

"The resort had to cancel Beatriz's original date. Didn't Angela or Beatriz tell you? I assume they received my email." Fiona drew her brows together, wrinkling her forehead. Her brows, although neatly shaped, were generous like her lips.

You're thinking of eyebrows? Get a grip.

"So." Carmen kept her voice steady, but she really wanted to lose it. She was supposed to be the calm, steady one of the family. "Now what?"

"We can offer Beatriz Sunday, November 22, instead."

"Does Beatriz know this?" Fiona had said she'd sent an email, but there was no way either of her sisters had read it. Carmen did not want to be the one to tell them the resort re-scheduled the wedding to the Sunday before Thanksgiving.

Fiona apparently had the good sense to look embarrassed. That wasn't fair. It wasn't Fiona's fault. Right? Didn't she say the resort cancelled it? Must be some bigwig's doing.

"Tell me again. Why was the wedding date cancelled?"

The woman looked away from Carmen toward the glass-walled office at the other end of the room. She sighed and turned back. "Corporate scheduled a re-model of the ball-rooms, and it will not finish in time for a November 7th wedding. Other events are also being moved. In fact, we've had a couple of cancellations if the bride and groom would like to move their wedding up to September. The remodel won't start until October 1."

She almost laughed at Fiona's comment. Pulling off a wedding within the next few weeks was ludicrous.

But moving the wedding to Thanksgiving week was also insanity. At least other events had also been cancelled by the resort, and Beatriz's wedding party wouldn't be the only one wallowing in madness. Some consolation. If the sisters knew of the scheduling change, they would have hammered the resort by now. Had Beatriz already ordered the invitations? She was well organized, and the wedding was only three months away.

Carmen groaned. Of course, the invitations were ordered. Her mind brought up the image of the Save the Date card hanging on her refrigerator at home. She groaned again.

"Unfortunately," Fiona said, "it also means the band we had secured for her is not available on the new date. And the suite she wanted is already booked, and due to Thanksgiving week, we have fewer sleeping rooms available for your guests."

With each additional problem, Carmen's stomach tightened.

"We have another lovely suite for Beatriz, and we can refer some of your guests to the Hyatt Regency just a block away. I do need Beatriz's signature on this updated order." Fiona, her face paler than when they first met, set a paper before Carmen with great care.

If Carmen hadn't been so agitated, she'd have felt sorry for the poor young woman. *Selfish. I'm more worried about myself and how Beatriz and Angela will take the news. They'll blame me.*

They walked the luxury carpeted halls to the front lobby, across the imported Italian marble floor, and shook hands as the door swooshed open. The wind rushed in and swept a hank of curls into her mouth. She spit the hair out as she wished she could spit out the disaster she was now responsible for.

Courage, chica.

What were Beatriz and Angela going to say?

––––––––

"Nooooo! Not the Sunday before Thanksgiving!" Beatriz's wail echoed through the corporate hallways.

Carmen, her courage waning, had caught Angela and

Beatriz between meetings, and Beatriz already warned her she must rush out after the next meeting for a dress fitting.

Apparently neither sister had seen Fiona's email.

"How could you have let this happen, Carmen? Just tell them no. It's unacceptable." Angela stood to her full 5'10," making herself even more menacing.

"Everyone is being shuffled around due to the re-modeling. The Sunday before Thanksgiving is actually a good day. A lot of family will want to take the time off to be here anyway for the holiday. Instead of traveling twice in November."

"We've booked a cruise for that week!" Angela ground out the words through a clenched jaw.

Beatriz let loose another wail. "Raúl will have to change our honeymoon reservations." She walked a few paces, then turned back. "But you do have a point. We'll encourage everyone to stay at the resort for the entire week." She smoothed her sleek chignon.

Did she just say "everyone"? "That might be another problem."

Two sets of brown, almost black, eyes stared at her.

"The resort is almost all booked that week, so we won't get all the guest rooms you originally requested. They've reduced our room block." She hurried on, knowing Beatriz would blow another gasket, so she might as well get it over with. "And you won't get the King's Suite. It's already booked."

Instead of blowing her top, Beatriz's eyes held a high sheen, and she whispered, "Everything's going wrong. I'll have to order new Save the Date cards. And the invitations!" Beatriz's shoulders sagged.

Carmen had never seen her sister this defeated looking. She wanted to hug her, but despite the affectionate demonstrations from their older generation, the siblings just didn't do that. "But they are giving you the next best suite, The Queen's Suite, plus giving you a discount. And they're procuring rooms at the Hyatt Regency down the street, also at a discount."

Angela's and Beatriz's smart watches buzzed in unison.

Her oldest sister nodded toward Carmen. "I don't like it. This never would have happened if I weren't so busy and had to leave you in charge. Let's go, Beatriz. The CFO and his team are waiting."

They turned and headed down the hallway. The two sisters were almost identical from behind. If you didn't count the six-inch difference in height.

Humph. No "thank you." No "goodbye." Well, she was used to it, wasn't she?

Beatriz looked back over her shoulder at Carmen and mouthed "Thank you."

Wonder of wonders. In return, Carmen gave a little princess wave.

She forgot to tell Beatriz she had to find a new band.

———

An afternoon western sun invaded the study, bouncing from the windows onto the papers Carmen was trying to understand, and ricocheting into her eyes. She loved her large craftsman-style home but wished the covered front porch wrapped all the way around the house to keep the sun out of the book-lined room.

Ok, fine. You win. I'll close the shutters.

Carmen marched to the windows, unfolded the shutters, and tugged them into place, leaving the room in shadows.

The children, seven-year-old Artie and five-year-old Gabe, were happily playing with their best buds Zoe and Dylan at their neighbor's house. Olivia had been a Godsend this past week while Carmen wrestled with the details of Beatriz's wedding, like tracking down a band that could play every style of music.

She snatched the resort paperwork off the desk and plopped into an easy chair. Maybe a new seat would give her a new perspective. Fiona at the resort had already called twice over the last five days asking for the signed revisions. She should have had Beatriz sign it days ago. Maybe reading the contract for the tenth time would tell her something new. If she could do something to pull good out of this, perhaps Beatriz and Angela would give her a little more respect.

A woman of thirty-three shouldn't be trying to prove herself to her family. She was made in the image of God and formed exactly the way God wanted her. Right? Yet somehow, she had never fit into her family's mold. Well, that was on them. Wasn't it?

The pages came back into focus. Getting the resort to finish their remodel on time and getting the original wedding date was probably out of the question. She snorted. *Stop dreaming of the impossible and find something practical.*

Her laptop pinged with an incoming email. She jumped up, eager for anything to drag her out of all the legalese. The last band she'd contacted and auditioned had agreed to the gig. What a relief! They were exactly what Beatriz and Raúl had been looking for and for less money than the original group. *Score one for Carmen!*

A knock at the front door drew her away from her laptop and down the hallway. She threw the door wide to four kids bouncing up and down and Olivia doing her best to herd them. The petite blonde's usually immaculate jeans and tailored shirt were wrinkled and showed spots that looked suspiciously like ice cream.

Gabe grabbed his mother around the legs with a tight hug. Artie, ever the ringleader, announced they were all going upstairs to his room.

Olivia put a hand up. "Okay, but only for a couple of minutes. I have to get Zoe to dance lessons. And Zoe, watch Dylan please." Her voice was soft but firm.

Carmen spoke over the children clattering up the stairs, three-year-old Dylan trailing behind them. "You okay? I hope

Gabe and Artie weren't too much today." Although she and
Olivia had been friends and neighbors for only two years, it
seemed as if they'd been friends forever. But she didn't want to
take advantage of her. The guilt for asking Olivia to watch the
kids so many times this week found a pain in the back of her
throat.

"It was Dylan. Twirling around with his ice cream cone
and crashing into me." She twisted her face into a smile.
"How'd your afternoon go?"

"Booked the band. Now if I could just figure out the resort
contract—"

"You do know what I do for a living? I work with hotels
and convention centers contracting for meeting space. You
knew that, right?" With hands on her hips, she fake glared at
Carmen.

"You what? How did I not know that? Of course, I knew
that. What's wrong with me?" She grabbed Carmen's arm and
dragged her to the study. "Can you look at this contract and
see what we can do to make up for the date change?"

Olivia skimmed through the pages. "I'll have to read these
more carefully, but maybe you can ask for more concessions in
exchange for the inconvenience. Maybe even get some major
discounts or extra goods and services. I'll take these home and
let you know. That is, if you want me to." She sounded almost
apologetic.

"*If* I want you to? Oh, my gosh. You don't know how
grateful I'd be."

Won't Angela and Beatriz be impressed? Not with her, but,
hey, that didn't matter. Olivia was her friend and the family
practically had adopted her, so she'd take just a little credit
and let some of Olivia's limelight rub off. She chuckled at
herself.

———

"I should have known it was too good to be true." Carmen's heart fell at Olivia's news the next afternoon.

"There's nothing in their contract that would force them to give you anything. I'm so sorry for getting your hopes up." Olivia's face was somber. "But..." Her voice lightened. "That doesn't mean you can't ask. All they can do is say no."

"Really? I should just ask?"

"Sure. I'm always asking for extras. Sometimes I get 'em, sometimes I don't. But I always try."

They stood in the atrium entryway of Olivia and Frank's home. Another large space to the left, filled with mid-century modern furniture, was open all the way to the back of the house where a tall bank of windows overlooked the garden and gazebo beyond. Carmen always admired the light and airy feel of the Eichler-designed house. But a chink in Olivia's demeanor this morning hinted at something not so light. Despite the upbeat vibe in her voice.

"You okay, *chica*?"

"Oh, sure. Just a little insomnia last night. Hey, don't worry about the kids. We'll be fine. You don't want to be late for your meeting at the resort. Remember what I said. Just ask. With a positive attitude."

Carmen said goodbye to Gabe and Artie and slipped out through the lushly landscaped outdoor atrium to her SUV in the driveway. Her phone pinged with an incoming text, so she slipped the device out of her pocket, hopped into the front seat, and opened her email app.

The florist's bill had doubled because it was a Sunday and Thanksgiving week. Ugh. Beatriz's salary from their sister's company was more than adequate for a single person, but taking on a husband in law school, with scads of student debt, meant their income as a married couple was not unlimited. No wonder they needed to adhere to a lean wedding budget.

"I'm sorry. I can't authorize anymore concessions." Fiona's voice was tender, her face full of regret.

Carmen sagged against the chair. Another defeat. "Nothing? Surely, there's something."

"You know what? Let me take this to my boss. Perhaps she can do something." Her smile didn't reach her eyes as she stood. "Would you mind waiting here for a few minutes? Or perhaps you'd like to wait in our lobby coffee bar. It has delicious cappuccinos and lattes. In fact—" She slid open a drawer and extracted a small piece of paper and handed it to Carmen. "Let the resort treat you."

Coffee did sound good, and the voucher made it free. Even better. Besides, it would busy her mind while she waited. Wouldn't it?

She easily found the coffee bar. All she had to do was follow her nose to the enticing scent of robust beans. The hiss of a machine greeted her as she stepped up and ordered. When it was ready, she found an empty bistro table and settled in. Well, settled being relative. Sipping the creamy latte with a hint of lavender should have been relaxing. But her mind bounced around among the uncertain details.

Remind me again why I'm taking on this stress? Because she loved her sisters, even if they often treated her like a second-class citizen. They claimed to be Christians, and maybe they were, but she couldn't shake her skepticism. It was not her place to judge something that was between them and the Lord, although she didn't see much fruit in their lives. Her loving actions toward them would model Christian behavior. Or so she hoped.

An incoming text alert drew her out of her thoughts. Beatriz.

WHAT'S UP? ANY GOOD NEWS?

Not a bit. She laid her phone screen, side down, on the table and tried to ignore it. But moments later the second alert sounded. Her shoulders hunched toward her ears, but she soothed herself with another sip of the lavender-scented goodness.

Another incoming text. This time from Angela.

ANYTHING NEW TO REPORT?

Ugh. This time she poked at the text to prevent a second alert.

"Carmen?" Fiona slipped into the chair next to her. This time a genuine smile lit her amber-colored eyes. "The director approved a few concessions for you. I think you and Beatriz will be pleased."

Fiona slid a handwritten list in front of Carmen. The Royal Suite, the best in the house, free? A twenty-five percent discount on table linens and chair covers. A voucher for a free wedding cake from the house bakery. A ten percent discount on catering the wedding dinner.

Carmen stared at the list in wonder. The concessions, plus the kindness of the young woman going to bat for them, made her almost giddy.

"I couldn't do anything about putting more rooms back into your room block. The rooms have been contracted to others."

Well, that wasn't so bad. They had the room block at the other hotel to make up for it.

"In the meantime, there two or three other details we need to handle."

Any giddiness evaporated.

"All items for the wedding must be brought in through the loading docks and handled by union labor. The wedding party may bring personal items from, say their hotel room, but only what can be carried in their arms."

Union? Sounded expensive. "I assume there is a charge for their services?"

Fiona sighed. "Yes, I'm afraid so." She pushed another form toward Carmen.

The list of prices, even without a total, was staggering. Had Beatriz accounted for this in her budget?

"Also—"

Carmen's head snapped up. More?

"I don't find an insurance certificate."

"Insurance?"

"Yes, each event must have a policy." She named a dollar figure that shocked Carmen all the way down to her toes. Another item unaccounted for in Beatriz's budget?

She swallowed the lump in her throat. "Anything else?" She sounded like a croaking frog.

"That's it for now." Fiona was way too cheerful.

Gathering her things, Carmen stood, thanked the young woman profusely for her help, and said she'd get back to her about the insurance. Now she had to break the news to Beatriz. At least she had some good news to soften the bad. And, just maybe, Beatriz already knew about the union and insurance costs.

Dreaming again, chica.

———

After a tense dinner that night, not for her husband and the kids, of course, just for her, and after leaving the kids at home with their father, she knocked on Beatriz's front door.

A faint "come in" reached her, and she entered her sister's condo with its view of the ocean. She hadn't been there for several months, and she had forgotten how luxurious it was. Beatriz had told her she and Raúl would live here after the wedding, and since he was a student without a job, no wonder the wedding was on a budget.

"That you, Carmen?" Beatriz's voice floated down the staircase.

"If not, you may be entertaining a serial killer or something."

"Ha! Ha! Funny, sissy."

No one had called her the family's pet name for her in years.

Beatriz descended the stairs brushing her ebony-colored hair so that it ended in a slight upward curl just above her shoulders. She looked less like a corporate vice president and more like a young bride.

"I'm really sorry you have had to take on my wedding and all its problems." She seldom apologized. Maybe being a bride was softening her up. If that was the case, they should get Angela married, too. Fast.

"That's what families are for. Right? Is Angela coming over?"

"Any minute." She laid her hairbrush in a china bowl on the entry table and headed to the kitchen. "Want coffee or a soft drink?"

Without waiting for Carmen's response, Beatriz arrived with a can of Coke snug in a soft cozy and handed it to her. She led them to the balcony where they watched the waves roll toward shore.

"I hope you have good news. I really need some tonight. The merger isn't going well, so beware. Angela will be in a snit." She pushed her hair back from face, took a long breath and, turned her back on the blue expanse.

Great. Just what she needed. To walk into an Angela tornado. "Well, about that—"

The front door banged open, and Angela flew in, a scowl on her face. Her face was a perpetual glower. "You didn't answer my text, Carmen."

Did she talk to her employees this way? If so, Carmen couldn't understand why they stuck around. Maybe she left talking to her staff to others.

Beatriz jumped in. "She was just about to give us good news. Right, Carmen?" She raised her brows.

"You want the good news or the bad news?" Carmen

attempted to make her voice light, trying to diffuse the coming storm.

"Oh, just get on with it! I don't have all night. I have to get back to the office." Angela huffed and didn't budge from the entryway as if she were ready to take flight.

"Back to the office? Why?" Now Beatriz frowned.

Angela waved her hand dismissively. "Nothing for you to worry about. Now let's get on with it."

Why was Angela so involved anyway? It seemed beyond sisterly care. Especially for this particular sister. Was she helping with expenses or something?

"Well, I'm sitting." Carmen sank into the corner of Beatriz's turquoise leather sectional. Beatriz joined her, but Angela still guarded the door. Carmen recited the resort's concessions, adding a triumphant note in her voice at the end. That would be short lived, of course.

The bride-to-be's face lit up. Two or three of Angela's frown lines disappeared.

"That is fantastic!" Beatriz clapped.

"So, what's the bad news?" Leave it to Angela not to dwell in one place.

Carmen breathed out and gathered her courage as she told them about the insurance.

"Already handled." Angela waved dismissively again.

She told them about the minimal room block. Another wave of Angela's royal hand.

"As long as we have the block at the hotel down the street, that's not a problem." Beatriz leaned forward. "And?"

Another steadying breath and she talked about the union rules and costs.

Now Angela stalked into the room. "That's just ridiculous. Can't we sign a waiver or something?"

"Angela." Beatriz put her hand up. "You of all people should understand about union rules. We deal with it all the time."

"But it's a wedding!" She spit out the words. "Besides." She glared at Beatriz. "Why should you worry about it? You're not footing the bill."

Aha!

Beatriz reared back as if she'd been slapped. "It was your idea not mine. If it's that abhorrent to you, Raúl and I will pay the union costs."

Their older sister had the grace to look embarrassed. "No, I'll pay for it. You know this merger has me on edge. If that's all, I better get to the office."

At Carmen's nod, Angela swept out as fast as she had come in.

"How do you put up with Angela?" Carmen's chest heaved for Beatriz's sake.

"She's not that bad. Really. Besides, you have to admit most of the time she and I are pretty evenly matched."

A sarcastic retort stuck in Carmen's throat. Instead, she just grinned.

"Besides." Now Beatriz looked a little gray. "Don't tell anybody. Promise?" She waited for Carmen's nod and continued. "Raúl wants to forget the whole thing."

And she thought she'd had all the shocks she could take today. "He doesn't want to get married?"

Her sister chuckled. "Oh, he still wants to get married. He just wants to chuck it all and go to Las Vegas."

So, what am I doing all this for? I'm only thinking of myself again, aren't I?

Poor Beatriz. Carmen hadn't often thought of Beatriz or Angela as poor. Was Beatriz caught in the middle? "And what do you want?"

"I don't know. No, I do know. I'm ashamed to say I want the wedding. The whole big enchilada. The glitz and glam. Problems and all." Beatriz stood and held her hand out for Carmen's Coke can. "Finished?" She took their cans to the kitchen and hurled them into a bin where tin clashed against tin.

Carmen followed her sister. "You don't need to be ashamed to want a nice wedding. Most girls dream of a beautiful, romantic wedding. So, what are you going to do?"

"Now *that* I don't know. But, if you don't mind, would you just carry on?"

"What about the sales order that needs your signature? Signing that would be locking you in. What would Raúl say?"

Beatriz gave a shuddering breath. "Can you delay a little?"

"I'll try, but the rep is already getting a little anxious. Especially after she worked so hard to get us those concessions."

"Oh, nuts. You're right. But can you give me maybe just two more days?" Her face was stoic, not pleading as Carmen's would have been.

Another difference between her and her sisters.

She left the papers on the counter. "I'll be praying for you."

Her sister nodded, and Carmen slipped out of the condo. She didn't want to be a mouse on the wall during Beatriz's and Raúl's conversation. And what in the world would Angela say?

———

Fiona had called the next day asking for the signed papers. Again. Carmen was able to tell her truthfully they were in Beatriz's hands. But she didn't add she had no idea when, or if, she'd sign them.

Now it was Sunday, five days later, and Fiona hadn't called back nor had Beatriz called with a decision. In the meantime, Carmen kept ticking items off her to-do list, that is items that didn't commit Beatriz, or Angela, to any more money.

The last Sunday of the month meant it was family Sunday dinner, and Carmen, Jorge, and the children piled into the

SUV and headed toward her parents' house. All the way from Villa Park to Santa Ana, Carmen worried about how the day would go. Had Beatriz and Raúl worked out their differences? Would there be a big wedding? And what would Angela say?

When the Luna family gathered, particularly if all her brothers, their wives, children, and sisters showed up, you could count on bedlam. Her parents' home, where all the Luna children had grown up, was modest and ready to explode with twenty or so bodies crowded into it for Sunday dinners. And by the cars crammed into the driveway and taking up all the nearby curb space, it looked like everyone was here today.

Remember, this is not your rodeo. You're only a helper. Good grief. Talking to herself was beginning to be a habit. She straightened her spine and shuffled her children into the house.

With lots of noise and activity getting the dinner on the table, the wedding was ignored. Beatriz and Raúl seemed happy, so no catastrophe appeared to be waiting in the wings. Angela, the only single sibling since Raúl came into the picture, was her usual sober self.

The rich spices of *pozole*, *menudo*, and *carnitas* hung over the kitchen and dining room, luring everyone to at least a short period of relative peace as they ate. When the cease-fire wore off, Carmen waited for the wedding bomb to be dropped. But it didn't come. Did everyone else know something she didn't?

Clean up almost done, Beatriz and Raúl took her by the arm and steered her into what used to be the girls' bedroom, still with the three single beds crammed into the small room. Their parents hadn't changed the pink walls or removed their teenage-era posters.

Beatriz's face glowed. "Do you think we could move the wedding to September?"

"You mean next year?"

"No. Next month." Beatriz leaned into her handsome groom-to-be."

"What? Oh, my. Well...Well." She'd said that. "That's pretty soon. I don't know."

"Can we at least try?"

Fiona's voice echoed in Carmen's head. *In fact, we've had a couple of cancellations if the bride and groom would like to move their wedding up to September.* Next month. But Fiona told her that nearly two weeks ago. Surely, someone had snatched the dates up by now.

"Have you told everyone this already?"

"No, I just told everyone I wanted no wedding talk today. We all needed a break."

And Angela complied, just like that? Hmm.

"I'll try."

Beatriz and Raúl beamed as if it were a done deal. She prayed it would be so.

———

Carmen nearly dropped her phone the next morning when Fiona assured her they had one date left in September. But, she added, it was in two weeks. It meant they could have the entire room block, and they'd still get all the concessions previously offered. Win/win. If they could pull it together that quickly.

Beatriz squealed into the phone when Carmen told her. "Beatriz, you realize we have fourteen days to get this done. Someone will have to call all the guests and get commitments to attend–"

"I have faith in you, Carmen. Look at the miracles you've already performed."

Wait? Me? All this was going to fall to her? Saliva pooled in her mouth, and it took three tries to get it down.

"I guess I better get started then." She must have swallowed a frog with that saliva.

"I'll have Angela take care of the insurance. Oh, and I

assume you'll get me a new contract to sign. And, if you can't get that new band, maybe you can get the first one. And maybe the florist will go back to her original quote. Oh, sorry, gotta run. We have a merger meeting right now. Oh, thank you, Carmen! You're the best. Bye!"

Beatriz thought she was the best? That was a miracle. How was she going to accomplish everything and keep the title of "the best"?

She poked at the cell phone screen. "Olivia? How would you like to help with a miracle?"

———

Guests were heading home, and the ballroom was emptying, while the resort staff cleared tables.

Still the bride and groom swayed ever so slightly in the middle of the dance floor. Didn't they realize the band had gone home?

Carmen couldn't believe they'd pulled off the wedding in the last two weeks. Everything fell into place as if it were the Lord's plans all along. And, of course, it was. Angela and Beatriz had even signed the merge deal.

She and Olivia sat with their feet propped up on nearby chairs, too exhausted to move.

"Thank you, *chica*. I don't know what I would have done without your help."

"You're welcome. But it was a good thing your sisters-in-law pitched in, too. Do you need anything else before I leave? I should probably scoot. Frank's already taken the kids home, and he'll get worried." A shadow passed over her eyes, but she blinked, and it was gone.

"Jorge just took the kids home, too. You get on home. I'll talk to you as soon as I recover."

They both stood and hugged each other. She should be able to do this with her sisters.

"Take care, *chica*. And thanks again." Carmen didn't know why, but Olivia seemed so fragile sometimes.

Olivia moved off, and Beatriz, Raúl, and Angela were by her side.

Beatriz grabbed her in a bear hug. Carmen was so shocked she couldn't move.

"You are the best, Carmen. Thank you. Thank you!" Beatriz moved back to her new husband's side. He nodded and grinned.

"I'm surprised, but you did indeed pull it off." Angela had a few less wrinkles in her forehead and, of course, didn't move in for a hug. "It's a miracle."

Maybe Carmen should feel insulted, but coming from Angela, this was high praise.

She laughed. "Yes, a miracle indeed."

The End

Celebrate Lit Publishing
Is proud to endorse

Finding the pictures to capture your words

http://www.roseannawhitedesigns.com/

Made in the USA
Columbia, SC
01 June 2021